The Dells

The Dells

A Joe Shoe Mystery

Michael Blair

A Castle Street Mystery

THE DUNDURN GROUP
TORONTO

Editor: Barry Jowett   Design: Alison Carr
Copy editor: Marja Appleford   Printer: Webcom

Library and Archives Canada Cataloguing in Publication
Blair, Michael, 1946-
    The dells / Michael Blair.
(A Joe Shoe Mystery)
ISBN 978-1-55002-752-5
    I. Title. II. Series: Blair, Michael, 1946- . Joe Shoe mystery.
PS8553.L3354D44 2008   C813'.6   C2007-904680-0

1   2   3   4   5   11   10   09   08   07

Canada ▪◆▪   🌳 Conseil des Arts   Canada Council   ᐁᐊ   ONTARIO ARTS COUNCIL
            du Canada   for the Arts   CONSEIL DES ARTS DE L'ONTARIO

We acknowledge the support of The Canada Council for the Arts and the Ontario Arts Council for our publishing program. We also acknowledge the financial support of the Government of Canada through the Book Publishing Industry Development Program and The Association for the Export of Canadian Books, and the Government of Ontario through the Ontario Book Publishers Tax Credit program, and the Ontario Media Development Corporation.

Printed and bound in Canada.
Printed on recycled paper.
www.dundurn.com

Dundurn Press   Gazelle Book Services Limited   Dundurn Press
3 Church Street, Suite 500   White Cross Mills   2250 Military Road
Toronto, Ontario, Canada   High Town, Lancaster, England   Tonawanda, NY
M5E 1M2   LA1 4XS   U.S.A. 14150

For Hugh Fairlie Blair (1921–2006)

Author's Note

Many of the locations used in this story exist, but not exactly as portrayed. All events and characters, however, are completely fictional, and any resemblance to actual events or people, living or dead, is entirely coincidental.

chapter one

There were things Joe Shoe missed about Toronto; August was not one of them. The moment he stepped out of the refrigerated interior of Terminal 1 of Toronto Pearson International Airport the heat and the humidity hit him like a truck. There was not the slightest breeze and the air hanging over the airport, trapped by the invisible bowl of a temperature inversion, was the colour of thin chicken broth. It tasted bitter on the back of his tongue, and he imagined he could feel it eating away at the lining of his lungs.

"Welcome to the Big Stink," muttered a man who had been on the same flight, to no one in particular.

Shoe removed his jacket and slung it through the shoulder strap of his carry-on. Despite the stench of engine exhaust, hot rubber, and sun-baked concrete, he caught the faint, delicate aroma of Muriel's scent, still clinging to the material. Five hours earlier, as he and Muriel Yee had stood outside the security gate in the departure concourse of Vancouver International Airport, she'd put her arms around him as she'd raised herself up onto her toes to kiss him.

"Have a safe flight," she'd murmured against his mouth. "And have a nice visit with your family. I will miss you, you know. A bunch."

Shoe wasn't convinced she would miss him at all. She wouldn't have time. Since Patrick O'Neill's and Bill Hammond's deaths the previous December, Muriel had become Hammond Industries' vice-president of corporate development. The job kept her busy and she loved every minute of it. They had tried living together for a while, but had kept getting in each other's way; both had lived alone for far too long to adjust easily to cohabitation. They spoke every day, tried to see each other at least once during the week, and Muriel usually spent weekends at Shoe's ramshackle old house in Kitsilano, when she wasn't working — or when he wasn't. They both pretended the arrangement suited them.

To his left, a car horn blared. Shoe turned, expecting to see Hal, his older brother. A woman with pale blond hair yahooed shrilly over the roof of a dusty black Volvo. She wasn't yahooing at him, but at the man standing next to him. Shaking his head and smiling self-consciously, the man grasped the handle of his wheeled suitcase and dragged it toward the Volvo.

"Taxi, sir?" asked a dishevelled, turbaned attendant, beads of perspiration on his bearded cheeks. "I'm sure I got one big enough," he added, looking up at Shoe's lanky six-foot-six frame.

"Not yet, thanks," Shoe replied. He'd give Hal another ten minutes.

He'd told his brother on the phone the week before that it would not be necessary to pick him up, but Hal had insisted. "There's something I need to talk to you about," he'd said.

"We're all having dinner together the day I arrive," Shoe had said. "Can't it wait till then?"

"Not really," Hal had said impatiently. "I want to talk to you before Rae does." Rae was their younger sister, Rachel. A long pause, then: "She hasn't called you, has she?"

"No. What's this about, Hal? Is everything all right?"

"Of course. Why wouldn't it be?"

"You sound a bit stressed, that's all. What is it you want to talk about?"

"I don't want to go into it on the phone," Hal had replied. "I'll see you at the airport." Then he'd hung up.

Shoe gave Hal fifteen minutes before signalling the attendant to get him a cab. Forty minutes later, the cab deposited him in front of his parents' house on Ravine Road in the northern Toronto suburb of Downsview. As the cab pulled away, Shoe stood for a moment at the foot of the driveway, one of the few on the block that was still unpaved. A bright yellow Volkswagen New Beetle was parked in front of the garage. Rachel's car, he assumed. Since getting her first VW at eighteen, she'd driven nothing else: the original Beetle, a Karmann Ghia convertible, a Rabbit, and two Golfs. She'd owned more cars than Shoe had owned suits.

He looked at the house in which his parents had lived for most of their married life. It was an unassuming three-bedroom bungalow, with an attached single-car garage, a red-brick facade, white wood trim, and aging grey-green asphalt shingles, patched here and there with newer ones. At one time it had been virtually identical to every fourth or fifth house on the street. Over the years, many of the other houses, those that hadn't been replaced altogether, had acquired new facades, bigger garages, covered verandas, even second stories and dormer windows, but Shoe's parents' house had hardly changed at all in the forty years since his father had enclosed the exterior porch to create a larger vestibule.

The front yard was surrounded by an old barberry hedge, badly in need of a trim. It was a nasty, spiny thing, Shoe knew, from having fallen into it on more than one occasion while growing up, and many municipalities had banned them, which likely explained why his father, ever the curmudgeon, hadn't long since uprooted it. The lawn hadn't been mowed in some time, and it was thick with bright dandelions and pale clover. While he was visiting, he could make himself useful and cut the grass.

Slinging his carry-on over his shoulder, he made his way past Rachel's car and along the uneven flagstone walk between the garage and the house next door to the backyard. Larger and even more raggedly unkempt than the front, the backyard sloped down into the thickly wooded ravines of the Black Creek Dells conservation area, popularly known as the Dells. The properties on either side of his parents' yard were surrounded by hideous chain-link "Lundy" fences, cutting them off from the neighbours and the woods, but his parents' yard was still open to the woods. A post at the bottom of the yard marked the start of an old footpath. The path crossed a shallow drainage ditch via a narrow bridge of greying two-by-ten planks, then ran for fifty metres or so alongside the crumbling fieldstone wall that partly surrounded what was left of the Braithwaite estate, out of which the subdivision had largely been carved in the early fifties.

Shoe saw movement in the woods, figures atop the rise near where the footpath from his parents' yard merged with the wider path that skirted the far side of the Braithwaite property. Dappled by the afternoon sun through the trees, they looked like uniformed police, half a dozen or more, and two men — Shoe assumed they were men — in suits, standing off to one side. As he watched, other figures appeared from the far side of the rise, ghost-like, clad head to toe in pale blue disposable coveralls. Just beyond the crest of the rise, Shoe could see what appeared to be the peak of a white tent. A camera strobe flashed, flashed again, then a third time, lighting up the interior of the tent.

He turned at the sound of approaching footsteps. Two uniformed police officers emerged from between the garage and the house next door.

"Sir," said the older of the two, a greying, round-faced senior constable whose name tag read "R. Smith." There was a sheen of perspiration on his upper lip, and beneath the lightweight Kevlar vest the underarms of his blue shirt were sweat-stained. "We'd like to ask you some questions, if you don't mind."

"Certainly, officer," Shoe replied.

"Can I have your name, please, sir?"

"Joseph Schumacher," Shoe replied.

"Do you live here, Mr. Schumacher?" he asked, eying Shoe's carry-on. "I mean, in this house?"

"No. It's my parents' house. I live in Vancouver."

Without waiting to be asked, Shoe took his Vancouver boarding pass from the side pocket of his carry-on and handed it to the constable. The constable examined it, then handed it back.

"I guess I don't have to ask you where you were last night between midnight and 2:00 a.m.," the constable said. "For the report, sir, would you mind giving me your home address and contact information?" Shoe did. The constable scribbled in his notebook, then looked up. "We'll need to speak with your parents, if that's all right."

"Does this have to do with the crime scene in the woods?" Shoe asked.

"Yes, sir. The body of a man was found early this morning by a woman walking her dog. We're canvassing the neighbourhood to see if anyone saw or heard anything suspicious. If we could speak with your parents ... "

The back door was unlocked. It opened onto a small landing from which a half-flight of stairs led up to the kitchen. Another stairway led down to the basement, from which there came a muted mechanical thumping. His parents' old washing machine, perhaps, Shoe thought, as he preceded the constables up the stairs into the kitchen. The house was centrally air-conditioned and the relief from the heat and humidity was instantaneous.

Shoe's parents were sitting at the kitchen table. Shoe's father sat with his back to the door, reading a fat large-print paperback. He wore hearing aids behind both ears. Shoe's mother had a pair of lightweight headphones clamped to her head and was listening to something on a portable CD player while she snapped green beans with her fingers. Neither heard Shoe and the two police officers as they entered the kitchen.

"Dad," Shoe said, gently touching his father's shoulder.

Howard Schumacher turned with a start. "Jesus Christ, son," he said, without rancour. "Are you trying to give me a goddamned heart attack?" Howard Schumacher touched his wife's hand. "Mother." Vera Schumacher took off her headphones and raised her head. Her eyes were sharp and clear but unfocused; damage to the occipital region of her brain as a result of a fall eight years before had rendered her almost completely blind. "Joe's here," her husband said. "And some policemen." He stood. Shoe's mother slid her fingers over the controls of the CD player and pressed the stop button.

Howard Schumacher was not quite as tall as Shoe. Lean and rangy, he was still straight despite his eighty-four years. His hair, thick and in need of a trim, was startlingly white and he hadn't shaved recently. Sticking out a big, knobbly hand to Shoe, he said, "Hello, son."

"Hello, Dad," Shoe said, shaking his father's hand. The old man's grip was strong.

"Joe?" Shoe's mother said, turning toward the sound of his voice, reaching out to him from her chair.

"Yes, Mum," Shoe said, taking his mother's hand and bending to kiss her pale, lined cheek. Her flesh was soft and warm against his lips. She smelled of lavender soap and talcum powder.

"Dad," Shoe said, "the police would like to ask you and Mum some questions."

"Sorry for the intrusion," Constable Smith said. "Did either of you notice anything unusual going on in the woods behind your house last night, or someone in your yard, say between ten in the evening and two in the morning?"

"You'll have to speak up, son," Shoe's father said. "My hearing aids aren't doing much good these days. What was that again?"

Constable Smith repeated the question, speaking clearly and slowly and loudly.

Shoe's father shook his head. "We were both in bed by ten. Weren't we, Mother?" Vera Schumacher nodded. "What's this all about, officer?"

Constable Smith repeated what he'd told Shoe.

"Oh, goodness," Shoe's mother said. "I hope it wasn't someone we know."

"Have you identified the victim?" Shoe asked.

Constable Smith looked at his partner, who was younger, probably not much older than Shoe had been when he'd joined the Toronto police. His name tag read "P. Pappas." He was sweating even more profusely than his partner. Consulting his notebook, he said, "His name was Marvin Cartwright."

"Oh, dear," Shoe's mother said.

"Eh? What was that?" Shoe's father said.

"He said, 'Marvin Cartwright,' dear."

"Marvin?"

"Do you know him?" Constable Smith asked.

"He used to live in the neighbourhood," Shoe's father said. "Four doors down. But he hasn't lived here for thirty-five years. Must be in his seventies now. I'll be damned," he added. "Marvin the Martian."

"Howard," his wife scolded.

"I think the detectives are going to want to talk to you," Constable Smith said. He unclipped the radio microphone from his shoulder tab and spoke into it.

chapter two

Constable Pappas went outside to wait for the detectives, leaving Constable Smith in the kitchen with Shoe and his parents. The police officer tried unsuccessfully to make himself inconspicuous during Shoe's reunion with his parents.

"How you doin', son?" Howard Schumacher asked. "How's work?"

"I'm fine, Dad," Shoe replied. "Work's fine too. Thanks."

"Sorry t'hear about your friend."

"Thank you."

"How was your flight, dear?" Vera Schumacher asked.

"Uneventful," Shoe replied.

"Today, that's a good thing," his father said.

"Is that Rachel's car in the driveway?" Shoe asked.

Shoe's father nodded. "She's out *jogging*," he said. "Gotta be nuts, in this heat, especially with the pollution in the air."

Constable Smith grunted softly in agreement.

"Would you like something, son?" Shoe's father asked. "Coffee? All we've got is instant, I'm afraid."

"I brought my own," Shoe said, taking a vacuum bag of dark roast coffee and a box of cone filters from his carry-on. He took a six-cup Braun automatic coffee maker out of the back of the cupboard over the fridge. It probably hadn't been used since his previous visit. He inserted a paper cone filter into the basket, then broke the seal on the bag of coffee, and scooped coffee into the filter.

"That smells good," Howard Schumacher said. "Maybe I'll have a cup after all."

"And be up all night," his wife said.

"Half a cup then. With lots of milk."

"Would you like some coffee while you wait for the detectives?" Shoe asked Constable Smith.

"No, thank you," the officer said.

Shoe added another scoop of coffee to the filter, then filled the reservoir, and turned the coffee maker on. He took a carton of milk from the fridge, poured some into a mug, and placed the mug into the microwave, but did not start it.

"Do you have any idea what Mr. Cartwright was doing out there in the woods at night?" Constable Smith asked.

"He spent a lot of time in those woods when he lived here," Shoe's father said. "He was a birdwatcher. Don't guess he was watching birds at night, though."

"Any idea why he came back to the neighbourhood after so long?"

"Nope," Shoe's father said. "Sorry."

"Howard, maybe he came for the homecoming festival," Shoe's mother said.

"I forgot about that," Shoe's father said. "We've had a neighbourhood Sunday-in-the-park every August civic holiday weekend for thirty years," he explained to the constable. "Before that we all got together in someone's backyard. This year they're having a homecoming festival for people who used to live here. Our daughter is on the organizing committee. I suppose she could tell you if Mr. Cartwright was on the list of people who registered."

The front doorbell rang, the classic ding-dong of the old "Avon calling" cosmetics commercials.

"That'll be the detectives," Constable Smith said.

Shoe went to the front door. A man and a woman stood on the steps, Constable Pappas behind them. The detectives both wore dark glasses, and suit jackets despite the heat and humidity. The man was in his thirties, doughy and overweight and beginning to lose his hair. He smelled of cigarettes. The woman was older, in her early forties, slightly taller than her companion, slim and long-legged. Her cropped dark hair had a reddish hue in the sunshine. Shoe had the feeling he knew her, but that didn't seem likely. Perhaps she reminded him of someone he'd once known.

"I'm Detective Sergeant Hannah Lewis," she said, showing Shoe her badge.

She put her badge away, then took off her dark glasses. She had the sharpest cheekbones Shoe had ever seen, which gave her a slightly fox-like appearance, but it was when he saw her eyes, oblique and a deep violet, that he knew who she was, and when he had last seen her. Her name hadn't been Lewis then. It had been Mackie.

"This is Detective Constable Paul Timmons," she said. Her violet eyes connected with Shoe's and held them for a moment. "Are you Mr. Schumacher?" she asked.

"One of them," Shoe replied. He wasn't sure if he was relieved or disappointed that she didn't appear to recognize him. "Come in."

The detectives followed him into the kitchen. Lewis nodded to Constable Smith. To Shoe and his parents, she said, "Would you mind waiting in here for a minute while I talk to the officers?" Without waiting for an answer, she went into the living room. Constable Smith followed. While Lewis and the uniformed officers conferred in low voices, and Timmons stood silently in the doorway, Shoe pressed the start button on the microwave and heated the milk for his father's coffee. He heard the front door open and close as Lewis came back into the kitchen.

Shoe poured his father's coffee, then held up the pot. Lewis shook her head. Her partner said, "No, thanks." Shoe filled a mug for himself.

"What can you tell us about Marvin Cartwright?" Lewis asked, addressing Shoe and his parents.

"What was that, miss?" Shoe's father said, turning his head. "You'll have to speak up."

"Sorry," Lewis said. She repeated the question while Howard Schumacher carefully sipped his coffee.

"Not much," Shoe's father said. "He moved away thirty-five years ago, after his mother died. No idea where to. Lived where the Tans live now. They've lived there for fifteen years or so. Before the Tans it was the Gagliardis and before them it was the Bronsteins. He bought the house new, around the same time we did, when the street was a dead end and there were farm fields where the junior high school is now. Joe found an Indian arrowhead. And a musket ball. Remember, Joe? Anyway, you wouldn't know the place. The woods haven't changed much, I guess, except they're a bit wilder now. City's let the park go to hell, if you ask me, especially along the creek."

"How long have you lived here?" Lewis asked.

"Just a few months shy of fifty years," Shoe's father said.

"That means Marvin Cartwright was your neighbour for fifteen years," Lewis said. "You must've come to know him pretty well in that time."

"You'd think so, wouldn't you? But he pretty much kept himself to himself, as they say. Not that he wasn't friendly, mind you. He just didn't mix much. He was a bit different. The odd man out, you might say. He wasn't married, for one thing, and he didn't have a nine-to-five job like everyone else in the neighbourhood. Not sure what he did for a living, actually, but if he worked, it was at home. Or maybe he just looked after his mother full-time. She was an invalid. Bedridden. A truck would deliver oxygen once a month or so, and every so often an ambulance would come, take her away to the hospital, I suppose, and bring her back a few days later. Only time anyone ever saw her was when they were moving her back and forth from the ambulance. Kids called him Marvin the Martian. You know? After the old cartoon character? Some of the older boys used to play practical jokes on him."

"What sort of jokes?" Lewis asked.

"Kid stuff mostly. Leaving flaming paper bags of dog poop on his front porch and ringing the doorbell, hoping he'd stomp out the flames. Letting the air out of his car tires. Wrapping his shrubs in toilet paper. Not Joe, though," Shoe's father added, smiling at Shoe. "You used to do yard work for him, didn't you?"

Shoe shook his head. "That was Hal," he said.

"Did you know him?" Lewis asked.

"Not really," Shoe replied. He'd been fifteen the summer Marvin Cartwright had moved away. He remembered a sturdy, sun-browned man, always friendly, but who didn't smile much. To Shoe, Cartwright had had an aura of mystery about him, but that had likely been a product of his standoffishness and a teenager's active imagination. Shoe had never spoken to him that he could recall, except to say hello. He hadn't played jokes on him, as Hal had, until he'd grown out of it, not long before Cartwright had moved away.

"The littler kids liked him," Howard Schumacher said.

Lewis raised her eyebrows.

"The city used to set up an outdoor skating rink in the park behind the houses across the street. In the summer there was a baseball diamond and playground. The entrance to the park was across from Marvin's house. In the winter he'd invite kids in for hot chocolate. In the summer he'd make them lemonade. For a while he used to go all out for Halloween, too, decorating his lawn with gravestones and plastic skeletons and such, but the older kids kept tearing it up, so he eventually stopped even giving out treats."

Lewis looked up from her notebook at the sound of the back door. A moment later, Shoe's sister, Rachel, came up the stairs into the kitchen. She was wearing shorts and an athletic top darkened with perspiration. She had a tiny white MP3 player clipped to the waistband of her shorts, the earbuds hanging around her neck on fine, white wires.

"Hey, Joe," she said brightly. "I smell coffee — " She saw Lewis and Timmons. "Oops, sorry. Didn't mean to interrupt."

Shoe introduced Detective Sergeant Lewis and Detective Constable Timmons. Rachel's expression darkened as Timmons's eyes moved quickly up and down her body. Her shorts and damp top clung like a second skin.

"What's happened?" she said.

"We're investigating the death of a man named Marvin Cartwright," Sergeant Lewis said.

"Marvin ... " Rachel blinked and for a moment she was far away. She blinked again as she returned to the present. "My god. I haven't thought of him in years." Her eyes narrowed. "How did he die? I mean, you wouldn't be investigating his death if he'd died of natural causes, would you?"

"Sometime late last night or early this morning he was beaten to death in the wooded area behind your parents' house."

"Beaten to death? By whom?"

"That's what we're investigating," Lewis said.

"Yes, of course." She shivered. "Would you mind if I got dressed? I'm getting chilled. The air conditioning is set too high again," she added, in a disapproving tone of voice.

"We just have a couple of questions ... "

"Which I'll gladly answer after I've changed." Without waiting for a reply, Rachel turned and strode down the hall toward the bedrooms.

Lewis looked at Timmons. He shrugged, as if to say, "What can you do?"

Lewis looked at her notebook, then at Shoe. "Were you one of the kids Cartwright invited into his house?"

"No," he replied. "But my sister was."

"How old was she?"

"She was eleven when he moved away." Shoe said. "I don't remember how long he'd been having the kids in."

"Couldn't've been more'n two or three years, eh, Mother?" Shoe's father said.

"She and the other children started visiting Mr. Cartwright around the time Rachel turned six," Shoe's mother said. "She was very upset when he left. She adored him."

"You said he left after his mother died. What was wrong with her?"

Vera Schumacher shook her head, dark eyes unfocused. "No one knew. No one ever saw her, except when the ambulance came. Not even the children who visited him. He'd shoo them out whenever she called to him. Then one day an ambulance took her away and never brought her back. A week later a moving van came and packed everything up. The people who bought the house, the Bronsteins, said that except for a broken basement window it was like no one had ever lived there. No one ever saw Mr. Cartwright again."

Rachel came into the kitchen, dressed in jeans and a T-shirt, her dark hair brushed back from her face. Shoe was struck by how much she resembled their mother when she was younger: her compact physique, her broad cheekbones, dark eyes, and slightly square jaw.

"For the record, Ms. Schumacher," Lewis said. "Where were you between midnight and 2:00 a.m. last night?"

"I was here," Rachel replied.

"You live here?"

"Sort of," she replied. "I have a house in Port Credit, but — "

"Thinks we're gettin' too old to take care of ourselves," Shoe's father grumbled.

Rachel sighed. "That's not it at all, Pop. It's just easier this way."

"Humph," Howard Schumacher said.

"Why do you think Cartwright came back after all these years?" Lewis asked.

"I haven't any idea," Rachel said.

"Your mother told the officers that there was a homecoming festival this weekend. Could he have come for that?"

"I suppose. We ran some ads in local newspapers. We also have a website. Maybe he saw it, but he wasn't registered."

"Have you been in touch with him at all since he left?"

"No."

Lewis studied her notebook, ostensibly reviewing her notes in preparation for her next question. Shoe recognized it as a common interview technique. Many subjects, to fill the silence, will volunteer information, often taking the interview in unexpected directions. It wasn't a tactic that was likely to work well with his parents, however, especially his mother. She had inherited her Native ancestors' distrust of unnecessary talk, and had passed the trait on to Rachel and him — he wasn't sure about their older brother, Hal. To some degree, it had also rubbed off on his father.

"Besides the boys who played practical jokes on him," Lewis said after a moment, "was there anyone who particularly disliked him or who had a run-in with him? Maybe someone who didn't like the little kids visiting him in his house?"

"Well," Shoe's father said slowly, hesitantly.

"What?" Lewis asked.

"Howard," Shoe's mother said. "Those were simply ugly rumours spread by people with nothing better to do than think the worst of others."

"Sorry, Mother," Shoe's father said uncomfortably. "It might be important." Shoe knew what his mother was referring to and didn't blame his father for being uncomfortable. "Maybe we could go into the other room," Shoe's father said to Sergeant Lewis.

"Howard," Shoe's mother said sternly. "I'm not a child to be sent to her room when the grown-ups want to talk."

"What is it?" Lewis asked, unable to hide her impatience.

"Well," Shoe's father said again.

Shoe put his hand on his father's shoulder, and said to Sergeant Lewis, "That summer, before Cartwright moved away, there were a series of sexual assaults in the woods. One of the victims died. The media dubbed the perpetrator the Black Creek Rapist. As far as I know, the case was never solved."

"God," Rachel said. "I'd forgotten all about that."

"Cartwright was a suspect?" Lewis asked.

"A lot of people in the neighbourhood seemed to think so," Shoe said.

"Damn fools, if you ask me," his father interjected.

"If for no other reason that he was different," Shoe continued. "A forty-year-old single man, with no apparent means of support — apparent to his neighbours, anyway — and living with his invalid mother. But the police interviewed most of the men and older boys in the neighbourhood. The thing is, to the best of my recollection, there were no more assaults after Cartwright moved away."

"Did you know any of the victims?"

"I was acquainted with three of them," Shoe said.

"How many were there?"

"Four, that I'm aware of."

"What can you tell us?"

Shoe cast his mind back. "The first victim was a girl I knew from junior high school. Her name was Daphne McKinnon." Shoe recalled a shy, slightly plump girl, a talented musician who played the violin in the school band. "She was a year behind me, which would make her thirteen or fourteen. One evening in late May or early June she was in the woods when she was attacked from behind, her shirt pulled up over her head, and raped. Her attacker then tied her up with her clothes and left her. She managed to get loose and go to the nearest house to report the attack. She wasn't able to identify her assailant."

Lewis wrote in her notebook, then said, "Go on."

"The second attack was two or three weeks later. The victim was a teacher from the junior high school named Hahn. I never knew her first name. She was my ninth-grade English teacher. About twenty-four or twenty-five. Similar MO, except that it happened at midday and in a different part of the conservation area. Her attack was more brutal than the first. She wasn't able to identify her attacker either."

Shoe paused while Lewis scribbled in her notebook. When she nodded for him to continue, he looked at Rachel.

"What?"

"The third victim was Marty," Shoe said gently.

"Oh, Christ," Rachel said, the skin around her eyes turning pale. "That's right. Marty — Martine Elias — was a friend of mine," she added to Lewis. "But she wasn't raped, was she, Joe? Just molested."

"She got away from her attacker before he could rape her," Shoe said.

"Not that it was any less traumatic for her," Rachel said.

"How old was she?" Lewis asked.

"Same age as me. Eleven."

Lewis's face tightened. "She wasn't able to identify the person who attacked her?" she said.

"No," Shoe said.

"Poor Marty," Rachel said. "She was my 'bestest friend,' as we used to say, until she was attacked. Then we kind of drifted apart. She — "

"Excuse me, Ms. Schumacher," Lewis interrupted. "I'll ask you more about your friend in a minute. First, though," she said to Shoe, "tell me abut the last victim, the one you didn't know."

"I don't remember her name," he said. "She was a university student who worked part-time for the city parks department. It happened in late July or early August."

"Same MO?"

"As far as I know," Shoe said. "Except that she was strangled to death, perhaps because she saw her attacker."

Shoe didn't remember much about Marty Elias's

attack or the park worker's rape and murder. He'd been too upset by Miss Hahn's attack. She'd been one of his favourite teachers, and because she'd been young and pretty, he'd had a massive schoolboy crush on her. The whole school had been in shock; her attack had occurred just weeks before the end of the school year.

"Did Marvin Cartwright know any of the victims?" Lewis asked.

"He knew Marty," Rachel said.

"She was one of the kids he invited into his house?"

"Yes."

"Does she still live in the neighbourhood?"

"I don't know where she lives now," Rachel said. "Like I said, we fell out of touch after her attack," she added. "It ... changed her. She was always a little precocious, but afterwards she turned slutty. She dropped out of school at sixteen and started hanging out with a pretty rough crowd." She looked at Shoe. "What was the name of that biker gang she ran with for a while?"

"The Black Skulls," Shoe said. "They were mostly weekend warrior types, though. Rough enough, but hardly Hells Angels material."

"Are her parents still alive?"

"I don't know. They retired to Florida or California, I think."

"Did she have any brothers or sisters?"

"No."

"Did Cartwright know any of the other victims?"

"Not to my knowledge," Shoe said.

"No idea," his father said.

Rachel said, "I don't know."

"Mrs. Schumacher?" Lewis said.

"I don't know," Shoe's mother said.

Lewis scribbled in her notebook, then asked, "Do the families of any of the other victims still live around here?"

Shoe's father said, "The only ones we knew were Marty's folks."

"The McKinnon girl and her family moved away not long after her attack," Shoe's mother said.

Lewis looked at Shoe.

"I don't know where Miss Hahn or the park worker lived," he said.

"All right," Lewis said. "We'll check it out. One last thing. Is there anyone else who still lives in the area who knew Mr. Cartwright?"

"Let's see," Shoe's father said slowly, rubbing his stubbly chin. "There's Dougie Hallam and his sister, Janey. Stepsister, actually. I'm pretty sure they knew Mr. Cartwright. Dougie did, anyway. He was one of the boys that played tricks on him. Don't know for sure if Janey knew him or not." He looked at Shoe.

"No better than I did," Shoe replied, as memories of Janey Hallam bubbled up from the recesses of his mind. Janey had been his first serious girlfriend, the one with whom he had shed his virginity — at a far too tender age, he recalled with a high degree of discomfort — and with whom he'd once believed he'd spend his whole life. He was surprised she still lived in the neighbourhood; the last time he'd seen her, shortly after she'd graduated from high school a year behind him, she'd told him she'd taken a job as flight attendant and was leaving Downsview forever. Did she remember him as well as he remembered her? he wondered. Or as fondly? Perhaps he would look her up, he thought, see how she'd turned out. Or was that a rock better left unturned? He had no desire to resume the acquaintance of her stepbrother, Dougie.

"And there's Tim Dutton," Shoe's father said.

The name triggered a memory of a stocky boy with freckles and unruly red hair. Tim Dutton's father had opened one of the first so-called "big box" hardware and building supply stores in the area and had become quite wealthy, although he'd continued to live with his wife and two children in the modest three-bedroom house they'd bought the year before Shoe's parents had bought theirs. At one time or another, Bart Dutton had provided most of the neighbourhood kids with summer jobs. Tim, though, had been the boss's son and had made certain that everyone understood and appreciated the fact.

"There's no one else I can think of," Shoe's father said.

"Ms. Schumacher," Lewis said to Rachel. "Do you remember the names of the other kids Cartwright invited into his house?"

Rachel was lost in thought for a moment, then said, "Besides Marty, the only ones I remember are Mickey Bloom and Bobby Cotton."

"Those are boy's names?"

Rachel nodded. "But I have no idea where they are now."

"Thank you," Lewis said. She closed her notebook and slipped it into the side pocket of her jacket. "That should do it for now. We appreciate your help. If we need anything else, someone will be in touch." She shook hands with Shoe's father, mother, and sister.

"I'll see you out," Shoe said.

Timmons had a cigarette in his mouth before the front door was even open, but he did not light it until he was outside. A plain grey Chrysler Sebring was parked on the street in front of the house, so nondescript it all but shouted "Police."

"Is there something else?" Lewis asked.

"You don't remember me, do you?" Shoe said.

"I have the feeling I should," she said. "Have we met before?"

He half hoped she wouldn't remember. She'd been just sixteen the last time he'd seen her, at Sara's funeral.

Then he saw the blink of recognition.

"Oh, shit," she said. "You're Joe Shoe."

"That's right. And you're Hannah Mackie."

"Lewis now, although I've been divorced forever."

She silently scrutinized him for a moment. He'd never seen anyone else with eyes quite like hers. Besides the unusual colour, there was something else about them, a quality he couldn't quite pin down, as though they were capable of perceiving things no one else could. He'd heard of people whose eyesight extended slightly beyond the so-called visible spectrum, like certain types of raptors. Was she one of them?

"Funny, my not remembering your full name," she said.

"Perhaps you never knew it. To everyone, I was always Joe Shoe. Or just Shoe." Even Sara had called him Shoe.

"You, um, look different. And not so tall."

He smiled. "You're taller. How's your brother?"

"Okay," she said. "He has a copy and print shop now. He tried security after — after leaving the police, but it didn't work out. I don't see much of him. This job keeps me busy and he's — well, we never were all that close."

In fact, Shoe remembered, Hannah hadn't got along at all with her older brother. Eighteen years her senior, and her legal guardian since their parents had died in a road accident when she was twelve, Ron Mackie had been overprotective to the point of tyranny. Not that Shoe had blamed him. In his short time with the Toronto police he'd seen far too many young women dead of drug overdoses, beaten to death by their pimps or jealous boyfriends or drunken husbands, raped and murdered by friends and strangers alike, or simply discarded like yesterday's trash. In his ten years as a street cop, Ron Mackie had seen much more.

"How does he feel about you being a cop?" Shoe asked her.

"He pretends he's okay with it, but he doesn't really like the idea of his baby sister being a cop any more than he liked his wife being one." A flush highlighted her sharp cheekbones. "Uh, sorry."

"Don't worry about it," Shoe said. "It was a long time ago."

"Yeah." There was a moment of awkward silence.

"What do you do in Vancouver?" Detective Constable Timmons said, cigarette smoke spilling from his mouth. "Not still on the job, are you?"

"No," Shoe said. "I do some consulting, but mostly I'm semi-retired."

"What sorta consulting? Security?" Timmons asked, dropping his cigarette butt onto the pavement, grinding it out under the sole of a steel-toed shoe.

"I investigate companies other companies are looking to acquire."

"Interesting work?"

"Can be," Shoe said. Timmons didn't look as though he thought so. He went round to the driver's side of the car and got behind the wheel.

"Well, thanks for your help," Lewis said.

"You're welcome," Shoe said.

She got into the car. Timmons started the engine.

"You were in the academy with Hank Trumbull, weren't you?" Lewis said.

"That's right," Shoe said. He and Hank Trumbull had also served their probationary period in the same downtown Toronto division. Shoe hadn't seen him since he'd left the force and moved to the West Coast, but he'd called him in January to thank him for his putting in a good word for him during the investigation into Patrick O'Neill's murder. "Do you know Hank?"

"He was my boss," she said through the open door.

"He put in his papers last month. He got tired of waiting for promotion. I don't blame him. He should've been deputy chief by now, or even chief, but — well, you know him," she added with a shrug. "Anyway, his retirement bash was last week."

"I'm sorry I missed it," Shoe said. "I'll call him."

"Better hurry," Lewis said. "He's taking his wife on a three-month vacation in Europe. They're leaving tomorrow. Thanks again for your help. I'll see you around."

She closed the door. Timmons put the Sebring in gear and pulled away from the curb without signalling. Shoe turned his back on the memories and went into his parents' house.

chapter three

"You keep looking at your watch, Hal," Jerold Renfrew said. "Is there someplace you have to be?"

"Uh, no," Hal Schumacher replied.

"You sure? Because if there is, we can do this later."

"No," Hal said. "Let's get it over with."

"Okay. Hal, you're fired!"

Don't I wish, Hal thought sourly, smiling at Renfrew's favourite joke nevertheless. "The severance will come in handy," he said, playing along, as was expected, even required. "I've had my eye on a nice little summer place in the Muskokas for a while now."

Renfrew slapped the top of his desk in appreciation. "Good one, Hal. And who knows? Maybe you'll even be able to afford it after this year's bonus. I'm sure I don't have to tell you that your quarterly numbers are great, Hal. Simply great. Up over fifteen percent from last year. I'm really proud of you, Hal. You've built a great team of people. Simply great. Their performance is outstanding."

Jerry Renfrew was president, CEO, and sole share-holder of Renfrew & Doherty Assurance, Inc. Although younger than Hal by nearly a decade, Renfrew affected a kindly, avuncular manner, which Hal found as annoying as it was fraudulent.

"Thanks, Jerry. I'll pass that along."

"The next quarter is looking good too," Renfrew said, as though he hadn't heard. "Could be our best ever, in no small part due to the efforts of you and your people. It's starting to look like a safe bet that you're going to be taking home the Oscar again this year, Hal."

Christ, but the man loves the sound of his own voice, Hal thought irritably, as Renfrew prattled on. He was careful to keep his impatience from showing, though. Under other circumstances, he would have been flattered by the effusive praise, even though he knew these sessions were just Renfrew's way of reminding everyone who was really in control. Truth be told, Hal was counting on the "Oscar," as Renfrew called the big annual bonus that went to the head of the most productive department. Too bad he wouldn't get to enjoy any of it; it was already spent, and not on a cottage on Lake Muskoka.

Hal had always considered himself pretty sophisticated when it came to the market. He knew that when a stock looked too good to be true, it likely was, and he'd have scoffed at the suggestion that he could be taken in by a smooth sales pitch. Until recently, that is. Jesus, how could he have been so stupid? It only went to show that no matter how smart you thought you were, there was always some slick operator out there who was just that little bit smarter.

And, on top of that, he had Dougie Hallam on his back. Hal sighed. He'd screwed up, there was no denying that, but damn, a little good luck wasn't too much to ask, was it? It would make a nice change ...

"Hal?"

"Uh, yes, Jerry."

Renfrew frowned. "Is something bothering you, Hal?"

"What? No, Jerry, everything's fine. Why do you ask?"

"C'mon, man," Renfrew said. "You sit there, inscrutable as a damn Sphinx, when I'm practically coming right out and telling you that if you keep this up you're a shoo-in for CFO when Phil Desmond retires next year."

Hal's heart jumped, as if an electric current had passed through his chest. "I thought Ray Levesque was your choice for Phil's job," he said, barely able to contain himself. So the rumours of Ray Levesque's fall from grace were true after all.

"Frankly," Renfrew said, "I've been disappointed in Ray's performance lately."

"I'm sorry to hear that," Hal said, careful to keep the smugness from showing in his voice or on his face. Ray Levesque had been Jerry's fair-haired boy. Hal wondered what Ray had done — or not done — to fall out of Renfrew's favour. Whatever, maybe Hal's luck was taking a turn for the better.

"But we were talking about you, Hal," Renfrew said. "You've been a bit distracted lately. Is everything all right at home? How's Maureen? I was saying to Alice just the other day, we've got to have Hal and Maureen over for dinner soon. Alice is dying to show off the new house."

"Everything's fine, Jerry," Hal said. "Maureen's fine. And we'd love to see the new house."

"So what's the problem, Hal?"

"There's no problem, Jerry."

"I wasn't born yesterday, Hal," Renfrew said. "I can see plain as the nose on your face that something's going on with you. You can level with me, you know. If there's something bothering you, all you have to do is tell me. We'll make it go away. Trust me."

Yeah, right. "Jerry, honestly, it's nothing. I'm just tired, I guess. It's been a tough couple of months, and I worked a little later than usual last night."

"So I understand. A little bird told me you were here till after midnight. That's not good. I'm a big believer in a proper balance of life and work, Hal, you know that."

Yes I do, Jerry, and I'm sure you believe it, too, until the numbers start to fall, then it's a different tune you play for us to dance to.

"You sure everything's all right between you and Maureen? Working late is often the first sign of problems at home."

"We're fine," Hal said blandly. How easily the lie came. But was Jerry even listening?

"Because I don't need to remind you, Hal, Renfrew & Doherty is a very family values–conscious firm. We pride ourselves on that, as you well know. Nothing is more important than a solid, stable, and *healthy* family life. Frankly, I worry about you, Hal. You're not a churchgoer, I accept that, because you're a good man nevertheless, but we all need a reliable moral compass to steer by. Appearances are important in this business, Hal, I don't have to tell you that. We must be vigilant, on constant guard against any failure of personal integrity or deterioration of morality and family values."

"You don't have anything to worry about," Hal said.

"Renfrew & Doherty may not be the biggest insurer in this city," Renfrew said, "but we've got a reputation for integrity that's second to none in the industry."

"I know, Jerry."

"There's a lot at stake here, Hal. I wouldn't want to see you throw away your future with the company because you can't keep your family together."

You bloody hypocrite, Hal thought, keeping his expression carefully neutral as he endured yet another lecture on morality from the man who'd driven poor old George Doherty to an early grave with totally trumped up allegations of mismanagement and malfeasance. *Family values, my hairy ass. All you care about is the damned bottom line. Profit, that's your moral compass, you sanctimonious bastard, not God or the church. Those are for appearances' sake, nothing else.*

Hal almost laughed out loud at his own hypocrisy. Appearances were important to him, too, he knew, maybe more than he'd ever realized, otherwise he wouldn't be in the mess he was in. Just thinking about it made his legs twitch and his guts churn. Maybe Jerry was right, he thought, that everyone needs a reliable moral compass. Unfortunately, Hal's seemed to be broken of late.

It was Renfrew's turn to look at his watch, a wafer-thin gold Patek Philippe timepiece that probably cost more than the average Canadian's annual after-tax income. "I hope you find these sessions helpful, Hal. I know I do. Remember, if there's anything you need, don't hesitate. My door is always open." He stood, elegantly trim in his perfectly tailored two-thousand-dollar suit.

Hal stood too, grunting with the effort and sucking in his gut in a useless attempt to look a little less like a rumpled blimp. "I appreciate that, Jerry."

"You really should join a gym, Hal," Renfrew said.

"I know, Jerry," Hal said. "I wish I had time."

Renfrew came out from behind his desk. He placed a hand on Hal's shoulder as he guided him toward the door. "Physical health is equally as important as spiritual health, Hal."

"There are only so many hours in a day, Jerry," Hal said.

"Hmm," Renfrew said. He opened the door, paused, then suddenly released it, letting it swing shut. His brow furrowed dramatically.

"Something wrong, Jerry?" Hal asked warily.

Renfrew liked to spring things on people at the last minute, operating on the principle that their immediate reactions revealed more than any interview. Hal had a feeling he knew what was coming and began thinking of ways he might squeeze even more hours out of a day.

"I wasn't going to bring this up today," Renfrew said. He hesitated, furrows deepening, feigning indecision.

"What is it, Jerry?" he said, unable to prevent impatience from sharpening his voice.

Renfrew affected not to notice. "I'm sensitive to the fact that Gord Peters is your friend," he said. "So I'll understand if you decide to recuse yourself and bring in an outside firm. But I'm afraid I've got to ask you to initiate an internal audit of his department. I don't like what I've been seeing in his numbers lately. Something doesn't add up."

Shit, Hal thought. Not what he'd expected, but no great surprise, either. Say what you will about Jerry Renfrew, he wasn't stupid. It had been only a matter of time before he caught on to Gord's shenanigans. But the timing could not have been worse.

Renfrew pulled the door open again. "Sorry to drop this in your lap on such short notice," he said, ushering Hal into the outer office. "Think about it, will you? Get back to me next week about how you want to handle it. Have a nice holiday weekend," he said and shut the door.

chapter four

Shoe was in his parents' kitchen, getting a beer out of the fridge, when his brother's wife came up the stairs from the back door.

"How are you doing, Shoe?" she said, reaching past him to take a bottle of white wine from the top shelf.

"I'm doing just fine," he said.

Maureen Ryan Schumacher was a strapping redhead, full-figured and sumptuously curved, but without a gram of apparent extra fat. Her shoulder-length titian hair was tied back in a flamboyant ponytail, emphasizing her strong, even features. She wore a green cotton T-shirt that set off her hair nicely. It had a half-dozen small buttons at the neck, all undone, revealing a couple of inches of abundant cleavage.

She handed him the wine bottle. "Here, you do the honours while I check the veggies."

Shoe took the bottle and Maureen bent to peer into the oven, where red, green, and yellow peppers roasted with garlic, onions, and sweet potato. The position seemed intended to offer him a view of her firm denim-clad rump. He wondered what she did to stay in shape.

She straightened and he handed her the opened wine bottle. "That man's murder put a damper on your home-coming, didn't it?" she said.

"It did," he agreed. She took a tumbler from the cupboard by the sink and held it out to him. He shook his head as he twisted the cap off the beer bottle. "The bottle's fine." She smiled and poured wine into the glass until it was half full.

Hal and Maureen had been married for twenty-five years. Shoe had attended their wedding, but had other-wise spent little time with them in the intervening years and had not come to know Maureen very well. He liked her. She had a cheerful disposition, a mischievous sense of humour — one that wasn't always appreciated, par-ticularly by her husband — and an earthy quality that Shoe found quite appealing. It didn't hurt that she was a knockout. His brother was a fortunate man.

"Maureen," he said.

"Mm?" She looked at him expectantly, leaning against the kitchen counter, folding one arm across her ribcage, resting her other elbow on her forearm.

"What's eating Hal?"

She sighed, obviously disappointed with the choice of topic. "Damned if I know. He hardly talks to me any-more. He's been in an absolutely shitty mood for weeks and it's getting tiresome. If he's having a belated mid-life crisis, I wish he'd get it the fuck — pardon me — over with. Buy a Porsche or have an affair with his secretary. As long as his life insurance is paid up," she added with a grin. "I don't think his heart could stand either expe-rience." She drank some wine. "I'm joking, of course. About the Porsche, anyway. Too expensive. His secre-tary's not. Expensive, that is."

Earlier, while Hal had been preparing the gas

barbecue, Shoe had asked him why he hadn't been at the airport, was everything all right. Hal had shrugged and said, "Something came up at work. My boss's quarterly rah-rah session. He likes to spring them on us. Sorry about that."

Hal was four years older than Shoe, and he looked every day of his fifty-four years. His hair was a lustreless iron-grey, still thick but lying flat and limp on his skull, and his complexion was sallow and waxy. He'd put on a few more pounds since Shoe had last seen him; it did not sit well on his heavy frame. His thick, dark-rimmed glasses kept slipping to the end of his nose.

"What was it you wanted to talk to me about?" Shoe asked.

"What? Oh, that. Waste of time, if Rae's already talked to you." He stooped to open the valve of the propane tank, then stood, breathing heavily. He pushed his glasses back up his nose.

"She told me you thought Mum and Dad should move into a retirement home."

"Well, they aren't getting any younger, are they?"

"None of us are. How do they feel about it?" Shoe asked.

"I haven't said anything to them yet. Rae, of course, won't hear of it. But they're getting too old to live on their own. Mum's arthritis is getting worse. And what if one of them gets sick or has another accident?"

"They seem to be managing all right."

"Damnit, it's bad enough that Rae gives me a hard time about this, don't you start. You haven't seen them since Christmas before last. When was the last time you even spoke to them?"

"I try to call them at least once a week," Shoe said. It could be a frustrating experience. His father's hearing aids frequently fed back through the phone, and as often as not his mother called him "Hal." She'd never been able to keep her sons' names straight; his father usually just called them both "son."

"Okay, I'm sorry," Hal said grudgingly. "But put yourself in my place. You're on the other side of the country and Rae's too goddamn busy being the family's social conscience, I'm the one who has to look after them."

"Isn't that why Rae moved in here with them?" Shoe asked. "To keep an eye on them?"

"Right," Hal said sourly. "And how long do you think it will be before she takes off to march in support of aboriginal land claims or chain herself to some ugly old building protesting the loss of our architectural heritage. You know she participated in the Gay Pride Parade this year? Jesus, you don't think she's a lesbian, do you?"

Shoe decided a change of topic was in order.

"How's Maureen?" he asked.

"She's fine," Hal replied. "She's got this silly idea about starting her own landscaping business."

"Why silly?" Shoe had worked for a landscaping company for a few months when he'd first washed ashore in Vancouver. It had been a satisfying although not especially lucrative experience.

"She was an office manager for a lighting supply company," Hal said. "What does she know about running her own business?"

It seemed to Shoe that that made her as qualified to operate her own business as anyone was. He kept the thought to himself.

"How about you?" Hal asked. "Are you keeping out of trouble?"

"Trying to," Shoe replied.

"That'll be a change. Are you enjoying retirement?"

"Such as it is."

"And, ah, Muriel?"

"Busy."

"You're still together, though, right?"

"After a fashion."

"What does that mean?"

"We just don't see much of each other these days," he said.

"Mm," Hal replied. "Tell me about it."

Shoe was relieved that Hal didn't pursue the subject of Shoe and Muriel Yee's relationship. "What's up with you, Hal? Two years ago you were talking about retiring at fifty-five." Hal would turn fifty-five in October.

"I've made VP since then," Hal replied. "I can't afford to retire." He laughed at his own joke, a little hollowly, Shoe thought. "I'm up for what my boss calls the 'Oscar,' the super-size bonus he gives out every year, basically to rub it in the noses of everyone who doesn't get it. I was thinking about using it to buy an RV and do some travelling, but ... " He shrugged.

"I thought you disliked travelling."

"On business," Hal said. "By plane, especially, and staying in hotels. But last year and the year before Maureen and I rented an RV for a month during the summer. We were hoping to do it again this summer, but, well, it didn't work out. There's some beautiful country out there and we'd like to see some of it before it's all paved over. Y'know, I've never seen the Rocky Mountains except from thirty thousand feet in the air. Anyway, it was just an idea," he'd added.

"You've had worse ones," Shoe had said.

"Eh?" Hal had replied. "What's that supposed to mean?"

"Nothing, Hal," Shoe had said. "Relax."

Maureen stood away from the kitchen counter with a thrust of her hips, picked up the wine bottle, and beckoned him with it to follow her down the stairs to the back door and out into the yard. The evening was warm, but the humidity had gone down. The sound of crickets and cicadas and tree frogs was an appropriate accompaniment to the easy jazz drifting from speakers Maureen had propped in the basement window. The music was occasionally overwhelmed by the squeals and shouts of the kids playing in the pool in the backyard of the house three doors down, next to the house that had once belonged to Marvin Cartwright.

Shoe's parents sat in lawn chairs at the top of the slope while Hal tended the barbecue. He turned marinated chicken breasts, spicy Italian sausages, and butterfly pork chops, the barbecue tongs in one hand, a beer in the other. He drained the bottle and set it down with the two other empties on the ground next to the barbecue.

"So where's mine?" he said to Shoe, eyeing the beer in Shoe's hand.

"Take this one," Shoe said, handing the bottle to his brother.

Maureen frowned at her husband, said to Shoe, "I'll get you another one."

"Don't bother," he said.

"We're almost done here," Hal said, moving the food to the back of the grill. "Where the hell's Rae got to?"

"She had some errands to run," Shoe said. "She said she'd be back in plenty of time for dinner."

"I'm here," Rachel said as she came around the corner of the garage, staggering under the weight of a large cardboard carton. "Help," she squeaked.

Shoe took the carton from her and set it on the bench by the back door. "Rae's kid stuff" was scrawled on the top in Magic Marker.

"Whew, thanks," Rachel said. She went to her parents, bent and kissed first her mother, then her father. "Sorry I'm late." She exchanged a hug with Maureen, gratefully accepted a glass of wine, and said, "I hope you and Hal can account for your whereabouts last night."

Maureen chuckled. Hal harrumphed. Howard Schumacher said, "Eh? What was that?"

Rachel raised her voice and said, "It's okay, Pop. I was just wondering if Maureen and Hal had alibis for last night. Joe, you're probably the only one of us with an absolutely airtight alibi for the time of Marvin Cartwright's murder."

"Hal was rattling the windows when I got home at two from a night out with a girlfriend," Maureen said. "Of course, who knows what he was up to while I was out."

"I was working," Hal said. "Someone has to." The remark earned him an angry glare from his wife. "I took the last train and didn't get home till half past one," he added, shutting down the gas to the barbecue. He began transferring chicken breasts, sausages, and pork chops to a platter.

Shoe looked into the shadowy woods. Marvin Cartwright's body had been taken away late in the day and the crime scene shelter had been dismantled.

"Where did they find the body?" Maureen asked.

Hal said, "Do we have to talk about this?" He banged the platter down onto the picnic table.

Maureen sighed heavily and turned toward the house. "I'll get the veggies."

"I'll give you a hand," Rachel said.

Rachel and Maureen went into the house, leaving Shoe alone with his brother and his parents. No one spoke, but Shoe was comfortable with silence. So were his parents, sitting close, his father's hand resting lightly on his mother's arm, as if to reassure her she was not alone. Hal, however, fidgeted and seemed on the verge of speaking, but evidently could not think of anything to say.

Shoe told himself he needed to make a greater effort to come home more often. Despite his father's increasing deafness and his mother's arthritis and blindness, his parents were remarkably fit for their ages, but they were, he reminded himself, both in their eighties. They were probably in better health than Hal, Shoe thought, judging from the pallor of his brother's skin and that the slightest exertion seemed to make him short of breath. When was the last time Hal had had a physical? Shoe wondered. *On the other hand*, he thought grimly, *when was the last time I had a complete physical?* He'd been checked out in the Vancouver General ER just before Christmas, after a martial arts expert named Del Tilley had tried his best to kick him to death. His injuries, albeit painful, had been minor, mostly superficial, and they hadn't done a blood workup or an EKG. To his credit, he tried to run at least ten kilometres three or four times a week, worked out with weights or swam as often as he could, and enjoyed walking. He'd never smoked, seldom drank alcohol, and watched his diet, although he wasn't obsessive about it. He wore the same size jeans he had at twenty-five. He supposed he had a few miles in him yet.

Maureen and Rachel came out of the house. Maureen carried the platter of roasted vegetables, Rae another bottle of wine in one hand and three bottles of beer in the other, the necks between her fingers. She handed one to Shoe, one to her father, and Hal took the third, which got him another frown from his wife.

"I guess I'm driving home tonight," she said. Ignoring Hal's sullen glower, she started dishing out the food.

"Be right back," Rachel said. Ignoring a conveniently placed gate, she effortlessly vaulted the chest-high, vine-covered fence into the backyard of the house next door, where the Levinsons had once lived, walked to the back door, knocked, and went inside. She emerged a moment later, accompanied by a portly, bearded man. He opened the gate, let Rachel through, then followed, carefully closing the gate behind them. Arm in arm, they walked across the yard to the patio. The man bore two bottles of wine in his free arm.

"Hey, Doc," Howard Schumacher said.

"Evening, folks," the man said. He set the wine bottles on the picnic table.

He was in his early sixties, Shoe guessed, with a neatly trimmed salt and pepper beard and longish greying black hair that was thinning on top. He wore rimless eyeglasses with thick lenses that lent him a slightly startled look. He was dressed in an oxford shirt, corduroy trousers that were slightly baggy at the knees, and rugged walking shoes.

"Doc," Rachel said. "Meet my brother Joe. Joe, meet Dr. Harvey Wiseman."

Shoe held out his hand. "How do you do, Dr. Wiseman?" Wiseman's handshake was firm and quick.

"It's a pleasure to finally meet you," Wiseman replied, lamplight glinting off the lenses of his glasses. "I've heard a lot about you from Howard and Vera and Rachel. And, please, call me Harv."

"Ignore him," Rachel said. "Everyone calls him Doc."

"Despite my best efforts," Wiseman said. "I'm a physicist, not a physician. In my opinion, PhDs who insist on being called 'Doctor' are far too full of themselves. Besides, like Stephen Leacock, I'm afraid that if people call me Doc, one of these days I'll be called upon to delivery a baby."

"Far be it from me to put a helpless infant or unsuspecting parents at risk," Shoe said. "Harv, it is."

"I'm told I should call you Shoe."

"Most people do."

"Well, if Shoe fits," Wiseman said, to an chorus of groans. "Now that that's settled, let's eat. I'm starved. Hal, those sausages look delicious. Blackened just the way I like them."

"Uh, I think they have pork in them," Hal said. "There's chicken."

"I appreciate the thought, really, but they definitely look kosher to me." He speared a sausage off the platter, dropped it with a hard clunk onto his plate.

No one spoke for a time, concentrating on the food, while the cicadas and tree frogs sang along with Diana Krall. Shoe wondered what Muriel was doing at that moment. Working, most likely. He missed her, wished that she'd been able to come with him, but she'd been too busy. Perhaps next time …

"Doc," Howard Schumacher said around a mouthful of chicken, finally breaking the lull. "You heard about the dead man in the woods?"

"Pop," Hal said sternly.

"Yes, I did," Wiseman replied. "The police spoke to me earlier today. Awful. Beaten to death. I understand he used to live in the neighbourhood. Did you know him?"

"Sort of," Shoe's father said.

"Look," Hal said. "Do you really think this is appropriate dinner conversation?"

"Oh, Hal," Rachel said. "Don't be such a stuffed shirt." She poked him in the gut with a finger. "Your shirt is already stuffed enough as it is."

Maureen choked and coughed, unsuccessfully stifling a giggle. Hal's face clouded. He threw down his knife and fork with a clatter, stood, and stalked away from the table.

Shoe's mother cast about worriedly. "Hal, dear, what's wrong? What's the matter?"

"Forget it, Mother," Rachel said. "Hal has left the building."

chapter five

Shoe and Rachel sat side by side in aluminum lawn chairs at the top of the slope of the yard. Fireflies sparked lazily against the backdrop of the dark woods. Rachel cradled a bottle of beer in her lap. Shoe had a mug of coffee, thus far in his life mercifully immune to the negative effects of caffeine. His parents had gone to bed and Harvey Wiseman was in the kitchen with Maureen, helping with the washing up. No one knew where Hal had got to, but at least he hadn't taken his car; it was blocked by Rachel's yellow New Beetle.

"Maureen has been after Hal to lose some weight for ages," Rachel said. She took a slug from the beer bottle. "I guess he's a little sensitive about it."

"I think there's more to it than that," Shoe said. "How are things between Maureen and him?"

"I like Maureen," Rachel said. "And I think she likes me. But we're not close. We hardly ever talk about personal issues. Maybe we should. The short answer is, I don't know. Given Hal's behaviour this evening, maybe not so great."

"He told me that you and he disagree about whether Mum and Dad should move into a seniors' residence."

"That's what he said, we *disagree* about whether or not they should?" She sighed heavily. "I'm not against them moving into a seniors' residence. In fact, it was me who brought it up after Dad fell on the basement stairs going down to do the laundry. He wasn't hurt, but it was a wake-up call that maybe it's time they considered selling the house and moving into some place a little easier to manage."

"So you're not moving in permanently?"

"Christ, no. I just stay here on weekends. More than that, I'd go nuts. So would Mum and Dad. I don't care if they move into an apartment or a seniors' residence. What I'm against is the dump Hal thinks they should move to. He says they can't afford anything else, but that's bull. Do you know what this place is worth? Half a million at least. If they sold it, they'd have over a million dollars in cash and investments.

"Our parents are fucking millionaires, Joe. Doc says a million dollars isn't what it used to be. I'll have to take his word for it. But a million is more than enough for them to move into a much better place than the one Hal thinks they should. I found a place that'd run them about seventy-five grand a year, everything included. Even at the miserable interest rates the banks are paying these days, a million would easily last them twenty years. Okay, it's not inconceivable that they could both outlive the money, but how likely is it? Hal's just worried that there won't be anything left over for him."

"And you're not?"

"I'm not a millionaire by any stretch of the imagination, but business is good and I'm doing all right." Rachel called herself a strategic marketing analyst, whatever that was, and worked out of her house in Port Credit, just west of Toronto, beside the GO train tracks. "I don't need their money," she went on. "Neither does Hal. At least, I don't think he does — I don't know what his financial situation is. You don't, do you?"

"I have no idea what Hal's financial situation is."

"Need money, I mean."

"No," he said.

If Hal's problems were financial, Shoe might be in a position to help. Unlike Rachel, he was a millionaire, a little more than twice over, in fact, even more on paper. It was a situation that made him acutely uncomfortable whenever he thought about it, which he seldom did. He had never been particularly interested in money for its own sake. He appreciated its usefulness, but was not the least bit acquisitive. Bill Hammond had paid well and Shoe lived simply, his only extravagance being his house in Kitsilano, purchased with cash two years before, after the *Princess Pete*, the converted logging tug he'd lived on for a decade, had burned to the waterline. During his twenty-five years with Hammond Industries, Shoe had invested cautiously but well, and had built up a moderately comfortable nest egg for his eventual retirement. He'd also received the equivalent of two years' salary from Bill Hammond for finding Patrick O'Neill's killer. What had pushed him over the top, however, had been the stock, cash, and property Hammond had left Shoe in his will. In addition to being a minority shareholder in Hammond Industries, Shoe was also the proud owner of a more than slightly rundown motel and marina on the Sunshine Coast, north of Vancouver.

"Doc says the decision should be up to them," Rachel said.

"Wise man," Shoe said.

"Haw."

"How long have you known him?" Shoe asked.

"Doc? Almost my whole life. Well, since I was sixteen, anyway. He and his wife moved into the Levinson's house around the time you moved to Vancouver. Jesus, almost thirty years."

"Are you and he romantically involved?"

She made a face at him. "Nosy bugger, aren't you? You want to know if we're sleeping together?"

"Not especially."

"Well, we're not. He thinks he's too old for me."

"And you don't?"

"No, I guess I don't. I've made that pretty clear to him. His wife died of cancer three years ago and I don't think he's over it yet. I'm not sure I am either. She was a great lady. Her name was Rachel too. That may also have something to do with it."

A comfortable curtain of silence dropped between them as a warm breeze rattled through the leaves overhead, punctuated by the distant trill of a woman's laughter, a man roaring at his kids to get the hell inside this very minute, a dog barking, a door slamming, car tires squealing, and the far-off banshee wail of a high-performance motorcycle accelerating through the gears.

"How well do you remember Marvin Cartwright?" Shoe asked.

"Earlier today, if anyone had asked, I'd've said, 'Not very well,' but a lot of stuff is starting to come back. Bits and pieces mainly. Drinking hot chocolate with marshmallow after skating. Watching *Mr. Blizzard* after school on a big console colour television set with Marty, Bobby Cotton, and Mickey Bloom. Mr. Cartwright teaching us how to play chess in a room lined with books and records and drawings of birds. And the smell of disinfectant and bleach and his mother calling from her room in the back of the house. But I don't remember what he looked like."

"It was a long time ago. You were pretty young."

"Do you remember him?"

"I don't recall ever speaking to him. I certainly never went into his house. Like you, I also remember bits and pieces, some more vividly than others." He had a sudden recollection of a man with his shirt sleeves rolled up, vigorously polishing the body of a dark green car as an awkward, gangly boy watched from the far side of the street. "For instance, I remember his car. It was English. A Rover, I think. British racing green. I have the impression it was old. Not new, anyway. He would work on it in his driveway. Change the oil, rotate the tires, tune it up. I always wanted to talk to him about it, but I never did."

"I don't remember it," Rachel said. "Boys and their toys. You never played tricks on him, though, like Hal and Dougie Hallam and Tim Dutton, did you?"

"No, I never did."

"How come? I remember you getting into trouble at school for playing practical jokes. Like switching the signs on the boys' and girls' washrooms during a district track-and-field meet."

"Not the same thing at all," Shoe said.

"No, of course not," Rachel said. She looked around as Maureen and Harvey Wiseman came out of the house. "I wonder where the hell Hal's got to?"

chapter six

Hal had not gone far. After storming away from the table, he'd walked to the small park behind the houses across the street, where the following day they would be setting up for the homecoming festival. He'd plopped himself down on a bench, out of breath, his anger dissipated, and with it his sense of self-righteousness. He tried to rekindle the feelings of resentment, but it was like trying to set a match to soggy paper, so he gave it up. God, he was tired. He felt as though there were a powerful vacuum in the middle of his chest, sucking the life out of him. He hadn't got a wink of sleep the night before and felt that if he closed his eyes he might never be able to open them again. Then again, maybe that wouldn't be such a bad thing. Oblivion sounded like a pretty good deal at the moment, all things considered. Good luck repossessing his soul.

He fished around in his pockets for his cigarettes, a habit he'd only recently reacquired, after more than twenty years of abstinence. He didn't find them; they were locked in the glove box of his car. What he found instead was a folded piece of notepaper. He unfolded it and peered at it in the dim light of the pseudo-Victorian lamppost a few feet from the bench. He couldn't read it without his glasses, which were back at the house, but he knew what was written on it.

Despite what he'd told that sanctimonious blowhard Jerry Renfrew, all was not well in the Schumacher household. Hal was certain Maureen was having an affair and the note was a list of the men with whom he thought she might be having it: Davy, the twenty-something kid who worked at the garden centre where Maureen seemed to spend an inordinate amount of time; Bob Nobbs, who lived two doors down from them in Oakville and who claimed to be some kind of writer, but since his divorce spent all his time reading magazines and drinking beer on a chaise lounge in his backyard; Ivan, the muscle-bound Neanderthal who worked at the gym Maureen went to three times a week; and Clark Sheppard, husband of Maureen's best friend, Dinah, and supercilious jerk of the first water. There were two other entries, men whose names Hal did not know: the man who jogged by the house every morning as Hal was leaving for work, whom Hal simply called the Sweater; and the Samaritan, a man Hal had never seen but who Maureen had told him had helped her when her car had broken down in the parking lot of Maple Grove mall.

Hal folded the notepaper and returned it to his pocket. He should go back to the house, he thought, face them, apologize for his behaviour. He could not move, immobilized by ennui.

If Joe hadn't lived in Vancouver, Hal would have included his brother's name on the list. The last time Joe had visited Toronto, two Christmases ago, he'd stayed with Hal and Maureen, because he hadn't wanted to impose on their parents, he'd said. It was all right to impose on him and Maureen, though, Hal had grumbled to Maureen at the time.

"Oh, Hal," she'd said, "don't be such an old poop. He's your brother, for heaven's sake. And he's no trouble, really."

"If he's no trouble, why doesn't he stay with my mother and father then?" Hal had replied.

"Why don't you want him to stay with us?" Maureen had asked.

Because I don't want him around you, he'd almost said. *Or you around him.*

A bubble of gas rose painfully in his chest. He squirmed and belched. The pain eased, but his stomach burned, as though it were being slowly dissolved in acid. Just what he needed, he thought glumly. A goddamned ulcer. Christ, his life was turning to crap. *Yeah*, he chided himself, *and whose fault was that? Face it, fat boy. You blew it. Now what're you going to do to fix it?*

Still, it wasn't fair. He'd worked hard all his adult life to build a secure future for himself and Maureen, only to see it all come crashing down around him because of a couple of bad judgement calls. What really rankled, though, was that his brother, who professed not to care about such things, had lucked into more money than he'd ever need simply by being in the right place at the right time. Things had always come easily to Joe, the grades, the jobs, the girls, whereas Hal had had to struggle for everything he'd achieved, including his wife.

Only to watch it all slip through his fingers ...

Hal's head bobbed and he realized he had dozed off. Jesus, he could've been mugged, he thought, nervously looking about. The small park was deserted. His bladder finally coaxed him off the bench and back to his parents' house. He went in the front door, hoping to use the bathroom before having to face the others, but Maureen and

Harvey Wiseman were in the kitchen, finishing up the dishes.

Maureen draped the dishtowel through the fridge door handle. "Well, where did you get to?" she said, in that accusatory tone she was so good at.

"I went for a walk," he said sullenly, continuing down the hall to the bathroom. The door to his parents' bedroom was closed. It was only ever closed when they were in bed.

After using the bathroom, he returned to the kitchen. It was empty. He got a beer from the fridge, scoffing down a couple of leftover barbecued pork chops while he was at it, then went out into the backyard. Rachel and Wiseman stood at the base of the yard, on the edge of the dark woods, talking quietly. Maureen and Joe sat in lawn chairs placed close together at the top of the yard, facing the woods. They stopped talking when Hal let the screen door slam shut behind him.

chapter seven

Very little surprised Hannah Lewis anymore. She had learned early to take things in stride. But that afternoon, she'd been knocked for a loop when she'd realized that the tall, dark-haired man with the battered face and distant eyes was none other than Joe Shoe. She hadn't let it show, of course, but it hadn't been easy; she'd spent so much of her teens listening to her brother's endless bitching about how Shoe had stolen his wife and destroyed his career that she'd almost come to believe it herself.

Shoe had done neither, of course. Shortly after Ron's "accident," and two months before her death, Sara had set Hannah straight, explaining that her marriage to Ron had ended long before she'd met Shoe because Ron had insisted that she choose between marriage and her career as a police officer. Likewise, it had been Ron who, in a jealous rage after discovering that Shoe and Sara were seeing each other, had gone after Shoe in the locker room with his nightstick. If Ron's injury and resulting forced retirement was anyone's fault, it was his own, not Shoe's.

Shoe had simply been defending himself. Moreover, had Shoe not told the division commander that he and Ron had been roughhousing and that Ron's injury had been an accident, for which Shoe had nevertheless received a reprimand, Ron would not have qualified for a disability pension.

"Most of Ron's troubles are of his own making," Sara had told her. "Maybe one of these days he'll realize it."

Hannah lucked into a parking space immediately in front of her three-storey row house in the Danforth, across from the old, scaffolding-encased Greek Orthodox church that was in its fifth year of restoration. She'd got the house in the divorce, otherwise she might not have been able to afford to live in the area. As it was, the upkeep and the taxes were slowly bleeding her dry. She loved her house, though, and the neighbourhood, even if parking seriously sucked.

As she locked up her ten-year-old Pathfinder, her cellphone began to ring. She swore when she saw the number on the call display, and pressed the button that sent the call directly to her voice mail. Florence De Franco had called at least twice a day for the past three days. Obviously, she'd weaselled Hannah's unlisted numbers out of her husband, who was a city councillor, as well as a member of the civilian Police Services Board. Dominic De Franco had denied giving Hannah's numbers to his wife, but there was no other way she could have got them.

Inside, the message light on her landline phone was blinking. She pressed the recall button and swore again. Her brother had called twice and Florence De Franco had called three times. Wearily, she accessed her voice mail. Both had left messages. She fast-forwarded and erased them all without listening to them. She knew what they were about.

In June, Councillor De Franco's wife had gone into Ron's copy and print shop to place an order for invitations to a charity event she was organizing. The day after the invitations had gone out, however, someone noticed that the date was wrong — August 12 had been transposed to read August 21. Ron was certain he'd used the date Mrs. De Franco had given him, but admitted it was possible he'd transposed the numbers when he'd filled out the order form. Either way, he offered to tear up the bill and mail out corrections at his own expense. Mrs. De Franco, however, would have none of it. She accused him of purposely trying to sabotage the event, claiming he'd made an indecent proposal, which she'd rebuffed, and that sabotaging the event was his way of getting back at her.

"It's crap," Ron told Hannah. "She's not bad looking, but nothing to write home about." As if it mattered.

Ron sent out the corrections, hoping it would end there. No such luck. A few days later, Mrs. De Franco filed a police report, alleging that Ron had vandalized her car and sprayed herbicide on her prize-winning roses. Likewise crap, apparently. The police couldn't find any damage to the car and the roses looked fine. According to a reporter friend of Ron's at the *Toronto Sun*, Mrs. De Franco had a history of making nutty allegations. She'd evidently accused mail carriers of reading her mail before delivering it, gas station attendants of making sexual advances by suggestively poking the pump nozzle into the gas filler, and her vet of injecting her dog with a drug that made it hump her leg. Her allegations against Ron were just more of the same. Now the woman was accusing Hannah of abusing her police powers to have her phone tapped and have her followed. Things were getting out of hand.

The doorbell rang.

"Christ, now what?" Hannah muttered as she went

to the door and peered through the peephole. "Shit," she said when she saw her brother's balding pate shining under the porch light. She was briefly tempted to leave him standing there, but he must have been waiting nearby in his car for her to get home. She opened the door.

"You're working late," he said.

"You know how it is," she said, stepping back to let him in. She closed the door behind him. "What's up?"

"Haven't you listened to your messages?" He followed her into the living room.

"No."

"The light on your phone isn't blinking. You erased them without listening to them, didn't you?"

She sighed. "C'mon, Ron. Gimme a break. It's been a long day."

"You know what that crazy bitch says I did now?"

"No," she said. "And I don't want to know."

But Ron wasn't listening. "She says that I hired someone to hide in her closet, videotape her getting undressed for bed, and post the videos on the Internet. I've had it up to here with this crap. I'm going to get me a lawyer."

"Save your money, Ron. The woman's obviously got psychiatric problems. No one takes her seriously. Just ignore her."

"Hell with that. I did some poking around and found out she was diagnosed with a borderline personality disorder. Hah! Nothing borderline about it. Last year, when her husband claims she was on vacation in Mexico, she was locked up in the psych ward of Mount Sinai. Sleazebag's been covering for her for years. She's been busted for everything from shoplifting to public indecency. If she doesn't stop this crap, I'm going to send what I got to my buddy at the *Sun*."

"Christ, you really are your own bloody worst enemy, aren't you?"

"What's that supposed to mean?" he demanded.

"If you go dragging her psychiatric history through the muck, you're going to need that lawyer. Let it go."

"You're afraid that if I make a stink it will wreck your chances of promotion."

"That's not fair," she said. But it wasn't entirely untrue. Being a cop, and a female cop at that, was tough enough without making enemies on the Police Services Board. "Have you eaten? I'm going to fix myself something."

"I'm okay. Wouldn't turn down a beer, though."

"Help yourself." He did, and when they were seated at the table in her kitchen-cum-dining room, Ron with a beer and a can of dry roasted peanuts, Hannah with a salad and a glass of white wine — a big glass — she said, "You'll never guess who I saw today."

"Okay, so tell me."

"Joe Shoe."

"No kidding. Where?"

"At his parents' house in Downsview."

"What were you doing there?"

"Working a case."

"Don't tell me he killed someone."

"No. He's in town visiting his family. Last night a man who used to live in the neighbourhood was beaten to death in the woods behind his parents' house."

"Bad timing. How is he?"

"I didn't recognize him at first. He's been living out west. Vancouver."

"He still a cop?"

"No. He's some kind of corporate investigator. He looks like he's taken his share of lumps, though."

"I hear the corporate world can be pretty dog eat dog. The vic … ?"

"What about him?"

"Any leads?"

"Nothing much so far. Early days yet."

"What was the name again?"

She smiled dryly. He smiled back. She hadn't mentioned the victim's name. She said, "Cartwright. Marvin Cartwright."

"Cartwright?" Ron said.

"That's right. What is it?"

"Nothing," he said. "Sounds familiar, that's all."

Hannah finished her salad and poured herself another glass of wine. Ron refused a second beer.

"I'm driving," he said. "Speaking of which, I should get going." He stood. "If you see Shoe again, say hello for me, will you?"

"Sure," Hannah said, walking him to the door.

"Tell him … " Ron paused, seeming lost in thought for a moment. Hannah let him find his own way back. "Tell him, if he's got time, to drop by the shop. We'll go grab a beer or something, get caught up. Tell him … " He hesitated, then said, "Tell him it'd be good to see him."

"I will," she said.

"Good," he said. He kissed her quickly on the cheek and almost ran down the steps.

No, nothing much surprised her anymore.

chapter eight

"Goddamnit, Hal," Maureen said, bracing herself against the dashboard as Hal braked suddenly. "What the hell is going on with you? And slow down, for god's sake. Or pull over and let me drive." She immediately regretted the offer, hoped he wouldn't take her up on it; she'd had a couple of glasses of wine too many herself.

"I'm not drunk," he snapped, mashing the horn button because the car in front of them had slowed to make a right turn without signalling.

"I didn't say you were drunk," Maureen said with a sigh. Sometimes talking to Hal was like talking to a five-year-old. "I wish you'd tell me what's bothering you."

"Nothing's bothering me," he growled.

"Oh, for god's sake, Hal, it's obvious something is bothering you. What is it? Is it work? Is it me? Have I done something to piss you off?"

"What were you and my brother talking about?"

"He was telling me about Marvin Cartwright, the man who was killed in the woods."

"I know who Marvin Cartwright was, for Christ's sake. What did he tell you?"

"He didn't get a chance to tell me very much at all before you came barging out and practically accused him of trying to fuck me. Frankly, it was bloody embarrassing."

"Not half as embarrassing as watching you fawn all over him like he was some kind of rock star or something."

"Oh, for heaven's sake, Hal, don't be ridiculous. I was not fawning all over him. I was just being polite. What's the matter with you?"

"Nothing's the matter with me," he barked. "What's the matter with you? Look at you. You're a forty-five-year-old woman dressed like a goddamned teenager. You're practically falling out of that shirt. And it's so thin I can see your nipples right through it, for god's sake."

"If I was dressed like a teenager, Hal, you'd see a lot more than my nipples. I'd have jeans so low I'd have to shave my pubic hair, tattoos, and a stud through my tongue. Maybe one in my clitoris, too. How's that, Hal? Maybe I should get a clitoral ring. I'm told it makes cunnilingus a lot more interesting."

"That's disgusting."

"What's disgusting, Hal, is that just because I'm forty-five you think I should dress like your mother."

"What's wrong with the way my mother dresses?"

"Oh, for god's sake, Hal, it was just a figure of speech."

Hal lapsed into a sullen silence. Did he really think she was interested in Shoe? Maureen wondered, staring out the passenger side window. Or, if she was, that she'd do anything about it? If she was honest with herself, and she tended to be, she'd be the first to admit that she found Shoe attractive. What was not to be attracted to? Well, lots, actually. He wasn't exactly handsome. His jaw was crooked, his nose was bent, and there was something oddly asymmetrical about his cheekbones. In fact, he looked as though someone had taken a baseball bat to his face. But he seemed to be in great shape, didn't drink much, didn't smoke, and, most refreshing, did not litter his speech with profanity, whereas she had a vocabulary that would make Tony Soprano blush. He wasn't a prude. Swearing just wasn't a habit he'd acquired. She wondered what his views were on cunnilingus.

"What's funny?" Hal asked tartly.

"Eh?"

"You laughed."

"Did I?"

"Yes, you did."

"Sorry."

Poor Hal. He was as unlike his brother as a man could be. He was overweight, drank too much, smoked (although he didn't know she knew), swore, albeit not as much as she did, and seemed to think that oral sex of any variety was disgusting. A man who doesn't like fellatio, her friend Dinah had said to her once, was as rare as a duck that doesn't like water. "Not that I'm especially keen on it," she'd added, "but I don't mind doing it if I know I can expect something in return. Fortunately, Clark is as happy to give as to receive." Maureen's experience with either was sadly limited.

Nor was Hal the same man she'd married twenty-five years ago. Maybe what she found so attractive and exciting about Shoe was that he reminded her a little of Hal when he'd been younger. Or maybe she was just making excuses for herself. There was an element of danger about Shoe that Hal had never possessed. There was also an odd, almost contradictory vulnerability about him. Shoe brought out the protective side of her that Hal never had, but at the same time he brought out her submissive side as well. Although she had never been a fan of the adventure romance novels Dinah consumed like air, Maureen laughed at the sudden and completely ridiculous image of herself on the heaving deck of a storm-tossed sailing ship, bodice of her gown ripped, clinging to Shoe's sinewy arm as he steered the ship between treacherous shoals to the safety of a sheltered bay, where they made tender passionate love on a white sand beach.

"What's funny now?" Hal demanded as he turned the car into the driveway of their house in Oakville and shut down the engine.

"You don't want to know," Maureen muttered, half under her breath.

chapter nine

The envelope fell from between the pages of a pink, vinyl-covered diary with a tiny clasp lock, which she'd had to break open with a nail file. It was a standard No. 10 business envelope, folded once. The crease was sharp and the paper crackled dryly as she unfolded it. There was no stamp, no return address, just her first name written large on the front. She lifted the flap of the envelope and extracted a single sheet of typewriter paper, folded three times. It was a letter, written in a neat, even hand.

Dear Rachel,

I'm sorry to have to say goodbye to you like this, rather than in person. Please forgive me. I hope you will not be too angry with me for too long. That would make me sad. Much sadder that I am already.

I will miss all you kids — you, Marty, Bobby, Mickey, and the others — but I will miss you most of all. I will never have children of my own

*and getting to know you and the other kids —
But mostly you! — made me realize how much
I will be missing.*

*Please tell the other kids goodbye for me.
Especially Marty. She's very lucky to have a
friend like you.*

*Say goodbye to your brothers, too. From
what you told me about Joe, he sounds like a
good boy. It's a shame he was too shy to talk
to me. I hope he and Joey can patch up their
friendship. And don't be too hard on Hal. He's
a good boy too. He just fell in with the wrong
crowd for a while.*

*Rachel, after I'm gone, you may hear peo-
ple say bad things about me, some of which you
may not understand until you are older. Please
remember, though, that things are not always as
they seem.*

*Thank you for being my friend. I will re-
member you forever.*

The letter was signed, *Marvin, your favourite
Martian*, and the signature was embellished with a simple cartoon of a little man with big feet and stubby an-
tennae above pointy ears.

The drawing blurred as tears filled her eyes. She
swallowed the hard lump in her throat. The sadness she
felt was an almost physical thing, not quite pain, not
quite emptiness, in the middle of her chest. She'd completely forgotten about the letter, just as she had all but
forgotten him. *I will remember you forever*, he'd written.
She touched the letter, running her fingertips along the
words. Had he remembered her? She hoped so.

She heard a noise behind her and turned. Joe was on
the basement stairs, caught in the act of reversing direction to go back up again.

"I'm sorry," he said. "I didn't mean to intrude."

"You're not," she said, wiping the tears from her eyes with the tips of her fingers.

"Are you all right?" he said, descending again.

"Yeah, I'm fine. I found a letter Marvin Cartwright wrote me when he left." She handed the letter to him. He read it quickly, then handed it back to her. "I don't remember how I got it. I mean, I remember reading it, I think, but not getting it." She looked at the letter again, scanning the text, then looked up. "I don't remember people saying bad things about him," she said.

"You were pretty young. A lot of people were sure he was the Black Creek Rapist."

"Not Mum and Dad, though."

"No, I think they knew him a little better than most. Or tried to."

Rachel looked at the letter again. *Please tell the other kids goodbye for me*, Mr. Cartwright had written. Had she? She didn't remember. She didn't remember telling anyone about the letter, not her parents, not Joe or Hal, not even Marty. Some best friend, she thought sadly. But she hadn't seen much of Marty after her attack; she'd stopped coming round the house, despite her gigantic crush on Joe. She could have tried harder to stay in touch, though, Rachel thought guiltily.

"I'm sorry I didn't say goodbye to you for him," she said to Shoe.

"That's all right," he said. "I hardly knew him."

"Were you too shy to talk to him?"

"I suppose I was," he said.

She glanced at the letter again. "You never did patch things up with Joey, did you?"

"No," he said quietly.

Joey Noseworthy had been Joe's best friend from the first grade until their final year of junior high school. People had called them Joe and Little Joe; by fourteen,

Joe was almost six feet tall, whereas Joey had barely made it past five feet. While their friendship lasted, they'd been virtually inseparable; Joey had spent as much time at their house as Marty, and Rachel had had as big a crush on Joey as Marty had had on Joe. In their final year of junior high school, however, Joey had stopped coming round and Joe had started spending more time with Janey Hallam. Rachel didn't know what had happened between them, and had never asked. She thought it might have had something to do with Janey. Despite being two years younger than Joe and Joey, "Calamity Janey" had become the third "j" of the triangle a few years before. If it wasn't a love triangle, it was the next best thing, and just as unstable.

With a jolt, Rachel realized that Joe and Joey had fallen out in the spring of the same year that Marvin Cartwright had moved away, a month or so before the attacks in the Dells had begun.

"What is it?" Joe asked.

She folded the letter and put it back into the envelope. "I'm going to have a drink before going to bed. Join me?"

"I'll keep you company," he said.

They went upstairs, where Rachel took a bottle of Glenmorangie single malt whisky down from the top shelf of a kitchen cupboard. "I keep this around for emergencies." She took a tumbler from the cupboard and poured herself a generous shot. The smoky aroma filled the room. "Sure you won't change your mind?"

"A finger," he said.

She got down another glass and poured him a shot, to which he added a few drops of water from the filter jug in the refrigerator. She knew that that was supposed to be the proper way to drink single malt, a drop or two of water to bring out the flavours, but she preferred hers unadulterated. They went back down to the basement, to what had been the TV room when they were growing up. The television had long since been relocated upstairs and the old overstuffed sofa and matching chairs smelled of dust and disuse. Her nose twitched as she stifled a sneeze. She sipped her whisky. It helped.

"A couple a years ago some wannabe gang bangers beat some poor bastard half to death in the main parking lot of the conservation area," she said. "Just for the hell of it, apparently. Do you think that's what happened to Marvin Cartwright?"

"Possibly," her brother replied. "He was a long way from the parking lot, though."

"Who do you think did it then?"

"I haven't any idea."

"But you've thought about it, haven't you? I can see it in your eyes. You can't help it. It's the cop in you."

"I haven't been a police officer for almost thirty years. There isn't any cop left in me."

"You don't believe that any more than I do, Joe." She couldn't bring herself to call him Shoe. "I remember when you graduated from the police college. You were so proud you almost actually smiled when your photograph was taken, and you never smiled when your photograph was taken. Being a cop was the perfect job for you. I'll bet a day doesn't go by that you don't — " Her mouth snapped shut, chopping off the words, but it was too late. She saw the brief flash of pain at the memory of Sara's death, killed on duty by a drunk driver the day after he'd proposed, and she'd accepted. Christ, could she have been any more stupid and insensitive? "Joe, I'm sorry."

"Forget it," he said. He sipped his whisky.

Maybe if he hadn't moved to Vancouver after Sara died, Rachel thought, if she'd seen more of him, she wouldn't keep forgetting that he wasn't the big, dumb lummox too many people seemed to think he was. Not by a long shot. He wasn't always so easy to read, though;

like that old *Star Trek* character, the half-alien Mr. Spock, Joe pretty much kept his feelings to himself. Which didn't mean he didn't have any. He'd simply learned early, maybe too early, not to let much, if anything, show. Why, how, or exactly when, Rachel wasn't sure. One incident stood out in her mind.

When Joe was thirteen, he'd fallen while playing capture the flag in the woods, landing on an old board and driving a rusty nail through the palm of his left hand. Rachel and Marty had been helping Rachel's mother bake cookies when Joe had walked into the kitchen and calmly proclaimed, "I think I need to go to the doctor." Rachel's mother had almost fainted at the sight of the rusty four-inch spike through his hand, but Joe had been so cool and matter-of-fact about it Rachel had said incredulously, "Doesn't it hurt?"

"Sure it hurts," he replied. "Look, it goes right through." He showed her and Marty the bloody inch of nail sticking out of the back of his hand.

"Neat," Marty said. "How come it isn't bleeding much?"

"The nail is plugging the hole, I guess."

Rachel's mother had been so shaken she'd had to get Mrs. Levinson next door to drive them to the doctor's office. Rachel and Marty went, too, and both watched, fascinated, as the doctor sprayed Joe's hand with something that smelled harsh and cold, pulled the nail from his hand with a pair of funny-looking pliers, then cleaned out the wound with a fat orange toothpick. All while Joe sat absolutely still and expressionless. After the doctor bandaged his hand and gave him a tetanus shot, he complimented Joe on how brave he'd been. Rachel thought he was incredibly brave too, even though she'd seen the muscles in his jaw twitch and the single tear that had escaped from the corner of his eye. Marty had just stared at him with an expression of total adoration on her face.

"Big deal," Hal, then seventeen, had said when Rachel told him of Joe's mishap. "What's he want, a medal or a chest to pin it on?" But Rachel had known even then that if it had been Hal, he'd have run whimpering to their mother for comfort, then bellowed and thrashed and cried as the doctor had tried to treat him.

"Rae?" Joe said.

"What? Oh, sorry. I was someplace else." She tossed back the remainder of her whisky and stood up. "I'm for bed. See you in the morning." She paused, one foot on the bottom step of the stairs. "Or not, if you sleep late. We have to start setting up for the homecoming festival at eight."

"Let me know if you need another strong back," he said.

"We've plenty of those," she said. "Most come with weak minds attached."

"So one more won't hurt."

She smiled. "G'night," she said, and climbed the stairs.

chapter ten

Saturday, August 5

Shoe was awakened by a spike of sunlight through the high window facing the foot of the bed. The bed was in the basement bedroom his father had built when Hal had turned twelve and had needed a room of his own. Shoe had inherited the bedroom when Hal had gone away to McGill University in Montreal to study business. His wristwatch, propped against the base of the lamp on the bedside table, read a few minutes to six. Still slightly jet-lagged, he thought about closing the curtain so he could catch another hour of sleep, but he could hear the creak of floorboards and the quiet mutter of morning radio from upstairs. He got up, showered, dressed, then followed the smell of coffee up to the kitchen. Rachel, dressed in loose drawstring pants and a body-hugging tank top that complemented her compact muscularity, stood barefoot at the stove. She was laying strips of bacon in an ancient and blackened cast iron frying pan.

"I found your stash," she said. "I hope you don't mind, I made a pot."

"Not at all," he said. He poured a mug of coffee and sat down at the kitchen table.

"Should I do you some bacon?"

"No, thank you," Shoe replied. He didn't go out of his way to avoid fatty meats, but he couldn't remember the last time he'd eaten bacon. It smelled good as it began to sizzle quietly in the pan. She put the package away in the fridge.

"In his letter, Mr. Cartwright wrote that he hoped Joey and I would patch things up," Shoe said. "I wasn't aware that Joey knew him." Even though Joey had been his best and closest friend, he added to himself.

"Mr. Cartwright had a shelf full of chess trophies in his living room," Rachel said, turning the bacon in the pan. "I remember Joey telling me that he gave demonstrations at the junior high school chess club. He'd play a dozen games at a time. When I asked Mr. Cartwright about it, he told me Joey was the only person who ever came close to beating him."

"Joey was a good chess player," Shoe agreed.

"You beat him, though, didn't you?"

"Once in a while."

"A lot, he said."

Shoe shook his head. "Not true at all," he said.

"Would you like to play a game or two while you're here?" Rachel asked.

"I haven't played in years," Shoe said.

"Then maybe I'll have a chance," Rachel said.

"Maybe."

When the bacon was crisp, Rachel put it into the toaster oven to keep warm, then broke two eggs into the pan. Hot grease popped and spit. Holding the pan at an angle, she basted the eggs with a spoon. The only cereal in the house was Cheerios, which to Shoe tasted like burnt cardboard. He got bread out of the fridge to make toast. Fortunately, it was whole wheat. And there was a jar of Robertson's Scotch-style orange marmalade.

"Do you want toast with your cholesterol?" he asked Rachel.

She made a face. "Carbs? No, thanks." She sat down and began to eat. When Shoe's toast popped, he sat down facing her. "What do you think of the chances he'll be at the homecoming?" Rachel asked.

"Joey? I'd be very surprised."

She picked up a strip of bacon in her fingers, delicately bit off a piece and crunched it between her teeth. "So you haven't seen him or spoken to him since ... " She hesitated.

"No," Shoe said. She lifted a forkful of egg, dripping yellow yolk, to her mouth. "Have you?" he asked.

Swallowing, she said, "No. His mother died two years ago. I took Mum and Dad to her funeral. Joey wasn't there. His father died eight or nine years ago. According to his sister, he wasn't at his father's funeral either."

Shoe watched her swab the last of the grease and yolk from her plate with the edge of her thumb. She then stuck her thumb in her mouth, sucking noisily. Wiping her thumb off with a paper serviette, she grinned sheepishly at him.

"Pretty disgusting, eh?" Their parents had tried for years to break her of the habit of cleaning her plate with her thumb, obviously without success. "Can I ask you something?" she said. He waited. "What happened between you and Joey? Did you fight over Janey?"

Shoe hid his surprise behind his coffee mug. Janey Hallam had had nothing to do with his falling out with Joey. At least, not directly. He supposed, though, to an eleven-year-old Rachel, it might have appeared that way.

"We didn't fight over Janey," he said.

"What then? For ten years you and Joey were

practically joined at the hip. What happened? You don't have to answer if you don't want to." she added.

"Good," he said.

Her disappointment was evident, but she said, "Okay."

"You're all right with that?"

"No," she said. "Not really. But if you don't want to talk about it, I understand."

"Do you remember when he was in the hospital for a week? It was in early May of our last year of junior high school."

"I think so," Rachel said. "He had an accident on his bike, didn't he?"

Shoe shook his head. "He was cutting through the Dells on his way to a chess club meeting at the junior high school when he was jumped by three boys, beaten up, stripped, and left naked and unconscious in the woods. Some kids found him and ran home to tell their parents, who called the police. Joey was hospitalized for a week with a concussion, a ruptured spleen, and a broken bone in his right hand. He never told the police who'd attacked him. Boys he didn't know, he said."

"Jesus, did he tell you?"

"No, but I knew."

"Who?"

"Dougie Hallam ... "

"Of course," Rachel said contemptuously.

"Ricky Marshall ... "

"Dougie's little toady."

"And Hal."

Her eyes widened with astonishment. "You're kidding. Hal didn't like Joey much, but that doesn't seem like him at all. What did you do?" The expression on his face must have been answer enough. "You beat him up, didn't you?"

"Yes," Shoe said.

Hal had been avoiding Shoe since Joey's attack, and when Shoe confronted him about it, he admitted he'd participated — reluctantly, he claimed. Although Hal was four years older than Shoe, and heavier, Shoe was slightly taller. He was also stronger, quicker, and in better condition. In a fair fight, Hal might have held his own, but Shoe had no intention of fighting fair. He sucker-punched Hal in the gut, growing soft even then, then proceeded to beat the stuffing out of him. He didn't beat him half as badly as Joey had been beaten, drawing only a little blood and breaking no bones; Hal was his brother, after all.

"Did you beat up Dougie Hallam too?" Rachel asked.

"Yes," Shoe said again.

Dougie Hallam had been the neighbourhood bully for as long as Shoe could remember. According to gossip, his father and stepmother, Freddy and Nancy, were just trailer trash who'd made good. No one was quite sure how, but the general consensus was that it hadn't been legal, a suspicion later strengthened by their gangland-style murders shortly before Shoe joined the police. Mrs. Hallam was a normally meek and mousy woman, but when she got a couple of drinks in her she became strident and sluttish. Freddy had beaten up more than one man who had become the unwilling focus of her attention. Rumour had it he beat her up regularly too. He was also virulently anti-Semitic.

Dougie Hallam was proof that apples seldom fall far from the trees; he was as loutish and bigoted as his father. At nineteen he was taller than Shoe was at fifteen, and more heavily muscled, with a reputation as a dirty fighter. On Sunday morning, the week after Joey's attack, as Dougie was washing his customized '57 Ford Fairlane convertible in the driveway of his parents' house, Shoe walked up to him and, without a word of warning, punched him in the nose, breaking it and spraying blood across the white vinyl convertible top of the car. Dougie tried to fight back, but he was blinded by blood and pain and anger and didn't have a chance. By the time his parents realized what was going on and came to the rescue, Dougie lay unconscious on the drive, a minor concussion to go with the broken nose, two missing teeth, and cracked rib.

"You didn't beat up Ricky Marshall too, did you?" Rachel asked. "He wasn't much bigger than Joey."

"No, but I scared him pretty badly."

After leaving Dougie bloodied on the driveway of his parents' house, Shoe rode his bike to the drive-in restaurant where Ricky Marshall worked. Ricky saw him coming and ran. Shoe caught him at the edge of the parking lot. He was so frightened, he soiled himself. Shoe left him there, huddled in a miserable heap, and rode home to wait for the police. The police never came, but a week later Shoe's father received a bill for Dougie's dental work. He paid it, and Shoe reimbursed him out of the earnings from his weekend job at Dutton's Hardware and Building Supplies.

"I take it Joey wasn't grateful," Rachel said.

"Far from it," Shoe said. "When I told him what I'd done, he called me a muscle-headed moron and told me to 'fuck the hell off' and mind my own business." Rachel's eyes widened, unaccustomed to his use of profanity. "I was hurt and confused. I'd done what I thought was the right thing, but eventually I realized I'd only compounded his humiliation. By then it was too late."

The following winter, two weeks after his sixteenth birthday, Joey dropped out of high school and got a job pumping gas at the Canadian Tire gas bar. Five months later he bought an old Harley-Davidson motorcycle and took to the road. He hadn't said goodbye.

"Well, you know what they say about good deeds, Joe," Rachel said. "They rarely go unpunished."

chapter eleven

"I have to go into the office," Hal said.

Maureen did not look up from the Home and Garden section of the Saturday paper. "Fine," she said coldly.

It was the first word she'd spoken to him since they'd got home the night before. He tried to swallow his anger, but it stuck in his throat like a fish bone. "I'll try to get away by lunchtime," he said.

"Fine," she said again. She turned the page of the newspaper, snapped it straight, then picked up her coffee mug and took a sip.

"But I can't promise," Hal said.

She banged the mug down and glared at him. "Oh, for Christ's sake, Hal, will you just shut the fuck up."

"Well, I'm sorry," he said. Even after twenty-five years of marriage, her language shocked him. "I still have to go to the office."

"No, you don't," she said. "You're just looking for an excuse to avoid going to the homecoming. I'm not sure why. Until a couple of weeks ago, you seemed to be looking forward to it. Or is it that you just don't want to spend the day with me?"

"That's not it. There are just some things I need to do to get ready for the quarterly performance evaluations."

"For god's sake, Hal. You'd think, after all these years, you'd've figured out I can always tell when you're lying. The rims of your nostrils turn red. The only time you can get away with lying to me is when you've got a cold or your allergies are acting up. The rims of your nostrils are always red then, so just to be on the safe side, when you've got a cold, I don't believe anything you tell me."

"What's with you this morning?" he said, as if he didn't know. "Look, I told you I was sorry about last night. I've got a lot on my mind these days."

"So you said. That doesn't excuse your behaviour." She made a dismissive shrugging motion. "Go to the office, Hal. No one's going to miss you. Certainly not me." She went back to her newspaper.

On the drive to the train station, he tried not to think about Maureen and his brother spending the day together. He almost turned back, figuring that maybe it would be better to go with Maureen to the homecoming after all. At least he'd be able to keep an eye on them. He didn't, though, but continued to the Clarkson GO Station, where he parked the Lexus in the huge, mostly empty lot, and trudged through the tunnel to the platform. He found an unoccupied bench and sat down to wait for the next train to Union Station, then remembered he'd forgotten to have his ticket stamped in one of the proof-of-payment machines. For most of the year he purchased a monthly pass, but he usually took vacation during July and August and it was more economical to buy ten-ride tickets that had to be cancelled for each ride. Wearily, he got up, inserted the ticket into a nearby machine, then slumped onto the bench again.

Maureen was right. No one would miss him. Sure, they might wonder where he was, why he wasn't there, click their tongues and comment on how all work and no play made Hal a dull boy, but that was it. They wouldn't give him another thought. Maureen. Joe. Rachel. That pompous old fart Wiseman. His parents, even though he'd promised to take them to the concert later that evening. The truth of the matter was, he was about as interesting and exciting as an old sofa.

And, he thought, looking down at his protruding gut, he was built a bit like an old sofa too. No wonder Maureen got all gooey-eyed over Joe. He didn't look as though he'd gained an ounce in thirty years. In fact, he seemed even trimmer than he'd been when he'd quit the police and gone out west. Hal had never been exactly skinny, even as a teenager, but he'd started gaining weight in his second year of university and had continued to gain until he'd topped out at his current weight five or six years ago. When was the last time he'd been able to see his own dick without a mirror? he wondered glumly. Not for some time, even erect. Good thing he could find it by feel, he thought with bitter humour.

The train came and he climbed aboard with the other Saturday morning commuters and shoppers. He trudged up the stairs to the upper level of the car because it was usually less crowded. The only other occupants were a foursome of teenaged girls who fell momentarily silent, staring at him as though he were an alien just arrived from Mars, then dismissed him utterly, as though he'd suddenly ceased to exist. Or had never existed at all.

He found a seat and tried to ignore the girls as thoroughly as they were ignoring him, but he couldn't keep his eyes off them. Try as he might to focus on his newspaper, his gaze was drawn back to them as inexorably as a compass needle is drawn to magnetic north. None of them was especially pretty, but they all wore skin-tight jeans that rode below their hipbones, and skimpy tops that revealed their midriffs and the shoulder straps of their brassieres, those wearing them. One girl, a chunky Chinese with shining black eyes and orange-striped hair, obviously wasn't, and the nipples of her plump, immature breasts were like dark pebbles below the surface of the sand. None of them had tattoos, that he could see, or obvious body piercings. With a shudder of revulsion, he wondered if any of them had pierced genitals. Surely they were too young for that sort of thing. On the other hand, they were too young to be dressed so provocatively. Didn't they realize the kind of message they were sending?

One of the girls became aware of his attention and whispered conspiratorially to her companions. They all looked in his direction and giggled. The Chinese girl glanced around the compartment, then locked eyes with him. His pulse raced. She plucked at the hem of her top, raising it higher on her midriff, as though she were going to reveal her breasts. Hal stared, mouth dry, perspiration pooling in his armpits and running down his sides, simultaneously fascinated and horrified. Then, laughing, the girl pulled the hem of her top back down. Her friends roared with laughter. Face flaming, Hal struggled to his feet and staggered down the stairs to the lower level, the girls' laughter chasing him like the taunts of Yonge Street whores.

Marty Elias had teased him like that once, he recalled, as he sagged into a seat on the lower level. One day, when he got home from playing softball, he found her sprawled on the sofa in the basement recreation room of his parents' house — she was Rachel's best friend and always hanging about — wearing shorts and a stretchy pink tube top.

"What're you doing here?" he said to her.

She looked at him. "Waiting for Rachel."

"Yeah," he said. "Where is she?"

Marty shrugged. Beneath the fabric of her top, her breasts were the size of half golf balls and shaped like foreshortened ice cream cones.

"How old are you now?" Hal asked, although he knew perfectly well how old she was.

"Same as Rachel," she said. "Eleven."

"You look, um, older," he said.

"Yeah? Really?" She sat up a little straighter, thrusting out her chest. "My boobies are bigger than hers," she said proudly.

"A little, I guess," Hal said, face hot.

A sly expression crossed her small face. "I bet you've never seen a girl's boobies before."

"What? Sure, of course I have," he lied. He had, but only in magazines.

"Gimme a dollar and I'll show you mine."

He swallowed dryly. He was certain she was teasing, but he dug into his jeans pocket anyway, feeling his erection as he fished out some change and a crumpled dollar bill. "I'll give you fifty cents," he said.

"Gimme the dollar."

Heart hammering wildly, he gave her the dollar. She smiled triumphantly as she shoved it into the pocket of her shorts. She fingered the upper edge of the stretchy tube top. There was an almost unbearable tightness in his chest.

"Well," he croaked.

Suddenly, she jumped up from the sofa and bolted up the basement stairs.

"Hey!" he shouted, starting after her.

Rachel came downstairs from the kitchen just as Marty flew out the back door. She frowned down at Hal from the landing. "What's wrong with Marty? What'd you do to her?"

"Nothing," Hal grumbled, then went into his room, locked the door, and masturbated into a dirty gym sock.

The train pulled into Union Station and he queued at the door to disembark. Without paying him the slightest attention, the four girls brushed past him as soon as the doors opened. He had ceased to exist for them, if he had ever existed at all.

chapter twelve

After breakfast, Shoe and Rachel walked to the small park behind the houses across the street. Shoe had never known its name, but a shellacked wood sign identified it as Giuseppe Garibaldi Park, a testament, he supposed, to the many people of Italian descent who'd lived in the area, and did still. He carried the heavier of a pair of file boxes of pamphlets and papers, and the rolled-up woven blue polypropylene kitchen shelter he'd helped Rachel get down from the rafters of the garage. There wasn't a cloud in the sky and, despite the omnipresent yellow haze of pollution, the mid-morning sun had a savage bite. Fortunately, the humidity had dropped a bit more overnight and there was a slight breeze, insufficient to disperse the pollution, however.

The park was a hive of activity. Where the outdoor skating rink had been every winter when he was growing up, a group of bare-chested, sun-baked men with bandanas tied around their brows was erecting a big white open-sided tent, driving two-foot metal stakes into the hard ground with sledgehammers, and stringing wire-rope guys to sturdy metal poles. A white five-ton truck stood nearby, "Rain or Shine Party Rentals" emblazoned on the sides, from which two men off-loaded folding tables and stackable chairs. Dozens of men and women and kids bustled about, setting up community action kiosks and crafts tables, portable garden gazebos and more camp kitchen shelters; dragging gas barbecues into position; lugging picnic coolers and boxes of hot dog and hamburger buns and cases of soft drinks from the backs of minivans and SUVs parked along the street on the south side of the park; and dumping bags of ice into a child's plastic wading pool next to which stood tall stacks of shrink-wrapped flats of single-serving bottles of spring water. Pennants fluttered and clusters of balloons bobbed from the Victorian-style lampposts scattered throughout the park. There were waste receptacles and recycling bins everywhere. Supertramp's "Breakfast in America" blasted from a huge boom box on a table in front of a first aid station manned by teenaged boys and girls in scouting scarves, shirts encrusted with merit badges.

"What can I do?" Shoe asked.

"You can help me set up the shelter," Rachel said. "Otherwise, everything seems to be under control."

Between them, they put up the kitchen shelter, banging the pegs in with his father's carpenter's hammer, unzipping and rolling up the bug-screen sides to let in some air. Between the extra-long poles of the door fly, Rachel strung a banner that read "Welcome to the Umpteenth Annual Black Creek Weekend in the Park." When Shoe commented on it, Rachel said, "Saves us from having to paint a new banner every year."

Shoe unfolded the legs of a rental table inside the kitchen shelter. Rachel laid out the contents of the file boxes. It was good to get out of the sun. Rachel placed an IBM laptop on the table, opened it, but did not turn it on. She placed a cellphone beside it.

"Tim Dutton is supposed to hook up a solar-powered battery charger for the computer and my phone," she said.

"I'm surprised he still lives around here," Shoe said.

"He likes being the big fish in a small pond," Rachel said, frowning. She shook her head. "I shouldn't be so hard on him. He contributed a lot of money and materials for the homecoming. But he's as big a jerk as he ever was. Wait till you see his house. When he took over his father's business, he moved his parents into a retirement home, a nice one, of course, then bought the houses on either side of his parents' house, tore all three down, and built a new place. It's hideous. A dog's breakfast of architectural styles. God knows who the architect was. It wouldn't surprise me if Tim designed it himself. Patty hates it."

"Patty?"

"Tim's wife. His second, actually. Wait till you meet her. She's absolutely stunning and smart as a whip. Tim doesn't appreciate her at all. She even calls herself his tarnished trophy wife. She and I have become pretty good friends. She's the chairperson of the homecoming committee. Patty's worked her ass off to make this weekend a success."

"Nevertheless," a woman said, as she came into the shelter, "it's still far too big." She placed a file box on the table next to Rachel's laptop.

"It is like hell," Rachel said with a smile. The woman was attractive, with fine, even features, medium-length blonde hair, and an excellent figure, albeit perhaps slightly too long-waisted. Rachel and she exchanged quick kisses. "Patty, meet my brother Joe. Joe, meet Patty Dutton."

"Joe," Patty Dutton said, taking Shoe's hand and gazing up at him with cool green eyes. "Pleased to meet you. Rae talks about you all the time." She held his hand a little longer than necessary. "What do you do for a living, Joe? Crush rocks with your bare hands?"

"Not quite," Shoe said. His hands were large and strong, like Shoe himself, but he'd been doing a lot of masonry and carpentry work on the marina and motel lately and his hands were harder and rougher than usual.

Patty smiled and released his hand. "Rae wasn't exaggerating about your size. How tall are you?"

"A fraction over two metres," he said. Patty Dutton crossed her eyes comically. "Six-six and a bit," he translated.

"You're what, Rae?" Patty said. "Five-four, five-five? You got shortchanged."

"There wasn't enough fertilizer left over for me after Mum and Dad grew Hal and Joe," Rachel said.

"It's quality that counts, eh, Joe? Not quantity," Patty said.

"That's right," Shoe said.

"Speaking of quality," Rachel said, grasping Patty by the shoulders and turning her around. "Tell her that her ass is just fine." Patty blushed and laughed and waggled her backside at him.

What could he do? "It is fine indeed," he said.

"Thank you, kind sir," Patty said, placing a finger under her chin and performing a quick curtsy.

"Where's Tim?" Rachel asked. "He was supposed to bring some stuff to hook up the laptop."

Patty lifted the lid off the file box she'd placed on the table. "I brought it, but I haven't a clue what to do with it. How about you, Joe? You're a guy. Guys know about these things."

"Not this guy, I'm afraid," Shoe said. "I'm a Luddite when it comes to computers."

"Modest, as well as handsome. How come you're not married?" She smiled. "Tim should be along soon.

When I left the house this morning he was still going on about that man who was killed in the woods the other night. Tim says he used to live where the Tans live now. He was a pedophile, Tim said. Is that true?"

"It's shit," Rachel snapped. Patty Dutton's eyes widened. "Sorry," Rachel said. "No, it's not true. Marvin Cartwright was not a pedophile."

"You knew him?" Patty said.

"Yes," Rachel said. "He — "

She was interrupted as a burly elderly man and a strikingly handsome middle-aged woman came into the shelter.

"Hullo," Rachel said brightly. "Welcome to the Umpteenth Annual Black Creek Weekend-in-the-Park."

"Thank you," the woman said, smiling.

She was in her mid-fifties, Shoe guessed, slim and elegant. The man was older, in his late seventies, grizzled and bear-like. They both looked familiar, but Shoe couldn't place them. Rachel handed them each a photocopied list of events and map of the park and asked them if they'd like to sign the guest book. The haunting strains of Carlos Santana's guitar introduction to "Samba Pa Ti" began to wail out over the park from the boom box by the first aid tent. Patty Dutton half closed her eyes, hummed softly to herself as she arranged material on the table. Her fine backside began to sway with the music.

The kitchen shelter was getting crowded, so Shoe went out into the hard, hot sunshine and purchased a bottle of water for two dollars from a Girl Scout sitting beside a plastic wading pool of ice in the shade of a beach umbrella. Most of the ice in the pool had already melted. He was standing in what shade there was outside the shelter when the man and the woman came out. The woman looked at him and smiled. He felt he should recognize her, but he didn't.

"You're Joseph Schumacher, aren't you?" she said. She had a faint British accent. "I thought so. You don't recognize me, do you?"

Suddenly, he did recognize her. Something in the way she'd spoken his name. He didn't recall that she'd had a British accent when she'd been his ninth-grade English teacher, however.

"Miss Hahn," he said. "It's good to see you."

"And you, Joseph," she said. They shook hands, his hand engulfing hers. She turned to the older man standing quietly beside her, whom Shoe had also recognized. "Jake," she said, "you remember Joseph Schumacher, don't you?"

"I'm afraid I don't," the man said in a rough, gravelly voice as he and Shoe shook hands. "But my memory isn't what it used to be. My apologies, Mr. Schumacher. I assume you were one of Claudia's students."

"Yes, sir, I was." Jacob "Nine Fingers" Gibson had been the principal of Black Creek Junior High School when Shoe had been a student there. He had been called Jacob Nine Fingers because he was missing the ring finger of his left hand. The legend was that he'd lost it during a school fire drill when he'd fallen on the stairs and his wedding ring had caught on a railing.

"There were so many students, Mr. Schumacher. And only one of me."

"I understand, sir."

"Joseph," Miss Hahn said. "Perhaps we could get together later and talk. Catch up. I expect you've led an interesting life."

"I'd like that very much," he said.

"Good," she said. She took Mr. Gibson's arm and walked him toward a craft table featuring hand-painted ceramic figurines.

Rachel came out of the welcome tent and stood beside him. "*That's* your old junior high school English teacher?" she said. "No wonder you had a crush on her. She's beautiful."

chapter thirteen

Patty had taken the Navigator, so Tim Dutton drove the Audi to the store. The heat and humidity had put him in a crappy mood, which wasn't made better when he saw the Harley-Davidson motorcycle parked by the employee entrance. He didn't especially like motorcycles, or generally have much use for people who rode them. He made a mental note to find out who it belonged to and tell him to park it somewhere else. Better yet, not to ride it to work at all.

Marty Elias was at her desk in the outer office when he went upstairs, pounding away at the keyboard of her computer. Even on a bad day she typed ten times faster than he did, and he was no slouch, if he did say so himself, but she was death on keyboards. How many had she gone through in the two years since they'd put in the new system? Three, at least. Still, it was worth it; she did the work of three people. She understood the business, too. Her father had been a general contractor and it had rubbed off. In the three years she'd worked for him, she'd become almost indispensable. She had other talents, too. She didn't usually work Saturdays, though.

"What're you doing here?" he said.

"Tim," she said, snatching off her reading glasses as she swivelled her chair to face him, as though she were embarrassed to be caught wearing glasses. "I thought you were supposed to be setting up Rachel's laptop at the homecoming this morning."

"I came to pick up the manual for the solar charger."

"I've got it here," she said. She rummaged through the papers on her desk, found what she was looking for, and handed Dutton a small booklet.

"Thanks," he said. He hesitated, then said, "Did you hear the news?"

"What news, Tim?" she said. "I don't have time to listen to the news, you've got me working all the time. Don't tell me they've finally repealed indentured servitude."

He scowled. "About Marvin the — about Marvin Cartwright?"

"Marvin Cartwright? No. What about him?"

"He was killed in the Dells the night before last."

For a moment, Marty stared at him, expression blank, then her eyes went wide and she raised her hand to her mouth. "No," she gasped. "Killed? How?"

"Beaten to death," Dutton said. "In the woods behind his old house."

"My god," she said. "That's awful. Why would anyone want to kill him? He was so nice." She took a breath. "He used to make Rachel and me and the other kids hot chocolate after skating."

"Oh, come on, Marty," Dutton said irritably. "He was a rapist and a murderer and a child molester, for Christ's sake."

The heat rose in her face. "He didn't rape anyone, Tim," she said angrily. She was immediately contrite. "I'm sorry," she said meekly, looking at her hands as they rested in her lap, fingers toying with the earpieces of her glasses. "I didn't mean to snap at you."

"Forget it," he said.

"Just don't let it happen again, eh?" She smiled tentatively.

"Yeah," he said. "Look, I'm sorry. I forgot. He raped you too, didn't he?"

"It wasn't him," she said insistently. "Anyway, I wasn't raped. Just ... " She shrugged.

"Just what? Molested? Never mind. Look, I'm sorry I brought it up, okay?"

"Sure, Tim."

She was wearing a sleeveless T-shirt and jeans that looked as though they had been washed ten thousand times. He had a rule about employees wearing jeans to work, just as his father had, but he didn't say anything; it was Saturday, after all, and if Marty wanted to wear jeans to work on Saturdays, it was fine with him.

The jeans didn't bother him half as much as the tattoos, a band of barbed wire encircling her upper right arm, and a blue spiderweb on the back of her left shoulder. She knew how he felt about them and usually kept them covered up. He was about to tell her to put a shirt on when he noticed the shiny black motorcycle helmet on the floor beside her desk and the motorcycle jacket on the coat rack by the door. He remembered the motorcycle parked by the employee entrance.

"Did you buy a new bike?" Marty had a smelly old Triumph, but he wouldn't let her bring it to work.

"The Harley?" Marty said. "I wish. No, it's Joey's. He lets me use it when he stays at my place."

"Your place? What the hell's Joey Noseworthy doing at your place?"

"He usually stays with me when he's passing through. You know that."

"The hell I do."

"There's no reason for you to be like that, Tim," Marty said.

"Like what?"

"You know. Jealous."

"I'm not jealous, for Christ's sake. I just don't think letting him stay at your place is a very good idea, that's all."

"What's wrong with him staying with me?"

"Besides him being a worthless drunken bum and ex-con, you mean? What if I wanted to come by?"

"You never have before," she said. "You don't own me, Tim. You have no right to tell me who I can be friends with. Or who I sleep with, for that matter."

"Are you sleeping with him?"

"Are you sleeping with your wife?"

"It's not the same thing."

"If you say so."

"Okay, look, never mind, all right?"

"Sure, Tim."

She stood up. She was only an inch or two shorter than him, a little thick-figured, but not too thick, with heavy, pendulous breasts, low on her chest. Although she'd been around the block a time or two, she was still a good-looking woman, wore her forty-six years well, but wore them nonetheless. Her hair was dyed an inky black and raggedly cut, as though it had been styled with a hedge trimmer.

"Is there something the matter, Tim? You aren't worried the police will think you had something to do with Mr. Cartwright's murder, are you?"

"What? Don't be stupid. Why would they think that?"

She made a clicking sound with her tongue. "Because

maybe someone will tell them about the jokes you used to play on him? You and Hal Schumacher and Dougie Hallam."

"I never played jokes on him," Dutton protested. "That was Ricky Marshall. He hung out with Hal and Dougie. I was friends with Joe Schumacher."

"I remember some of the stuff you used to do, Tim. They might not have been as bad as the things Dougie and Hal did, but they weren't very nice, either. I never understood why you boys teased him the way you did."

"Because he was a pervert."

"He wasn't like that at all," she said. "Maybe some people thought he was different, because he stayed home and looked after his mother, but he was nice. You and Hal and Dougie made him mad, but he never said anything bad about you, even when one of you pooped in his living room when he was visiting his mother in the hospital."

"Come on, Marty," Dutton said. "It was thirty-five years ago. You were just a little kid."

"I've got a good memory, Tim."

She did, too. She remembered how much of a particular item was in stock, who was behind on their payments, what they'd had for dinner on any particular day when they were at trade shows, and the name of every motel they'd ever shacked up in.

"Anyway," he said pointedly. "I was home all Thursday evening, except when I had to come here because *someone* didn't close up properly and that fucking alarm went off again in the middle of the goddamned night."

"Everything was fine when I left," Marty said with a sigh. "And if you aren't happy with the way I close up, stay and do it yourself for a change."

"All right, never mind. Forget it." He went into his office. She followed. "What are you doing here, anyway?" he said.

"Trying to get caught up on some paperwork. Which reminds me ... " She returned to the outer office, took a handful of printouts from the printer beside her desk, and came back into his office. "Since when did Dougie Hallam have an account with us?"

"Eh? He doesn't."

"Then maybe you can explain these." She handed him the printouts.

He took them, glanced at them, said, "Oh, these," and dropped them onto his desk. "Don't worry about it."

"They're six months overdue."

"It was a special order. A sort of favour. He paid cash. I guess I just forgot to enter it. I'll take care of it."

She retrieved the printouts from his desk. "Look at this stuff. Pumps. PVC piping. Electrical fixtures. What was he doing, anyway?"

Tim took the printouts out of her hand. "He was renovating an old greenhouse for some guy. Under the table. You know Dougie."

"Yes, I know Dougie," Marty said. "I also know that it's — "

He cut her off with an angry gesture. "I *said* I'd take care of it."

She flinched. "Okay, Tim."

"I should go set up Rachel's computer," he said.

He didn't make a move to leave, however. He just stood in the middle of the cluttered, windowless room, facing his desk, which was as messy as the office. Marty looked good in her jeans, a lot better than she did in the frumpy skirt and blouse she usually wore to work. They made her look younger, and it was sexy the way they rode low on the slight roundness of her belly and how the crotch seam emphasized her sex. He pulled the big executive chair out from behind his desk, dropped into it, and swivelled to face her.

"Close the door," he said, unzipping his Dockers.

chapter fourteen

Shoe was at loose ends, and trying to decide how to rectify the situation, when Maureen brought his parents to the park. Despite their ages and his mother's arthritis, both were still fairly spry, but they tired easily and after a short while were content to sit quietly in the shade of the big tent shelter.

"Hal didn't come with you," Shoe said to Maureen.

"He's out shopping for that Porsche," she said. She was wearing a lightweight wraparound floral skirt that hung below her knees and a loose raw cotton peasant blouse. Her flamboyant red mane was tied up off the back of her neck with a twist of yarn the same colour as her hair.

"He told me he was thinking about buying an RV," Shoe said.

She snorted. "I'd rather it was a Porsche. At least I could drive it." She smiled. "He had to go into the office. Something about quarterly performance evaluations. Maybe he's having an affair with his secretary, after all.

If it helps him get whatever's bugging him out of his system, I'm all for it. He thinks I'm in love with you, you know."

"Pardon me?"

"And that the feeling's mutual. We argued about it on the way home last night. Am I making you uncomfortable?"

"Yes, indeed," he said.

"Sorry," she said. "I guess I can be a bit too forthright sometimes. Let's change the subject. Last night you started to tell me about Marvin Cartwright. I get the impression that he was something of a neighbourhood character. A recluse or something."

"I wouldn't call him a recluse," Shoe said. "He just didn't mix much with the other folks in the neighbourhood."

"Did he have any friends at all?"

"I'm sure he must have," Shoe said. He moved closer to his father, who was watching some kids pitching rubber horseshoes while Shoe's mother dozed in a lawn chair. "Dad?"

"Mm?"

"Do you remember if Marvin Cartwright had any friends in the neighbourhood? Someone who might be at the homecoming?"

Howard Schumacher rubbed his chin. He still hadn't shaved and his jaw was bristly with grey stubble. "That was a long time ago, son," he said. "I don't recall anyone in particular. Your mother and I, we tried to be neighbourly, invited him to a backyard barbecue or two. He was never unfriendly or rude, but he never accepted. I don't think he liked leaving his mother alone too long, in case she took a bad turn. I felt sorry for him, a young man in his prime burdened with taking care of his sickly mother. Had to admire him for it too, though. How many kids these days would do it? Stick old folks in homes nowadays, hire someone to look after them, instead of doing it themselves."

"What about the Braithwaites?" Shoe's mother asked. She hadn't been asleep after all. "He was friendly with Ruth, wasn't he?"

"Now that you mention it," Shoe's father said, "I did use to see him in the woods with Ruth Braithwaite now and again. I remember thinking that they made a queer couple, her family being so religious and all and him being an atheist."

"If you didn't know him very well, how do you know he was an atheist?" Shoe asked.

His father looked thoughtful for a moment, then said, "Not sure, actually. Maybe it was just talk."

"Takes one to know one," Shoe's mother said, not unkindly.

"Now, Mother," Howard Schumacher said. "I'm not an atheist. I'm just not a believer."

"Braithwaite?" Maureen said. "They live in that house off by itself at the end of the little cul-de-sac that sticks into the woods behind your place, don't they? The one with all the religious statuary in the yard."

"That's them," Shoe's father said. "The twins, Naomi and Judith, and Ruth. She's the youngest. She'd be Hal's age or so, I'd say, Naomi and Judith a year or two older. Mr. Braithwaite came from money. Liquor or tobacco, I think. His family owned most of the land around here before the war, but he sold it off to developers and started doin' missionary work in Africa with his wife. They got themselves killed in the Congo or someplace. Left those girls pretty well off, too, I suppose. Financially, anyhow. Didn't leave 'em very well equipped to get on in the world."

Shoe remembered Mr. and Mrs. Braithwaite. Older than his parents, they'd been drab and stern and aloof. He had no recollection of ever having seen the twins,

Naomi and Judith, but he'd seen Ruth in the woods a few times, usually with a drawing pad. Never in the company of Marvin Cartwright, though, or anyone else. He'd thought she was pretty, in a nervous, awkward kind of way, and had tried to speak to her once, but she'd fled from him as if pursued by demons. Neither she nor her sisters had gone to public schools, receiving their schooling at home from their parents or from the even drabber and unsmiling woman who'd looked after them when their parents were away, which they often were. Shoe had been in university when Mr. and Mrs. Braithwaite had died.

"Far as I know," Howard Schumacher was saying, "none of 'em has set foot out of that house in daylight in thirty years. Get their groceries delivered. Front yard is more like a field than a lawn. Every so often kids'll knock over some of the statues, or spray paint graffiti on 'em, but in the next few days they'll all be standing again or painted over. I remember some talk, too, that Ruth may have been the first victim of the Black Creek Rapist, but if she was, she or her father never reported it."

"The Black Creek Rapist?" Maureen said.

She'd grown up in another part of the city, Shoe remembered, and would have been only ten at the time. "There were a series of sexual assaults in the woods the summer Marvin Cartwright moved away," he explained. "One of the victims died."

"And Marvin Cartwright was a suspect?" Maureen said.

"Not the only one," Shoe said.

Howard Schumacher harrumphed. "No one with a lick of sense really believed Marvin did it."

"Do you remember how you heard that Ruth may have been attacked?" Shoe asked.

"It was just talk," Shoe's father replied, with a dismissive shrug.

chapter fifteen

At noon, Shoe took his parents back to the house, where he helped his father fix lunch, tomato soup, mild cheese, and crackers for them, a meatloaf sandwich and an apple for him. He returned to the park while his parents took their afternoon nap. He found Maureen and Rachel in the kitchen shelter. With them was a stocky man with freckles and thinning red hair, and a woman with shaggily cropped inky black hair and light brown eyes. Shoe knew who she was as soon as she smiled at him.

"Well, speak of the devil," Tim Dutton said. "How the hell are you, Shoe? People still call you Shoe?"

"I'm fine, Tim," he said as they shook hands. "And, yes, I'm still called Shoe."

"Shoe?" Marty Elias said.

"A nickname I gave him in high school," Dutton said.

It had been Janey Hallam who'd started calling him

Shoe, but Shoe chose not to contradict him. "How are you, Marty?" he said instead.

"You remember me," she said, her face lighting up with surprise and delight.

"Of course."

She opened her mouth to speak, but Dutton cut her off. "What're you doing with yourself these days? Not still a cop, are you?"

"No."

"Still living on the left coast? Not back to stay, uh?"

"Yes and no," Shoe said.

"Isn't that a kicker about Marvin the Martian?" Dutton said. "Coming back to the old neighbourhood after all these years just to get beaten to death by some wacko in the woods. Too bad. He was a bit weird, I guess, but he was okay."

Marty frowned and shook her head. Dutton glared at her. Dutton had been one of the neighbourhood boys who'd played some of the nastier pranks on Cartwright, Shoe remembered. He'd once bragged about breaking into Cartwright's house when Cartwright's mother was in the hospital, and the house was empty, and defecating in the middle of the living room carpet. Shoe again chose not to contradict him.

"You gonna be in town for a while?" Dutton said. "We should get together for a beer or two some time. Right now, though, I gotta get this computer working or I'll never hear the end of it. No rest for the wicked, eh?"

They left Tim Dutton to his devices. Outside the tent, Maureen excused herself to check out some of the crafts tables and flower displays. Rachel said to Shoe, "Claudia Hahn came by looking for you. I can't believe she was one of your junior high school teachers. She hardly looks old enough. How old was she? Twelve?"

"She'd have been in her mid-twenties," Shoe said.

"That would make her at least sixty now. She doesn't look it."

"No," Shoe agreed.

Tim Dutton called to Rachel from the tent. Rachel excused herself, leaving Shoe alone with Marty.

"I'm surprised you remember me," Marty said.

"Why wouldn't I? You were like a second sister, you were at our house so much." Until her assault, he reminded himself, after which he'd hardly ever seen her. "How have you been?"

"Kicked around some for a time," she said. "And got kicked around some too. But things are okay now. Been worse, lots worse, that's for sure." She scrunched up her face and suddenly, for a brief moment, she was eleven again. "You look like you've gone a round or two yourself. I might not've recognized you if Tim and Rachel and your sister-in-law hadn't been talking about you. I'd forgotten you were a cop."

"A long time ago."

"I lived with a cop for a while ten, twelve years ago. Met him when they busted a strip joint where I was working in Vancouver. Some of the girls were doing more than taking off their clothes, if you get my meaning." She laughed. "What a hoot, eh? Can you imagine this old broad a stripper. Listen to me. God. Give me another five minutes and I'll be telling you about — well, never mind. Always sort of hoped we'd run into each other, but — well, Vancouver's not as big as Toronto, but it's big enough. And it's not like we hung out in the same social circles, is it?"

Shoe smiled. "It's good to see you again, Marty."

"You too. I had an awful crush on you, you know."

"No, I didn't know."

"You never wondered why I could hardly talk when I was around you?"

"Yes, I noticed that."

"I was going to marry you, Rae was going to marry Joey, and we were all going to live happily ever after." She scrunched up her face again. It seemed to be her way of shrugging. "What is it they say about expectations? If you don't have any, you'll never be disappointed. But hell, what's life without a little disappointment, eh? Have you seen him?"

"Seen who, Marty?"

"Sorry. Joey."

"Not for a long time."

"Typical Joey," she said. "Out of the blue, he shows up at my place at half past two in the morning, half in the bag and smelling like he'd slept in a dumpster. He's got a bit of a problem with drink, does our Joey," she added with a mock British accent, straight out of *Coronation Street*. "Anyway, he has a shower, then insists I have a drink with him and get caught up. At three in the morning, can you believe? He was still sleeping it off on my couch when I left for work in the morning."

"You and Joey have stayed in touch then."

"On and off for — well, a long time. He stays with me when he's passing through, every couple of years or so. That's Joey. Always passing through. He used to crash with me when I was in Vancouver, too, before I hooked up with Robby. I like him, even if he's got enough baggage for half a dozen guys. He's asked me to go on the road with him more than once. Not sure why I don't. He's — "

She was interrupted by Tim Dutton's voice from the shelter, not quite shouting. "What the hell'd you do, anyway? I told you not to screw with this stuff till I got here. Shit!"

"Oh, fuck off, Tim," Rachel replied, not quite shouting back. "I didn't touch a goddamned thing."

"Oops," Marty said. "Tim thinks technology works better if you yell at it. People, too, sometimes. I'd

better get in there before they start beating on each other
with the chairs. It's real good seeing you again, Joe. Uh,
Shoe."

She went into the tent. On his own, Shoe strolled
through the small park. It was crowded and bright with
colour and noise. Kids of all ages ran three-legged races
and played ring toss and splashed in inflatable wading
pools. Barbecues, attended by sweating men in aprons
and drinking beer from bottles or cans in brown paper
bags, flamed and smoked and filled the air with the aroma of singed meat and burning bread. Competing boom
boxes blasted out rock and country and opera. A band
was setting up on the raised platform at one end of the
big tent shelter, two men and two women, all middle-
aged, all a bit overweight, and all dressed in jeans, baggy
T-shirts, and sandals. Shoe couldn't guess what kind of
music they played, but judging from the size of the am-
plifiers and speakers, it was loud.

It saddened him, but didn't surprise him, that Joey
Noseworthy had apparently become an alcoholic. The
first time he and Joey had tried alcohol, taking a bottle of
rye that Joey had swiped from his father into the woods,
they'd both hated it. Nevertheless, Joey had taken a second sip, then a mouthful, then another, before it had
gone to his head and he'd fallen down, smashing the bottle. He'd had an awful headache the following day, and
he'd vowed never to try it again. Obviously, he had.

Shoe was browsing at a table selling second-hand
LPs, cassette tapes, and CDs — his music collection, such
as it had been, had gone down with the *Princess Pete*
and he hadn't replaced much of it — when Miss Hahn
appeared at his side. She tilted her head to look at his
selections.

"Kiri Te Kanawa and Pink Floyd. I prefer Placido
Domingo and early Rolling Stones myself." She examined the rows of CD jewel cases on the table. "Oh, look,"

she exclaimed, picking up a pair discs bound together by an elastic band. "Tom Waits's *The Asylum Years*. Every time I hear 'The Heart of Saturday Night' I'm eighteen again and cruising down Yonge Street in Billy Hunter's convertible. And I could never respect a man who doesn't tear up just a little the first time he hears 'I Hope That I Don't Fall In Love With You.'"

"I'm not familiar with either, I'm afraid," Shoe said.

"Let me buy them for you."

"What if I don't like them?" he said. "I don't know if I want to risk losing your respect."

"Perhaps I'll adjust my standards. After all, Tom Waits is something of an acquired taste. Please accept it, Joseph. Consider it a belated graduation present."

"In that case, it would be ungracious of me to refuse," he said. "Thank you."

Transactions concluded, carrying the discs in a used supermarket bag, Shoe reciprocated by treating her to a soft drink and a bag of potato chips, which she called "crisps." They sat in the shade of a garden umbrella. Despite the August heat and the rising humidity, she managed to look cool and comfortable in an off-white shirtdress that parted on her knees when she crossed her legs. Her dark hair was cropped short and streaked with grey at the temples, whereas when she'd been his teacher, her hair had been long and wavy. Her complexion was pale, smooth, and clear. Had he not known her age, he would have guessed that she was younger than he was.

She returned his appraisal unselfconsciously. "When I look at you," she said, "I see both the awkward fifteen-year-old boy I knew thirty-five years ago and the man he's become. Almost like a double-exposed photograph, taken years apart. It's quite disconcerting."

"I don't know whether to be flattered you remember me," he said, "or embarrassed. Was I that difficult a student?"

"Not at all," she said. She smiled. "I was very young and it was quite unsettling to have a student of such apparent maturity in my class."

He smiled. "Have you kept in touch with any of your other students?"

"I didn't return to teaching after my rape," she said, coolly matter-of-fact. "I got married, got divorced, got some counselling, then moved to England, where I got married again, divorced again, and got more counselling. I came back to Canada two years ago. I'm an editor at a small publishing house. The only person with whom I maintained contact was Jake. Mr. Gibson. I had no family of my own and he and his wife took me under their wings following my rape. They arranged for me to stay with his wife's sister when I went to England after my first divorce. He's been very lonely since his wife died, but our relationship is strictly platonic — and not altogether satisfying for either of us. There you have it. My life in a nutshell. What about you, Joseph? They say the face is the map of one's life. The road you've travelled appears to have been a bumpy one, if you don't mind me saying so."

"I was with the police for a while after graduating from university," he said. "But resigned after my fiancée, also a police officer, was killed on duty by a drunk driver. I've lived in Vancouver for almost thirty years. Until last year I worked for a man named William Hammond, first as his chauffeur, bodyguard, and general dog's body, then more recently as what my personnel file called a 'corporate development analyst,' which was just a fancy title for a sort of corporate snoop. I took early retirement after Hammond died last Christmas. I'm currently the proud new owner of a rundown marina and motel north of Vancouver. I've never been married. I could probably use some counselling."

"You seem quite well-adjusted to me," she said.

"Looks can be deceptive," Shoe said. "Miss Hahn — may I call you Claudia?"

"Certainly. I may have been slightly more than half again your age when I was your teacher, but now nine or ten years seems hardly any difference at all, does it? But what shall I call you? You seem to wince whenever I call you Joseph. Do people call you Joe?"

"Most people call me Shoe."

"My, what an intriguing name. I like it. Shoe. If you'll pardon the expression, it fits." She smiled. "You hear that a lot, I'm sure. Now, you were about to say … "

"You must be aware that the man suspected of being the Black Creek Rapist was killed in the woods behind his old house the other night."

"Marvin Cartwright. Yes, Jake Gibson told me this morning that he'd heard on the news that Marvin had been murdered. Beaten to death, he said. How sad. But Marvin wasn't the man who attacked me, I can assure you of that. The police briefly considered him a suspect, but he was definitely not the man who raped me. And it follows that he did not attack the others, either. I knew him, you see."

"Did you know him well?"

"Well enough to be certain he wasn't the man who attacked me. Jake knew him better than I. They shared a keen interest in birdwatching. Actually, to call it 'keen' is an understatement. Given half an opportunity, it's all they would talk about." She laughed, light and musical. "They were so incorrigible that we set aside the first five or ten minutes of every meeting for them to get it out of their systems. It usually took longer."

"Was he a teacher?"

"No, he was a writer. Whether he was a good writer is open to interpretation. Jake Gibson thought so. Marvin was an authority on the birds of east-central North America. He also wrote historical adventure and romance novels under a number of pen names. Jake liked the adventure novels. I read one of each and while they were competently written, as I recall, they were not my cuppa. He could have done well, I think, had he continued — the genres are popular these days — but Jake thinks he must have stopped writing fiction after his mother died. I got to know him because he spoke regularly at schools in the area, about writing and birds and chess."

"My sister told me he was a chess player," Shoe said. "Quite a good one, she thinks."

"Yes, I believe so."

"His interest in birds was common knowledge, but no one in the neighbourhood knew he was a writer or lectured at schools. I don't recall attending any of his talks, but I wasn't particularly interested in chess, birds, or writing. Did you or Mr. Gibson keep in touch with him after his mother died?"

"I was suffering from the aftermath of my rape then. I didn't learn of his mother's death until months later. It was Jake who finally told me about it, but by then Marvin had dropped out of sight. I regret not trying to contact him. It was likely because of him that I became interested in editing and publishing. I don't have the patience, or perhaps the talent, to be a writer."

Shoe looked over Claudia's shoulder, then stood as Jacob Gibson approached, a worried look on his deeply lined face. Claudia turned, then also stood.

"I'm sorry to interrupt," Gibson said.

Claudia looked at her watch, a large stainless steel and masculine timepiece, worn loose on her slim wrist. "I'll be right along, Jake," she said. She looked at Shoe. "I'm afraid we have to run. I'm to deliver Jake to his daughter and son-in-law's house for a family do. But I would like to talk with you further. How long will you be in town?"

"Till the end of the week," he said.

When he shook hands with her, she drew him close and leaned up to kiss him on the cheek.

"I look forward to seeing you again," she said.

chapter sixteen

Shoe was about to go into the kitchen shelter, to tell Rachel that he was going back to the house for a while, when a woman emerged. Smooth and sleek as a greyhound, she was wearing snug black jeans and a fitted western-style shirt with snap fasteners, undone to the tops of her breasts. She had mannishly short hair, bleached almost white, wide shoulders, and narrow hips. Her face was square and chiselled. When she smiled at him, nests of fine wrinkles formed at the corners of her mouth and eyes.

"Hey, Shoe," she said.

"Hello," he replied. It was his day for not recognizing people he knew he should recognize.

The woman's smile did not falter. "I don't know whether to be pissed or pleased that you don't remember me. I've changed in thirty years, but I didn't think I'd changed that much. You haven't. I'm Janey. Janey Hallam."

"I haven't forgotten you, Janey. I didn't recognize you. You have changed. A lot."

"For the better, I hope."

"I'd say so," he said.

"No more baby fat," she said, placing both hands on her trim waist. He didn't remember that she'd had any excess fat, baby or otherwise. "And I got my teeth straightened. Otherwise, all natural. Lots of exercise and clean living. Well, not too much clean living," she added with a mischievous grin. "How's life treating you?"

"As well as can be expected," he said. "How are you, Janey?"

"I'm good. Keeping busy, at least. I teach marketing a couple of nights a week, do a little music management on the side, and give fitness classes at a gym in the Jane and Finch mall." She looked him up and down. "I'd suggest you come by, but you don't look like you need to work out more than you already do. Or are you just one of the lucky ones?"

"A little of both," he said.

"You want to go get a beer or something? Get caught up?"

"I was just on my way back to my parents' house to check on them," he said. "Rain check?"

"Sure. I'll be around. Come find me later."

She waggled her fingers and smiled coyly over her shoulder as she walked away, taut backside twitching. In some ways, Shoe thought, it appeared Janey Hallam hadn't changed at all.

Shoe didn't remember precisely when the Hallam family had moved into the neighbourhood, but his memory of his first encounter with Janey Hallam was still vivid after nearly forty years. He and Joey Noseworthy had been twelve. They were shooting marbles in the schoolyard when Shoe became aware they were being watched by a scruffy, tomboyish girl of nine or ten. She had raggedy dark blonde hair, slightly crooked teeth, and scabbed knobbly knees.

"Hi," she said. "I'm Janey. Can I play?"

"Sure," Shoe said. "Where're your marbles?"

"I don't have any."

"Well, stupid, you can't play then, can you?" Joey said. "Go 'way."

"I'm not stupid," she said. "I have a quarter. I can buy some marbles."

"So go buy some," Joey said dismissively.

"I mean from you."

Shoe was trying to work out how many marbles he'd be willing to sell her for a quarter, and which ones, when Joey stood up. He looked Janey in the eye, and said, "I'm not going to sell you any marbles, and neither is he, so why don't you just go *away*." He put his hand on her chest and pushed.

Janey staggered back a step or two, face clouding and eyes smouldering. Shoe saw it coming, but before he could warn him, Janey stepped up and slugged Joey, a roundhouse right to the cheek that knocked him onto the tarmac. She then grabbed his blue Crown Royal bag of marbles and ran. She didn't get far. One of the teachers monitoring recess had witnessed the altercation and cut off her escape. The teacher returned Joey's marbles to him, then dragged all three of them to the principal's office.

"He should've just sold me some marbles," Janey later said to Shoe. He agreed.

It was the beginning of a triangle that challenged Shoe's loyalties more than once. Joey was his best and oldest friend, but the better he got to know Janey, the more he liked her, despite the two-year difference in their ages. She was smart and feisty and tough. The first time Shoe heard the term "take no prisoners" used to describe a personality trait, he thought it applied perfectly to

Janey. She called him Shoe from the first day he told her his last name. Needless to say, Janey and Joey did not get on at all, and as often as not, Shoe was caught in the middle.

If Dougie Hallam was his father's son, Janey was, albeit to a much lesser degree, her mother's daughter. She did well in school, though, and somehow managed to avoid inheriting the worst of her parents' trailer trash attitudes. By the time she turned thirteen, she'd discarded most of her tomboy ways. Not quite pretty, she was sexually mature for her age, and attracted boys like bees to clover. She seemed to enjoy the attention, and it wasn't long before she acquired a reputation as easy.

While his friendship with Joey lasted, Shoe relegated his feelings for Janey to the back burner, where they simmered quietly, intensifying slowly but inexorably. Despite her reputation, the extent of their physical relationship was holding hands while watching television in Shoe's parents' basement. Sometimes she would let him put his arm around her in the movie theatre, but only after the lights went down, so they wouldn't be seen by her friends. She ran with the "tough" crowd, girls in tight clothing, high school boys who wore leather jackets with the collars turned up and who rode Japanese motorcycles or drove old cars. But after Shoe and Joey's falling out, things began to change. Janey started holding his hand when they went walking in the woods. One evening, as they sat on the swings in the park across the street from his parents' house, she leaned over and kissed him. He needed a little coaching — he had kissed girls before, but never one that put her tongue in his mouth — but he caught on quickly. A week or so later, while they kissed in the dark on a bench the same park, she took his hand and placed it on her breast. A week or so after that, in his parents' basement, she unhooked her bra and guided his hand under her sweater to her bare breast. He was astonished at the warmth and softness of her flesh, the feel of her nipple in the palm of his hand. He ached for her to touch him, but he was terrified to ask, lest she refuse or, worse, be offended.

Daphne McKinnon was raped a few weeks after Joey was released from the hospital. Janey spent a lot of time in the Dells and Shoe was concerned for her safety, but when he called her, she would not come to the phone. He tried talking to her in the hall between classes or in the schoolyard after school, but she told him to leave her alone. He left notes in her locker, and even wrote her a letter; all went unanswered. Desperate to learn what he'd done wrong, he even went so far as to wait outside her parents' house one morning, hoping to catch her on her way to school, but her father came out and threatened to set the dogs on him if he didn't go away.

In mid-June, Claudia Hahn was raped as she walked in the Dells during her lunch break, almost within sight of the school. Two weeks later, Marty Elias was attacked, but she managed to get away from her attacker before she was raped. Then the park worker was raped and strangled to death by the big tree that had fallen across the creek years earlier to form a natural bridge. The neighbourhood was frantic. Parents kept their daughters — and their sons — home, forbidding them to go into the woods. On Saturday afternoon, three weeks after the park worker's murder, Shoe's father knocked on Shoe's bedroom door.

"Janey's here to see you. She's downstairs."

Shoe almost knocked his father down in his rush to get to her before she got away. She wasn't in the basement. His brother was sitting on the sofa.

"Where's Janey?" Shoe asked.

"Outside," Hal said. His voice was strained and he was red in the face.

"What's wrong with you?" Shoe asked.

"Nothing," Hal replied curtly.

Shoe went into the backyard. Janey was sitting on the picnic table, feet on the bench seat.

"Let's go for a walk," she said.

Before he could reply, she got up and headed into the woods. He thought about telling her he had better things to do, that he was through being jerked around, but went after her instead. He hadn't been in the woods since Miss Hahn's rape.

"Aren't you afraid to be in the woods?" he said when he caught up with her.

"Not when I've got you to protect me," she said. "You'll protect me, won't you?"

"Sure," he said, even though the idea of encountering the monster the newspapers and TV called the Black Creek Rapist frightened him. "I won't let anything happen to you." They descended into a narrow ravine, then began to climb the high, wooded ridge that overlooked the big ravine through which Black Creek ran. "Where are we going?"

"You'll see."

She took his hand as they began to descend the steep north side of the ridge toward the creek. It was as if they'd never been apart, as if the preceding two months had never happened. He wanted to ask her what he'd done to make her so angry with him, but he didn't. He was just grateful that she'd apparently forgiven him.

Two large boulders, one roughly the size and shape of an automobile, the other only slightly smaller, were embedded in the hillside, hanging thirty feet above the creek, deposited millennia before by a retreating glacier and partly exposed over the centuries by erosion. The larger boulder lay almost horizontal atop the smaller one. Someday both would tumble into the creek. Janey stepped onto the top of the large boulder and walked to the end overlooking the creek. A dead tree leaned at a steep angle beside the car-sized boulder, about three feet away. Leaning out, Janey took hold of the stub of a branch, swung out, and clambered lithely down the tree, disappearing out of sight beneath the boulder. Shoe followed more clumsily.

A shallow cave had formed under the large boulder, behind the supporting pillar of the smaller boulder. The entrance was hidden by brush and brambles. In his explorations of the Dells, Shoe had never discovered the cave. He wondered how Janey had found it. She had enlarged it, digging deeper into the hillside. It smelled of earth and old leaves, but it was dry, despite the recent rain. It had an old canvas tarpaulin for a door, another on the floor.

A kitchen match flared as Janey lit a candle. She'd outfitted the little cave with an orange crate larder, stocked with canned soup, baked beans, and Irish stew, along with bottled water and soft drinks, and a single-burner camp stove. There was also an air mattress and a sleeping bag. It was cramped; Shoe could not stand up straight.

"When did you find this place?" he asked.

"Last year," Janey said.

"Where do you go to the bathroom?" he asked, ever practical.

She laughed. "A little farther down toward the creek."

It was there, on the musty sleeping bag, that Janey relieved him of the burden of his virginity. Given her reputation, and certain physiological evidence about which he'd only read, he wasn't under any illusion that it was the first time for her. Nevertheless, he assumed that it meant they were boyfriend and girlfriend. She quickly dispelled that misconception.

"I like you," she told him afterward. "You're the only boy who doesn't treat me like a tramp. But don't think this means we're going steady or anything like that. In fact, if you tell anyone we did this, I'll call you a liar and it'll never happen again. Understand?"

"I think so," he said, but he didn't really.

"Good," she'd said, rolling over and straddling him. "Now let me show you something girls really like. And it won't get them pregnant. I think you'll like it too." She was right. Then she returned the favour.

Later, when they were dressed, she said, "I want you to do something for me."

"We just got dressed." He still had the taste of her on his lips, the scent of her in his nostrils.

"Not that. I want you to help me break into Marvin the Martian's house."

Two weeks earlier, an ambulance had taken Marvin Cartwright's mother away for the last time. A few days later, a moving company had cleared out his house. There was a For Sale sign on the lawn.

"What for? There's nothing there. The moving company took everything away."

"Maybe not everything. Will you do it?"

"What if we get caught?"

"We won't get caught. Not if we're careful. I'll — I'll make it worth your while."

He knew what she meant, and it made his heart beat faster and the heat flow in his loins, but he said, "You don't have to do that. I — I love you."

"Don't say that," she said angrily. "You don't love me. You just fucked me, that's all. Look, will you help me or won't you?"

That night they broke into Marvin Cartwright's house through a basement window, but the house was as empty as the day it had been built. She never told him what she was looking for. She never mentioned Marvin Cartwright again.

Shoe never again told her that he loved her. Janey

reverted to her previous behaviour, refusing to publicly acknowledge their relationship, treating him in front of her friends, and his, as though he were a complete stranger.

It didn't matter. All that mattered to him was the time they spent together.

chapter seventeen

Shoe's parents sat in the shade of a garden umbrella in the backyard. His father was reading the Saturday paper aloud, dramatizing and adding the occasional wry editorial aside. The lawns were looking more ragged than ever. Shoe got his father's old power mower out of the garage. When he was done mowing the front lawn, his shirt was soaked and sticking to his back. His father had finished reading the paper, so Shoe took off his shirt and mowed the back lawn. In spite of the thin yellow haze of pollution, he could feel the mid-afternoon sun baking the skin of his shoulders. His one-eighth Native ancestry made him almost impervious to sunburn, but he didn't suppose it afforded any protection from skin cancer.

Lawns cut, clippings added to the compost heap by the edge of the woods, and the mower hosed off and put away, he took a shower in the downstairs bathroom, made a phone call in the kitchen, then walked across the street to the park to look for Janey Hallam. He found her behind the stage in the large tent. She was drinking beer from a can in a brown paper bag with the members of the band.

"Hey, Shoe," she said. "Guys, meet my old friend Shoe."

"Hiya, Shoe," the members of the band chorused. The women, although likely unrelated, nevertheless looked as though they'd been cast from the same mould, both blond and full-figured. The men, as different from each other as the women were the same, both had a vaguely dissolute look about them.

"Janey, can I have a word with you?"

"Sure," she said, bouncing to her feet. "Later, guys." She started to follow Shoe out of the tent, then said, "Hang on a sec." She tipped up the beer, draining it in three quick swallows. "Okay, let's go," she said, dropping the empty can and paper bag into a trash barrel. "Man, it's hot," she said, blinking in the sun as they left the tent. She popped another snap of her shirt, revealing the inner curves of her breasts. Subtlety had never been part of Janey's repertoire when they were teenagers, and it didn't appear she'd changed much in that regard.

"Is that one of the bands you manage?" Shoe asked her.

"Yeah." She leaned close. "Not one of my better ones," she said, lowering her voice, even though they were well out of earshot of the band members. "But they work cheap." She straightened and, after a few silent paces, said, "What did you want to talk about?"

"How well did you know Marvin Cartwright when we were kids?" Shoe asked.

"I hardly knew him at all. I heard he was killed in the Dells. I don't know anything about it, believe me, officer." She chuckled.

He wondered how many beers she'd had with the band. "Do you remember breaking into his house the week after he moved away?"

"The way I remember it, you were there too."

"Reluctantly," he said. "What were you looking for?"

"Nothing. It was just a lark. Fun. And, well, maybe I just wanted to see if you'd do it, you know." She bumped him with her shoulder. "You'd've set your own hair on fire for me that night, if I'd asked you."

"Had you ever been in his house before the night we broke in?" he asked.

"No."

"Had you ever spoken to him?"

"I may have. I don't remember."

"He used to give talks at the junior high school about writing and chess and birdwatching. Perhaps you attended one of them."

"Right. Chess and birdwatching. Fascinating subjects. Look, what is this? I told you, I didn't know him. Why do you care anyway? You're not still a cop. You writing a book?"

"I'm curious, Janey. It's in my nature."

"Yeah, well, go be curious somewhere else, all right?"

"I'm sorry, Janey. I didn't mean to upset you."

"Forget it. Look, let me sort out a couple of details with the band, then we can go have a drink or two and talk about old times. Who knows," she added archly, "maybe we'll do more than talk."

"Maybe some other time," he said.

"Sure," she said blithely. "I'll be around. Just whistle." She gave him a sultry look. "You remember how to whistle, don't you, Shoe?"

chapter eighteen

Shoe was sitting in a lawn chair in the blue-tinted shade of the welcome tent when Tim Dutton sat down beside him. Dutton was drinking beer from a can, but instead of hiding it in a brown paper bag, he was using a cotton gardening glove. Shoe had a bottle of water.

"I saw you talking to Janey," Dutton said. "She's looking pretty damned good, isn't she? Better 'n she did as a kid, I'd say. She's still the same old Janey, though; when she's got an itch ... " He shrugged.

Shoe chose not to respond to Dutton's innuendo.

"She doesn't look half as good as Miss Hahn, though," Dutton went on. He whistled through his teeth. "Man, can you believe she's, what, sixty? I remember how she used to stand behind her desk, with the back of the chair pressed against her crotch. Drove me nuts. Spent most of my time in her class with a fucking woody." He drank from his gardening glove, belched softly, and dabbed at his mouth with the thumb of the glove. "There was a story in the news a while back about this teacher out west who got fired for screwing one of her students. He was fifteen and she was, like, thirty. We should've been so lucky, eh?"

"Tim," Rachel said as she came out of the kitchen shelter. "Don't be a bigger jerk than you have to be."

"Get fucked, Rae," Dutton said good-naturedly over his shoulder. "It'll do you good. If you can't find any takers, I'm always ready to help out a friend."

"Asshole," Rachel muttered, and headed in the direction of the row of blue portable privies set up at the back of the park.

"Rae needs to get out more," Dutton said.

"And you need to show a little more respect," Shoe said.

"Yeah, well," he said with a shrug. "Regular sex will do wonders for her disposition. Maybe she should get married again, not that that's any guarantee of regular sex. How many husbands has she been through? Two? Might as well go for the hat trick," he added, and took another swallow of beer.

"Do you remember if Janey knew Marvin Cartwright?" Shoe asked.

"Did she?"

"I'm asking you."

"I dunno if she did or didn't. Maybe she was fucking him. She was fucking everyone else in the neighbourhood. Right?"

"Tim."

"What?"

Shoe sighed. "Never mind."

"I know. Show more respect."

"At least try."

"Sure, okay. The only person I know for sure Janey was fucking was you. For sure she wasn't fucking me. Hell, no one was fucking me. At any rate, maybe Cartwright was the Black Creek Rapist and maybe he wasn't, but Janey was, what, thirteen when you and her started doing it? That's young, particularly for those days. She had to learn it from someone. Marty and Rae claim Cartwright wasn't a kiddy diddler, but maybe he just hadn't gotten around to them yet. Liked 'em older. Either way, Janey was a pretty screwed-up kid, right?"

Shoe had never thought of Janey as particularly screwed up. Temperamental, a little wilder and more unpredictable than most, himself included, but also tougher, smarter, and more imaginative than most, himself included again.

"You know that for last couple of years she's been living in the apartment in the basement of her parents' old house, eh?" Dutton said. "Dougie lives upstairs. You should see the place. Janey keeps her part of the property pretty neat, but Dougie lives like a goddamned pig. The front yard's a dump. Worse than it ever was when his old man was alive. It's worth a few bucks, though. Janey would like to sell, use the money to get back on her feet, but Dougie isn't interested in selling and won't agree to buy her out."

"Get back on her feet how?"

"She had her own advertising agency a few years back, but I heard she tried to fuck over her business partner, and got her ass sued off. Had to declare bankruptcy and move into her folks' old house with her brother."

"Stepbrother," Shoe corrected.

"Yeah, right." Dutton was silent for a moment, then said, "Hey, did Marty tell you that Joey Noseworthy is staying at her place? Man, now there's a pair and a half."

"What do you mean?" Shoe asked.

"Well, you know … "

"No, Tim, I don't."

"If it wasn't Cartwright that diddled her in the woods when she was a little kid, I'd put my money on

Noseworthy. She let everyone think it was Cartwright, or whoever the Black Creek Rapist was, but I figure it was Joey that molested Marty."

"Based on what?" Shoe asked.

"I know he was your friend and all, but even you have to admit he was a pretty weird kid. Remember how he used to dress, like it was always Halloween? His socks never matched and one time he even came to school in a fucking *cape*."

"It was a Tyrolean cloak his aunt sent him from Austria for Christmas when he was eleven or twelve," Shoe said. "He wore it only once, but you and some of the other kids" — including Janey, he thought — "made so much fun of him, he threw it away and told his parents someone had stolen it. I don't remember anything about his socks not matching."

"Marty says it wasn't Cartwright that diddled her," Dutton insisted.

"That doesn't automatically mean it was Joey," Shoe said.

"I remember she used to tease him all the time," Dutton said, "on account he was a sissy and not a lot bigger that she was. Maybe he just got pissed off at her one day."

"I seem to recall that you were always after Marty and my sister to play doctor with you," Shoe said. "Maybe you got tired of them saying no."

"Hey," Dutton protested. "I was just kidding around. Geez, what do you take me for?"

Shoe was saved from having to answer by the arrival of a massive, barrel-bodied man carrying a large blue and white thermal lunch box.

"Oh, Christ," Dutton moaned loudly. "Lock up your wife and daughters and bring in the cat."

"Up yours, Dutton," Dougie Hallam said.

"Good repartee, Dougie."

"Repartee yourself, limp dick," Hallam said. "How you doin', Shoe? I heard you were back. Lotta beer through the bladder since the last time we went a round, eh?"

"Yes, indeed," Shoe said as he stood up. He was a hand taller than Hallam, but Hallam more than made up for it in girth. He carried himself well, however.

"Still living out there on the coast?" Hallam said. "I was out there couple years ago. Too many queers for my taste, but they're everywhere these days, aren't they?" He opened the big lunch box. "Wanna beer?"

"No, thanks," Shoe said.

Hallam took a can of Molson Export out of the lunch pail. He popped the tab and guzzled noisily, wiping his mouth with the palm of his hand. He slapped his huge gut. It sounded as if he were slapping a concrete wall. "Gotta keep up the old Molson muscle, eh? Wanna take a shot? Go ahead. I won't feel a thing."

"Some other time," Shoe said.

"Let me get my truck," Tim Dutton said.

Hallam ignored him. "You look like you're in pretty good shape. What do you press? I'm up to 425."

"Is that all?" Dutton said.

"Fuck off, Dutton. You couldn't bench press my dick."

"Nor would I want to," Dutton said. "No telling where it's been."

"Places yours'll never be."

"I can believe that."

"Like your wife's ass."

"In your dreams, Dougie," Dutton said with a laugh. "I gotta get back to the store. See you later, Shoe."

When Dutton had gone Hallam said, "We oughta get together while you're in town. Maybe go a couple of rounds. You still box?"

"I never did."

"No? I thought you boxed. Anyway, you should try it. It's great exercise and keeps your reflexes sharp. A man's sport. The sport of kings, right? Not like kung fu or karate, eh? That stuff's for faggots."

"The sport of kings is horse racing, Dougie, not boxing."

"What? Really? You sure? Oh, well. Learn something every day, I say. So, what say? Might be fun."

For whom? Shoe wondered. "No thanks, Dougie. I don't fight for fun."

"Fighting's always fun. Or are you chicken? Buck buck b-buck," he crowed.

"That must be it," Shoe said.

Rachel came round the kitchen tent on her way back from the line of portable privies. When she saw Hallam, she did an abrupt about-face. Too late ...

"Hey, Rae," Hallam called out. "Great job. Let's get together. Have a few. You can sit on my face, how's that sound?" He stuck out his tongue and waggled it obscenely.

Face flaming, Rachel snapped, "Stick your dick in a meat grinder, Dougie. I'm sure we can find someone to turn the handle." She ducked into the kitchen shelter.

Hallam laughed. "Your sister's as juicy as ever. I like 'em small. Nice and tight. Too bad she never learned to keep a civil tongue in her head. Like I say, though, they can't talk with their mouths full."

Shoe stepped close to Dougie Hallam, invading his personal space. "Don't you ever talk to my sister like that again," he said, with quiet intensity.

Involuntarily, Hallam backed away a step, then stood his ground. "Yeah, or what?"

"Or I'll have to teach you to mind your manners. Again." He stepped back. "Have a nice day, Dougie," he said, and walked away.

chapter nineteen

On a frigid Saturday night in the middle of January, shortly after his sixteenth birthday and a month before her fourteenth, Shoe and Janey had gone ice skating on the outdoor rink in the park across the road from his parents' house. At ten o'clock they left the little unheated shack by the rink, ice skates slung over their shoulders. Janey's stepbrother and two other boys were waiting outside the shack.

"Go home," Hallam said to Janey. "We got some personal business with Cochise here."

"Leave us alone, Dougie," Janey said.

Her stepbrother punched her in the chest and knocked her to the frozen ground.

Hallam hadn't learned anything from his previous engagement with Shoe. Almost before Janey hit the ground, Shoe had broken Hallam's nose again and knocked out another tooth. On his knees, Hallam coughed and spit blood, black on the moonlit snow. The other two boys backed off, then turned and ran as Shoe took a step toward them, brandishing his skate blades.

"Look out!" Janey cried.

Pain exploded across Shoe's back. He twisted sideways, staggering, slipped on the icy ground, and fell onto his back. He felt a rush of air as the end of a three-foot length of two-by-four slashed by his face.

"Okay, tough guy," Hallam said. "Let's see how tough you really are." He swung the makeshift club again.

Shoe blocked the two-by-four with a skate, the blade slicing deep into the wood. Hallam's friends, emboldened by his recovery, came back. The three of them circled Shoe like wolves, as Shoe tried to get to his feet. Hallam swung the two-by-four, slamming it into Shoe's shoulder, knocking him onto his back again. One of the other boys darted in, kicked him in the side, and jumped back. Not quickly enough. Shoe slashed his shin to the bone with the blade of his skate. He fell, shrieking and writhing and holding his leg as blood spattered onto the snow.

Hallam, with a bloody grin, swung the two-by-four at Shoe's head. Shoe parried with his skate again. He grabbed the board. Something stabbed through his glove into the palm of his hand. Hallam wrenched the board out of Shoe's grasp, swung again, batting the skates aside. Shoe scrabbled backwards, away from Hallam and the board. He'd forgotten about the third boy.

"Look out!" Janey shouted again.

Too late. Something smashed hard into Shoe's back, just above his kidneys. The pain was excruciating, but it propelled him to his feet. Janey threw herself at the boy who'd kicked him, clawing at his eyes. He tossed her aside. She fell and Shoe went after him. He ran. Shoe heard a grunt of exertion behind him, reflexively ducked and hunched his shoulders as he turned. The two-by-four struck his shoulder and glanced off the side of his head. He fell again, head ringing.

"Hey, you boys," a man bawled from the back of one of the houses bordering the park.

Hallam swung the two-by-four. Shoe raised his arms to protect his head. The wide edge of the board smacked into his left forearm, otherwise his arm surely would have been broken. It hurt nonetheless, but Shoe grabbed the board with his right hand and yanked it out of Hallam's grasp. Hallam backed off. Using the two-by-four as a support, Shoe struggled to his feet.

"You boys," the man shouted again. "I've called the police."

Disarmed, Hallam's grinning bravado had disappeared. "Fight fair, Cochise. Get rid of the board."

"You've got a funny idea of fair," Shoe said. "I think I'll keep it."

"Go home," Hallam said to Janey. "This is between me and him."

Janey stepped to Shoe's side. "Leave us alone, Dougie."

Hallam made a grab for her. He yowled as Shoe slashed him across the knuckles with the two-by-four. Shoe threw the board aside.

"All right, Dougie. You want a fair fight, you got it."

Hallam hesitated. Then he lowered his head and charged. He might as well have sent Shoe a note. Shoe sidestepped and hit him on the side of the head. Hallam staggered a couple of steps and sank to his knees. As Hallam struggled to his feet and turned unsteadily toward him, Shoe stepped up and drove his fist straight into Hallam's nose again. He felt cartilage split under his knuckles. Hallam grunted and fell onto his back, rolled over, but did not try to get up. Blood ran onto the snow. Janey tried to kick him, her face contorted with anger, but Shoe hauled her back. The anger in her face faded, to be replaced by fear.

Shoe's back hurt as he bent to pick up his and Janey's skates. Holding his left arm to his chest, gritting his teeth against the pain, he slung both pairs of skates over his shoulder. He pulled off his right glove with his teeth. The knuckles of his right hand were starting to swell and there was a two-inch splinter of wood in his palm. He plucked it out with his teeth and closed his fist on the blood. He heard sirens.

"Let's go," he said to Janey.

She shook her head. "I gotta take him home."

"The police will take care of him. Won't they, Dougie?" He nudged Hallam with the toe of his boot. Hallam moaned.

"I gotta take him home," Janey said again. She started to help her stepbrother up, but he lashed out at her, hitting her in the chest. She sat in the snow, wheezing for breath.

"Leave him," Shoe said, pulling her to her feet with his good arm.

"Go home. Please," she pleaded. "Let me take him home." She pushed him toward the park exit. "Go. Go. Please."

Reluctantly, Shoe left her with her stepbrother.

The following Monday, Janey wasn't in school. She didn't return until mid-week. She had a black eye, a bruised jaw, and a bandage on her right wrist. She'd fallen down the stairs, she told anyone who asked. Shoe knew better.

"He did this to you, didn't he?" The look on her face was answer enough. Shoe's anger ran deep and hot. "I'll kill him," he said, through clenched teeth.

"Please, Shoe, don't do anything. It'll only make things worse. He'll only beat me up again."

"Not if he knows what's good for him he won't."

"Don't be stupid," she said. "He's not worth it. I'm not worth it."

"Don't say that. You tell him, if he touches you again, he'll be sorry."

"It won't do any good. Stay away from him. Please. I had to beg Freddy not to come after you. You might be able to take Dougie, but you wouldn't stand a chance against his old man. He'd kill you, believe me. Let it go. Please. For my sake, at least, but yours too."

It hadn't been easy, but Shoe had let it go, hoping things would go back to the way they'd been. They hadn't, of course.

chapter twenty

At a few minutes past four, as Shoe was leaving the park, a plain grey Sebring sedan pulled up to the curb. A Toronto Police Service scout car pulled up behind it. Detective Sergeant Hannah Lewis and Detective Constable Paul Timmons got out of the Sebring and two uniformed constables got out of the scout car. Hannah Lewis's fox-like face was serious. Timmons had an unlit cigarette in his mouth. The uniformed constables looked wary.

"Good day, Detective Sergeant," Shoe said. "Detective Constable Timmons. Officers."

Timmons nodded curtly, lighting the cigarette.

"Mr. Schumacher," Lewis said, manner brusque and businesslike. "Have you seen Martine Elias?"

"She's in the park, talking with my sister." Rachel and Marty had been sitting outside the welcome tent, catching up and reminiscing about Marvin Cartwright. Shoe, feeling like an eavesdropper, had left them to it.

Lewis nodded to Timmons and the uniformed constables and proceeded into the park. Shoe fell in beside her. She glanced up at him.

"Do you mind if I tag along?" he asked.

"Just remember you're a civilian," she said.

Shoe looked at her out of the corner of his eye. Her face was too sharp and angular to be called pretty, but she was far from unattractive. And there was a keen intelligence behind those seemingly all-seeing violet eyes. There was a toughness, too, in the way she held herself, a sense that she would brook no nonsense. Like a lot of cops, it was a pose, a pretence one learned early and which eventually became habitual. Survival often depended on giving the right first impression.

"She's good," Hank Trumbull had said during Shoe's brief conversation with him earlier in the day. "She was on the fast track for a while, but, well, she can be something of a loose cannon. Comes by it honestly, I suppose; her brother wasn't exactly the poster boy for *esprit de corps*, was he?" A sigh. "I tried to be a good influence on her," he said, words heavy with irony. He paused for a moment, then said, "This Cartwright case could come back and bite her."

"How so?"

"Do you remember a rape/homicide case in that area about thirty, thirty-five years ago? Three sexual assaults and the rape and murder of a female park worker."

"The Black Creek Rapist," Shoe said. "Yes, I remember."

"Cartwright was a suspect," Trumbull said.

"Not a very good one."

"The best of a bad lot, maybe, but a suspect nonetheless."

"All right," Shoe conceded. "But how could that hurt Hannah?"

"Her brother was part of the investigation."

"He was?" Shoe said, surprised. "I didn't know that."

"No reason you should. It's not something he'd be inclined to brag about. According to a retired sergeant I play golf with, who knew him back then, Mackie had a major hard-on for Cartwright. He was convinced Cartwright was the Black Creek Rapist. He went way overboard, though, and got himself an official reprimand for harassment and insubordination. There was also something about him trying to pressure a witness into making a false statement. He's lucky they didn't kick him off the force. Might've saved himself and others a lot of trouble if they had."

"Are you suggesting that Ron Mackie may have killed Cartwright?" Shoe said.

"Hell, no, but — " A woman called Trumbull's name. "Be with you in a sec, love," Trumbull called in return. "I gotta go," he said to Shoe. "Listen, if there's the slightest hint Mackie is connected to this Cartwright murder, there's going to be some serious hell to pay, and Hannah is going to get stuck with the check. The smart thing would be for her to recuse herself, but — "

"Hank!" the woman called again.

"Tell her to keep her head down and play this one by the book."

"Hank! We're going to miss our goddamned plane!"

"Okay, okay," Trumbull had shouted as he'd hung up the phone.

Lewis became aware of Shoe's sidelong scrutiny. "What?"

"Did you know your brother was part of the investigation into the old rape/homicide case I told you about?"

She stopped in her tracks. "What? No. Where'd you hear that?" When Shoe hesitated, she sighed and said,

"Right. Hank. Shit."

"According to Hank, your brother was convinced Cartwright was the Black Creek Rapist and came close to being dishonourably discharged for harassment, insubordination, and possibly attempting to suborn a witness. He was concerned that Ron's connection to the case could compromise your investigation. He asked me to tell you to keep your head down and play it by the book."

"He's hardly the one to give that kind of advice." She was deep in thought for a moment, then said, "Was there a witness? Besides the victims?"

"I don't know," Shoe said.

"But you don't think Cartwright was the Black Creek Rapist, do you?"

"No."

"How can you be so sure? Maybe Ron wasn't wrong."

"Not according to Claudia Hahn." Or Marty Elias, according to Tim Dutton.

"Hahn was the second victim?"

"Yes. I spoke with her this morning. She knew Cartwright and is certain he wasn't the man who raped her."

"She wouldn't be the first woman to be raped by someone she knew but couldn't — or wouldn't — identify him."

"No, but she's extremely compelling. Talk to her yourself."

"Count on it." She sighed. "All right, so Ron screwed up. It wouldn't be the last time, would it? On the other hand, maybe you're wrong about Hahn."

"I'm frequently wrong about many things," Shoe said agreeably. Lewis smiled thinly. He knew what she was thinking: Claudia had denied that Cartwright was her rapist in order to remove a possible motive she might have for killing him. "But I'm inclined to believe her," he added.

"Mm," Lewis said. After a moment of contemplative silence, she resumed walking.

Rachel and Marty Elias were in the kitchen tent, sitting at the folding table, heads close together, looking at the laptop screen. Both stood when Shoe, Lewis, and Timmons entered. The uniformed constables waited outside, already attracting curious glances.

Rachel glared at Timmons. "Would you put that out, please?"

Timmons dropped his cigarette to the grass and ground it out beneath the toe of his shoe.

Lewis took a notebook out of her jacket pocket. She looked at Marty. "Are you Martine Elias?"

"Yes," Marty replied, looking at Shoe, then at Lewis again.

Lewis introduced herself and Detective Constable Timmons, then said, "Do you have a few minutes to answer some questions?"

"What about?" Marty asked, a little warily, Shoe thought.

"Are you acquainted with a Joseph Charles Noseworthy?"

Marty's eyes widened. "Sure, I know Joey. We all do. Why?"

Lewis looked at Shoe. "You know Joey Noseworthy?"

"He was my closest friend until our first year of high school. I haven't seen or spoken to him since."

"Why are you asking about Joey?" Rachel asked.

Lewis didn't reply. Shoe knew the answer. In the jargon of police speak, Joey had become a "person of interest" in the investigation into Marvin Cartwright's murder, possibly even a suspect.

"Miss Elias," Lewis said. "We understand he's been

staying at your apartment. Is that right?"

"So?" Marty said belligerently.

"How long has he been staying with you?" Lewis asked.

"Since Thursday night," Marty replied. "How — "

"What time did he get there?"

"I dunno, um, around midnight, I guess." She avoided eye contact with Shoe; earlier in the day she'd told him that Joey had shown up at her door at two-thirty in the morning.

"Are you certain of the time?" Lewis said.

"Look, I ... " Marty was flustered. Like lawyers, Shoe knew, cops also asked questions to which they already had the answer.

"Because when we canvassed your neighbours, they told us that a man who appeared to be quite drunk was banging on your door and shouting your name at two-thirty Friday morning."

Marty flushed. "Okay, so it was two-thirty."

"Thank you. What was his demeanour?"

"Like you said, he was drunk."

"Was there any blood on his clothing or on his person?"

"Not that I saw. He smelled like a dumpster, so I made him take a shower and threw his clothes in the washer. I didn't see any blood on them. Look, I know what this is about now, but there's no way Joey killed Mr. Cartwright."

"I hope you're right," Lewis said.

"Sure you do," Marty replied sarcastically.

The two uniformed officers standing patiently in the hot sun outside the welcome tent were attracting attention from passersby. Nor did the kitchen shelter, with its bug-screen walls rolled up, afford any privacy. Shoe wasn't surprised when Lewis suggested a change of venue.

"Perhaps we should continue this at the division," she said.

"I'm not going anywhere with you," Marty said.

"Miss Elias," Lewis said patiently. "This will go a lot easier if you co-operate."

"Easier for who?" Marty shot back. She looked at Shoe. "What should I do?"

Shoe said, "You should co-operate with them, Marty."

"I don't want to get Joey into trouble."

"It may be too late to worry about that," Shoe said.

"Mr. Schumacher is right," Lewis said. "But if you help us, you'll be helping Joey. You want to help him, don't you, Marty?"

"Don't patronize me," Marty snapped, temper flaring. "I'm not stupid. I know what cops are like."

"I apologize if I was condescending, but you should listen to Mr. Schumacher. He's giving you good advice. We can compel you to come to the station to make a statement, but we'd rather you came voluntarily. What will it be?"

Marty stared at Lewis for a moment, then said, "Okay, I'll go with you. But only if Shoe comes with me."

"Fuck that," Timmons grumbled.

"Shut up, Paul," Lewis said.

Timmons scowled. Was Lewis playing good cop, Shoe wondered, to Timmons' bad cop? If so, it was a convincing act.

"I don't have a problem with that," Lewis said to Marty. "Assuming it's all right with Mr. Schumacher."

"It's fine with me," Shoe said, wondering what he was getting himself into.

Lewis looked at her wristwatch. Like Claudia Hahn's, Lewis's wristwatch was also a very mannish timepiece, worn on the inside of her wrist. Masculine watches for women must be in vogue, Shoe thought.

"Would it be convenient for you to come to the station now?" Lewis said.

"I guess," Marty said.

Outside the kitchen tent, Lewis asked Shoe, "Do you have a car?"

"I can borrow my father's," he replied.

"Paul," she said to her partner. "I'll ride with Mr. Schumacher. Show him the way. Miss Elias, do you mind going with Detective Constable Timmons?"

"I guess not," Marty replied uncertainly, looking at Shoe.

"It'll be all right," he said. "I'll see you at the station."

"I won't talk to anyone till you get there," Marty said defiantly.

"Paul," Lewis said. "Make Miss Elias comfortable until we get there. And if you must smoke in the car, leave the goddamned windows down, will you?"

"Yeah, yeah," Timmons groused. "C'mon," he said to Marty.

Marty, Timmons, and the two uniformed constables trooped toward the park exit. Marty looked anxiously back over her shoulder at Shoe. He smiled at her, reassuringly, he hoped.

"I'll be just a minute," he said to Lewis, and went back into the kitchen tent. "Is Dad's car roadworthy?" he asked Rachel.

"Sure. Hal's been after him to sell it, but Dad won't hear of it. He hasn't driven it in months, though, so the battery's probably flat. You can use my car, if you like."

"Thanks," Shoe said. "I don't think I'll fit. I'll need to move it, though." Rachel's New Beetle was parked in the driveway, blocking the garage.

Rachel dug the keys out of her backpack, handed them to him. "Just leave them on the kitchen table," she told him.

"Are you all right?" Shoe asked her.

"Yeah, except I feel like I'm trapped in an episode of *The Twilight Zone*." She looked at Lewis, standing just a few feet away outside the kitchen shelter, and lowered her voice. "Do you think Joey killed Mr. Cartwright?"

"I don't want to," Shoe said. "But people change, often in ways we don't expect."

chapter twenty-one

Shoe's father's car was a ten-year-old Ford Taurus station wagon. Bought new, it looked as though it had just been driven off the lot, with less than sixty thousand kilometres on the clock. The battery was indeed flat, but there was a booster pack plugged into an outlet over the work bench at the back of the garage. When Shoe hooked it up, the car started instantly.

"I put gas treatment in the tank every time I fill up," Howard Schumacher explained to Hannah Lewis. "Keeps the gas from going bad and clogging the jets if she sits for too long. Usually turn her over every couple of weeks to keep the battery from going flat. Guess I been neglecting her lately."

Lewis smiled tolerantly. Shoe's father was proud of his knowledge of automobiles. He liked them, whereas Shoe considered them a necessary evil. His own car, an aging Mercedes, was nearly twice as old as his father's car, somewhat less well maintained, and showing its years.

Lewis gave him directions to the 31 Division police station. It had moved from its old location next to the fish and chips takeout in the mall at Jane and Wilson, but he wouldn't have had any trouble finding it on his own.

"Not that I mind the company," he said, "but is there some reason you wanted to ride with me, besides keeping Marty and me apart until you complete your interview?"

"No, that's pretty much it. And it'll give Paul an opportunity to work on her."

"Good cop, bad cop?"

"More like good cop, better cop. Don't worry. He won't be hard on her. He may look like a dumb, fat slob and smell like an ashtray, but he has a knack for getting people to open up to him. He's just not particularly good at putting it all together."

Shoe glanced over at her. "You haven't arrested Joey, have you?" he said.

She sighed. "I was hoping you wouldn't twig to that. Do you think Marty has?"

"Don't underestimate her," Shoe said. "She was a pretty smart kid, as I recall."

"I'll remember that."

"Is it because you haven't got enough evidence to arrest him, or because you don't know where he is?"

She looked at him. He concentrated on the Saturday afternoon traffic, imagining he could feel her violet gaze penetrating his hide like X-rays. An image popped into his mind, of an awkward, long-limbed girl with glasses, pigtails, braces on her teeth, and tears on her cheeks, holding a white rose. She stood stiffly beside a choleric-faced man in a wheelchair, a cervical collar on his neck, surrounded by men and women in police dress blues.

"I tried to talk to you after Sara's funeral," he said. "Ron wouldn't let me near you."

She looked at him for another moment before

replying. "I know. It probably wouldn't have done any good. I was pretty angry with — well, everyone. You. Ron. Even Sara. I was angry with you and Ron because I blamed you both for her death. And I was angry with her for dying." She smiled self-deprecatingly. "What did I know? I was just a dumb kid. It took me a long time to realize that it was no one's fault. I missed Sara. I still do. She was the mother I'd lost, the big sister I'd never had, and the best friend I could have asked for, all rolled into one. I missed you, too," she added. "You were the sort of big brother I wish Ron had been."

"If you were my sister, you might feel differently," Shoe said.

"You seem to get along. Are you a close family?"

"We haven't seen much of each other since I went out west," he said. "My fault. In twenty-seven years I've been back only five times, including this trip, and when I did return, I never stayed more than a few days."

Lewis was silent for a moment, expression thought-ful. "How well did you know Joey Noseworthy?"

"Probably not as well as I thought."

"Is he capable of murder?"

"I imagine we all are," Shoe said. "In the right cir-cumstances."

"You got that right."

"Do you have any evidence to connect him to Marvin Cartwright's murder?"

She looked at him, violet eyes darkening. "You really expect me to tell you, don't you?"

"I don't expect you to tell me anything that will compromise your case."

She sighed. "It may not be my case for very much longer. As soon as my new boss finds out there's a link between my brother and Cartwright, he'll pull me off it faster than you can say 'circumstantial evidence.' In fact, I should have backed off the moment you told me, let Paul take over. I just hope Ron's got a good alibi for Thursday night."

Lewis fell silent and looked out the passenger side window as they drove past the strip malls, parched parks, and apartment complexes that lined that section of Jane Street. When Shoe had been growing up, the Jane and Finch area had been mostly farmland, just beginning to develop. In less than forty years it had devolved, if the media could be believed, into an ugly and gang-ridden concrete sprawl. It wasn't a pretty area, Shoe conceded, but it looked peaceful enough, at least by daylight. Most of the people he saw on the streets were of African or Asian descent, but there were those of European extraction, too, as well as many whose ancestors might have swum in a dozen different gene pools. Multiculturalism and the melting pot were not mutually exclusive.

Lewis cleared her throat. "We found Cartwright's car in the Dells' main parking lot," she said. "His body was about a kilometre and a half away, on the other side of the creek, in the wooded area behind his former house — and your parents' house. He'd been struck repeatedly with a blunt object, likely a tree bough, which we haven't yet located. FIS — Forensic Identification Services — puts the time of death at between midnight and 1:00 a.m., but he may have been attacked as early as 11:00 p.m. He didn't die immediately. He walked or crawled some distance through the woods, perhaps trying to reach one of the houses for help, before collapsing. FIS says he lay there for at least half an hour before succumbing to his injuries. Official COD is exsanguination. He — "

"Bled to death," Shoe said. "I remember the jargon. What makes you suspect Joey?"

"His prints were all over Cartwright's car. He has a record, two misdemeanour convictions for assault, and two for drunk and disorderly. He's done jail time, but no hard time. There were other prints, too.

Cartwright's, naturally, and a couple we can't identify, but Noseworthy's prints in Cartwright's car was enough cause to bring him in for a talk." She paused.

"But you had to find him first," Shoe said. "How did you connect him and Marty? Wait. Don't tell me. You got an anonymous tip."

She shrugged. "You know how it is," she said.

He did. Luck frequently played a part in homicide investigations. It came in many forms, from an anonymous tip, as often as not from an associate, a rival, or a jealous girlfriend, to the serendipitous arrest of the killer for an unrelated and frequently relatively minor infraction, such as a traffic violation or drug possession. Of course, no amount of luck compensated for sloppy police work; good cops had to know how to make their own luck.

"The caller was a woman. She told us the person who killed the man in the Dells was a biker-type riding a Harley-Davidson Sportster, smallish, with long grey-blond hair, and that he was probably shacked up with Marty Elias."

"Did she give you Joey's name?"

"We already had his name from his prints, but yes. Good call. It indicates she may have been acquainted with Noseworthy, but wasn't necessarily a witness to the crime itself."

"It could also mean someone is trying to fit him up or misdirect the investigation."

"All anonymous tips are suspect," Lewis reminded him. "Anyway, we put eyes on Elias's place last night, but she took Noseworthy's Harley to work this morning and they followed her. It wasn't until she got off the bike at her work that they realized their mistake."

Not all luck, Shoe also knew, was the good kind.

"Then a truck delivering beer to the restaurant on the ground floor of Elias's apartment building backed into the new team's vehicle. They got into a bit of a ruck-us with the driver and Noseworthy must've made them. When we executed our warrant and got the building manager to let us into Elias's apartment, he was gone."

Sometimes, Shoe thought, the universe unfolded ac-cording to Murphy's Law, rather than Newton's.

"He didn't jump out a window in his underwear, but he left without his saddle packs or camping gear. We didn't find his wallet, or any money, so he's not without resources. We did find a book about birds, written and autographed by Marvin Cartwright, and a small travel-ling chess set with Cartwright's name engraved on the case."

"Joey's fingerprints in Cartwright's car and a book and chess set that apparently belonged to Cartwright aren't enough to get a conviction," Shoe said. "All they prove is that Cartwright and Joey were acquainted."

"Maybe we'll find traces of blood on his clothing," Lewis said. "Elias did his laundry, but a normal wash-ing doesn't necessarily remove all traces of blood. Could screw up DNA, but it'll take a few days before the crime lab can get back to us with results. In the meantime, he's in the wind, possibly armed and dangerous."

The idea that Joey Noseworthy could be considered armed and dangerous seemed ludicrous to Shoe, until he remembered what he'd told his sister about people changing, sometimes in unexpected ways.

chapter twenty-two

Marty's interview was conducted in a small, windowless room that smelled of powerful disinfectant that did not mask the rank, flat stink of the accumulated human misery to which the room had borne witness. Shoe hadn't been in a police interview room in almost thirty years, and then they had been the domain of detectives, not wet-behind-the-ears uniformed constables. With the exception of the no smoking signs and the video camera, which evidently had replaced the traditional mirrored observation window, they hadn't changed appreciably.

Marty and Shoe sat on straight-backed grey steel chairs across a scarred grey steel table from Detective Sergeant Hannah Lewis and Detective Constable Paul Timmons. Timmons chewed vigorously on a stick of nicotine gum that made his breath smell like rotting sawdust. Lewis had removed her contact lenses and donned glasses with rectangular black plastic frames that did little to soften the angularity of her face. She had made it clear to Shoe that he was there strictly as a courtesy. He was to observe only. Interfere and he was out; Marty would be on her own.

Lewis started off easy. "Do you know where Noseworthy was before he got to your place?" she asked.

"A bar?" Marty said, voice full of mockery.

"Which bar?" Lewis said evenly.

"I don't know."

"Does he have a regular hangout?"

"I don't know."

"When he arrived at your apartment, did he seem particularly agitated or nervous, upset about anything?"

"No," Marty said. "He was drunk."

"What kind of drunk is he? Is he a mean drunk?"

"No."

"He's got a temper, though."

"Yeah, I guess."

"Is it worse when he's drunk?"

"Not especially."

"Would you say he's a happy drunk then?"

Marty shook her head. "He gets a little sappy sometimes when he drinks, I guess, but mostly he just talks a lot. He's not very careful about what he says, either. Like, if he thinks someone's an asshole … " She shrugged.

Lewis made a note on the pad in front of her. "Tell me about his movements between his arrival at your apartment Friday morning and when you left for work this morning."

"I don't know if he had any."

Lewis's expression didn't change. Timmons grunted. It was an old joke. They'd both seen it coming. So had Shoe.

Marty shrugged. "I work half days on Fridays," she said. "When my boss lets me. Joey was still asleep on my couch when I got home."

"What time was that?"

"About one. He got up about two, I guess. We hung out at my place till five, got something to eat, then went to the show."

"A movie?" Lewis asked. It had been years since Shoe had heard going to a movie theatre referred to as "going to the show."

"Yeah," Marty said. "At Yorkdale. After the show, we had a few drinks before going back to my place. Joey had some more to drink and fell asleep around midnight. He was still asleep when I left for work this morning."

"Where did you have these drinks?"

"At a bar on Bathurst, near Lawrence. I don't remember the name, but they have live country music."

"Could it have been where he was drinking on Thursday night?"

"I don't think he'd been there before."

Lewis took off her glasses, put them down on the table, then massaged her temples. Shoe had the feeling the questions were going to get a little more difficult. Lewis put her glasses back on.

"You lied to us about the time Joey got to your place Friday morning. Why?"

"I dunno," Marty replied with a shrug. "You're cops?"

"Or perhaps you lied because you knew Noseworthy needed an alibi."

"Yeah, well, he does, doesn't he?"

Lewis's expression conceded the point. "Why did you take his Harley to work this morning?"

"My bike isn't running too good," Marty said. "Joey was supposed to look at it while he was here."

"Whose idea was it that you take the Harley? His or yours?"

"Like I said, he was still asleep when I left. I took it because he lets me use it when he's in town."

"You and Noseworthy are close to the same size, wouldn't you say?"

"Yeah, I guess. He's not big and I'm not small. So?"

"In leathers and a helmet, you could easily pass for him from a distance. Are you sure you didn't take the Harley because you knew the police would follow you, giving him a chance to escape?"

"Why would I do that?" Marty said. "I didn't know you were watching him. Anyway, they'd've probably followed my bike, too, if they didn't know I owned one."

"As it happens, you're probably right," Lewis said. "We didn't know you owned a motorcycle."

Score another one for Marty, Shoe thought. At least she had the good grace not to smirk.

"Where's Noseworthy's bike now?" Lewis asked.

"At the store where I work, in the loading bay. My boss made me park it there so no one could see it. He doesn't like motorcycles."

"We'll need to impound it."

Marty dug into the pocket of her jeans and took out a set of keys on a rabbit's foot keychain. She removed one key from the ring and put it on the table. Neither Lewis nor Timmons made any move to touch it.

"What are the other keys for?" Lewis asked.

"These are my keys," Marty said. She held them up, one at a time. "This one's for my bike, this one's for the garage in my apartment building, this one's for my mailbox, this one's for my apartment, these are for work."

"Okay," Lewis said.

Marty returned her keys to her pocket.

"Where were you on Thursday evening?" Lewis asked.

Marty nodded, as though she'd been waiting for the question. "I worked till nine-thirty, locked up, then went home. I watched TV till eleven-thirty, then went to bed. And, yeah, I was alone, till Joey got there."

"Can anyone verify you were home between ten o'clock Thursday evening and one o'clock Friday morning? A friend or neighbour?"

"No, I guess not."

"When was the last time you saw Marvin Cartwright?"

"I haven't seen him in, like, thirty-five years, since he moved away."

"The last time you saw him, was that when he molested you in the woods?"

"No," Marty said, spots of colour rising on her cheeks. "It wasn't him."

"Who was it?"

"I don't know. I never saw his face. Someone just tried to grab me and I ran. I know it wasn't Mr. Cartwright. He — he wasn't like that." She stood, chair scraping across the floor. "I'm not going to answer any more questions."

"I'm sorry, Marty," Lewis said. "I didn't mean to upset you. Please, sit down. Would you like some water? Paul, get Miss Elias some water."

"I don't want any water. I want to leave."

"Soon. Just a couple more questions. Sit down. Please."

Lewis looked at Shoe and nodded almost imperceptibly. Shoe stood. He put his hand on her arm.

"Sit down, Marty," he said. "Just answer the questions."

"I didn't kill Mr. Cartwright, if that's what they're thinking. And neither did Joey." She slumped into the chair.

"Do you know where Joey might go?" Lewis asked, as Shoe sat down beside Marty again.

"No," Marty said.

"Besides yourself and Mr. Schumacher, does he have any friends he might go to for help?"

"Well, there's Rachel," Marty said. "But she told me she hasn't seen him in a long time. And Janey Hallam maybe."

"Janey Hallam," Lewis said, flipping back the pages of her notebook. "She was acquainted with Mr. Cartwright, wasn't she?"

"If you mean, did she know him, sure, everyone in the neighbourhood knew him. She wasn't friends with him, though, not like me and Rachel."

"I see. Anyone else?"

"Not that I know of."

"Does he hang with any other bikers?"

"I don't know what he does when he's here. He never stays long. Usually just a couple of days."

Lewis thrust her fingers under her glasses and rubbed her eyes. She settled her glasses, then said, "Does he own a gun?"

Shoe wasn't surprised by the question, but Marty was. "A gun? No, of course not. Why would he have a gun?"

"For protection, perhaps. He lives pretty rough, doesn't he?"

"He travels around a lot, but what would he need a gun for? He works straight jobs. He's not a criminal."

"So you've never seen him with a gun?"

"No," Marty said firmly.

Lewis made a note, then said, "All right, that should do it for now. If you think of anything, give us a call. Okay?" She handed Marty a business card.

"Sure," Marty said. She didn't seem very sure, Shoe thought.

"If we have any more questions, we'll be in touch."

Timmons was the first to stand, perhaps desperate for a cigarette, Shoe thought, but he held the interview room door for Marty, Lewis, and him. Lewis escorted Marty and Shoe to the reception area, where she turned to Marty.

"I appreciate your help, Marty. And if Joey should happen to contact you, tell him the best thing for him would be to turn himself in."

"Yeah," Marty said. "Sure."

"I'd like a word with Mr. Schumacher," Lewis said. "Would you mind waiting? It won't take a minute."

"I'll be outside," Marty said to Shoe.

"She's hiding something," Lewis said, when Marty had left the building.

Shoe thought Lewis was probably right. Whatever Marty was hiding, though, it was obvious she didn't wholeheartedly believe Joey hadn't killed Marvin Cartwright, but despite her doubts, she would do the absolute minimum to help the police. But that wasn't what Lewis wanted to talk to him about.

She took off her glasses and massaged her eyes with the tips of her fingers. "Bloody contacts," she said. "I'm never going to get used to the damned things."

Shoe waited. She'd get to it sooner or later.

"About what we were talking about in the car," she began tentatively.

"Yes?"

"I spoke to Ron yesterday," she said. "I told him I'd seen you. He said to say hello. Do you ever think about getting back in touch with him?"

"I've thought about it," Shoe said.

"You should," she said. "He … wonders how things turned out for you."

"Maybe I will."

She handed him a card. "Those are his particulars, home and work."

He looked at the card, then slipped it into his shirt pocket. "Is there something else?"

She looked up at him, violet eyes steady. "I appreciate your help with Marty," she said.

"But … ?"

"You won't forget you're still a civilian, will you?"

"Certainly not," he said.

chapter twenty-three

"**I**s there something going on between you and Sergeant Lewis?" Marty asked as Shoe drove out of the 31 Division parking lot and turned south toward Finch. "You act like you know each other."

"I knew her a long time ago," Shoe replied. "When I was a cop, she was my partner's kid sister. But, no, there's nothing going on between us." Marty looked skeptical. "Where would you like me to take you?" Shoe asked.

"Home, I guess," she said.

"Where do you live?"

She told him, and gave him directions, which he didn't need. There was much about the city he'd forgotten, but much he remembered.

"Rae invited me to a barbecue at your folks' place tonight," Marty said.

"You're coming, I hope. I'm sure you and Rachel have a lot of catching up to do."

"Yeah, it'd be great," she said. "But, well, there's something else I gotta do." She fluffed her raggedly cut hair with her fingers. "It sure is hot. Does this car have air conditioning?"

"It might," Shoe said. He took his eyes off the road for a moment and looked at the dashboard controls. "Maybe you can figure it out."

She played with the controls, then said, "Guess not."

She shrugged out of her shirt. Under it, she was wearing a sleeveless T-shirt. She had a blue spiderweb tattoo on the back of her left shoulder and a band of barbed wire encircling her right upper arm. They looked like jailhouse tattoos. Had Marty, like Joey, done time? Shoe wondered.

"That other detective," she said. "The fat one? He told me they searched my place and took all of Joey's clothes and stuff. Mr. Cartwright was beaten to death with a tree branch or something, right? On television, when someone beats someone else to death like that, they have blood on them. Joey didn't have any blood on him when he got to my place. His clothes stank, so I threw them into the washer before I left for work the next morning. I'd've noticed blood."

"He might watch television, too. He could have changed before he got to your place, ditched his clothes somewhere."

"Yeah, I guess he could've done that, but when he got to my place he was so drunk he could barely get undressed by himself. Besides, he didn't *act* like he'd killed someone. We spent most of Friday afternoon together. Friday night too. I'd've known if he'd killed someone. He likes to think he's tough, but he isn't. Not that kind of tough. Not the kind of tough it takes to kill someone and not show it."

What kind of tough was that? Shoe wondered. "People can fool you sometimes, Marty."

She sighed. "Yeah, I guess."

"When Sergeant Lewis asked you if Joey had any other friends he might go to for help, you mentioned Janey Hallam."

"He used to stay with her sometimes, he told me, before she had to move into in her folks' old house. Dougie and Joey don't get along, which isn't news to you, I suppose. You seem surprised that Joey and Janey are friends. The three of you were pretty tight, weren't you, back when we were all kids?"

"Joey and I were friends, and Janey and I were friends, but Joey and Janey fought like cats and dogs from the day they met."

"Maybe they fought because they liked each other. Kids do that, you know?"

Shoe laughed. Marty looked hurt. Shoe said, "I'm not laughing at you, Marty. I'm laughing at myself for not seeing it."

"You're smarter than me," Marty said. "Sometimes smart people see things as more complicated than they really are."

"Maybe I'm not as smart as you think I am," Shoe said. "You've heard of Confucius, haven't you?"

"Chinese guy, lived a long time ago. Philosopher or something, right? Wrote a lot of sayings, anyway."

"One of Confucius's sayings goes something like, 'Common men marvel at uncommon things, while wise men marvel at the commonplace.'"

She thought about it for a moment, then chuckled. "If you're saying you think I'm smart, thanks. Now tell me why I ain't rich. Anyway, Joey told me Janey and him were friends; I didn't figure it out on my own. She was the first girl he ever had sex with, he said." A flush highlighted her cheekbones. "I guess that was after you and her broke up."

"Perhaps," Shoe said. "But I wouldn't bet on it."

Marty was silent as they continued east along Wilson

Avenue, past small, shabby strip malls crowded close on both sides of the street. All seemed to feature the same types of establishments: restaurants or coffee shops, small grocery or convenient stores, video rental stores, beauty salons, discount clothing or shoe stores, cheque-cashing services, plus the occasional bar or pool hall. How did they all stay in business? he wondered. The signs over the storefronts were in Chinese, Korean, Vietnamese, with a sprinkling of English, Italian, and Arabic. Many of the signs seemed to have been painted over more than once.

"Turn in here," Marty said, pointing left to a three-story apartment building with a restaurant, a health food store, and a bank on the ground floor. "I live over the bank," she said. He parked in front of the bank, but she made no move to get out of the car.

"Would you like me to come up?" he asked. "Just to make sure everything's all right?"

"No, I'll be okay." She paused. He waited. Finally, she said, "This may sound funny," she said. "But I want to hire you."

"Hire me?"

"You're some kind of private detective, aren't you?"

"Where did you hear that?"

"Rae told me."

"I'm not that kind of detective, Marty."

"But you used to be a cop."

"A long time ago, Marty." He paused. "What is it you want to hire me to do?"

"Help prove that Joey didn't kill Mr. Cartwright. We get along pretty good, him and me. I think he might be ready to settle down. I dunno, maybe we could have a life together." She looked at Shoe. "He's a pretty good motorcycle mechanic — he's good at a lot of things, actually — and I've got a good job too. Tim says he couldn't get along without me, and maybe that's true, but, well, even if it doesn't work out, I know the business and his isn't the only building supply company in town. Anyway, I've got a little money put away," she concluded hopefully. "I could pay you."

"Keep your money," he said.

"You'll — you'll do it?"

"I'll do what I can. But what if it turns out he did kill Cartwright?"

"I'll have to take that chance, won't I?" She leaned across the centre console. "Thank you," she said, and kissed him on the corner of the mouth. She pulled back, blushing. "Sorry."

"No problem at all," he said.

chapter twenty-four

For her fourteenth birthday, which fell on St. Valentine's Day, Shoe had bought Janey a ring. It had cost him two month's earnings from working part-time in the lumberyard at Dutton's Hardware and Building Supplies. When he gave it to her, in his parents' basement family room, she looked at first as though she were going to cry, then she laughed.

"What am I supposed to do with this?"

"You don't have to wear it all the time," he said. "Just when we're together."

"Why would I want to wear it at all?"

He wanted to tell her that he loved her — he had the naive notion that it made a difference — but he knew it would just make her angry. He desperately wanted to say something, anything, but he sat there, looking at her, his world crumbling.

"God, you're so *dumb*," she said. She stood up. "Don't call me anymore." She left.

Shoe spent a miserable week, again wondering what

he'd done wrong. On Friday, after school, he was in his room doing his homework when his mother called him to the telephone in the kitchen. "It's Janey," she said.

Shoe took the handset and looked at his mother. She smiled, hung the dishtowel through the handle of the refrigerator door, and left the room.

"Hello," Shoe said into the telephone.

"How come you haven't called me?" Janey said.

"You told me not to."

"Do you always do what you're told?" When he didn't answer, she said, "Do you still have it?"

"What?" he asked.

"The ring."

"No. I gave it to Sandy Dykstra."

"You did not." A pause: "Did you?"

"No."

"I won't wear it all the time, you know," she said. "I'll only wear it when we're together."

They started seeing each other again, and when they were together, she wore the ring. She insisted he keep it when they were apart, but she never missed asking him for it when they met.

Joey Noseworthy quit school in March, two weeks after his sixteenth birthday. Shoe and Joey hadn't spoken for almost a year, but Shoe had seen Janey talking to him outside the movie theatre in Yorkdale mall, where she refused to go with him for fear that her friends might see them together. They seemed to be arguing. A few days later, while they were walking in the Dells, Shoe asked her what she and Joey had been arguing about.

"Are you spying on me?" she demanded.

"No, I — "

She yanked the ring off her finger. "Take your stupid ring."

She threw it at him. It bounced off his chest and fell to the ground. She scuffed at the leaves and twigs and rotting branches where it had fallen and ran off. He started after her, but she had always been able to outrun him. He went back and tried to find the ring. He looked for it for almost an hour before giving up. The next day he went back again. Janey was on her hands and knees on the ground, grubbing through the decomposing leaves, and crying.

"Don't bother," he said. "I found it and took it back to the store."

"No you didn't. I watched you. Help me find it."

He got down on his knees and together they looked for it. They didn't find it.

"I'm sorry," she said.

"It doesn't matter," he said, helping her to her feet. The knees of their jeans were wet and muddy.

She took him to her cave. There were still patches of snow on the north-facing slope, where the sun didn't reach. The spring runoff hadn't been kind to Janey's cave, and Shoe thought that one of the boulders had shifted slightly, but the air mattress and sleeping bag were relatively dry.

They made love. Shoe had recently been introduced to the mysteries of the female orgasm from reading a copy of *Lady Chatterley's Lover* he'd found in Hal's bedroom.

"What are you doing?" Janey asked.

"I'm trying to make you come," Shoe said.

"Girls don't come. Only boys. Stop it."

"I thought you liked this," he said. "Maybe I'm not doing it right."

"I said, stop it!" she said angrily, and pushed him away.

"I'm sorry," he said.

"Never mind," she said. "It's okay." She reached for him.

He took her wrist, so slim it was like a child's in his

large hand. "No."

"Why not?"

He didn't know how to answer.

"How do you know girls come?" she said.

"I read about it."

"You read too much. Okay," she said, shifting around in the small space. "Let's do it to each other."

He'd read about that too; the reality was more interesting. Did Janey have an orgasm? He didn't know. She didn't say and he wasn't sure what to look for. And it was difficult to concentrate. She never stopped him again, though.

Things started looking up. He wanted to buy her another ring. She said, no, she didn't need a ring. She was his girl, she said, no matter what anyone thought, but it still had to be their secret.

Shoe obtained his driving permit in April and, with it, use of the family car — at least when his mother, father, or older brother weren't using it. Naturally, Janey wouldn't let him pick her up at her house; she didn't want her stepfather or stepbrother to know she and Shoe were seeing each other. Shoe thought it was unlikely that Dougie didn't already know, but he knew it was useless to argue with her. She wouldn't let him take her to the local drive-in restaurant, where there was too great a risk of being seen with Shoe by someone she knew, or park in the Dells at first, for the same reason, but she eventually relented on the latter.

Shoe bought gasoline at the Canadian Tire station where Joey worked. Five or six dollars, about what he earned in an afternoon at Mr. Dutton's store, would fill the tank. Joey refused to serve him, always getting someone else to do it. Unless Janey was with him. Then Joey would fill the tank, check the oil, clean the windshield, and take Shoe's money, all without a speaking a word to him. Shoe tried to engage him in conversation a few times, to no avail.

"Why do you keep buying gas there?" Janey asked him.

"I don't know," Shoe said.

Late one Sunday afternoon in July, after a drive in the countryside north of the city, Shoe dropped Janey off near her house, then drove to the gas station. As he pulled up in front of the pumps, he saw Joey in the next lane, sitting astride a rumbling Harley-Davidson motorcycle. Their eyes locked, and for that brief moment, Shoe thought Joey was going to say something to him. He didn't. He gunned the bike, dropped it into gear, and roared away. That was the last time Shoe saw him.

On a warm and wet Saturday night, a month after Joey had left, Shoe and Janey were parked in the Dells. It was about eleven o'clock, before there were gates at the park entrance. They'd been to a movie — she still wouldn't let him take her to the theatre at Yorkdale — after which they had driven to the Dells to park and make out. They were snuggled together in the front seat, occasionally talking, but mostly just content to be together. Lights washed over the rain-spotted windows as another car arrived or departed. The Dells was a popular spot. Suddenly, the dome light came on as the passenger side door burst open. A man hauled Janey out, almost literally by the scruff of her neck. Shoe surged out of the car, to be confronted by Dougie Hallam and his stepfather, Freddy. Freddy handed Janey to Dougie. He held her by the arm. She squirmed helplessly in his grasp.

"You fucking my little girl, punk," Freddy Hallam said to Shoe. He was slightly shorter than Shoe, but thick and powerful and aggressive. Shoe smelled alcohol on his breath.

"Sure they're doin' it, Pop," Dougie said. "I can smell it on them."

"Shut up," Freddy Hallam snapped. "Kid," he said

to Shoe, stabbing him in the chest with a hard stubby finger. "You're lucky there's other cars here, 'cause if we were alone I'd put some serious hurt on you for what you're doin' with my little girl. You come sniffin' around her again, I'll for sure kill you. Understand me? Your own mother won't recognize your corpse."

"I'm not afraid of you," Shoe said, with more bravado than good sense. Engines roared to life and headlights came on as cars began to head for the exit.

Freddy Hallam laughed. "You oughta be. Maybe you're tough enough to take my boy here — "

"I told you, Pop," Dougie said. "He took me by surprise."

"Shut up. He still took you." He rounded on Shoe again. "Believe me, kid, you ain't tough enough by half to take me. You wanna find out right now, go ahead. Take your best shot."

"Shoe, don't," Janey cried.

"Buck buck b-buck," Dougie Hallam crowed.

"Shut up," Freddy Hallam snapped.

He took Janey and held her by the arm as Dougie got behind the wheel of the car. With a feeling of complete helplessness, Shoe watched as Janey's stepfather threw her into the backseat of the car and slammed the door.

"Stay away from her," he said again as he got into the car and pulled the door closed.

The car fishtailed as Dougie accelerated away in a spray of gravel that spattered like hailstones against the side of Shoe's father's car. Shoe waited a few minutes, until his heart stopped pounding and his hands stopped shaking, then got into the car and drove home.

Shoe didn't see Janey for more than three weeks. She didn't return to her summer job in the stockroom at Dutton's. Hoping to at least catch a glimpse of her, he walked or drove or rode his bike by her house two or three times a day, or watched from the woods. He never once saw her. He tried leaving notes in the cave, but it seemed she'd abandoned it; a family of raccoons had moved in. On Saturday afternoon of the Labour Day weekend, he was sitting disconsolately on the old tree that had fallen across the creek, trying to compose another letter to her, when he heard someone slipping and sliding down the steep path from the top of the ridge. A moment later Janey emerged from the underbrush. She was not alone.

His name was Will. He was older than Shoe by a year or two. He rode a motorcycle and had a job driving a Pepsi-Cola delivery truck. After Will came Tony, and after him, Don, then Jimmy, Steve, Jack, and so on. None of them lasted more than a week or two, a month at most. All were older, most had full-time menial jobs, and rode motorcycles or drove souped-up cars or pickups. It took a while, but Shoe eventually gave up hope that he and Janey would ever get back together, even temporarily. They remained friends, though, of a sort, until she graduated from high school with the second highest average in the history of the school. The last time he saw her was the day she told him she'd taken the job with the airline.

chapter twenty-five

It was almost eight o'clock. Sunset was still forty minutes away, and the sky was tinted a strange shade of
pink-tinged saffron. In Hal's absence, Shoe had been con-
scripted to man the barbecue. "Girls don't grill," Rachel
had told him. "These girls, anyway." She and Maureen
sat at the picnic table, an almost empty bottle of Chilean
Merlot on the table between them. Shoe's parents sat
next to each other in lawn chairs, Shoe's father with a
bottle of beer, his mother with a glass of Rachel's single
malt whisky and plenty of water. Shoe had a bottle of
beer, which he'd barely tasted, on the end of the picnic
table next to the barbecue.

Shoe had turned the flame to low, and had started
moving the hamburger patties to the back of the grill,
when he heard the clatter of a motorcycle engine in the
driveway. The bike shut down with a rattle, and a moment later, Marty Elias came round the corner of the garage. She was wearing a slightly too big black leather

motorcycle jacket and carrying a full-face helmet. Her inky black hair was flattened to the shape of her skull.

"Hi," she said, smiling uncertainly, running the fingers of her free hand through her hair.

"Marty," Rachel said, with a smile. She got up. "I'm so glad you decided to join us. Sit. Would you like a glass of wine or a beer?"

"Um, well," Marty said. She looked at Shoe, an expression close to panic on her face.

"What's wrong, Marty?"

"Could I talk to you for a minute?"

"Of course," Shoe said.

"In private?" she added apologetically.

Shoe handed the barbecue tongs to Rachel and followed Marty to the front of the house. A road-weary, two-cylinder Triumph motorcycle stood in the drive. The bike smelled of old oil and dried gasoline and the paint was chipped and peeling from the dented fenders and fuel tank. The tires looked new and the bike was equipped with oversized saddlebags. Marty laid her helmet on the cracked leather of the saddle and unzipped the jacket. The front of her T-shirt was sweat-stained below her breasts.

"Joey called me," she said. "He wants me to meet him, bring him my bike. Do you think — I mean, could you maybe come with me?"

"I could," Shoe said. "If you're sure that's what you want to do."

Marty lifted the motorcycle helmet off the saddle, held it for a moment, as if she were going to put it in, then put it down again. "I know Sergeant Lewis told me I should call the police if I heard from him, but I — I can't do that. I was thinking, maybe you could talk him into turning himself in."

"I could try."

"He didn't do it, y'know."

"Did he tell you that?"

"Uh, no, but he got real mad when I asked him. 'What do you think?' he said. I told him I didn't think he did it. He said, 'Well, there you go.'"

Not exactly a vigorous denial, Shoe thought. "Where does he want to meet?" he asked.

"At Downsview Park," Marty said.

Downsview Park was a former Canadian Forces base east of Keele Street. Decommissioned in the early 1990s, the huge area included a film production centre, an aerospace assembly plant, a municipal airport, and a vast public park. In 2003, the Rolling Stones had performed in the park for half a million people, along with AC/DC, the Guess Who, Blue Rodeo, and a number of other bands, as part of a daylong open-air benefit concert to reassure the world that Toronto was still safe following the SARS outbreak. Pope John Paul II had performed there for even more people on World Youth Day in 2002.

"The police may have been watching you," Shoe said.

"Maybe," she said. "But I took a couple of detours getting here a car couldn't follow."

Shoe didn't think it would take much imagination on the part of the police to guess she might be coming to see him.

Marty zipped up the motorcycle jacket, donned the helmet, and threw her leg over the Triumph. "You shouldn't have any trouble following me." Her voice was muffled by the face shield of the helmet. "Just watch for the smoke."

Shoe asked her to wait a moment. He made his excuses to the others, without going into detail, then got his wallet and car keys from the house and went out to the car. Marty flipped the start lever out with her foot, stood on it, and bounced. The Triumph coughed and emitted a thin cloud of blue smoke, but with a little coaxing, started on the first kick.

He didn't have any trouble following her. The Triumph did indeed burn oil, but Marty also took it easy, staying well within the speed limits, coming to a full rest at stop signs, and respecting yellow lights. She was a cautious rider, or a considerate one, or both, and Shoe was still right behind her when they turned into the main entrance to the big park. They followed the winding access road to the large — and apparently full — parking lot, where Marty stopped and gestured for Shoe to pull alongside her. She raised the face shield of her helmet.

"He said to meet him behind the bandstand," she said.

She pointed in the direction of a tall structure on the far side of a large open area that thronged with people, half of which seemed to be children. Many people stood, swaying to the beat of Celtic dance music produced by the dozen or so musicians fiddling and jigging on the stage. Far more people sprawled on the grass or sat in folding chairs. Hawkers moved through the crowd selling soft drinks, bottled water, and snacks. The sun was a dark, burnt orange, huge and low over the western suburban skyline.

Marty found room for the Triumph in a space occupied by a big gleaming Harley-Davidson with a teardrop-shaped sidecar, and a small, hot pink Honda scooter, stowing the helmet in a saddlebag. Shoe circled the lot until he finally gave up and was forced to squeeze the Taurus into a space on the access road only slightly longer than the car itself. He and Marty then set out through the crowd and across the field toward the bandstand. They made their way to the edge of the crowd gathered close to the front of the stage, and worked their way round to the rear of the bandstand.

"That's him," Marty said. "Sitting by that big electrical cabinet."

Shoe wouldn't have recognized him if Marty hadn't pointed him out. His face was lean, deeply etched by wind and sun and time, and his thinning grey-blond hair fell straight to his shoulders. Noseworthy evidently recognized Shoe, however; as they made eye contact, his face tightened and his mouth compressed into a grim line. He stood, clutching a green canvas backpack. For a moment, Shoe thought he was going to bolt, but he waited as Shoe and Marty walked toward him. Although he was still quite a bit shorter than Shoe, he was taller than he'd been the last time Shoe had seen him — the result of a late growth spurt, perhaps — and slightly thick through the middle. He was wearing black jeans and an old, naturally distressed jean jacket.

"What's this shit?" Noseworthy said to Marty, anger making his voice shrill. "What the fuck'd you bring him for?"

"Hello, Joey," Shoe said. "It's been a long time."

Ignoring Shoe, Noseworthy grabbed Marty's arm and pulled her into the deeper shadows between the tall electrical cabinet and the underside of the bandstand.

"Goddamnit, Marty. He's a fucking *cop*."

"No, he's not, Joey," Marty said. "Shoe, tell him."

"I'm not a cop," Shoe said. "I haven't been one in a very long time."

"Once a cop, always a cop, far as I'm concerned," Noseworthy said.

"Sorry, Marty," Shoe said. "I guess this wasn't such a good idea after all. Good luck, Joey." He turned to leave.

"Wait," Marty said. "Shoe. Please. Joey, talk to him," Marty pleaded.

"We got nothing to talk about," Noseworthy said.

"How about Marvin Cartwright's murder?" Shoe said.

"What about it?"

"Did you kill him?"

"Get to the point, will you?" Noseworthy said. "I got a busy schedule."

"Did you?"

"Like I said, once a cop," Noseworthy said. He looked around. "Where are they? I don't see 'em. My allergies must be acting up. Usually I can smell 'em a mile away."

"We didn't bring the police," Marty said.

"So what're you doing here?" Noseworthy asked, looking at Shoe.

"Trying to help a friend," Shoe said.

"All things considered," Noseworthy replied, "I'd rather be poked in the eye with a stick."

"I get it," Shoe said. "You're still angry with me. But it's a long time to carry a grudge, Joey. What could I do? I wasn't going to let them get away with what they did to you."

"What the fuck do you know about what they did to me? Nothing like that ever happened to you. No one ever bullied you in the school yard, stole your lunch or the money you collected for UNICEF at Halloween. You ever wonder why I never had a bike? Because every time I had one, it got stolen or smashed and my parents couldn't afford to keep buying me a new one. Anyone ever pull down your shorts in front of the girls' gym class, piss in your gym shoes, or glue the pages of your math book together? You ever get beat up by a girl? No? Well, that kind of thing happened to me all the time."

"What can I say, Joey?" Shoe said. "I did what I thought was right. You were my best friend. I had to do something."

"Yeah, well, maybe what Dougie Hallam and that shit-for-brains brother of yours did was worse than most times, but you didn't make it any better. Okay, so it was a lose-lose situation. I'd've been pissed at you if you hadn't done anything and was pissed at you when you did. That's life, though, right? One thing I've learned, you gotta carry your own water." He shrugged and some of the anger left his face. "Who knows? Maybe what you did helped me learn it."

"Can we put it behind us, Joey?"

"I ain't that guy anymore, so I guess it's behind me. I don't know about you."

"I'll let you carry your own water," Shoe said. "But does it make sense to carry more than you have to?"

He shrugged again. "You carry what you got."

Shoe changed tack. "Have you been on the road since you left?"

"I move around a lot. My driver's licence says Canmore, Alberta, but I don't really live there. My sister's place, an address of convenience, like, so I can register the bike, that sort of thing."

"What do you do for money?"

"This and that. Taught shop in the Northwest Territories one summer and worked for the phone company in Louisiana the next winter. My folks would be proud." Joey's father had worked for Bell, Shoe recalled, as he saw a brief flash of regret beneath Joey's mask. According to Rachel, he'd missed both his parents' funerals. "I visited their graves the other day," he said, as if reading Shoe's thoughts.

"How well did you know Marvin Cartwright when we were kids?"

"I visited his house once or twice. I didn't hang out, like your sister and Marty did, if that's what you mean. His old lady gave me the creeps, the way she was always calling to him from her room in the back in that whiney voice of hers. Marvin do this and Marvin do that, Marvin bring me this and Marvin bring me that. It was pathetic. He was pathetic, how he never stood up to her. And the place stank of medicine. We either met at the school or in the park and all we ever did was play chess and talk a little."

"Did you keep in touch with him after he moved away?"

"I ran into him about fifteen years ago when I was working in Sandbanks Provincial Park in Prince Edward County. He moved to Picton after his old lady died. I think he grew up around there. I'd stop by his place every couple o' years, whenever I was in the area. He was always good for a hot and a cot. And a few bucks if I was short."

"The police found your fingerprints in his car, and when they went through the stuff you left at Marty's, they found a signed book and an engraved chess set that belonged to him."

"He gave me those things."

"When?"

"The day they say he was killed. We met in the Dells in the afternoon, in the parking lot on the other side of the old flood control dam. We sat in his car because he said the sun bothered him, played a couple of games — tried to, anyway. He couldn't concentrate, kept forgetting whose move it was. That's when he gave me the chess set and the book. And, well, some money. A lot more than usual. Later we walked up to the dam and talked for a bit more. He talked, anyway. If I was gonna kill him, I'd've done it there and buried him in all the old tires and shit that's washed up against the back side of the dam."

"The police didn't find any money at Marty's apartment."

Noseworthy patted his stomach. "I keep my money and ID in a money belt and the essentials in my rucksack. You never know when you're gonna need to move on in a hurry."

"What did you and Cartwright talk about?" Shoe asked.

"Like I said, he mostly did all the talking. He rambled on about all sorts of stuff. Rachel and Marty and the other kids he used to invite into his house. His mother, how hard he tried to be a good son to her, but how he was always a disappointment to her. The kids — Dougie Hallam, your brother, Tim Dutton — that used to play practical jokes on him. Some weird shit about making amends to someone, atoning for his sins before it was too late. I asked him what sins, but he wouldn't tell me. Most of the time he didn't make a lot of sense, like he couldn't finish his thoughts or they were all jumbled and mixed up inside his head. Every so often, he'd sort of drift off and stare into space. It was the meds, he said. He looked like shit."

"Did he tell you what was wrong with him, what the meds were for?"

"No."

"Do you remember the sexual assaults that occurred in the woods that summer?"

"Sure," Noseworthy said.

"Marvin Cartwright was a suspect."

"Yeah," he said again, dragging the word out warily.

"Do you think he was guilty?"

"Why ask me? How would I know?"

"Do you remember a cop named Ron Mackie? He would've been in uniform, about twenty-five."

"I talked to a lot of cops that summer," Noseworthy said. "I didn't ask their names. Why? What's that got to do with anything?"

"There may have been a witness to one or more of the rapes or the park worker's murder," Shoe said.

"Well, it wasn't me, if that's what you're thinking. I'd've told the cops, man. Anyway, I never went back into those damned woods." He turned to Marty. "You bring the bike?"

Before Marty could reply, Shoe said, "If you didn't kill Cartwright, why run?"

"Force of habit. I don't trust cops. Ex-cops either, for that matter. They don't care if you're guilty or innocent, they just want to make an arrest so they can go on TV and say they're winning the war on crime."

"Some are like that," Shoe said. "Most aren't. The detective in charge of Cartwright's murder, she's one of the good ones."

"Ain't no such thing as a good cop. Not in my experience."

"She's a friend of Shoe's," Marty said.

"Bully for her."

"Where were you when Cartwright was killed?" Shoe asked.

"When was that?"

"Say between eleven Thursday night and one Friday morning."

"I ain't got any idea, man. I remember bein' thrown out of a bar sometime between eleven and midnight. Next thing I know I'm wakin' up on Marty's couch. Don't remember anything in between. Hate it when that happens," he added casually.

"Does it happen often?"

"Depends on what you mean by 'often.'"

"Do you remember the name of the bar?"

"I think it was Hallam's."

"As in Dougie Hallam?"

"Yeah."

Shoe was about to ask in what sense Joey meant 'Hallam's bar,' was he the owner or just a regular, but Joey turned to Marty again and said, "Did you bring the bike or didn't you?"

"It's in the parking lot," she said. "But it isn't running so good, Joey."

"It's a good bike. You just don't take care of it like

you should."

"It needs a valve job, maybe new rings."

"But it's running?"

"Yeah, but ... "

"Gimme the keys."

"Joey ... "

"What?"

"Nothin'," she said miserably, and handed him the key to her motorcycle. She shrugged out of the leather jacket and give it to him as well.

Shoe said, "Joey, this is what I meant about carrying more weight than you have to. If you didn't kill Cartwright, all you're going to accomplish by running is convince the police that you're guilty. They'll focus their efforts on apprehending you, not finding the real killer. If you turn yourself in and proclaim your innocence, they'll be more likely to pursue other avenues."

"You got a lot more faith in them than I do," Noseworthy said. He shook his head. "I'd rather take my chances on the road. If your lady cop friend is as good as you say she is, maybe she'll 'pursue other avenues' anyway, find out who really killed Marvin, and take the heat off me."

"And if she's not ... "

He shrugged. "It's all about karma, man. Things have a way of workin' out."

"If that's the way you feel, why run?"

"I ain't too keen on the idea of sittin' in jail while they do. What if they don't?" He put Marty's motorcycle jacket on over his jean jacket and shouldered his backpack. "I gotta get going." He looked at Marty. "I'll send you some money for the bike as soon as I can. Meantime, take care of yourself, kid."

Tears spilled from her eyes. "Take me with you."

"You bring another helmet?"

"No."

"Well, there you go, then." He started around the bandstand, then paused. "If you don't mind waitin' here while I make my getaway … "

Shoe and Marty watched Joey walk away, merging with the crowd, then they followed a dozen or so metres behind. They watched him cross the parking lot to where Marty had parked her Triumph. He stood looking at the Harley-Davidson with the sidecar for a moment, shaking his head, then he settled his backpack more comfortably on his shoulders, took the helmet from the saddlebag, and threw his leg over the Triumph. Donning the helmet, he turned on the ignition and the fuel cock, and kicked the starter. It took him three tries before the bike started. He popped the throttle a couple of times. Oily smoke belched from the exhaust. He rocked the bike off the kick stand, walked it backwards out of the parking space, toed it into gear, and drove away.

"Shit," Marty said quietly.

chapter twenty-six

In the car, on the way out of the park, Marty's voice was thick as she asked, "Are you going to tell the police you talked to him?"

Shoe glanced at her. Sadness was deeply stamped on her face. Her sleeveless T-shirt was grey and sweat-dampened, and she exuded a musty, not unpleasant odour of perspiration and soap, spiced with the residual scent of leather. "I think I should, don't you?"

"I s'pose," she said miserably. "But, well, maybe you could give him some time to get away?"

"You don't really believe he's going to make it, do you, Marty?"

"No, I guess I don't, not really, but would it hurt to give him a couple of hours' head start?"

Against his better judgement, he said, "I'll wait till tomorrow morning, how's that?"

"Thanks," she said.

"Joey called the bar he was thrown out of Hallam's.

How did he mean it? Does Dougie own it? Or just drink there?"

"He owns it. Well, him and the bank. Not many people know about it. I do because Tim helped him get his liquor licence and, well, I hung out there for a while when I first came back. Till Dougie bought it."

"What about Joey's bike?" Shoe said. "If he was as drunk as you say, surely he didn't ride it to your place from the bar?"

"I've seen him ride his bike when he was too drunk to walk," she said. "He says he doesn't drink and drive because you need both hands to drive a motorcycle, so he drinks before he drives. He might've dumped it in my garage while I was at work on Thursday, before going to the bar. But ... " She lifted her shoulders slightly as she scrunched up her face.

"Where is the bar?" Shoe asked.

"Jane, north of Finch. Not far from the cop shop. It's called the Jane Street Bar and Grill. Imaginative, eh?"

For the second time that day, Shoe dropped Marty off in front of the bank on the ground floor of her apartment building. It was nine-thirty when he got back to his parents' place. Hal's Lexus was in the driveway, so he parked on the street. Steeling himself, he joined his family in the backyard. The evening was still and warm and muggy. Moths fluttered and swooped around the flickering flames of the smoky citronella mosquito torches planted at the top of the slope, many of them perishing in their mindless attraction to the light. An electric bug zapper in the yard next door hissed and popped. Rachel, Harvey Wiseman, and Maureen were playing cards at the picnic table, by the light of a portable fluorescent lantern that was attracting its share of bugs. Hal was slumped in an aluminum lawn chair that looked on the verge of collapse under his weight, three empty beer bottles on the ground beside him. He cradled a fourth in his ample lap.

Shoe's parents' lawn chairs stood at the top of the yard, unoccupied; they retired early.

Maureen stood when she saw Shoe. She glanced at her husband, who appeared to be asleep, then said to Shoe, "Is everything all right? Can I get you something to eat? We managed to save you a couple of burgers."

"Thanks," Shoe said. "One will do fine."

"What did Marty want?" Rachel asked.

"Company," Shoe said.

Hal, who wasn't asleep after all, snorted and saluted Shoe with his beer bottle. "Here's to those who boldly go where many men have gone before." He lifted the bottle to his mouth, only to find that it was empty. Dropping it onto the grass with the others, he said, "While you're up, hon."

Maureen's face was like stone as she went into the house.

"Where did you go?" Rachel asked.

"Downsview Park," Shoe said. Rachel raised her eyebrows. "To meet Joey," Shoe added. Rachel's eyebrows went up even more as her eyes widened in astonishment. "She wanted me to try to talk him into turning himself in."

"Were you successful?" Wiseman asked.

"No."

"God, he didn't kill Marvin Cartwright, did he?" Rachel said.

"I don't think so," Shoe said. "But I could be wrong. He doesn't remember anything between being thrown out of a bar around midnight and waking up on Marty's couch the following morning. He may be prone to alcoholic blackouts. Marty asked me to look into his alibi, even tried to hire me, but … "

Maureen came out of the house, carrying a plate and three bottles of beer. She passed Shoe the plate, on which there was a thick hamburger and a small pile of salad.

"The hamburger may be a little dry, I'm afraid," she said. "And there wasn't much salad left."

"It's fine," Shoe said.

She handed him a bottle of beer, then held another out toward Wiseman. "Doc?"

"No, thank you, Maureen."

"All the more for me," Hal said as he took the two remaining bottles from Maureen.

"Are you going to help her?" Rachel asked.

"I don't know," Shoe replied. He bit into the hamburger. The meat was dry and rubbery, reheated by microwaves. He washed it down with a swallow of beer.

"Where would you start?" Rachel asked.

"Did you know that Dougie Hallam owns a bar?" Shoe said.

"You're kidding," Rachel said. "No."

Shoe looked at his brother. He was studiously picking at the label of the beer bottle with his fingernails. "Hal?"

Hal looked up. "What?"

"Do you know about Dougie Hallam's bar?"

"Sure," Hal replied. "It's a dive, just the kind of place Marty would frequent."

"Goddamnit, Hal," Rachel snapped. "If you don't have anything useful to contribute, keep your fucking mouth *shut!*" She looked at Maureen. "Sorry."

"Don't be. I was thinking exactly the same thing."

"Humph," Hal grunted, raising the bottle to his mouth and drinking.

Harvey Wiseman broke the uncomfortable silence. "Don't murder investigations usually start with the victim?" he asked. "Who he was, who are his friends, what he did for a living, did he have enemies, that sort of thing?"

Hal scoffed. "You read too many detective stories, Doc."

"Knowing the victim is the first step in understanding why someone would want to kill him," Shoe said. "Also, where he was and who he spoke to in the hours immediately preceding his death. But I'm not investigating Cartwright's murder. The police are doing that. I'm just going to try to establish whether Joey has an alibi."

"And if he doesn't?" Rachel said.

"You don't have much of an alibi for the time of Cartwright's death, either," Shoe said. "That doesn't mean you killed him."

"No, of course not, but if you can't establish Joey's alibi, you'll have to find Mr. Cartwright's real killer in order to prove Joey's innocence."

"I'll leave that to the police," Shoe said.

"Sure you will," Rachel replied.

"What's your alibi, Doc?" Hal said. "We know everyone else's. What's yours?"

"Hmm," Wiseman said, looking under the picnic table, the bench, searching through his pockets. "I know I had one a minute ago. Where could it have gone? Oh, dear, I'm always misplacing things when I need them most."

"Very funny," Hal grumbled.

"If you must know," Wiseman said. "I don't really have one. I was at home all evening. And, no, I can't prove I didn't go out."

"You spend a lot of time in the woods, don't you?" Hal said. "I've seen you with binoculars, too, haven't I?"

"I enjoy walking in the woods," Wiseman said. "I find it relaxing. But not usually at night. I do not own a pair of binoculars, but I do occasionally carry a camera."

"Oh, shut up, Hal," Rachel said tiredly.

Hal shrugged. "Just trying to be helpful."

"What about Marty?" Maureen asked. "If she was

molested by Mr. Cartwright as a child, she'd have a reason to kill him, wouldn't she?"

"Both Marty and Claudia Hahn insist that Cartwright was not the man who attacked them," Shoe said. "The suspicion that Cartwright was the Black Creek Rapist was largely based on the opinion of one misguided cop."

"I remember when Marty was attacked," Rachel said. "Mr. Cartwright was quite upset about it. Angry. Maybe even a little scared."

"Of what?" Shoe asked.

Rachel's brows knit. "I'm not sure. I think Marty's father may have come to his house and threatened him."

"Marty's old man was drunk most of the time," Hal said.

"I spent as much time at her house as she did ours," Rachel said. "I never saw him drunk."

"You were just a kid," Hal countered. "How would you know? Tim Dutton's screwing her, you know."

"Oh, for god's sake, Hal," Maureen said.

"Well, he is."

"Who's Tim screwing?" Patty Dutton asked as she came around the corner of the garage into the backyard. "Or maybe I should ask, who isn't he screwing?"

"Don't pay any attention to him, Patty," Rachel said, getting up to greet her friend. Shoe and Harvey Wiseman also stood. Hal remained slumped in the lawn chair.

"Okay, I won't," Patty said. She was carrying a bakery box, which she thrust into Rachel's hands. "Cheesecake," she said.

"Yum," Rachel said. "I'll get plates and stuff." She went into the house.

"Shoe, be a sport and pour me a glass of that wine, would you, please?" Patty fell into the lawn chair Shoe had vacated. "What a day," she sighed. "And more of the same tomorrow. I don't know how I let Rae talk me into organizing this thing." Shoe handed her a glass of white wine. "Thank you, good sir," she said, favouring him with a come-hither smile that almost made him laugh, it was so theatrical.

"Patty," Rachel chided, returning from the house with plates and cutlery for the cheesecake. "Behave yourself."

"Spoilsport. Why should Tim have all the fun? How 'bout it, Shoe? How'd you like to have Tim's cake and eat it too?"

"Best offer I've had all day."

"Hey, you two," Rachel said.

Maureen giggled.

Hal heaved himself to his feet, the lawn chair falling over behind him. "Let's go," he said to Maureen, taking her arm and pulling her up from her chair.

"Hal," she said, removing her arm from his grasp. "We've both had too much to drink. We should stay here tonight." She looked at Rachel. "Assuming there's room."

"Scads of room," Rachel said.

"If you don't want to drive, we'll leave your car here," Hal said.

"Stay here tonight," Shoe said. "I'll sleep in the spare room upstairs. You and Maureen can have your old room." The basement bedroom had a queen-sized bed, while the spare upstairs bedroom had two singles.

"I don't want to stay here tonight," Hal said. He took Maureen's arm again. "C'mon."

"I don't think you should drive either," Maureen said, resisting.

"I don't care what you think," her husband said.

"Hal, you're hurting me."

He released her. "Fine, suit yourself. I'm going home."

"Hal," Shoe said, looking at the empty beer bottles beside Hal's overturned chair. "You've had at least six beers. You're in no condition to drive."

"I'm not drunk."

"I didn't say you were, but your blood alcohol is probably over the limit. It would be irresponsible of you to drive and irresponsible of us to let you."

"You self-righteous prick," Hal snarled. "You holier-than-thou bastard. You sanctimonious — "

"Okay, you've made your point," Shoe said.

"Hal," Maureen said. "What the hell is wrong with you? Stop behaving like an ass."

Hal thrust his hand into his pocket and took out his keys. "Fine. Here. Take my keys." He flung his keys at Shoe. Shoe let them sail into the dark of the lower lawn; they'd be easy to find in the morning. Hal stamped into the house, slamming the door behind him.

Maureen slumped into her chair. "I don't know what's wrong with him. He won't tell me and whenever I try to talk to him about it, he flies off the handle and tells me it's me. I'm spending too much money, I'm never home, I don't dress my age, I'm too sexually demanding, or I'm not interested in sex at all. I don't know how much longer I can take it. *Fuck*!" she added angrily.

"Honey," Patty said, putting her hand on Maureen's arm. "My advice, for what it's worth, is to just say to hell with him and find a twenty-year-old who lives to give you orgasms."

"Hear! Hear!" Harvey Wiseman said.

Rachel threw a half-eaten dinner roll at him.

chapter twenty-seven

All that remained of the cheesecake was crumbs. Patty Dutton said good night and left. Rachel looked at Maureen, who stretched and yawned and said, "I guess I'll turn in." She stood and looked down at Shoe. "Would you mind checking on Hal? To be honest, I don't think I can face him."

Shoe and Maureen said good night to Rachel and Harvey Wiseman and went into the house. Inside, Maureen said, "It's all right. I'll check on him. Rachel just wanted a chance to be alone with Doc."

"I saw the look she gave you," he said. "I think I'll check on him anyway."

Hal was nowhere to be found. He wasn't in the spare upstairs bedroom, nor was he on the sofa in the living room, or in the basement recreation room, or in the basement bedroom.

"Perhaps he took a cab home," Shoe said.

"Hal spend fifty dollars on a cab? Not likely. Damn, I'll bet he took my car." They went out the front door and checked the street. Maureen's car wasn't where she'd parked it. "I forgot he had a spare set of keys for my car. I thought he gave up his own keys a little too easily."

"I'm sure he'll be all right," Shoe said.

"He won't be after I get through with him," Maureen said grimly. Inside again, she said, "I don't know what to do, Shoe. I want to understand, to help him through whatever he's going through, but he won't let me."

"If it's financial," Shoe said, "I might be able to help."

"That's kind of you," she said. "But I don't think that's it. Hal's always been careful with money. No, I think it's me. I'm sure he thinks I'm having an affair. God knows with who." She smiled weakly. "Hell, maybe I should take Patty's advice. Things haven't been, well, very active in the sex department lately." Her smile wavered and she looked sidelong at him. "What do you think?"

"I'm not qualified to comment," he said uncomfortably. His experience with long-term relationships was essentially non-existent; he'd never had one. Since Sara died, the longest he'd been in a relationship was less than a year. He'd been with Muriel Yee almost as long as he'd been with any woman, although he'd known her for fifteen years. It was a stable and satisfying relationship, for both of them, he hoped, but where it was headed was anyone's guess. I couldn't imagine what it was like to live with someone for twenty-five years, let alone nearly sixty, as in the case of his parents.

"Maybe you could talk to him," Maureen said.

"It might only make matters worse," Shoe said. "As you may have noticed, we don't get along very well."

"When I met him," Maureen said, "it was months before I knew he even had a brother or a sister. He never talked about either of you. It was only when I asked him point-blank if he had any siblings that he said he did, but that you weren't very close. I couldn't really understand that. My family was so close it was stifling. What is it? Was he jealous of you because when you and Rae came along he was no longer the centre of attention?"

"I doubt it's that simple," Shoe said.

"No, I suppose not," Maureen said. "I've never thought of Hal as a particularly complicated person. His life always seemed to revolve around work, his power tools, and me. Not necessarily in that order. I usually came before his power tools. Now he doesn't seem to give a damn about anything, work, his power tools, or me. He's changed so much lately, become so moody and remote. It's like living with a totally different person. And not a very nice one."

"How are things at work?"

"It's hard to say. He seldom talks about work anymore, in any meaningful way, and I've been so busy with school — I'm taking business management and landscape design courses — that I haven't really been paying very much attention to him. Maybe that's all it is, he's feeling neglected. Hal isn't as self-sufficient as you or Rachel."

Shoe wasn't sure he was as self-sufficient as everyone seemed to think.

He said goodnight and went downstairs. It was just past eleven o'clock, eight in Vancouver. He thought about calling Muriel, but the bedroom did not have a telephone and he did not own a cellphone. There was only one telephone in the house, and that was the old black rotary-dial wall phone in the kitchen that must have been almost as old as the house itself. Change was not something his parents embraced. As near as Shoe could tell, with very few exceptions, everything in the house was exactly as it had been when he'd moved out thirty years ago. One of the exceptions was the television in the living room. It was relatively new, purchased, he supposed, when his parents began to find it difficult to manage the stairs to the basement recreation room, where the television had been from the day his father had bought their first one, years after everyone else on the block had one.

Being in his parents' house was like being caught in a time warp. The place was drenched in the past. Lying on his back on the bed with his hands behind his head, staring at the ceiling, the years seemed to melt away and he felt sixteen again, could almost remember what it was like to look into the future with wonder and awe and fear at what it might hold. For the life of him, though, he could not remember what he'd thought his future might have held, what he'd expected of life at sixteen, or wanted from it. Perhaps he'd learned early that the only thing one could reasonably and reliably expect from life was the unexpected.

He turned off the light and went to sleep.

chapter twenty-eight

"You okay there?" the barman asked, gesturing toward Hal's half-empty glass of beer.

"I'm fine," Hal said. The barman turned away, but not before Hal saw his scowl of displeasure. He couldn't blame the barman for being unhappy. He was still working on his first beer, but he'd gone through two bowls of nuts. "Sorry," he muttered, but the barman wasn't listening.

God, this was an awful place, Hal thought morosely. A cinder block had more character. In fact, the walls were just that, cinder block painted a dull, medium brown, a colour his father called "shit brindle." The only decorations that weren't ads for beer or liquor, or government-issue posters proclaiming the province-wide ban on smoking in public places, were a few stark, black-and-white, mass-produced photographs of early-twentieth-century city scenes, maybe Toronto, maybe New York or Chicago. The beer was watery, the barman was surly, and the waitresses were thick and coarse. But the clientele didn't come for the ambience. Or to watch sports or music videos on the big projection TV screen. They came to drink and be with other drinkers. Although he was drinking more than usual lately, Hal didn't really consider himself much of a drinker. He certainly wasn't in the same league as most of his present company.

He looked at his watch. It was past eleven. He wanted a cigarette. He drained his beer glass instead, and signalled the barman for refill. The barman drew him another draft and placed it in front of him without a word. Hal smiled his thanks, but the barman walked away without acknowledging him. *I guess he doesn't like me*, Hal mused sourly. He looked at himself in the mirror behind the bar and didn't particularly like what he saw either, an overweight middle-aged man with lank hair and bags under his eyes and sallow skin. He liked what he saw even less when Dougie Hallam walked through the front door.

He had a woman on his arm, a big, soft-bodied blonde whose billowy breasts overflowed the bodice of her short, too-tight dress. Hallam was in full good-old-boy mode, backslapping and fanny patting as he and his companion made their way toward the bar. He seemed to know everyone, and everyone seemed to know him. Not everyone appeared happy about it, though. After Hallam clapped him on the shoulder, a thin-faced man with a droopy moustache under a huge hooked beak of a nose looked at his table mate and silently mouthed, "Asshole." At another table, a man saluted Hallam's back with a raised middle finger. One of his companions grabbed his hand, and surreptitiously pointed out the video cameras positioned in all four corners of the bar. The man who'd given Hallam the finger looked sick as he got up and left, abandoning a full glass of beer. If he was smart, Hal thought, he'd never come back.

Hallam clamped a hand onto the shoulder of the

man on the stool next to Hal's. "Hey, partner, be a gent and let the lady have a seat."

"Sure, Dougie, no problem," the man said, wincing slightly.

Flexing his shoulder, he picked up his beer and relinquished his stool. The blonde eased onto the stool, her skirt riding high on heavy thighs. She smiled at Hal. It had been a while, he thought, since she'd visited a dentist.

"Syd," Hallam said, snapping his fingers at the barman. "Give the lady a beer."

"Sure thing, Dougie," he said.

"Doll," Hallam said to the woman, "Gimme a minute. I gotta have a word with my buddy here."

"Whatever you say, Dougie."

"Let's find us some privacy," he said to Hal.

Hal picked up his beer and followed Dougie to a booth in the corner by the door to the kitchen and washrooms. The booth was occupied by a man and a woman, sitting side by side on the same bench. The man was nuzzling the woman's neck and fondling her breasts. She had one hand buried in his lap, the other around her drink. Hal thought she looked bored.

"How 'bout you two get a room," Hallam said.

"How 'bout you mind — " When the man looked around and saw Hallam, he quickly changed his tune. "Oh, hey, Dougie, sure," he said, scrambling out of the booth. "C'mon, babe." He unceremoniously yanked the woman out after him. She didn't spill a drop of her drink.

"So," Hallam said, when they were seated. "You're a little out of your territory, aren't you, old son? To what do we owe the pleasure?"

"Just slumming," Hal said.

A scowl briefly darkened Hallam's face, then he smiled and said, "You looking for some action?" He leaned forward and lowered his voice. "Or are you here to take care o' business?"

"No, I ... " Hal paused as one of the waitresses placed a bottle of Molson Export in front of Hallam. *Christ*, Hal thought rhetorically, *how did I ever let myself get into this mess?* "About that," he said. "I'm going to need some more time."

Hallam picked up the bottle and half emptied it in three long swallows. He looked at Hal across the table as he took the bottle from his mouth. "You're not having second thoughts about our arrangement, are you? You know I'm always happy to help a pal out of a jam, but I'm a lot happier when I know there's something in it for me. I ain't no altruist."

Hal was surprised Hallam even knew the word, let alone the concept. But, he reminded himself, Hallam wasn't quite as stupid as he liked to have people believe.

"You make it sound so simple," Hal said.

"It ain't rocket science," Hallam said. He leaned forward. "Look, don't make it more complicated than it needs to be. Just think of it as an investment or one of your insurance policies. Business as usual."

"It may be business as usual for you, but not for me. Thing is, money is a bit tight right now."

"Not my problem," Hallam said dismissively. "I ain't running a charity. It was you who called me, remember."

"Don't worry," Hal said. "You'll get your money."

"Oh, I ain't worried about *that*. I am concerned about when, though. Like I said, I'm not into altruism. Motivated self-interest is more my style. And money is a great motivator. You want me to be motivated, Hal. It's in your best interest too."

"Don't you mean enlightened self-interest?" Hal said.

"Enlightenment don't pay the bills, old son. You're

a smart guy, Hal. Smarter than me, maybe. More edu-
cated, anyway. But look at where all that book learning
has got you. Up to your ass in alligators. You gotta learn
to relax."

"Easy for you to say," Hal said. "You're not the one
who's up to his ass in alligators, as you so colourfully
put it."

"You just gotta hang in there. Look, what you need
is to let off some steam. You probably haven't seen any
action at home in a while, especially since you got so
fat. Look at that gut, man. It's like a huge fucking bowl
of jelly. Must be a real turnoff for your old lady, all that
jiggling. My lady friend over there — " He waggled his
fingers at the blonde at the bar, who waggled back, smiling vapidly. "Her and her friends ain't as fussy as your
old lady. Suck on your dick for the price of a drink, let
you fuck 'em in the ass for a couple more. What say we
have us a little party somewhere?"

"Being with one of your whores isn't going to make
me feel any better."

"How do you know? You ever been with a whore?"

He had, after a fashion, three or four years before,
when he and Gord Peters had been in Montreal on business. It had been a humiliating experience. He'd been so
nervous and afraid that he hadn't been able to get an
erection, no matter how hard the woman had tried to
arouse him. She'd even taken him into her mouth, something he'd never had the courage to ask Maureen to do.
Although she'd spent the better part of the hour with
him, and had more than earned her fee, he'd asked for
his money back, which had been pretty stupid thing to
do. She'd laughed so hard she'd had tears in her eyes
when she left the hotel room with his $500.

Hallam beckoned to the woman at the bar. She stood
and walked to the booth, wobbling on her high heels.

"It's late," Hal said. "I should be getting home."

"Relax," Hallam said. "Have another beer. Think of it as my way of maintaining good customer relations. I'll be right back. Doll, keep my friend company for a couple of minutes." He winked broadly.

"Okay, Dougie," she said accommodatingly, as she slipped onto the bench and slid close to Hal's side.

chapter twenty-nine

When Shoe went upstairs in the morning, Rachel was sitting at the kitchen table, one leg tucked under, eating Cheerios by the handful from the box. The Sunday paper was spread out on the table in front of her. She was drinking instant coffee.

"I didn't want to take too many liberties with your supply," she told him. "Oh, and Hal's car is gone. Likewise Maureen. She must have got up at the crack of dawn and gone home."

Shoe started coffee, enough for two, and ate two pieces of whole wheat toast with peanut butter and a banana while it brewed. At a few minutes to eight the telephone rang, the familiar loud ratchety clatter he hadn't heard in years. Rachel snatched the handset off the hook before the second ring.

"Hello? Oh, hi, Moe. What's — " Her brows knit. "No, we haven't seen him." She put her hand over the mouthpiece and said to Shoe, "Hal didn't go home last night." She took her hand away, listened for a moment, then said, "All right. If you're sure. See you later." She hung up the phone. "She sounds pretty worried," she said. "And more than a little pissed."

Maureen had a right to be upset with Hal, Shoe supposed. Shoe didn't like the idea, nor did he believe it would do much good, but it looked as though he was going to have to have a talk with his older brother after all. He'd rather have his teeth cleaned.

"What's on your agenda today?" Rachel asked around another fistful of Cheerios.

"I'm going to go for a walk in the Dells," he said.

"Haven't changed much," Rachel said indifferently. "Still full o' trees. And bugs," she added. Rachel hadn't enjoyed the woods the way Shoe had. She'd preferred the sports field or the public library. "But, um, what about Joey?"

"I thought I'd pay a visit to Dougie Hallam's bar later, see if anyone remembers him."

"Better you than me," Rachel said with a grimace. "I don't want to think about the kind of place Dougie Hallam would drink at, let alone own."

After cleaning up his breakfast dishes, Shoe called Hannah Lewis's cellphone, but got her voice mail. He left a message for her to call him at his parents' number, then put on his trail shoes, slung a water bottle from his belt, and set out into the woods. The path from the bottom of his parents' yard was somewhat overgrown — it likely hadn't been used much in recent years — but it was still clearly visible. Shoe followed it to the narrow bridge of aging grey planks that crossed the drainage ditch, then alongside the low, half-collapsed fieldstone wall at the western boundary of the Braithwaite property. The large lot was so wildly overgrown that had it not been for the wall, and the unkempt cedar hedges inside it, Shoe would have been hard pressed to say where the woods ended and the Braithwaites' backyard began. At the northwest corner of the Braithwaite property, he came to the main footpath from the turnaround at the end of Wood Lane. He angled left and followed the well-beaten path deeper into the woods.

Until he'd outgrown A. A. Milne, Shoe had spent endless hours in his own "100 Aker Wood" behind his parents' house, pretending he was Christopher Robin, setting traps for heffalumps with Pooh and Eeyore and Piglet. As he'd grown older, he'd ventured farther afield, imagining he was exploring uncharted wilderness with the La Vérendryes, Lewis and Clark, or Alexander Mackenzie. By his mid-teens, he'd learned to simply enjoy the quiet and the relative solitude. He attributed his love of hiking in the rainforests and mountains of the Pacific Northwest, something he hadn't done nearly enough of recently, to the time he'd spent in the thickly wooded ridges and ravines of the Dells.

The Dells had always been popular with dog walkers, and evidently still was, some of whom were less than conscientious about scooping up after their pets. He was leaning with one hand against a tree, scraping the sole of his shoe with a twig, when a voice interrupted the quiet.

"Don't you just hate that?"

He turned to see Claudia Hahn. "I do." He tossed the smelly twig aside.

She looked very adventuresome, in a pale blue shirt, sleeves rolled above her elbows and secured with tabs, tan shorts with thigh pockets, and sturdy, well-worn hiking boots with bright red laces. She had a professional-looking digital SLR camera slung over her shoulder and waist pack fitted with two water bottles.

"I took your photograph," she said, showing him his image on the camera's screen. "I can erase it, if you like."

"I'll leave that up to you," he said.

"I'll add it to my collection on the hazards of suburban hiking." She looked at him. "What is it?"

"To be honest," he said, "I'm a little surprised to see you here. I would have thought these woods held some unpleasant memories for you."

"Unpleasant memories tend to fade with time, don't you find?" she said. "Good memories, on the other hand, such as the taste of dark chocolate or your lover's touch, often grow even stronger." She smiled. "It didn't happen overnight, of course, but learning to appreciate these woods again helped me come to terms with my rape. What about you? You must have spent a great deal of time here when you were growing up. Did the rapes and Elizabeth Kinney's murder change how you felt about them at all?"

"I suppose so," he said, recalling that Elizabeth Kinney had been the name of the park worker who'd been the fourth and, with any luck, final victim of the Black Creek Rapist. "For a long time afterward many people in the neighbourhood, particularly the women and girls, avoided the woods. Things eventually returned to normal." He looked around. "They will again."

"Was it near here that Marvin's body was found?"

"Yes. See. There's still some crime scene tape on that tree over there."

She shuddered. "Do you mind if we move along? Or would you rather I left you alone?"

"No," he said. "I'd enjoy the company."

Together, they descended through the trees into a narrow ravine, then climbed to the top of the higher wooded ridge that formed the southern boundary of the wider, deeper ravine — a small valley, really — through which Black Creek meandered, at places cutting deep into the base of the ridge. Below them, on the other side of the creek, the open meadows of the valley floor had been landscaped into parkland. The grass hadn't been mowed,

except in the picnic areas along the entrance road and
by the parking lot, and the creek bank was weedy and
the footpaths overgrown. Shoe and Claudia Hahn turned
left and proceeded along the path atop the ridge, shafts
of morning sunlight spearing through the leafy canopy
and dappling the ground ahead of them.

"Do you live nearby?" Shoe asked.

"No," Claudia Hahn replied. "I live in Riverdale,
east of the Don Valley. I bought a little row house there
when I moved back from England. I'm staying the weekend with a friend who lives near the junior high school."
She placed the emphasis on the second syllable of "weekend," in the British manner.

The ridge slowly descended and narrowed, until it
terminated on a low knoll overlooking a muddy flood
plain. A huge and gnarly old tree had once stood on the
tip of the knoll, an elm or a maple, but it had fallen, or
been cut down, and no sign of it remained. The knoll was
overgrown with young trees, saplings, brush, and wild
grasses. Visible through the new growth, a few hundred
metres farther down the ravine, the creek disappeared
into the detritus of tree branches, old automobile tires,
and at least one supermarket shopping cart washed up
against the jumbled rock of the flood control dam erect-
ed forty years earlier to protect Jane Street, another half
a kilometre west of the dam. On the far side of the busy
four-lane road lay the surreal and gently rolling lawns
of the Black Creek Golf and Country Club. Beyond
that, almost lost in the haze of pollution, the great grey
sprawl of industrial development and the wide slash of
the northbound Highway 400.

"Do you remember Joey Noseworthy?" Shoe asked.
They stood where the tree had once stood. From their
vantage point, they could see the housing developments
that crowded close on the hills to either side of the conservation area. Out of sight over the brow of the hill

to the south was Black Creek Middle School, formerly Black Creek Junior High School. "He was in your other English class."

"Smallish? Very intense? You and he were friends, as I recall. Why do you ask?"

"The police believe he may be able to help them with their inquiries into Marvin Cartwright's death."

"Does that mean what I think it means? They suspect him of killing Marvin? Oh, dear. He didn't, did he?"

"I don't think so."

"But you're not sure."

"No."

From the knoll, they descended and followed the path that ran between the creek and the high ridge, heading east again, back the way they had come. The path was overhung with maple and elm and willow. Where the creek curled up against the base of the ridge, the path became narrow, occasionally steep. Claudia Hahn was nimble and sure-footed. Her legs were strong and straight and muscular. She stopped on a slight rise and stared down at the sluggish brown stream.

"Have you ever been to the Lake District in northwest England?" she asked.

"No," he said. "I've heard it's very beautiful."

"The water in the streams there is so clear it looks like lead crystal."

"There are rivers like that in the Rockies," he said. "And glacial lakes that from above look like liquid turquoise."

"We'll just have to pretend we're in the Lake District or the Rocky Mountains then, won't we?" she said. She resumed walking.

"Is there anything else you can tell me about Marvin Cartwright?" Shoe asked.

"I don't know," she replied. "It's been so long. What would you like to know?"

"What kind of man was he? Was he a warm person?"

"No, I wouldn't say he was warm, but he wasn't cold, either. Cool, perhaps, and a little distant. I suppose you could say he was neutral."

"And yet he was passionate about chess and birds."

"So it would appear, I suppose, to the casual observer," she said. "However, chess is a very precise, logical discipline, is it not? And his interest in birds was more scientific than it was aesthetic."

"You said he wrote adventure romance novels. They're passionate, aren't they?"

"But it was make-believe, the imaginary passion of fictional people, idealized and romanticized. It was with real people and real life Marvin had difficulties."

"You said you didn't think he had many friends. What about enemies?"

"I wouldn't know. But hatred, like friendship, is an emotional response, wouldn't you say? Are people who don't have close friends likely to have enemies?"

"My sister remembers a warm, friendly man, a sort of real-life Mr. Rogers, with slippers and cardigan, not the cool, distant man you describe."

"Perhaps he felt more at ease around children. Did your friend Joey know him when you were growing up?"

"Yes. And later too. Joey dropped out in our first year of high school, bought a motorcycle, and took to the road. He's been on it ever since. He ran into Cartwright some years ago, while working in a park in Prince Edward County, near where Cartwright was living. After that, he stayed with Cartwright whenever he was in the area."

"On what grounds do the police suspect Joey of Marvin's murder?" she asked.

"They received an anonymous tip, a phone call, possibly from a witness who doesn't wish to be involved.

Also, Joey has a criminal record, and his fingerprints were found in Cartwright's car."

"Joey and Marvin were friends, you said."

"They were acquainted with each other," Shoe said. "I don't know if they were friends. Joey was also in possession of a book and a chess set that belonged to Cartwright. He told me Cartwright gave them to him."

"Is he telling the truth?"

"I think so."

"I wish there was something I could tell you that would help, but I honestly can't think of anything more."

"Does the name Ruth Braithwaite mean anything to you?"

"No. Who is she?"

"She and her two sisters are semi-recluses who live in an old house in the woods behind my parents' house. Cartwright and Ruth Braithwaite may have been friends, possibly even lovers."

"Sorry. No. I don't recall the name. I have a difficult time imagining Marvin having a lover, though. From what I remember of his novels, I don't think he had much direct experience with sex, if any at all."

They walked in silence for a few minutes, eventually coming to a part of the creek that did not match his memories. Where once the creek had flowed more or less straight for twenty or thirty feet or so, it looped around a pair of automobile-sized boulders. Shoe paused and looked up the hillside. The path the boulders had taken when they'd tumbled down into the creek was barely evident, long since overgrown. It had obviously happened some years before, perhaps even decades.

"What is it?" Claudia Hahn asked.

"These two boulders used to be thirty feet up the hillside," he said.

"Goodness," Claudia said. "I do hope no one was

on the path when they fell."

The footpath angled up the hillside, around and over the shoulder of the bigger of the two boulders. Shoe wondered if there was any evidence of Janey's little hideaway buried beneath the boulders — a rusting can of Irish stew, the remnants of an old sleeping bag.

"You told me that Mr. Gibson knew Cartwright," Shoe said as they continued along the path on the other side of the boulders.

"As well as anyone did," Claudia said, with a smile.

"Do you think he'd talk to me?"

"I'm sure he would," she said.

The dry season was at its height and the creek was reduced in places to a mere trickle of water a few handbreadths wide. The wet mud gave forth a dank, foul odour that evoked memories in Shoe of his youthful explorations. They came to a sharp bend, where once a big elm tree, roots undermined by erosion, had fallen to form a natural bridge, near which Elizabeth Kinney had been killed. The tree was gone, replaced by a pressure-treated timber footbridge, the wood greying with age. Shoe stopped at the approach to the footbridge.

"You're not lost, are you?" Claudia Hahn asked.

"When I was a boy, there was a path to the top of the ridge," he said. To their right, the steep embankment was eroded and crumbling and no sign of the path remained. "Unless you're prepared for a nasty scramble, it looks like we're either going to have to go back the way we came or cross the bridge and take the long way round. If I remember, there's a place we can cross again a little farther upstream, then a path that will take us up to the old sewage treatment plant, if it still exists. From there we can pick up a path that will take us back to the top of the ridge." That must have been the route Marvin Cartwright had taken to get from the parking lot to where he'd been killed; Shoe couldn't imagine a seventy-five-year-old man scrambling up the hillside, especially if he'd been in poor health.

"Lay on then," Claudia said.

Shoe started across the bridge, then stopped, looking over the side of the bridge along the weedy bank of the creek.

"What is it?" Claudia asked.

"Go back," he said, but too late. She stood beside him, peered over the bridge railing.

"Oh, my."

The body of a woman lay face down in the creek bed, legs in the shallow water, head and shoulders under the bridge. She was barefoot and dressed in jeans and a sleeveless T-shirt, covered in mud and weeds. Shoe continued across the bridge and sidestepped down the embankment. Claudia Hahn followed, stood over him as he squatted in the muddy water by the body. Despite the smear of mud, Shoe could make out the spiderweb tattoo on the back of her shoulder. He leaned under the bridge and rolled her onto her side. He gently scraped weeds and grasses from her face with his fingers. Her eyes were partly open and filled with black mud. Dark slime oozed from between blackened lips.

Claudia inhaled sharply and said, "Didn't I see you talking to her in the park yesterday?"

"Yes," Shoe said.

"Who is she?"

"Her name is Marty Elias." He eased Marty's body back into its original position under the bridge and stood.

"Marty Elias? That was the name of the little girl who was attacked after I was."

"Yes," Shoe said.

"Bloody hell."

He looked round. There were no signs of discarded personal effects or her shoes. He climbed the embankment and took Claudia's hand as she climbed out after him. Her hand was like ice. She had a cellphone in her waist pack and called 911, but Shoe had to explain to the operator precisely where they were.

They waited for the police by the footbridge. A woman walking a brace of tiny Yorkshire terriers came along the path from the parking area. She was indignant when Shoe intercepted her before she could cross the bridge and politely suggested that she take another route. She started to argue, but his size and the grimness of his expression changed her mind. Muttering about reporting him to the park attendants, she dragged her dogs back the way she had come.

chapter thirty

After taking her statement, the police sent Claudia Hahn to her friend's house in a scout car. Shoe was asked to wait at the scene for the detectives. Detective Sergeant Hannah Lewis and her partner arrived a few minutes later, walking from the parking lot, even though the first responders' scout cars and the Forensic Identification Services truck had driven across the grass, leaving deep ruts in the turf. Shoe and Hannah Lewis watched from a distance as the FIS officers cordoned off the site and began erecting the crime scene shelter over Marty's body. Timmons was on the footbridge, smoking and talking to a man in rumpled slacks and a sports jacket, the local coroner, who'd pronounced Marty officially dead.

Marty's death saddened Shoe deeply. It was not his fault that she was dead, he knew, but he felt responsible nonetheless. If he'd seen her to her door the night before, or if he'd insisted that she come back with him to his parents' house after meeting with Joey, perhaps she'd still be alive. If he'd called the police immediately upon returning to his parents' house and informed them of his and Marty's meeting with Joey, Lewis might have had Marty picked up, thereby also likely preventing her death. If he'd refused to go with Marty in the first place, called Lewis instead, told her where Marty was supposed to meet Joey, the police would have picked both Joey and Marty up, with the same result. If only …

"Crap," Lewis said.

"Pardon me?"

She looked tired, her eyes red-rimmed and slightly bloodshot, the flesh around them pale and dry. "I said, 'crap.'"

"I heard what you said," Shoe said. "I was just curious why you said it."

"How would you feel if someone you'd interviewed in the course of a homicide investigation turned up dead less than twenty-four hours later?"

"No worse than I'd feel finding the body of someone I'd been talking to less than twelve hours earlier, who was almost a second sister to me when I was growing up, and who I very much liked."

"Yeah," Lewis said. "Sorry."

"Are you all right, sergeant?"

"Damnit," she said. "I should've insisted on maintaining surveillance on her apartment."

"Why didn't you?"

"I agreed with my boss that there probably wasn't any point. Noseworthy wouldn't have risked going back there. He would have assumed we were watching her." She sighed. "We have to prioritize resources. Sometimes we prioritize wrong." She looked at him. "I got your message this morning. What did you want?"

"You're not going to like it," he said.

"Tell me anyway. How much worse can my day get?"

"Marty and I met with Joey Noseworthy last night in Downsview Park," Shoe said.

"Last night? Shit, and you're telling me this *now*? Goddamnit, if you'd told me last night — better yet, if you'd called before meeting Noseworthy — maybe Marty would still be alive."

"I know that."

Detective Constable Timmons, cigarette in his mouth, walked over to where Shoe and Lewis were standing.

"I could have you charged with obstructing a police investigation," Lewis said.

Timmons raised an eyebrow.

"I know that too," Shoe said.

"Jesus Christ," Lewis said. She took two or three deep breaths in an effort to calm herself. An errant breeze blew smoke from Timmons's cigarette into her face. "Put that damned thing out," she snapped.

"Sorry, boss." Timmons dragged hard on his half-smoked cigarette, then flicked it into the creek, downstream of the crime scene.

Lewis wasn't done with him. "I've had it up to here with your smoking, constable. You get the goddamned patch or I'll put in a request for a new partner and recommend you for a desk job, where you'll be inside and not able to smoke at all. Understand?"

"Look, boss, I — "

"*Understand?*"

"Yeah," he grumbled. "I understand."

"Stay here and keep an eye on things. You — " She stabbed a finger at Shoe. "Come with me."

"Boss," Timmons said, "maybe I should — "

"Do what I say without bloody arguing for a change," Lewis barked. She turned and strode up the footpath toward the parking lot. When they got to the Sebring, she yanked open the passenger side door, leaned in, and took a bottle of water off the seat. Twisting off the cap, she poured water into her cupped palm and scrubbed her face with her hand. Her colour improved. She drank, then offered the bottle to Shoe.

"Thanks," he said, taking the water bottle from his belt. "I've got my own." He pulled out the spout, squeezed water into his mouth, and hooked the bottle back onto his belt.

Lewis leaned against the side of the car, took another sip of water, and said, "All right. This had better be good."

Shoe told her about his and Marty's meeting with Joey, keeping it simple, but leaving out nothing.

"Describe her bike," Lewis said, when he'd finished.

"It's an old two-cylinder Triumph Bonneville. Dark blue. Big saddlebags. Pretty beat up. It burns oil."

"Did Noseworthy tell you the name of the bar he was thrown out of?"

"He thought it might have been a place called the Jane Street Bar and Grill. It's owned by a man named Douglas Hallam."

"I know it. It's a dive. And Noseworthy claims he doesn't remember anything between getting thrown out of the bar at midnight and waking up on Marty's couch the following morning."

"That's what he said. He may suffer from alcoholic blackouts."

"When were you going to tell me about this? You *were* going to tell me, weren't you? Never mind. Don't answer that. I'll assume that's why you called. You could've called earlier, though. Has it occurred to you that Noseworthy may have killed her?"

"Yes," Shoe said. He had accepted the possibility that Joey had changed his mind about running, or changed his mind about taking Marty with him, and had called her to meet him again, or gone to her place.

Perhaps they'd argued. Perhaps Joey's temper had got the better of him. Perhaps …

"But … " Lewis said.

"I don't believe he did." He almost added that the reason he didn't believe Joey had killed Marty was because Joey loved her, but he knew that love, in one form or another, was all too often the motive for murder.

Timmons trudged up the path to the parking lot. He was breathing hard and perspiring heavily under his jacket. Shoe could almost feel the man's need for a cigarette.

"Ident says COD looks like manual strangulation," he said. "Bruises on her neck. Too much mud on the body to tell if there's any petechial haemorrhaging or if she was sexually interfered with."

"Okay," Lewis said. She stood away from the car. She opened a back door. "Get in," she said to Shoe. "We'll take you back to your parents' place. I want to talk to your sister."

Fifteen minutes later, Lewis and Timmons waited in the living room of parents' house as Shoe went into the kitchen. Rachel was at the sink, washing dishes. Through the open window, Shoe could see his mother and father sitting in their lawn chairs, and hear his father's voice as he read the Sunday paper aloud in his usual wry style.

"The police would like a word with you," Shoe said to Rachel.

"What about?" she asked, drying her hands with a dish towel as she followed Shoe into the living room. "Christ, is it Hal? Has something happened to Hal?"

"It's Marty," Shoe said. There was no easy way to say it. "She's dead. Claudia Hahn and I found her body in the creek an hour and a half ago."

Rachel slumped onto the sofa. "Oh, god."

"When was the last time you saw her?" Lewis asked.

Rachel looked at Shoe. "She came by early yesterday evening to talk to Joe."

"Before that ... "

"When she left the park with you. Oh, god, was she raped?"

"We won't know for certain until after the post-mortem," Lewis said. "You and she spent some time together yesterday." Rachel nodded. "What did you talk about?"

"Mostly we reminisced about growing up."

"Did she seem troubled, worried about anything, or anyone?"

"No. There was some problem with work, but otherwise she seemed fine."

Lewis nodded and scribbled in her notebook. "What sort of problem?"

"She didn't say, but I think it had something to do with how her boss, Tim Dutton, runs the business."

"He owns a hardware and building supply company, is that right?"

"His father started it more than forty years ago. Tim runs it now, but the family still owns it. I don't think they're doing very well. There's a lot of competition from the big chains nowadays. Marty's father was a general contractor, so she knows — knew the business, in some ways probably better than Tim. Tim isn't the kind who takes advice very well, though. Especially from a woman. Um ... " Rachel hesitated.

"What?"

"I think she was having an affair with him, too."

"Dutton?" Rachel nodded. Lewis thanked her for her help, then she and Timmons left.

"I've got to get over to the park," Rachel said. She collected her file box and computer from the dining room table. "You know where I'll be if you need me. Despite what Hal thinks, Mum and Dad will be okay on their own if you have better things to do than hang around here." She stood in the doorway, holding her boxes. "Jesus Christ, Joe," she said, eyes glistening with tears. "Poor Marty."

"Will you be all right?"

"Yeah, I'll be okay," she said. She was lost in thought for a moment, then focused and said, "What are the chances there's a connection between Marvin Cartwright's murder and Marty's?"

"Too good," Shoe replied.

chapter thirty-one

When Hal regained consciousness — you couldn't call it waking up; it was much too painful — he had no idea where he was. He barely knew *who* he was. His head was splitting, an almost unbearable stabbing pain behind his eyeballs and down the back of his neck. When he tried to sit up, he broke into a cold sweat and nausea clawed at his guts. He fell back with a moan, then stiffened as pain lanced through his head. Was he having a stroke? he wondered. If he was, he wished it would kill him and get it the hell over with.

He lay as still as possible, breathing shallowly through his mouth, trying to control the nausea and the pain. When both had subsided a little, he dared slowly crack open his eyes and look around. He was in a motel or a hotel, but where it was located was anyone's guess. He closed his eyes again.

Thirst finally drove him to get out of bed and stagger half blind with pain into the bathroom where, unable to find a glass or a cup, he drank handful after handful of tepid, bitter-tasting water from the faucet. He'd have traded his soul for a bottle of Tylenol.

He raised his head and stared at himself in the mirror over the sink. He looked even worse than he felt, as if he'd been dead for a week and only recently dug up. His skin was pasty and oily and his eyes were bloodshot, red-rimmed and crusted. There was what looked — and smelled — like dried vomit in his hair. He was wearing only his underwear. He didn't know where his clothes were.

Gritting his teeth, he removed his underwear and wristwatch and started the water in the bath. There was no shower curtain, just hooks. "Screw it," he muttered, and pulled the knob that diverted the water to the shower head. The spray was weak and uneven, and the temperature kept changing, but he stood under it for a long time before unwrapping the tiny bar of soap and washing himself from head to toe. He dried himself with a towel that was coarse and smelled of bleach.

Christ, where was he anyway? More to the point, how had he got here, wherever the hell here was?

He trudged into the bed-sitting room. His clothes were in a heap on the floor beside the rumpled bed. His wallet was in his pants' pocket and he seemed to have all his credit and debit cards. There was no cash, even though he remembered withdrawing $200 from an ATM after leaving the office on Saturday. He went to the window and parted the curtain to squint out on an unfamiliar commercial street a storey below, awash in brilliant sunshine. He looked at his watch. It was 12:35. Sunday? God, he hoped so.

He sat on the edge of the bed to dress. Each movement brought a fresh wave of nausea. Between struggling into his shirt, damp and smelling of beer and vomit, and pulling on his equally soiled trousers, he tried to recall how he'd come to be there. He didn't remember arriving or checking in. In fact, he didn't remember much of anything after leaving his parents' house in a huff because everyone thought he'd had too much to drink — he hadn't then, but he'd obviously had more later — and meeting Dougie Hallam at his bar. He supposed he was suffering from some form of retrograde amnesia from drink.

Dressed, he sat on the side of the bed, breathing hard and fighting off the nausea, concentrating on the carpet beneath his feet. When it passed, he went into the bathroom and drank some more water. He urinated, left arm braced against the wall over the toilet. His bowels churned and he knew he was in for a bout of diarrhea, which was his usual punishment for drinking too much.

Returning to the main room, he sat down again on the edge of the bed to catch his breath. He noted for the first time that there were a dozen or more empty beer bottles scattered about, as well as an empty Canadian Club bottle on the coffee table. There were also a dozen butts of his brand of cigarettes in the ashtray beside the bed. Some of them were ringed with dark red lipstick. Then he saw the empty blue foil condom packet on the floor under the edge of the bed. There were two more on the floor by the easy chair.

"Oh, god," he moaned aloud, as he remembered the blonde woman squatting over the great spill of his gut, heavy breasts bouncing and breathing hard as she pumped up and down on thick thighs, muttering, "Come on, you fat bastard, come on." He barely made it to the bathroom before he threw up into the toilet.

Other disjointed fragments of memory surfaced as he hunched over the sink, rinsing and spitting: making another withdrawal from an ATM while Dougie and the blonde waited in Maureen's car; Dougie slumped in the easy chair in the motel room, trousers around his ankles, the blonde crouched between his knees, his big hands clamped on either side of her head; and another woman, this one with dark hair and a garish tattoo at the base of her spine, performing oral sex on the blonde while Dougie Hallam knelt over them on the bed, masturbating.

Hal's stomach heaved and he retched into the sink. Acid burned in his throat with each painful spasm. Slumping to the floor, he curled into a ball, arms wrapped around his head, moaning. He squeezed his eyes closed until red sparks flashed, but he could not eradicate the image of Dougie Hallam, Canadian Club bottle in one hand, erect penis in the other.

He curled tighter, moaning aloud again as he remembered Dougie Hallam slapping him, cursing him, while he whimpered and moaned on the bed. "Come on, you fat fuck. Get your ass in gear. Shit! Well, you're on your own, lard boy." And his relief when Dougie finally left him alone.

More memories of the night, of Dougie and his two whores, circled through his mind, spinning, then slowing, then dimming as he slipped into unconsciousness ...

Some unknown time later, he awakened on the bathroom floor, head throbbing, mouth foul, body aching. Dragging himself to his feet, he slurped water from cupped hands, then staggered into the other room. He let himself out of the motel room and walked unsteadily along the connecting balcony to the stairs down to the parking lot. Maureen's car was on the other side of the lot, baking under the hot August sun, parked between a rusty pickup and a mud-encrusted four-by-four with oversized tires. He unlocked the car and squeezed in, collapsing onto the driver's seat with a sigh of relief.

He sat for a moment, catching his breath, before shakily inserting the key and trying to start the engine. Nothing happened when he turned the key. He remembered that Maureen's car was equipped with a safety interlock that prevented the engine from starting unless the brake pedal was depressed. When he put his foot on the brake pedal, he found that the seat was too far back. He located the control, and moved the seat forward. Had someone else been driving the car because he'd been too drunk?

He started the car and reached for the air conditioner controls, but Maureen's car did not have air conditioning. He rolled down both the driver and passenger side windows. He wondered if he should check out. He didn't have a key to the room, though. To hell with it. It was the kind of place where one paid in advance.

Next to the motel there was a small strip mall with a pharmacy. He turned off the engine and, without locking the car or winding up the windows, walked to the pharmacy, where he used his bank card to buy Extra Strength Tylenol and a litre bottle of water. He also got $20 in cash, the most the cashier would allow. Returning to the car, he took four Tylenol and drank half the water. He then started the engine, put the car in gear, and wondered where to go.

chapter thirty-two

Shoe cruised slowly south along Weston Road, looking for place to park. He was in what should have been familiar territory — when he and Joey Noseworthy had been in their early teens, they'd gone to the Biltmore movie theatre almost every Saturday for the afternoon matinee — but he didn't recognize a thing. The Biltmore was long gone, of course, had been for some time even when Shoe had walked a beat in this area for the final months of his short career as a police officer. Everything else about the area was different too: more plastic and steel and glass, less brick and stone and wood; bars and licensed restaurants in a district that had once been one of the last so-called "dry" areas of the city.

Shoe parked on a side street, in the shade of a row of mature trees overlooking the deep green gash of the Humber River ravine, into which Black Creek merged a few kilometres farther south. He locked the car, and walked back two blocks to his destination. The lettering on the storefront window read "RM Printing &

Reproduction, Ronald S. Mackie, Prop.," and promised
business cards in an hour, passport photos while you
waited, and instant digital photo printing. "We're Open
Sundays" proclaimed a sign hanging above the push-bar
of the door. A buzzer rasped as Shoe pulled open the
door and went inside.

A counter divided the shop into a small waiting area
at the front and a larger production area in the back. The
waiting area contained a row of half a dozen contoured
fibreglass chairs under the window facing the street, a
magazine-strewn coffee table, a water cooler, and a small
work table. Above the work table hung a cork board
crowded with business cards, event flyers, and notices
advertising items for sale — from cars to computers
to office furniture — garage sales, and babysitting and
house-painting services. Shoe went to the counter. There
was no one in the production area. A Ricoh copy machine, about the size of a small chest freezer, worked
unattended, chugging away, *cat-a-chunk*, *cat-a-chunk*,
cat-a-chunk, spitting page after page after page into the
sorter. Three other machines, ranging widely in size and
age, from a small, state-of-the-art Canon desktop machine to a huge Xerox 9500 that hadn't been state of the
art for twenty years or more, sat idle. The red eye of a
security camera glared from high in the far corner of the
room.

A push button on the wall at the end of the counter was labelled "Press for Service." Shoe was about to
press the button when a door at the rear of the production area opened and a man stood in the doorway. He
hesitated when he saw Shoe at the counter. Beyond him
Shoe could see a ten-inch web printing press and other
machinery. The man stepped into the room and the door
hissed closed behind him. He was in his early sixties, six
inches shorter than Shoe and soft around the middle. He
had a round, open face and an unruly fringe of greying

brown hair surrounding a shiny pink dome. He wadded up the paper towelling with which he'd been wiping his hands and dropped it into a waste basket beside a cluttered desk. He stepped up to the counter.

"My sister told me you were in town," he said, putting his strong, pale hands flat on the counter top. He was wearing an ink-stained grey work coat. A slight chemical odour emanated from him.

"How are you, Mack?" Shoe said.

"Not bad, all things considered." He raised his hands from the counter top, then, as if unsure what to do with them, put them down again. "No one's called me Mack since I left the job. What's in a name, eh?"

"Have you got a few minutes?"

The copy machine stopped with a final *cat-a-chunk*, followed by a grating whine as the sorter retracted. Ron Mackie lifted his hands from the counter and dropped them to his sides. "Gimme a couple of minutes to finish up this job, then we can go get a coffee."

Ten minutes later, Shoe and Mackie were sitting under an umbrella on the sidewalk terrace of a coffee and sandwich place across Weston Road from Mackie's print shop. Mackie was drinking a frothy iced coffee concoction from a tall glass. Shoe had regular coffee.

"I was surprised when Hannah told me you weren't still a cop," Mackie said. "Not sure why I was surprised, now that I think about it. You miss it at all?"

"No," Shoe said. He didn't want to ask Mackie if he missed being a cop, since he was responsible for ending Mackie's career.

"I did," Mackie said. "For a while. I got over it. I still keep in touch with some of my old pals, though. Like street gangs, the cops isn't a club that's easy to quit." He sipped his iced coffee, wiped his mouth with a wadded-up serviette. He seemed nervous, Shoe thought. What did he have to be nervous about?

"Things turned out okay for me, though," Mackie went on. "Between the disability and some good invest-ments, I'm doing okay. More'n okay, actually. I don't really need to keep working, but the shop pays for it-self and the wife says it keeps me out from underfoot. Some days, though, I think seriously about packing it in. Hannah tell you about this crazy woman who's been giving me grief?"

"No," Shoe said. He didn't remember Mackie being so talkative. They'd been well-paired; on patrol, hours had gone by without the exchange of but a few words. Except toward the end, when Mackie had learned that Sara was seeing someone else, probably some "suit," he'd said, and had started talking obsessively about find-ing out who.

"The wife of a city councillor who's also on the po-lice services board," Mackie continued. "The councillor, not the wife. Claims I hit on her, then said I purposely put the wrong date on invitations for a charity thing she was organizing when she blew me off. Maybe I should retire, take up fishing or curling or whatever. Wanna buy a print shop? Nice little business, except for the occa-sional wacko customer." His hand shook slightly as he raised the glass of coffee to his mouth and drank.

Why is he so nervous? Shoe wondered. With a start, he realized that Mackie was afraid that Shoe had come to settle old scores.

"Ron," he said. "Relax."

"Yeah," Mackie said. Exhaling, he bent his spine and eased against the chair-back. "I am kind of running off at the mouth, aren't I?" He leaned forward again, but his hands and his voice were steady. "Look, let's get this out of the way. I know I was an asshole, all right."

"No, you weren't," Shoe said.

"Yeah, I was. I knew Sara and me were never gonna get back together, but I was too much of an asshole to let it go. What happened between me and her was my fault, not hers. Or yours. I don't blame you for what happened between you and me either. I'm sorry, okay. For, well, for a lot of things."

"Likewise," Shoe said. "I'm glad things turned out for you."

"Thanks. How about you? Things turn out okay for you?"

"Yes, I'd say they did."

"Hannah told me you're some kind of corporate investigator. Like I said, was a little surprised you didn't stay a real cop. I always thought you could've been a good one, if you'd tried. Ever thought about hanging up a shingle as a PI or security consultant?"

"Not seriously." After a moment of silence, Shoe said, "I'd like to talk to you about an old case you worked, the Black Creek Rapist."

"Yeah, Hannah asked me about it. Wasn't much I could tell her. It was a long time ago."

"Did Hannah tell you about Marvin Cartwright's murder?"

"Yeah, she did. Son of a bitch finally got what he deserved, didn't he? Couldn't've happened in a better place, too."

"Did you know there was another murder in the Dells last night?"

"No. Christ, this city's turning to shit. Besides being in the Dells, is it connected with Cartwright's murder in any other way?"

"The victim was a woman named Marty Elias."

"Elias? She was one of Cartwright's victims, wasn't she? The kid, right?"

"Yes. Claudia Hahn and I found her body this morning."

"Claudia Hahn?" Mackie's brow lowered in thought for a moment, then he said, "She was Cartwright's second victim. The schoolteacher. Like my old rabbi used to tell me, everything's connected some way or another. You just gotta find how."

"You still think Marvin Cartwright was the Black Creek Rapist then?"

"When I think about it at all. Any reason I shouldn't?"

"Claudia Hahn is certain it wasn't Cartwright who raped her."

"She was what, twenty-two, twenty-three back then? Pretty shook up, as I recall. And she knew him from the school where she taught, didn't she? I remember thinking, people don't like the idea that people they know would do that kind of thing." Mackie lifted his glass of coffee and drank.

"Most rapists have a victim preference, don't they?" Shoe said.

"So the experts claim. Your point being?"

"The age of the victims in this case ranged from eleven — Marty Elias — to mid-twenties — Claudia Hahn. Daphne McKinnon was fourteen and Elizabeth Kinney was nineteen or twenty. How alike were they physically? Marty Elias was prepubescent and Claudia Hahn was a grown woman, tall and slim. What about the other victims? I remember Daphne McKinnon as being plump and blond. What about Elizabeth Kinney?"

"The parks department worker?" Mackie said. "She was black as the ace of spades. Look, I know where you're going, and if this was a television cop show, I might agree with you. But you know as well as I do — or maybe you don't; you weren't a cop as long as I was — that you gotta be careful about making too many assumptions about things. Yeah, some of the investigators thought that the lack of physical similarity between victims meant there was more than one perp. Me, I figured Cartwright was either just getting started and hadn't established his preferences yet, or he was an opportunist, jumped anything that happened by."

"None of the other investigators seemed to think Cartwright was guilty."

"Yeah, well … "

"According to Hank Trumbull, you almost lost your job over it."

"So I was a little overzealous in my pursuit of justice. I was young and green and stupid, and it was my first big case. But I wasn't wrong. I just went about it the wrong way." His tipped up his glass to drink, but it was empty. He put it down. "What do you want me to tell you? That it wasn't Cartwright? He was innocent as fresh fallen snow? Fine. Someone else attacked the teacher and those girls. Someone else raped and murdered the black girl. Happy?"

"Hank Trumbull is worried that your connection to Cartwright might compromise Hannah's investigation."

"Is that right?"

"Or that you may have even had something to do with his murder."

"Trumbull's an old pal of yours, isn't he? Hope you won't be too upset then when I tell you he's an asshole."

"It would help Hannah's investigation if you had an alibi for the night of Cartwright's murder," Shoe said.

"You're starting to make me regret talking to you," Mackie growled. Then he shrugged. "Hannah's already asked me if I had an alibi for that night. Not that it's any of your business, but as a matter of fact, I don't. Not much of one, anyway. I was working in the shop till around midnight or a little after, then got home about one, maybe a little before. My wife's visiting her sister — I think she half believes I got it on with the councillor's crazy wife — so there's no one to vouch for the time I got home. But in the real world alibis aren't worth shit unless they're absolutely airtight. Nothing lawyers like better than creating reasonable doubt around someone's alibi."

"Cartwright wasn't the only suspect in the case. Why were you so certain he was the Black Creek Rapist?"

"Jesus, it was thirty-five years ago. Let's see. He spent a lot of time in those woods. He didn't have a credible alibi for the time of the attacks." He smiled thinly. "And, yeah, I remember, now — there was a complaint."

"A complaint? From whom?"

"The father of some girl in the neighbourhood. I forget the name, but they lived in an older house at the end of a little dead-end road that stuck into the woods behind your parents' place."

"Braithwaite."

"If you say so. I don't remember. All I remember is that the girl's father didn't want Cartwright hanging around his daughter, but there wasn't anything we could do about it because he wouldn't let us interview her. In any case, she was over twenty-one. He was some kind of preacher."

"Pretty circumstantial," Shoe said.

"When circumstantial is all you've got, circumstantial is all you've got."

"Hank said there may have been a witness to one of the rapes or the homicide, and that you were accused of suborning a false statement. Was there a witness?"

"There were three," Mackie said.

"The surviving victims, you mean? None of them was able to identify her attacker."

"That doesn't mean they didn't know him. It only means they wouldn't identify him."

"Or couldn't."

"Yeah, well, maybe, but I was sure the kid knew who'd attacked her. She was a lousy liar. I tried to get her to open up, but her parents complained to the lead investigator that I was trying to get her to say it was

Cartwright who'd attacked her even though she kept saying it wasn't."

"Do you remember an assault that occurred in the Dells a month or so before the first rape?" Shoe asked. "The victim was a fifteen-year-old boy."

Mackie's eyes narrowed. "Not sure. Sounds sort of familiar."

"His name was Joey Noseworthy."

"Noseworthy. Noseworthy. He was interviewed for the rape case, too, wasn't he? Small for his age, with a big mouth? Queer, though, right?"

"Smallish and sharp-tongued," Shoe agreed. "But he wasn't homosexual."

"If you say so. What about him?"

"Hannah has him down as prime suspect for Cartwright's murder."

"Is that right?" Mackie said. "Maybe it's a case of what goes around comes around then. Maybe it was Cartwright that attacked him. Was he raped? Always figured Cartwright for a shirt-lifter."

"It wasn't Cartwright who attacked Noseworthy," Shoe said.

"No? Who was it then?"

"My brother and a couple of his friends: Dougie Hallam and a boy named Ricky Marshall. They were the neighbourhood bullies. Hallam was, anyway. My brother and Ricky Marshall just went along for the ride."

"How do you know it was them? Seems to me I remember the Noseworthy kid couldn't or wouldn't say who beat him up."

"My brother admitted it. So did Ricky Marshall. I didn't give Dougie Hallam a chance. Joey Noseworthy was my best friend."

"Your brother," Mackie said slowly. "Hal, right?" He was lost in thought for a moment, then said, "I remember him. He had a smart mouth too, but he was kind of fat and whiney. I could see him beating up a smaller kid, but I never figured him for having the balls to rape a grown woman, if you'll pardon the expression. Christ, you don't think your brother was the Black Creek Rapist, do you?"

"No," Shoe said.

"I don't remember the Marshall kid, but I remember Hallam. He was a punk. Thought he was tough, but I remember something about him getting the crap beat out of him around the time the rapes started. That was you? Payback for Noseworthy?"

"Yes," Shoe said.

"Hallam or his old man would've been my second choice for the rapes, except they were both out of town when the first two attacks occurred. The old man — Eddy? Freddy? — he was a real piece of work. He had a couple of convictions for assault and battery, and both him and his old lady had a dozen arrests between them for robbery and receiving stolen goods, but skated on them all, as I recall. Insufficient evidence, witnesses losing their memories, changing their stories, that sort of thing. The son wasn't much better. There was a daughter, too, wasn't there? I don't remember much about her, but if she was anything like her old lady ... " He left the thought unfinished. "Hallam and his old lady, weren't they killed around the time you joined up?"

"A little before. Their bodies were found in the trunk of their burnt-out car, wrists wired together and .22 bullets in their heads."

"Shows what can happen when you keep bad company. No great loss to the gene pool."

"There must have been other suspects in the rape/homicide case," Shoe said.

"Sure. Just about every male in the area over the age of twelve. But none of them panned out." He examined his stubby, powerful hands for a moment. "All right, so maybe Cartwright didn't do the Noseworthy kid, but he was guilty as hell for the sexual assaults — and for the homicide, although I was off the case by then. Just talking to him I knew it was him. You could see it in his eyes. You know the look. They all have it, the guilty ones. They can't hide it. It's like a stigma on their souls. Of course, we may never know for sure now, eh?"

"Perhaps not," Shoe agreed.

"Why are you so interested, anyway? You figure Hannah's looking at the wrong guy, is that it? Her and me, we haven't had a lot to say to each other, but the word I hear is, she's a good cop. Better'n most."

"Hank Trumbull thinks so too."

"I never had much use for what Trumbull thought, but he's right about that. Maybe Hannah hasn't closed all her cases, but every one she has closed was rock solid. Crown prosecutors love catching her cases. Most of them get pleaded out and hardly ever go to trial. Saves us beleaguered taxpayers a bundle. I hear she's tough on partners, though. She's on her second this year."

Mackie regarded Shoe for a few seconds through half-closed eyes. The expression made him look as though he were falling asleep, but Shoe remembered that it was a sign Mackie was thinking, trying to make up his mind about something.

"How's the saying go?" Mackie said at last. "If you hear hoofbeats, think horses, not zebras? For someone who says he isn't interested in PI work, you sure sound an awful lot like a PI. You're working for someone, is that it? Noseworthy?" When Shoe didn't answer, he went on: "It's a good bet whoever killed Cartwright also killed the Elias girl. Two murders in a matter of days in more or less the same location, and a history between the victims. This city gets maybe sixty murders a year, give or take. Subtract the gang-related killings and the domestics, the number drops significantly. You'd have to be a complete idiot to rule out a connection. And my sister's no idiot."

"No, she isn't," Shoe said.

Mackie looked at his watch and stood. "I gotta get back." He offered his hand.

Shoe stood and took it. "I don't remember you from the Black Creek Rapist case."

"No?" Mackie said, releasing Shoe's hand. "I remember you."

"When we were partners, why didn't you ever tell me you'd worked the case?"

"I was supposed to be training you to be a good cop," Mackie replied. "Not a fuck-up."

"Thanks for talking to me," Shoe said.

"Yeah," Mackie said. "See you around." He turned away and strode across the busy street as if traffic did not exist.

chapter thirty-three

"Rae?" Patty Dutton said.

"Uh?" Rachel said. Patty had been speaking, but Rachel couldn't for the life of her remember what she'd been saying. "Sorry. I guess I'm not really with it," she said with a wan smile.

"If you want to take off," Patty said. "I can handle things. It's not like there's a whole lot happening." They were sitting in lawn chairs outside the kitchen shelter, in the shade of the door fly.

"I'm all right," Rachel said. "A little stunned. I can't help thinking about Marty. Why would anyone want to kill her?"

"Not that I wished her ill," Patty said, "but she was having an affair with my husband. I know she was your friend, but it's hard to get too worked up about the death of the woman who was sleeping with your husband."

"The police are going to want to talk to him, you know," Rachel said.

"Well, he's made his own bed, hasn't he?"

"Was he there when you went home after leaving my parents' place last night?"

"Rae," Patty said incredulously. "You're not seriously suggesting Tim killed her, are you?"

The flesh of Rachel's face prickled with the heat of her embarrassment. Naturally, she had considered it, but how seriously, she wasn't sure. "God, no," she said, with as much sincerity as she could muster.

"As a matter of fact," Patty said, "he did go out after I got home. The security company called. The alarm at the store went off and Tim had to go down and check it out. He's been having a lot of trouble with it lately. The slightest thing seems to set it off."

Convenient, Rachel thought, and chided herself for her suspicious nature. "What time did he get home?" she asked nevertheless.

"I don't know," Patty replied. "I took a pill and went out like a light."

"How long have you known about Tim and Marty?" Rachel asked.

"A while," Patty said. "What I don't know is what Tim saw in her. She wasn't particularly attractive, was she? I mean, men weren't attracted to her because she was pretty, were they? It was because she would, well, do things."

"For heaven's sake, Patty. Do things? Such as?"

"You know what I mean," Patty said, cheeks reddening.

Rachel was shocked by Patty's uncharacteristic priggishness. She was so vivacious, flirty, and sexy, it was hard to believe she was a prude. Then, although she realized she was stereotyping, she remembered that Patty's father was a retired minister and her mother a librarian.

"You think I'm a prude, don't you?" Patty said. "All right, fine. If not wanting a man to come in my mouth or screw me in the ass is being a prude, then I'm a prude."

"Not wanting to do those things doesn't make you a prude, Patty, but disapproving of other women because they do, that's prudish. I didn't like anal sex the one time I tried it, and won't do it again. As for a man ejaculating in my mouth, I'm not crazy about it either, but, well, there are times when it just seems like the right thing to do."

"Okay," Patty admitted with a sheepish grin. "I guess you're right about that, but I haven't felt that way with Tim for a long time. You know, a couple of months ago he asked me if I'd be interested in, um, a three-way with another woman. I told him no bloody way."

"Did he have another woman in mind?" Patty didn't answer. "Was it Marty?"

"Guess again." She raised her eyebrows meaningfully.

"Me?" Rachel laughed and almost choked. "You're joking."

"What's the matter? I'm not your type?"

"Huh. No. I didn't mean … "

"It's all right, Rae. I'm just kidding." She hesitated, then said, "Did you and Tim ever — well, you know?"

"No way," Rachel said. "Tim's a … " She shut her mouth.

"Tim's a what?" Patty asked. "You were going to say pig, weren't you?"

"I've never told you this," Rachel said. "Because we're friends. But Tim must've made a dozen passes at me in the last couple of years or so. They were all pretty clumsy and crude and when I told him to drop dead, he'd pretend he was just joking around. He wasn't, though. He was serious. I finally told him that if he didn't cut it out, I'd tell you."

Patty laughed, but it was a thin, self-conscious sound. "Tim's congenitally incapable of being within ten feet of a woman without making a pass at her."

"Patty," Rachel said sternly. "That's what the shrinks call 'enabling.' Don't make excuses for his philandering. It's okay to be pissed at him because he fools around. In fact, it's more than okay; you *should* be pissed at him."

"Of course I'm pissed at him, but what can I do? He's a guy. Guys have a problem with sex. They need it more than we do."

"With all due respect, Patty, that's bullshit, and you know it. Tim's a selfish, insensitive prick, if you'll pardon the redundancy. You don't know what Tim saw in Marty. Well, I don't know what you see in him."

"Sometimes I ask myself the same thing."

"Why *did* you marry him?"

"It seemed like the thing to do at the time?" Patty said, with a self-deprecating smile.

"Right," Rachel said, laughing. "Been there. Done that. Twice. Use the T-shirt to wash my car."

"Tim's no better or worse than a lot of men I've known," Patty said. "Worse than some, better than others. How'd you like to be married to Dougie Hallam?"

"Ugh. I'd rather be celibate the rest of my life."

"Then there are guys like your brother."

"Hal? I'd rather be celibate the rest of my life."

"I meant Joe. Shoe."

"Yeah, I know who you meant."

"How come he's not married?"

"Just lucky, I guess."

chapter thirty-four

After leaving the motel and getting his bearings, Hal found a Wal-Mart, where he bought a pair of slacks, a polo shirt, socks, and underwear, plus a cheap overnight bag. He changed in a public washroom, placing his soiled clothes into the shopping bag, knotting it, and stuffing it all into the overnight bag. By the time he walked across the huge parking lot to Maureen's car, his new shirt was soaked and sour with sweat. He wasn't any drier or sweeter smelling when, twenty minutes later, he parked in front of Gord Peters's Spanish-style ranch house in Mississauga.

"Hey, Hal," Peters said when his wife, Clara, showed Hal into the backyard. The yard was surrounded by a six-foot fence and tall hedges, affording almost complete privacy. Peters was lounging in a beach chair by the small, kidney-shaped, in-ground pool, beer bottle propped on his small, hairy belly — he looked like a man who'd swallowed a soccer ball. He was wearing a black

Speedo bathing suit that barely contained his bulging genitals, his feet dangling in the water. Gord and Clara, like Hal and Maureen, didn't have children, but their ancient standard-bred poodle, Puddles, liked to cool off in the pool. At the moment, though, Puddles was lying in the shade of a parched-looking evergreen shrub, panting as though he were breathing his last. "Jesus," Peters said. "You look like death. Clara, get the man a beer."

"No, thank you," Hal said, stomach lurching.

"Get me another, then, will you, pet? That's a dear." He absently scratched at his privates with stubby, hairy fingers.

Clara Peters smiled thinly as she turned toward the house. Hal watched her walk away. She was a quietly pretty woman, a bit serious, perhaps, the vice-principal of an elementary school. About forty, she had an absolutely stunning figure, Hal knew, from having seen her in a bathing suit at company picnics. Most times you wouldn't know it to look at her, though; she tended to wear baggy, shapeless clothing. Peters constantly complained that she dressed like a washer woman.

"Sit down before you fall down at least," Peters said, indicating a lawn chair. Hal sat heavily, placing the empty overnight bag at his feet. "To what do we owe the honour of your visit, O wise one? Or'd you just come to lech Clara?"

"I have a favour to ask."

"Ask away, old chum."

Clara came out of the house with Peters's beer. She also had a tall glass of ice water. She handed the bottle of beer to her husband and held the glass out to Hal. "You looked like you could use this," she said.

"Thank you," Hal said, taking it. She smiled down at him.

"Yeah, thanks, pet," Peters said, toasting her with his beer bottle, then raising it to his mouth. When his wife had gone into the house again, he said, "So, what can I do for you, pal of mine?"

"I need some money."

"Clara!" Peters bellowed, so loudly Puddle's head popped up and Hal flinched. "Bring my chequebook." At a more reasonable volume, he said, "How much do you need?"

"Oh, five hundred thousand ought to do it."

"Five hundred — Clara," he called. "Forget the chequebook." Lowering his voice: "You're joking, right?"

"I'm perfectly serious."

"That's a hell of a lot of money, Hal."

"I know it is."

"The stuff doesn't just grow on trees."

"As I figure it," Hal said, "your fraudulent claim scheme has netted you at least three times that much in the last two years."

Peters sat up. "For god's sake, Hal, keep your voice down."

"Clara doesn't know?" Hal said.

"Of course not. Miss Goody Two-Shoes. She'd freak. Then turn me in for the finder's fee. Look, we had a deal, Hal. I did you a pretty big favour — "

"And I can't tell you how much I appreciate it, Gord," Hal said.

" — because if that girl had filed a complaint, Hal, Jerry would've fired your ass faster than you could say 'family values.' He sure as hell wouldn't've made you a VP."

"Yes, I know, Gord," Hal said tiredly. "I don't need you to remind me that it was an incredibly stupid thing to do."

"But I made it all go away, didn't I?" Peters said.

"Yes, you did," Hal said. For all he knew, though, it had been a setup from the start, orchestrated by Peters;

the girl had made it a point to prove to him that she never wore underwear. "And in return, I turned a blind eye to your embezzlement, even covered your tracks a couple of times."

"And thanks for that, but a deal's a deal, Hal. I do you a favour, you do me a favour. We both win." His expression sharpened. "Rumour has it Jerry is considering you for CFO next year. No one deserves it more. Thing is, Hal, it's always possible that the little cock-teaser could come back for more. You never know with blackmail, do you?"

"No," Hal agreed. "You never do."

"What do you need the money for, anyway?"

"That's my business."

"All right, look," Peters said. "We're friends. I want to be fair. I can let you have a few grand. Say twenty. In the spirit of friendship."

"You must think I'm pretty stupid."

Peters feigned hurt. "Hal, Hal. I don't think you're stupid at all. All right, twenty-five. But that's it."

"We're both in the insurance business, Gord."

"What's that supposed to mean?"

"Think about it," Hal said. Peters's tan was beginning to look a little greenish and a sheen of perspiration glistened on his upper lip. "I need five hundred thousand dollars, Gord, but in that spirit of friendship you mentioned, I have something to offer in return."

"I'm listening."

"Jerry has requested an audit of your department."

Peters looked as though he were going to throw up. "Oh, shit."

"You've been pretty slick," Hal said, "but not quite slick enough. Did you really think you could get away with it indefinitely?"

"No, of course not, but I figured I had a little longer. You're the VP of finance, Hal. Isn't there anything you can do?"

"To stop it? Sorry. It's out of my hands. You know Jerry. When he gets a bee in his bonnet, he isn't happy till it stops buzzing. The best I could do is delay it for a week, maybe two. That would give you a little time. Or ... "

"Or what?" Peters's colour still wasn't good, but his face was hard, his grey eyes as lifeless and cold as ball bearings.

"I could go to Jerry first thing Tuesday morning and serve him your head on a platter."

"What good would that do you?"

"No good at all. In fact, it would in all likelihood cost me my job, wouldn't it?"

"Damn right. I took out some insurance too, Hal. I've got you and your little friend on tape."

"I assumed as much," Hal said. "And who could blame you? But I've been thinking about retiring anyway. You, on the other hand, would lose everything — your house, your savings, perhaps even Clara — and, in all probability, go to jail for a good long time."

"You son of a bitch. You're enjoying this, aren't you?"

"No," Hal said. "I'm not enjoying it at all."

"You know," Peters said, "if you weren't my friend, I'd bash your brains out with this beer bottle and bury you in Clara's garden."

"Then I'm thankful you consider me a friend," Hal said. "It's because you're my friend I'm just asking for five hundred thousand."

"Some friend. I don't keep that much just lying around, you know."

"I know. Let's start with the fifty thousand you keep in that safe in your recreation room."

"How the hell do you know about that?"

"You told me, Gord. At last year's Christmas party.

Your emergency fund, you called it."

"Well, that was stupid of me, wasn't it?" Peters said with a thin, ironic smile.

"It was," Hal said. "We'll go to your bank first thing Tuesday morning and get the rest out of your safe deposit box. Would you like me to tell you the number?"

"Go fuck yourself, Hal," Peters said, without feeling. He stood. Beneath his round, hairy belly, his genitals protruded grotesquely in the ridiculous bathing suit, the shape of his fat penis clearly evident through the thin material, level with Hal's eyes.

Hal stood with a grunt. He followed Peters into the house and down the back stairs into the basement recreation room. It was finished like a British pub, complete with dartboard and ornate beer pump handles labelled with names such as Smithwick's and Courage. Hal had helped with the woodwork. Peters went behind the bar and swung aside a mirror to reveal a small safe set into the wall. He spun the dial and opened the safe. He handed Hal five one-inch stacks of bills bound by thick blue elastic bands.

"There's ten grand per bundle," Peters said.

Hal fanned one of the stacks. The top bill in each stack was a hundred. So, apparently, were the rest. He put the money into the overnight bag and zipped it closed. The $50,000 would get Dougie Hallam off his back. The remaining $450,000 would go a long way toward covering his loses.

Peters gestured for Hal to precede him up the stairs. Hal almost complied, then shook his head.

"After you," Hal said. Outside, he turned to Peters and offered his hand. "Thanks."

"You bastard," Peters said, ignoring Hal's hand. "Like I had a choice."

"Sure you did. Just not a very good one. What are you going to do?"

"I've always thought it would be nice to live in Costa Rica."

"What about Clara?" Hal asked.

"She'll be all right. The house is in her name. If she's careful, she won't have to sell it. She might have to get a second job, though."

"You're a prince among men, Gord," Hal said.

"You'd know," Peters said churlishly.

"See you Tuesday," Hal said, and walked to the car, heart hammering and sweat spilling down his sides. As he got into the car, he caught a whiff of himself. He didn't like what he smelled.

chapter thirty-five

When Shoe lived in Toronto, bars weren't open on Sundays. The current situation wasn't an improvement, especially in the case of the Jane Street Bar and Grill. The only positive thing one could say about it was that it didn't pretend to be anything but what it was — a drinking establishment. The décor was uninspired, to say the least, and the music was bland modern pop, played just loud enough to be annoying. The only customers that Sunday afternoon were four solitary men, ranging widely in age and dress, but all white and all drinking beer from the bottle. No sooner had Shoe settled onto a stool than the barman was in front of him, wiping the stainless steel surface of the bar with a damp rag. He was about Shoe's age, with brown, thinning hair, sharp eyes, and a mouth that turned down at the corners. He wasn't wearing a name tag.

"What can I get you?" he asked, placing a coaster on the bar.

"I'll have a club soda," Shoe replied.

"You want that with a twist?" the barman asked.

"No, thanks."

"Good. 'Cause we're all out and I hate disappointing a customer."

While the barman was drawing Shoe's club soda, no twist, Shoe asked, "What's your name?"

"Syd," the barman said, placing the tall glass of soda and ice on the bar.

"Pleased to meet you, Syd. I'm Shoe. Is Dougie around?"

"Dougie who?" the barman asked.

"How many do you know?"

"You'd be surprised." He half closed one eye, peered at Shoe sideways with the other. "I know most all the regular cops around here. You're either new, visiting from downtown, or private. Which is it?"

"None of the above. I'm just a citizen."

"Well, citizen, what do you want with this Dougie guy?"

"He's an old acquaintance."

"What makes you think you're gonna find him here?"

"I heard a rumour he owned the place."

"Oh, *that* Dougie. Why didn't you say so? Sorry, he ain't here. Most of the time he's what you might call an absentee owner. Hardly ever in before eight or nine at night. If you're an old friend of his, like you say, you'll know where he lives. Try him there."

"I did. He wasn't home." Neither was Janey. And Tim Dutton had been right, the place was a dump. Except for a small patch in the back, facing the woods, the yards were uncut and full of trash, decaying lawn furniture, rusting car parts, even the corpse of a discarded washing machine.

"Well, I ain't his keeper," the barman said. "I just work for him."

"Were you working last Thursday night?"

"Might've been, maybe."

"Was Dougie around that night too?"

"I thought you said you weren't a cop."

"I'm not."

"Well, you sure ask questions like you're a cop. If you're not a cop, get lost. If you are a cop, get lost. I talked to enough cops today already. I got a very low tolerance threshold."

Shoe looked him in the eye. He returned Shoe's stare, not intimidated in the least. After a long moment, keeping his voice low and friendly, Shoe said, "I'm just trying to help out a friend who's got himself into a bit of trouble with the law. I'm sure you can appreciate that. You seem to be a decent fellow."

"Maybe I am and maybe I'm not, but I make it a point to keep my nose out of other people's business. Especially if it involves Dougie Hallam. No offence, Mr. Shoe, but you got questionable taste in friends."

"It's just Shoe. And Dougie Hallam's not the friend I'm trying to help. I'm hoping he might be able to help me help my friend."

"Then you don't know him as good as you think you do." Syd thought for a moment, then said, "Okay, yeah, I was working Thursday night. Our other bartender quit and I'm workin' double shift till Dougie finds a replacement. Wish he'd hurry it up. Dougie was here too."

"Do you remember a man about five-six or five-seven, my age, long greying hair, getting a bit thin on top? He might've been pretty drunk."

"The cops asked me about a guy like that this morning."

"What did you tell them?"

"What makes you think there was anything to tell them?"

Shoe feigned disappointment. "Syd, Syd. And here

I thought we were developing a rapport. I guess I was wrong. Or is it just general contrariness on your part?"

The barman smiled dryly. "Do you watch television?"

"Not much," Shoe replied.

"Well, on TV it's usually at this point that the guy asking questions — that's you — takes out his wallet and offers the bartender — that's me — a hunnerd bucks."

"As I said, I don't watch much television." Shoe took out his wallet. "How's fifty sound?"

"What? You'll have to speak up." He stuck a pinkie into his ear and jiggled it. "I got bad wax build up."

Shoe rolled the fifty-dollar bill into a tight cylinder. He held it out. "Use this to clean it out."

Syd took the rolled-up bill. "I hear you better now," he said. He unrolled the bill, folded it, and tucked it into his shirt pocket. "Yeah, there was a guy like that, about as tall as me, but he looked older'n you. No question about him being drunk. Not that that's so unusual around here. He was runnin' off at the mouth about how him and Dougie were old pals from way back, tellin' everyone how dumb Dougie was then, and wondering if was any smarter now. Talk about dumb, I thought Dougie was going to kill the silly fucker when he asked Dougie if he was still porking his sister. That's when Dougie threw him out."

"What time was this?"

"Eleven, eleven-thirty."

"Did you see him after that?"

"You mean, did he come back in after Dougie left? Shit, no. He wasn't that dumb — or that drunk."

"How long after he threw him out did Dougie leave?" Perhaps Hallam had seen Joey later that night, Shoe thought hopefully.

"Half an hour, maybe," Syd said. "He got a call from someone. I remember because it pissed him off. He was puttin' the moves on some blonde he's had his eye on for a while."

"Did he leave alone?"

"No. She left with him."

"Do you know who the call was from?"

"I didn't ask. I ain't his social secretary. A guy is all I can tell you."

"How long was he gone?"

"An hour, maybe a little longer."

"What kind of vehicle does he drive?"

"Big black Hummer. Windows tinted real dark. Keeps a mattress in the back. Sometimes he takes women to some local park in it — he's got keys to the gates, apparently. Other times, he just takes 'em out back. He's a class act, knows how to treat a woman right."

A pair of men dressed in jeans and boots and western shirts, and sporting huge bellies and big silver and gold belt buckles, climbed onto stools at the far end of the bar.

"Be right back," Syd said, and moved down the bar to serve the men. They ordered a pitcher of draft. Shoe sipped his club soda. The ice had imparted to it the stale flavour of refrigeration. Syd came back. "Anything else I can help you with?"

"How long have you worked here?"

"Ten years or so. Started working for the previous owner. Nice old guy. I didn't think he was interested in selling — I'd've bought the place myself. Instead, I wake up one morning a couple of years ago workin' for Dougie Hallam." He shrugged. "Didn't like him much when he was a customer and like him even less as a boss." He tapped his shirt pocket, wherein nestled Shoe's fifty-dollar bill. "The owner of a little pub up in King City says he's thinking about retiring soon, so I'll be moving on before long."

"Do you know a woman named Marty Elias?"

"Marty? Yeah, I know Marty. Why?"

"How well did you know her?"

"Pretty good. She used to be a regular. Ain't seen her lately, but around the time Dougie bought the place, she used to come in most every Friday night. She didn't have to buy her own drinks, if you get my drift, but she usually did." His eyes sharpened. "Why are you asking me how well I *knew* her?"

"If she was your friend, I'm sorry to be the one to tell you this," Shoe said. "She's dead. Her body was found this morning in the Dells."

The man's face drained of colour. "Aw, crap," he said. He twisted the cap off a single-serving bottle of mineral water and drank. His colour improved somewhat.

"She was more that just a regular, wasn't she?" Shoe said.

"We went out a couple of times," Syd said. "She was good people."

"She was," Shoe agreed.

"You knew her?"

"Yes," Shoe said. "A long time ago. She was my kid sister's best friend. We almost grew up together." He felt a sudden chill. "Was she in here last night, maybe asking about my friend?"

"No. Like I said, I haven't seen her in a while."

"How long is a while?"

"A year, more or less."

"Was Dougie Hallam here last night?" Shoe asked, for no particular reason, except a tingle of curiosity.

"He's here most nights."

"Was he alone?" Where was his subconscious taking him? he wondered.

"When Dougie's here, he's never alone. He's got lots o' friends in this place. I think that's why he bought it. It came with them built in."

"Was he here the whole time?"

"He went out for while around ten or so."

"How long was he gone?"

"An hour, maybe a little less. He came back with the blonde. He left again around eleven, eleven-thirty, with the blonde and another guy."

"This other guy, what did he look like?"

"Bit bigger'n Dougie, but soft. About fifty, fifty-five. Glasses. Short greying hair kinda lyin' flat on his head."

The description fit Hal to a tee, Shoe thought unhappily. The Jane Street Bar and Grill hardly seemed like the kind of place Hal would patronize. On the other hand, he added to himself, glancing at the big-bellied men at the end of the bar, overweight middle-aged men weren't exactly in short supply.

"Did Dougie came back later?" he asked.

"Yeah, he was back by closing time. I don't think he trusts me."

"And the other guy?"

"Don't remember seeing him later. This place is pretty busy on a Saturday night."

Shoe stood up. "I appreciate your help. The police might be by again to ask you about Marty. I hope you'll be as helpful to them as you've been to me."

"I dunno ..."

"Would another fifty help you to make up your mind?"

"Keep your money. I'll tell the cops whatever you want. If Dougie and that other guy you're lookin' for killed Marty, they deserve what they get."

"Just tell the truth," Shoe said. "Thanks for your help." He took out his wallet and dropped two twenties and a ten on the bar.

"I told you to keep your money."

"That's for the club soda," Shoe said.

Syd picked up the bills. "The next one's on the house."

chapter thirty-six

Through the glass wall, Shoe watched Janey Hallam conducting an aerobics class. At least, he thought it was an aerobics class. It might have been a martial arts class, as it involved a lot of kicking, spinning, and air boxing, except that it was being performed to the mind-numbing thud of techno-rock dance music. The average age of the class appeared to be about forty-five. Women outnumbered the men two to one. With a few notable exceptions, most of both genders were ten to twenty pounds overweight, some much more. And, with more or less the same exceptions, most were having a difficult time of it. They missed steps, floundered, staggered, recovered, only to miss another step, like marionettes operated by a drunken puppeteer. Shoe hoped they were enjoying themselves, but judging from their expressions, they didn't appear to be. The majority looked as though they were in pain.

Janey was tireless, lean and muscular in bright, sweat-stained Spandex that fit her like scales on a snake.

She wore a microphone headset, into which she whooped encouragement and shouted instructions as she kicked and punched and spun, and the music pounded. When she saw Shoe through the glass wall, she waved and held up both hands, fingers splayed. Shoe acknowledged with a nod, then retreated to a nearby waiting area, where he leafed through fitness magazines, the contents of which consisted mainly of ads for dietary supplements, complex exercise machinery, and expensive exercise clothing, until Janey's class ended.

As her class headed for the showers, Janey came into the waiting area, mopping her neck and upper chest with a towel. She smiled up at him. "Hey, Joe." Her colour was high and she was breathing deeply and slowly. An artery pulsed in her neck.

"Have you got a couple of minutes?" Shoe asked.

"For you, sure," she replied. She paused, then added, "Did you hear about Marty Elias?"

"Yes," he said.

"Can you believe it? What's the world coming to?"

"I don't know," Shoe said. He'd heard a report of Marty's murder on the car radio, but the police hadn't released Marty's name, "pending notification of next of kin." How had Janey heard about it? He asked her.

"One of the girls in my exercise class is married to a cop who works out of the local station. It's just around the corner." He was relieved she hadn't heard that he and Claudia Hahn had found Marty's body. "Give me a minute to grab a quick shower and change," Janey said. "Then I'm all yours for the price of a drink."

She touched his arm, as if for reassurance that he was really there, then went back through the exercise room, where a slim young Asian man in a white judo *gi* with a black belt was arranging exercise mats. A group of about two dozen boys and girls between the ages of five and fifteen, wearing *gis* with belts of various colours, trouped into the room and began helping him. Shoe watched them work out for a few minutes, then felt a gentle touch on his back and turned. Janey was wearing a short skirt, flared slightly to accommodate her muscular thighs, and a snug, stretchy top with a scooped neckline. The tops of her breasts were dusted with fine freckles. Her hair was still damp from the shower and slicked back, emphasizing the shape of her skull and the starved-orphan gauntness of her face. Was there such a thing as being too fit? Shoe wondered.

"All set?" he asked.

"Yep," Janey said. She slung a nylon sports bag over her shoulder and took his arm, pressing her breasts against him. The message couldn't be clearer. "Where would you like to go?" she asked.

"Anywhere's fine with me," Shoe said, as they walked toward the exit. "As long as it's not the Jane Street Bar and Grill."

"God, no." She ducked through the door as he held it for her. "Don't tell me you've been there."

"I was looking for Dougie." He gestured toward his father's car, parked in the lengthening shadow of the building.

"As good a place as any to start, I suppose." In the car she said, "Head south. There's a decent pub not too far from here. So," she said, when they were underway, "why are you looking for Dougie?"

"I want to ask him a couple of questions."

"Nothing too hard, I hope."

"Any idea where he might be?"

"It shouldn't come as any surprise to you that I don't keep track of his whereabouts. In fact, the less I see of him, the better."

"Living in the same house must make that difficult."

"Yeah, but fortunately he isn't around much. Neither

am I, between the gym, my bands, and my teaching gig."

"You said yesterday you taught marketing," he said. "I always imagined you doing something more adventuresome."

"Such as?"

"When you graduated, you told me you'd got a job as an airline flight attendant."

"I did? Really? I thought about it, I suppose — I guess it seemed like a cool job — but I ended up in advertising. Close to twenty-five years. Not exactly, um, adventuresome, but it had its moments. Had my own company until — well, it's a long story and I don't want to bore you with it."

"Tim Dutton said something about losing your advertising business in a dispute with your partner."

"I suppose you could call it a dispute," she said. She sighed. "What happened was, five years ago my business partner, who I also happened to be married to at the time, ran off with his bimbo of an assistant, most of our clients, and what was left of our cash reserves after he'd talked me into upgrading our image and moving into a new space that was costing us ten grand a month. I divorced him, of course, and sued to recover the money he'd stolen, but by the time the dust settled, I'd lost all my clients and I was over two hundred thousand in debt. Don't ever try to declare bankruptcy when you owe money to lawyers. It's not a lot of fun."

She pointed through the windshield toward the parking lot of a tidy little strip mall set back from the road. Shoe turned into the lot.

"Patty Dutton's a snob," Janey said, as Shoe manoeuvred the Taurus into a parking space. "But I feel sorry for her, married to Tim. He was fucking Marty, you know, right under his wife's nose. Rumour has it his business isn't doing too well, either, and he's in hock up to his eyeballs. Wouldn't surprise me if it went toes up soon."

"Tough on the employees."

"Tell me about it," Janey said. "I had twenty people working for me when I had to close up shop. Tim isn't his old man, that's for sure. I don't know how he's managed to stay above water as long as he has. It must drive the old man crazy, seeing Tim run the business he built into the ground. Old Bart ran a pretty tight ship, but he cared about the people who worked for him. The only person Tim Dutton cares about is Tim Dutton."

The pub was cool and quiet, except for the occasional roar from the people watching a soccer match being played on a big-screen TV in a corner. Janey led him to a table at the far end of the room. The waitress knew her by name.

"Hiya, Janey. The usual?"

"Yeah, Dee, thanks," Janey said.

"And what can I get you, big fella?" the waitress said to Shoe, dropping a pair of coasters on the scarred tabletop.

Shoe asked for a half-pint of Double Diamond. There was a large array of single malts lined up behind the bar, and he was tempted by the Lagavulin, but this was neither the time nor the place for a sixteen-year-old malt whisky.

"Here's to old times," Janey said when their drinks arrived, lifting her gin and tonic.

Shoe sipped his beer.

"I'm probably going to regret asking," Janey said, "but what did you want to ask Dougie about anyway?"

"The police are looking for Joey Noseworthy."

"Joey? Why? Jesus, they don't think he killed Marty, do they?"

"They want to talk to him about Marvin Cartwright."

"You mean they think Joey killed him? That's nuts. They were friends."

"So I've recently learned," Shoe said. "Nevertheless, Joey is the prime suspect in Cartwright's homicide."

"What's it got to do with Dougie?"

"Joey can't account for his whereabouts at the time of Cartwright's death, but evidently he was in Dougie's bar on Thursday night until between eleven and twelve, until Dougie threw him out."

"You're kidding. Joey's always been a little crazy, but I didn't think he was suicidal? He's lucky Dougie didn't kill him. Well, good luck." She drank, ice rattling.

"Marty told me that you and Joey were lovers."

"Did she? Well, I guess you could say Joey and I had a kind of love-hate relationship. It was a long time ago. After you and he had fallen out. You and I had broken up — again — and, well, I guess we both sort of missed you in our own ways."

"What about more recently?"

"I haven't seen Joey in three or four years," she said. "Not since I went bankrupt. Before that, he'd give me a call sometimes when he was passing through and we'd get together. He crashed at my place once or twice, too, after my ex took off." She shrugged. "Things led to things."

"Were you and Marvin Cartwright lovers?"

"No," she said, with a sigh. "I told you, I hardly knew him."

"Where were you around the time he was killed?"

"You're not serious. You're asking me if I have an alibi?"

"Yes, that's what I'm asking you."

"Well, for your information, I was in Hamilton with one of my bands. Stayed overnight in a hotel. Alone, if you must know, but I can show you the receipt. I didn't get back to Toronto till around noon on Friday. Satisfied?"

"Yes, but don't lose that receipt. The police may want to see it."

"C'mon, Shoe, don't spoil the mood. Drink up. You've hardly touched your beer. Aren't you having fun?" She waved at the waitress and pointed to her empty drink glass.

He raised his glass and took another sip of beer. Janey was lying to him about her relationship with Marvin Cartwright. It may not have been sexual, but he was sure there was more to it than she was admitting. There was no point in pursuing it. He knew from experience that if Janey didn't want to talk about something, she wouldn't.

"Just a few more questions, then we'll talk about anything you want." The waitress brought Janey's second drink. "When was the last time you saw Marty?" he asked when the waitress had gone.

"About a year ago, I guess. She came to the club for physiotherapy when she sprained her shoulder at work. I hadn't seen her since she dropped out of high school, so we came here for a drink and to catch up. Now there was someone who'd had an adventuresome life, maybe a little too adventuresome. Did you know she used to be a stripper?"

"She mentioned that," Shoe said.

"She also lived with a vice cop in Vancouver for a while, until he killed himself."

"She told me she'd lived with a cop," Shoe said. "She didn't tell me he'd committed suicide. What else did you talk about?"

"Mostly she wanted to talk about Joey. She was hoping she could get him to settle down. I wished her good luck with that."

"What can you tell me about Joey's relationship with Marvin Cartwright?"

"Like I said, they were friends from back when we were kids, but Joey didn't talk much about growing up. He didn't have a happy adolescence. Hell, who did?"

Michael Blair

I did, Shoe thought. *Mostly*.

"I know they played chess a lot," Janey said. "He told me Marvin thought he could've played professionally if he'd applied himself. I didn't know there was such a thing."

"What about later? Joey told me he ran into Cartwright fifteen years ago when he was working at a provincial park in Prince Edward County. He stayed with Cartwright whenever he was in the area."

"Joey told me they'd reconnected," Janey said, "but I think as far as Joey was concerned, Marvin was just another source of a 'hot and a cot,' as he put it."

"Did you ever have any contact with Cartwright after he left the neighbourhood?"

"No."

"Did Marty?"

"I don't know."

"Janey, be straight with me. How well did you know Marvin Cartwright?"

"I didn't know him any better than you did."

"I don't believe you."

"Tough." She shook her head. "I don't want to talk about this anymore."

"What did you expect to find when we broke into his house?"

"I didn't expect to find anything. I just wanted to see if you'd do it." She tossed back her drink. "You've asked your questions. It's my turn now." She started to signal the waitress, but changed her mind. "Let's talk about the good times we used to have, Shoe. We used to have some pretty good times, didn't we? Before — well, never mind that."

"Before what, Janey?"

"Forget it. C'mon, tell me what you've been doing with your life. You don't look like you've put on an ounce since you were eighteen. I'm not surprised, if that's the way you drink beer. You married? You aren't wearing a ring, but a lot of men don't. It cramps their style."

"I'm not married."

"Ever?"

"No."

"Haven't turned queer on me, have you?" She winked broadly.

She couldn't have been more obvious if she'd been wearing a sign around her neck. Was he tempted? No more than he had been by the Lagavulin.

Janey chattered on, uncharacteristically, about "the old days." The problem was, she didn't seem to remember them the same way he did. It was as if she were talking about two people Shoe didn't recognize at all. The boy she spoke of was smarter and more confident, *cooler* than Shoe had ever been; the girl was sweeter and more innocent; and the times were good and full of promise, not the dark and uncertain teenage years Shoe remembered. She ordered another drink.

"How come we stopped seeing each other?" she asked, when the drink came. "We were pretty good together, weren't we?"

"When we were together," he said.

"What do you mean? We were going steady."

"That's not the way I remember it," he said. "You had lots of boyfriends." Including, evidently, Joey Noseworthy.

"Okay, maybe there were a few others, but no one I liked as much as you. And it wasn't like you didn't have other girlfriends. What about Mandy or Candy or whatever her name was? The one with the glasses and the teeth."

"Sandy? I went out with her once, and only after you and I broke up for the last time."

"Maybe I'm not remembering it the way it really was," she said, hazel eyes bright and moist. "Maybe

I'm remembering it the way I wish it was. You and me against the world. It was a little like that, wasn't it, Shoe? The local hero and the girl from the wrong side of the tracks."

"I was hardly a local hero, Janey, and you lived just down the road."

"I may as well have been from wrong side of the tracks," she said. "I know what people said about my parents. Trailer trash in a nice house. Never mind that it was true, it still hurt."

"I never thought you were trash, Janey."

"I know. You didn't think I was a slut, either. I was, though. I still am. I think … " Her voice trailed off.

"What?"

"Never mind. Forget it." She leaned toward him, gestured for him to lean closer. She hunched her shoulders, deepening her cleavage. Her breath smelled of juniper and quinine. "Why don't we get out of here? Go back to my place. There's beer in the fridge and a couple of steaks in the freezer we could throw onto the barbecue. How's that sound?"

"I don't think so, Janey. Not tonight."

"There might not be another offer."

"I'll have to live with the disappointment."

"Sarcasm. Shoe. I didn't think you had it in you."

"I should be going. Can I drop you somewhere?"

She sat back. "I think I'll hang around for a while. Who knows? Some other guy might get lucky. But you haven't finished your beer. Stick around. Maybe I can change your mind. I'm as good as I ever was. Maybe better. Hell, definitely better."

"It's a tempting offer," he said. And it was, too, more that he cared to admit. A lot more. He stood. "But I'm going to have to decline."

"Too bad."

"You're sure I can't give you a ride home?"

"I'm sure." She downed her drink and waved at the waitress.

Shoe went to the bar to pay the tab. As he was leaving the pub, he saw two men in business suits approach Janey's table. One spoke to her, then the other. She smiled up at them with an air of boredom, but nodded. Both men sat, smiling at their good fortune. Shoe wondered which of them would get to scratch Janey's itch. Or was he underestimating her? Maybe it would take both of them to satisfy her itch.

chapter thirty-seven

Rachel emerged from the woods onto the turnaround at the end of Wood Lane. The narrow cul-de-sac was aptly named; it was more like a driveway than a street. In fact, it may have once been an entrance drive, before Mr. Braithwaite had sold the surrounding property to the developers and used the money to perform his missionary work. The Braithwaite house stood by itself at the end of the road, surrounded by woods, next to the turnaround. A sprawling single-story precursor to the typical Toronto bungalow, it was fifteen or twenty years older than the other houses in the neighbourhood. To Rachel, it looked as it always had: sagging eaves; curtains drawn across unwashed windows, some of which appeared to be boarded up; trim desperately in need of scraping and painting; old flower beds choked with weeds and a few struggling shrubs. The overgrown front lawn was littered with cheap religious statuary: plaster or cement casts of the Madonna, with and without child; Christ figures, some blessing unseen supplicants, some bearing a cross, some on the cross; plus numerous effigies that meant nothing to her, but which could have been saints or apostles or, for all she knew, characters from *The Lord of the Rings*. They were scattered haphazardly about in the long grass and weeds, some leaning drunkenly, some fallen, most stained and scabrous with neglect, like the house and lawns. There was no discernible path to the front door.

Earlier in the afternoon, Joe had come to the welcome tent in the park, where he'd told her that Ruth Braithwaite's father had evidently filed a complaint with the police about Marvin Cartwright. "It was the main reason Ron Mackie was so certain Cartwright was the Black Creek Rapist," he'd said. "Dad said he thought Cartwright and Ruth Braithwaite might have been sweethearts. Perhaps Cartwright kept in touch with her and she can tell us why he came back."

"You said you were going to leave that part of it to the police," Rachel had reminded him.

"Hannah — Sergeant Lewis — told me that they haven't had any luck contacting Ruth or her sisters. No one answers the door or the telephone. I thought I'd give it a try, but Dad thought there probably hasn't been a man in that house since their father died."

"Do you want me to try to talk to her?"

"They might be more likely to open the door to a woman."

"Sergeant Lewis is a woman," Rachel had said. "In case you hadn't noticed."

"Her partner isn't," he'd replied.

The house had no porch, just a broken concrete slab at the front door. The varnish of the door and doorframe was crazed and peeling. Three small triangular panes of frosted glass were set into the door at eye level. Two were cracked. There was no doorbell, just a pair of frayed, corroded wires protruding from a hole in the doorframe.

There was a brass knocker, green with age and so stiff that she could barely move it. She rapped on the door with her knuckles, and stood back. She waited a minute and rapped again. There was still no answer, but she thought she saw the curtains in the living room window twitch.

Rachel knocked again, harder. She leaned close to the door and called, "Hello." Still nothing. She was about to turn away when she saw a shadow of movement behind one of the cracked triangular windows, followed by the grinding click of the lock. There was a tortured creak from the rusted hinges as the door opened a couple of inches.

"Who are you?" a woman asked, peering through the gap. She looked to be in her mid- to late-fifties, with wide-set blue eyes, a small nose, and full, pale lips. Her hair was shoulder-length and thick and the colour of ashes. Her voice was light and papery, as if she were unaccustomed to speaking.

"My name is Rachel Schumacher. My parents live on Ravine Road. Their backyard is opposite yours. Are you Ruth?"

"What do you want?" The woman leaned close to the gap as she spoke. Her breath was stale and her teeth were small and yellow. Once she might have been pretty. "Go away," she hissed, but she didn't close the door.

"I want to talk to you about Marvin Cartwright," Rachel said.

"Marvin," the woman said, inflection flat. She blinked quickly, spasmodically. "Marvin."

"Marvin Cartwright," Rachel said again. "He lived down the street from my family, with his mother. Are you Ruth? Did you know him?"

"You're that tall boy's sister," the woman said. "The one who tried to talk to me about my drawings."

"You mean Joe? Yes, I'm his sister."

"Is that his name? He didn't tell me his name. He was nice, but I ran away. Father told me that wasn't polite, but I wasn't supposed to be in the woods, and he punished me. I like the woods. He doesn't let me go into the woods, but I do. I know I shouldn't, but I do."

"Do you still go into the woods? Were you in the woods last Thursday? Did you meet Marvin in the woods, Ruth?"

"Thursday. Marvin."

"Yes. Thursday. Three days ago. Did you go into the woods to meet Marvin?"

Ruth didn't answer, or even appear to have heard or understood. Her blue eyes shifted as she looked past Rachel toward the road. Rachel turned. A stout, elderly woman, dressed in flowered shorts and carrying a green plastic pail, stood watching them from the middle of the road. She nodded slightly, then resumed walking toward Cantor Street. When Rachel turned back, Ruth was closing the door.

"Wait," Rachel said, putting her hand on the door.

"Go away," Ruth said, leaning close to the gap in the door. "He doesn't like us to have visitors. He'll punish us. He'll punish you, too. Go away."

"Who? Who will punish you? Your father? Your father is ... " She hesitated. She couldn't say it.

"Father." The woman's eyes became unfocused in confusion for a moment, then she blinked and said, "Yes. Father. Father will punish us. We aren't allowed visitors."

"Did Marvin visit you?"

"Marvin." Again, the inflection was flat. "He's writing a book about Africa, you know. Mother and Father are in Africa. Have you been to Africa?"

"No," Rachel said.

"Neither have I. Father said he'd take me, but Mother won't let him."

"Marvin talked to you about Africa? When?"

"Father got angry and sent him away. He came back, though." She pressed her pale face close to the gap and there was fear in her eyes. "He doesn't know," she whispered urgently. "He'll get angry and punish us. Please. Go away. He'll punish you, too, if you don't go away." And she closed the door with enough force to rattle the cracked triangular panes of glass.

Rachel stared at the door for a moment, then turned and made her way through the statuary to the road. There was no sidewalk and she walked in the road to the corner. The woman in the floral shorts was sitting on the steps of the screened porch of the house on the corner, sorting through the contents of her pail. Rachel didn't remember the woman's name, but she'd lived in the neighbourhood for some time. She looked up as Rachel stopped at the end of her driveway. She was the Braithwaites' nearest neighbour. What the hell, Rachel thought.

The woman watched as Rachel walked up her short driveway. "Hello. I'm Rachel Schumacher."

"Howard and Vera's daughter?" the woman said. She was about seventy, with sharp, dark eyes in a face like a crumpled brown paper bag that had been poorly smoothed out.

"Yes," Rachel answered.

The woman set aside the plastic pail, which was half filled with wild mushrooms. "I thought I recognized you. I'm Flora Zaminksi. I used to babysit you and your brothers when you were little."

"I'm afraid I don't remember."

"You wouldn't. You were very young. I'm sorry. I didn't mean to be rude, but it's been ages since I've seen any of the Braithwaite girls. That was Ruth, wasn't it?"

"I think so. Did you know the Braithwaites?"

"No, not really. Once in a while I'd see him or her

on the street or in the yard, and they always said good morning, but that was all. Bert — he was my husband — he helped Mr. Braithwaite push his car out of a snowbank one winter. Otherwise they kept to themselves and their kind. Each to his own, as Bert used to say. We were in Turkey, I think it was, when Mr. and Mrs. Braithwaite died." She looked down the road toward the Braithwaite house and shook her head. "I wish the girls would take better care of their yard."

"You've lived here a long time."

"Forty-six years, on and off. Bert was an engineer. He built hydroelectric dams all over the world. We didn't have any children, so I went with him. We kept this place, though, to come back to, between Bert's projects. Bert reckoned it would be worth a lot of money when it came time for him to retire and we'd sell it and buy a place in Mexico or Costa Rica or St. Lucia. When Bert died of a heart attack in India, I came back here. That was eighteen years ago. Except for visiting my brother in Ireland twice and my sister in Florida for a month every winter, I've been here ever since."

"Do you remember Marvin Cartwright?"

"About as good as I remember Mr. and Mrs. Braithwaite. It's a shame about him getting killed in the woods like that."

"Do you remember if he was a friend of the Braithwaites?"

"I'm not sure the Braithwaites had many friends in the neighbourhood. I didn't think Marvin Cartwright did, either. Except the little kids. You were one of them, weren't you, dear?"

"Yes." Rachel hesitated. She looked toward the Braithwaite house. She could see it quite clearly, hunched by itself in the woods at the end of the cul-de-sac. She turned back to Mrs. Zaminski. "Have you noticed if anyone has visited Ruth and her sisters recently?"

Mrs. Zaminski's face crumpled as she smiled. "I admit I'm something of a busybody, dear. I do try to mind my own business, but television is so boring and stupid these days, and I find it harder and harder to read for any length of time now. I don't sleep very well, either, anymore, so I spend a lot of time just sitting on my porch or in my window, depending on the weather." Rachel waited, curbing her impatience. "There were a lot of police bustling about on Friday morning," Mrs. Zaminski went on. "After Mrs. Mahood found poor Mr. Cartwright's body. They parked their cars and trucks in the turnaround at the end of the road, right next to Ruth's house. It was exciting, really, but she and her sisters must have been quite upset by all the activity. The police knocked on the door several times, but no one answered. I'm really very surprised Ruth opened the door for you."

"Do they have any regular visitors?"

"Sobeys delivers groceries every Monday afternoon — the driver leaves the boxes in the breezeway — and once in a while the Jehovah's Witnesses will knock on the front door. No one ever answers, of course. And Dougie Hallam. I've seen that truck of his, like the ones the American army uses, only shinier, parked in their driveway. He does odd jobs for them."

"Dougie Hallam?" Rachel said. That was a side of Dougie Hallam she'd never seen. Or imagined. "What kind of odd jobs?"

"A few months ago I saw him going into the house carrying a big tool box and what looked like plumbing supplies, pipe and whatnot. He does work for a lot of older people in the neighbourhood. I hired him once myself to replace a broken front step. His work was less than satisfactory, and I didn't like the way he looked at me. Like he was sizing me up for something. It 'creeped me out,' as my grandniece says. He also overcharged me."

That seemed more Dougie's style, Rachel thought.

"He visits the house at night sometimes, too," Mrs. Zaminski added. "At least, I'm pretty sure it's him, sneaking around in the dark. He comes through the woods and goes in the breezeway door."

"Did you see anyone last Thursday night?" Rachel asked.

"Thursday? No, dear. I can't be at the window all the time."

chapter thirty-eight

Janey knew she should be pissed with Shoe for bailing on her. She wanted to be pissed with him. She even tried to talk herself into being pissed with him, recalling the look he'd given her as he'd left the bar and Fred and Barney — she couldn't remember their real names, if they'd even told her their real names, which was doubtful — had invited themselves to join her. But no matter how much she wanted to be, or tried to be, she just couldn't be pissed with him. And that worried her; it usually didn't take much for men to piss her off.

Take Fred and Barney. Please. They pissed her off plenty. Fred — or maybe it was Barney — kept putting his hand on her thigh and trying to reach under her skirt. Barney — or Fred — just stared at her tits and practically drooled. Like this was supposed to do something for her, for Christ's sake. She'd finally had enough and, on the pretext of seeing a friend at the bar, excused herself and left them sitting there, with stupid looks on their faces and their dicks in their hands, which must have really spoiled their evening. Like she gave a shit.

Maybe the guy at the bar thought he'd died and gone to heaven when she squeezed into the space beside him and pressed her tits against his arm, or maybe not, but he was keen enough to play along when she told him she was being hassled by a couple of drunks and would he be a sport, pretend to be her friend, and buy her a drink. He was a bit on the geeky side, but nice enough, in an eager-to-please, doggy kind of way, and he smelled okay, so she showed her gratitude later in his car, letting him rub her through her panties while she gave him the tug job of his life, using the lubricating jelly she carried in her athletic bag. She didn't get off, of course, and she briefly considered inviting him to her place so he could do a proper job of it, but she had a rule about taking first dates home: she didn't. She let him drive her to the gym to pick up her car, though, where she kissed him on the cheek, and told him she'd see him around. As she got into her beat-up old Firebird, she made a mental note to wait a few weeks before going to that pub again.

She'd had a little more than usual to drink, but for some reason wasn't feeling it. When she got home to the downstairs apartment in her stepbrother's house — she thought of it as Dougie's house even though they owned it jointly — she stuck a Lean Cuisine in the microwave, stripped, and took another shower. Afterwards, she ate the Lean Cuisine straight from the plastic tray, sitting at the kitchen table in her panties and T-shirt with the air conditioning on full blast. As she was rinsing the tray at the sink, there was a knock on the door at the bottom of the stairs to the apartment.

"Shit," she swore under her breath. Louder, she called, "What do you want, Dougie?"

"Open the door."

"I'm tired, Dougie. I just want to go to bed."

"Open the goddamned door," he said. "I'm out of beer."

She sighed. He wasn't going to go away and he'd kicked the door in the last time she'd refused to open it for him. "Just a minute," she said.

She went into her bedroom and put on jeans and an old none-too-clean sweatshirt, then went back into the kitchen. When she opened the door, he pushed past her into the kitchen and yanked open the refrigerator door. He took out two bottles of beer and slammed the door shut.

"I don't know how you can drink this microbrew piss," he said, twisting the cap from a bottle and upending it. He guzzled down half the bottle.

"You seem to manage all right," she said.

"It's still beer." He guzzled down the rest of the first bottle, then opened the second.

Janey opened the fridge and took out two more bottles. She handed them to him. "Here, take them with you. I was just getting ready for bed."

"The night's still young. Have a beer with me." He went into the living room, dropped onto the sofa, and propped his feet on the edge of her coffee table.

"Dougie, please," she said, knowing the futility of pleading with him. "I'm tired."

"What's the matter, Janey? You used to be a real party girl. You slowin' down in your old age or what?"

"I guess that's it," she said.

"Well, have a beer. That'll get your motor running."

He finished his second beer and opened a third. Where does he put it? Janey wondered. He'd undoubtedly had a few already. More than a few. She'd seen him consume a dozen or more before settling down for some serious drinking. She didn't like being around him when he was drunk. She didn't much like being around him anytime.

"I'm going to bed," she said. "Don't forget to turn out the lights." She started toward the bedroom.

He snapped his legs straight, propelling the coffee table into the middle of the living room, almost knocking her down. When she sidestepped around it, he reached out and grabbed her wrist. "I said have a fucking beer." With a force that almost dislocated her shoulder, he hauled her down onto the sofa.

"All right, Dougie," she said, trying to sit up, to move away from him, but he would not let go of her arm. She knew better than to struggle, to try to get away. "All right," she said. "I'll have a beer with you."

"That's better," he said. To her profound relief, he let her go. He twisted open a bottle and handed it to her. He knocked his bottle against hers. "That's my party girl."

She took a mouthful. Fear made it taste sour on the back of her tongue, as if it had gone bad. She drank it anyway. Better that than make Dougie angry. Dougie drunk was one thing. Dougie drunk and angry was another thing altogether.

"How come you're not out partying with your boyfriend tonight?" he said.

"Which boyfriend would that be?" she said casually, although she knew who he meant.

"That prick Schumacher," he said. "Who the fuck d'you think? I saw you talkin' to him yesterday in the park, practically shoving your rack in his face. What's the matter? You losing your touch?"

"I guess so."

"Or maybe he's turned into a fag."

"Maybe." It was always safer to agree with whatever he said, otherwise he might just go off on her.

"Figures," he said, with a satisfied belch. "Fags never fight fair."

She thought about telling Dougie that Shoe had been looking for him that afternoon, but decided it would be better to get off the subject of Shoe. Even after thirty-five years, it still pissed Dougie off to remember that every time he and Shoe had squared off, he'd come out the worse for it.

"I've got an early class tomorrow, Dougie," she said.

"You don't think I can take him?" Dougie said. She didn't, but she wasn't crazy enough to say so. "Next time I'll be ready for his tricks," he said.

Sure you will, she thought.

Dougie drained the beer and tossed the empty bottle toward the other end of the sofa. "Get me another one," he ordered. She got up and started toward the kitchen. "And while you're at it, get the money you keep in that coffee can in your fridge."

She went to the fridge, got the last beer, opened it, and took it to him. "I don't do that any more, Dougie," she said, handing it to him. "Not since someone" — Guess who? — "broke in last year."

He grabbed her wrist. The beer bottle fell to the floor, rolling across the carpet, spewing foam. He heaved himself to his feet, still holding her wrist. With his free hand, he took a handful of her hair. He forced her to her knees and unzipped his jeans.

She'd been eleven the first time her stepfather had raped her. When he was done, he'd whipped her for not being a virgin. "Who you been with?" She told him. Then he beat Dougie, who'd been raping her since she was ten, for depriving him of what he regarded as his prerogative to deflower her. They'd both continued to abuse her on a regular basis until she was sixteen, when Freddy lost interest in her, transferring his attention to a young Korean girl Janey's mother had brought home to help with the housekeeping chores. When the Korean girl disappeared after a few months, Janey was afraid Freddy would start coming to her room again, but he didn't.

She was too old and no longer attractive to him. Dougie continued to force himself on her until a few months after Janey's nineteenth birthday, when Freddy and her mother had been found in the trunk of their burnt-out car, wrists wired together and shot in the head. Janey told Dougie that she'd got one of her biker friends to kill them. He hadn't believed her, of course, but hadn't touched her since. She'd sworn to herself then that if he ever did, she'd kill him.

"Goddamnit, Dougie," she said, turning her face away from his erect penis. "I'll bite your fucking dick — "

She cried out as he jerked her to her feet by the hair. "I got a better idea," he said.

Taking her by the arm, he dragged her into the kitchen alcove and began rummaging through the cupboards. He took down a bottle of olive oil.

Oh, god, she thought.

"I swear, Dougie," she said. "If you don't leave me alone, I'm going to sneak into your bedroom some night, handcuff you to your bed, and set you on fire. I might cut your balls off first. Don't think I — "

He backhanded her across the face, knocking her over the kitchen table. She tasted blood in her throat. He came round the table and lifted her by the neck, fingers and thumb behind the hinges of her jawbone, like the jaws of a steel trap. He squeezed and her breath locked in her throat.

"I could kill you as easy as this," he growled, breath hot in her face. He squeezed harder. "Pop your head right off your fucking neck. Stop wriggling!" he commanded.

She forced herself to go limp and he relaxed the pressure on her throat. She sucked in a ragged breath.

"Drop your jeans," he said. When she didn't comply immediately, he gave her neck a brief squeeze. "Do it!"

"No, Dougie," she croaked, but she unsnapped her

jeans and let them fall. "Don't. I — I'm HIV-positive."
She wasn't, but she was terrified Dougie might be.

"Bullshit," Dougie said, turning her over, pushing
her face down across the table. "Only fags get AIDS."
With one hand clamped to the back of her neck, he tore
off her panties as though they were made of paper.

She tried to do what she'd done before, whenever
Freddy or Dougie had raped her, go somewhere else in
her head until it was over, pretend that it was happening
to someone else, not her. It hadn't always worked then,
and it wasn't working now. Nor would it do any good to
put up a fight, she knew; he'd just beat her half to death
and rape her anyway. So she went limp, enduring the
searing pain by imagining herself sneaking up the stairs
to his bedroom with a knife and a can of gasoline.

chapter thirty-nine

"Are you sure it was Ruth?" Shoe asked. He, Rachel, their parents, Harvey Wiseman, and Maureen sat around the picnic table in the backyard. Hal was still missing in action. During a dinner of salad and cold cuts, Rachel described her encounter with Ruth Braithwaite and her subsequent conversation with Flora Zaminski.

"I think so," she said. "She seemed pretty, um, well, nuts, though, talked as if her parents were still alive in Africa. She remembered you. She told me her father chastised her for running away from you in the woods, then punished her for being in the woods in the first place. She also said that Marvin Cartwright was writing a book about Africa."

"Claudia Hahn told me he wrote historical adventures and romances," Shoe said. "Perhaps he was researching a book with Ruth's parents."

"I think she used to sneak out and meet him in the woods," Rachel said. "Until her father complained to the police about him. She said her father made him go away, but that he came back. She still seems terrified her father will punish her for going into the woods. Maybe she met Marvin in the woods on Thursday night and killed him because, I dunno, she was afraid her father would find out and punish her."

"Whoa," Shoe said, reining her in. "Slow down. Cartwright was beaten to death with a blunt object, most likely a tree limb. Do you think the woman you spoke to was capable of that kind of violence?"

"I don't know. I didn't get a good look at her, but she didn't seem especially frail. Still, he was an old man and you said Joey told you he was sick. He might not have been able to put up much of a fight."

"My grandmother was quite frail toward the end," Maureen said. "But her Alzheimer's made her paranoid and very physically aggressive. She gave my mother a black eye once and another time broke an orderly's finger. She had to be restrained for much of the last year of her life."

"Ruth certainly seemed paranoid enough," Rachel said.

"On the other hand," Wiseman said, "to the best of anyone's knowledge, Ruth hasn't set foot outside of that house in thirty years. I doubt Marvin Cartwright simply knocked on her door and said, 'Hello, Ruth. Long time no see. Would you like to go for a walk in the woods?' Even if he did, is it likely she'd go, especially given that she still evidently believes her father would punish her for doing so?"

Rachel slumped. "Okay, I admit, I'd make a lousy detective."

"On the contrary, m'dear," Wiseman said, beaming theatrically. "You may have cracked the case. What do you think, Shoe? Was it the handyman in the garage with the plumber's helper?"

"I'm not sure I'd go that far," Shoe said. "It might be worth looking into, though."

"What little I know of Dougie Hallam is mostly hearsay," Maureen said, "but it's hard to imagine him as the neighbourhood Mr. Fix-It."

"Some Mr. Fix-It," Rachel said. "The house looks like it's about to fall down."

"Someone must do some maintenance for them," Wiseman said. "I don't imagine Ruth or her sisters are the handy types. Mrs. Zed told you he sneaks into the house at night? What sort of maintenance is he doing then?"

"Maybe he's handy with more than just his hands," Maureen said.

"And Dougie's always got his tool with him," Rachel said, with a straight face.

"Rachel," Maureen admonished. "You should be ashamed."

"Anyway," Rachel said, "Mrs. Zaminski said she only thinks it's Dougie who visits the house at night. It could be anyone."

After dinner, they all went across the road to the park for the homecoming gala concert in the big tent shelter. Claudia Hahn was there, looking cool and composed despite her ordeal in the Dells that morning.

"When I said you looked as though you'd led an interesting life," she said to Shoe, "I didn't really expect to become part of it."

Rachel and Maureen excused themselves to help backstage, leaving Shoe with his parents, who sat close together in lawn chairs, enjoying the show, and Claudia Hahn and Harvey Wiseman, who seemed to instantly hit it off. Shoe, the odd man out, excused himself and went for a walk.

He missed Muriel. Nevertheless, he realized with a twinge of guilt, he hadn't called her since he'd arrived.

It was not quite eight o'clock, five o'clock in Vancouver. Muriel would be at the office. Shoe went to his parents' house to use the phone.

After the concert, Maureen asked Shoe if he wouldn't mind driving her home.

"You're welcome to stay over," Rachel said.

"Thanks," Maureen replied. "But I should go. Hal might come home." Her smile was weak and tentative, wavering. "Shoe, if it's not too much trouble … "

"No trouble at all," Shoe said.

In the car, after a long silence, Maureen said, "I'm sorry to put you out like this. I should've brought Hal's car, but he doesn't like me driving it."

She fell silent again and Shoe concentrated on driving, the nighttime expressway traffic heavier and faster than he was accustomed. Vancouver proper did not have expressways and those in the surrounding municipalities were mostly only four lanes wide. The 401 at some points was sixteen lanes wide. Muriel would have hated it. She disliked driving on anything wider than Marine Drive.

Muriel had been happy to hear from him, but harried. "I'm beginning to appreciate why Bill was so grouchy all the time." After Shoe quickly brought her up to speed on the last two days, she said, "And you thought your visit would be dull." They chatted for a minute or two, then duty called and she had to say goodbye. "Come home soon," she'd said. "I miss you." Then she'd hung up. He wondered if they should try living together again.

"Would you like to come in?" Maureen asked as Shoe turned the Taurus into the driveway of Hal and Maureen's house in Oakville, a mostly residential community — ignoring the great sprawl of the Ford assembly plant — some fifty kilometres west of Toronto.

He levered the transmission into park and turned off the engine. The house was dark but for the yellow bug light over the front door and a faint glow from the upstairs hall window. "A few minutes," he said, the need in her voice outweighing his reservations.

Maureen unlocked the front door. "Hal," she called as she opened it. "Are you home?" There was no answer. Shoe was relieved that he would not have to deal with his brother quite yet, and felt guilty that he did so.

Maureen looked around the living room, as if to check that everything was in order. It was a comfortable room, if somewhat over furnished for Shoe's liking. "I'm going to have some wine," Maureen said. "Will you have some? Or I can make you some tea, if you like."

"Please don't go to any trouble," Shoe said.

He followed Maureen into the gleaming white kitchen, where she got a bottle of white wine out of the refrigerator, deftly opened it with a lever-action corkscrew, and poured a large glass.

"Better times," she said and drank half the glass.

"I should be heading back."

Her face fell. "Must you? Won't you stay a little longer? Please."

"I'll keep you company for a while."

"There's some Scotch. I don't know if it is the kind you like. It was a gift."

"No, thank you," he said.

She picked up the bottle of wine and went into the living room. She set the bottle and her glass on the coffee table and sat on the sofa. Shoe sat in an easy chair by the fireplace. The grate was empty and the ashes had been swept.

"It's been an eventful weekend," Maureen said, topping up her wineglass. "You'll probably be glad to go home to some peace and quiet. I was sorry to hear about your friend. Patrick?"

"That's right."

"Hal told me he'd been murdered and that you discovered who'd done it. You also caught the man who killed your employer."

"I had some help."

"And now two more murders. As Claudia said, you do live an interesting life."

"Unlucky, more like it," he said. Particularly for others, he added to himself.

The wine bottle was half empty and Maureen was slightly flushed. She got to her feet, a bit unsteadily. Shoe started to get up. She gestured for him to stay seated.

"Excuse me for a minute," she said. "I've got to visit the little girls' room."

She went upstairs, although there was a bathroom off the kitchen. Shoe heard the hiss of water in the pipes, a door opening and closing, footsteps on the stairs. He looked up as Maureen came back into the living room. She'd changed into a dressing gown, burgundy satin, cinched tight around her waist and hanging to her ankles. She stood for a moment, looking at him.

"I hope you don't mind," she said finally. "I changed into something more comfortable."

"Not at all," he said.

Sitting down, tucking her legs under her, she picked up her wine glass. "Tell me about your marina," she said.

chapter forty

Dougie Hallam slammed the fridge door in Janey's apartment; there was no more beer. And she hadn't been lying when she'd told him that she didn't keep her emergency money in a coffee can in the freezer anymore.

"Stop that goddamned crying," he snarled. He flicked the tips of his fingers across her face. His nails left a row of parallel welts on her cheek.

"You bastard," she sobbed. "I wish I really did have AIDS."

He laughed and raised his hand. She flinched and he laughed again.

Still laughing, he went upstairs. He got a flashlight and left the house, descending into the ravine. The woods were dark, but he didn't turn the flashlight on. He didn't need it to find his way; the moon was almost full and there was plenty of light from the houses bordering the woods. Underfoot, rotting branches and twigs snapped and dead leaves crackled, until he came to the well-trodden main path. Then he moved in almost complete silence, a massive wraith in the moonlight.

The footpath ran alongside the Braithwaites' big backyard, emerging onto the turnaround at the end of Wood Lane. The single streetlight at the entrance to the footpath was burnt out; each time the city fixed it, Hallam would shoot it out with Freddy's old air rifle. They'd eventually given up repairing it.

Just before the turnaround, he clambered over the low stone wall into the overgrown yard and made his way to the side door, in the covered breezeway between the house and the garage. There was no light over the door — he'd removed the bulb himself — and the rotting wicker lawn furniture he'd stacked beside the door shielded him from view from the street, as well as from the prying eyes of that old busybody who lived up the road. He rapped on the door with the butt of the flashlight and in a matter of seconds, Ruth opened the door. Dim light spilled into the breezeway from the 25-watt bulb he'd installed in the small back foyer. He stepped inside, closed the door behind him, and twisted the deadbolt. He left the key in the lock.

Ruth peered silently up at him. In the poorly lit hall she looked almost like she had when he'd first started visiting her and her sisters more than twenty-five years ago. While the twins had turned fat, Ruth had somehow stayed slim and firm, god knows how. The only exercise she got was from housework, tending the crop, and sex. Not that he personally gave a damn what she looked like. His stepmother hadn't been any great shakes in the looks department, either, but she'd more than made up for it in other ways. Nevertheless, that Ruth had retained her looks helped sales of their videos.

He went into the living room. Ruth trailed obediently after him, slippers whispering on the threadbare carpets. In the brighter light of the living room, she looked palc and dry, but it must have been true, what they said about the sun damaging a woman's complexion, because the skin of her face was smoother than that of a lot of younger women. She was wearing an old housccoat over a flannel nightgown that had once buttoned up the front, but it had lost its buttons and he could see her tits when she turned. Small and pink-tipped, they hardly sagged at all. Despite having just had sex with Janey, he felt himself swell and stiffen. It had been more than a month since they'd done a Little Ruthie Show. First things first, though.

"Time to pay some bills," he said. Ruth silently watched as he opened the rolltop desk and took a chequebook from one of the interior drawers. From his pocket, he took the invoices he'd prepared earlier, for services rendered, plus materials. He put them on the desk beside the chequebook, then pulled a chair over. Ruth sat down.

He watched over her shoulder as she took a fountain pen and marked each bill paid, then wrote a separate cheque for each invoice. She wrote slowly and carefully, forming each letter perfectly. Even her signature — Ruth A. Braithwaite — looked like a handwriting example from a schoolbook. When she'd finished writing the cheques, she capped the pen, rose, and waited for instruction.

"Go to the bedroom," he told her.

She left the room. Hallam folded the cheques, totalling slightly more than $10,000, and put them into his shirt pocket. He added the invoices to others in a folder labelled "Expenses," then put the chequebook back into the drawer, and closed the desk. On his way to the bedroom, he went into the kitchen and took a couple of bottles of beer from a refrigerator that was at least as old as he was. He also grabbed a bottle of Canadian Club from the cupboard. Although Ruth didn't normally drink, she

usually needed a couple of shots before she could perform. More than that and she got sick.

She was waiting for him on the bed in the bedroom
at the end of the hall, naked, surrounded by the sex toys
he'd purchased on the Internet, and getting herself ready
with lubricating jelly. She'd brushed her hair and made
up her eyes and mouth and looked years younger. He
checked the positioning of the video cameras mounted
on tripods around the bed and that the DVD recorders
were loaded and ready to go. He made her take a couple of slugs from the bottle of Canadian Club. He drank
a beer as he undressed. Then he set the timer for half
an hour, started the recorders, put on his Lone Ranger
mask, and got onto the bed with her. He had an erection
like a steel pole and, thanks to the lessons his stepmother
had taught him, he could stay that way for pretty much
as long as he wanted. It was Ruth's job to do whatever
she could to make him come before the timer went off.
She'd become pretty good at her job, too, because she
knew he'd beat the crap out of her if she didn't succeed.
Sometimes he beat that crap out of her anyway.

He let her succeed, but just barely. Afterward, when
he came out of the shower, she was standing outside the
bathroom wearing the same tattered nightgown, housecoat, and slippers. She hadn't cleaned herself up and
there was drying semen on her face and in her hair. Her
lips were bruised and swollen. There was fresh blood on
the front of her nightgown; she'd needed motivating.

"That girl was here." she said, speaking for the first
time since he'd arrived.

"Eh? What girl?"

"Her brother tried to talk to me in the woods, but I
ran away. Father — "

"What did she want?" Hallam snapped, cutting her
off.

Ruth shook her head, would not speak.

Hallam grabbed her by the throat and pinned her against the wall. She clung to his massive wrist with both hands, but otherwise did not struggle. "Did she come into the house?"

"No, no. Father would have been angry. He doesn't let us have visitors."

"Tell me what she said," Hallam demanded.

"Please. I won't go into the woods again. I promise."

With a growl, he threw her aside. She fell to the floor and lay quivering and sobbing. He knew it was useless to try to make sense of anything she said. Ruth's mind was mush. Whatever marbles she had left were cracked and broken.

"She said his name was Joe," she whimpered.

"Whose name was Joe?" When she didn't answer, he reached down and pulled her to her feet as easily as if she were made of straw. He slapped her. Sometimes, when she was having trouble writing the cheques, slapping her helped focus her attention, but not always. "The girl's brother," he said. "His name was Joe?"

"Yes," Ruth said. "He talked to me in the woods. Father was very angry at me for going into the woods."

"When was she here?"

"Before."

"Before what?"

"Before. Before."

Hallam slapped her again. Her eyes went out of focus and she would have fallen had he not been holding her up.

"I'm sorry," she whimpered in a small voice. "I won't ever do it again, Poppa, I promise. Please, don't punish me." Suddenly, she began to thrash wildly in Hallam's grasp. "Go away," she shrieked. "Go away. He'll be angry if he catches you here. Father made Marvin go away because he liked my drawings and told me I was pretty."

Hallam slapped her again, harder. Her head rocked and her eyes rolled up until all he could see were the whites. Then they closed.

"Fuck," he said, releasing her. She collapsed in a heap at his feet.

After a quick check of the basement and the security cameras, he collected his flashlight and left the house, using his own key to lock the side door behind him. He was halfway home when he realized he'd left the DVD discs on the table in the living room. Hell with them, he thought. He'd pick them up later. He had other things on his mind. What was Schumacher's sister doing nosing around? And when, exactly? Ruth's sense of time was crap. Mostly, when she talked at all, it was about things that had happened twenty or thirty years ago or within the last few hours. Everything in between was scrambled like the pieces of a jigsaw in a box, and too many of them were missing. Rachel Schumacher might have come round thirty years ago or just that afternoon. Hallam was pretty sure it had been the latter.

He had a good thing going with Ruth. Between the fake invoices, the crop in the basement, and selling videos of his games with her on the Internet, he was making a small fortune. He was goddamned if he was going to let some do-gooder dyke bitch screw things up. He was going to have to keep an eye on her.

chapter forty-one

Shoe looked at his watch. It was past one o'clock. The wine bottle on the coffee table was empty and Maureen had fallen asleep on the sofa. One minute, they'd been talking about his plans for his motel and marina, and her hopes for her own landscaping business, then she'd put her head back, closed her eyes, and started snoring softly. He was spreading an afghan over her when the headlights of a car turning into the drive lit up the drapes drawn over the living room window. A moment later a key grated in the lock.

"Well, isn't this cosy," Hal said when he saw Maureen on the sofa and Shoe standing in the living room.

Maureen's eyes fluttered open and she sat up. "Hal." She scrubbed her face with the palms of her hands. "You're home?" She stood, clutching the front of her dressing gown.

"And just in time, too," he said. "Or am I too late?" He was wearing what appeared to be new clothes, tan trousers and a polo shirt with the hang tag still attached to the back of the collar. He was carrying a small overnight bag.

"Where the hell have you been?" Maureen demanded. "You've had us all worried sick. Isn't that right, Shoe?"

"Not so worried that it prevented you two from having a little fun, I see. Is my wife as good a shag as Marty, Joe? I wouldn't know. It's been so long since she bestowed her favours on me, I've forgotten."

"Don't be an ass, Hal," Maureen snapped. "Shoe has been a perfect gentleman."

"And gentlemen don't kiss and tell, do they? Well, don't let me interrupt. I hope you'll be very happy together."

"Oh, for god's sake, Hal," Maureen said. "I've got a splitting headache and I'm not in the mood for your foolishness. Nothing happened."

"Fine, nothing happened. Now, if you'll excuse me, I'm going to bed." However, instead of going upstairs, he went into the kitchen and down the basement stairs.

Maureen slumped onto the sofa and put her face in her hands. "Christ, what am I going to do?"

"Get some rest," Shoe said. "I'll call tomorrow."

She raised her head. "Are you leaving? Please don't. It's late. You can sleep on the Hide-A-Bed downstairs. I — I don't want to be alone with him in the morning."

Shoe was also uncomfortable at the thought of being in the house when Hal woke up in the morning. He considered suggesting that if Maureen didn't want to be there when Hal woke up, she could come back to his parents' house with him, but all he said was, "I should go."

"Fine," Maureen replied coldly, and stamped petulantly from the room and up the stairs.

Shoe turned to leave as Hal came into the living room. "Where's Maureen?" he said.

"Upstairs," Shoe said.

"Well, you can let yourself out," Hal said. He started up the stairs.

"Hal," Shoe said.

"What?" Hal stared down at him.

"You're my brother, whether I like it — or you — or not, and at the moment, I don't. Whatever it is you've got yourself into, or whatever's got into you, I'll do whatever I can to help you."

"I appreciate that," Hal said, voice dripping with false sincerity. "There is something you can do for me."

"Name it," Shoe said, with a sinking feeling.

"Get the fuck out of my house." He turned his back and went up the stairs.

Shoe let himself out.

It was almost three o'clock by the time he got back to his parents' house. Despite his fatigue, sleep eluded him. It was an hour before he finally fell asleep, only to awaken some time later from an explicitly carnal dream — of Muriel or Sara or some anonymous succubus conjured up by his imagination — achingly erect and on the brink of orgasm. He lay awake for another hour then, until finally sliding into sleep as the sky outside the high window began to lighten.

He awakened again a few minutes before eight o'clock. The house was silent except for the quiet hum of the central air conditioning system. He lay in bed for another twenty minutes, drifting in and out of sleep, until he heard movement overhead, then got up, showered, dressed, and went upstairs. Rachel was in the kitchen, washing her breakfast dishes.

"What time did you get in last night?" she asked.

"Late," he said, as he took the coffee out of the fridge.

"Any sign of Hal?"

"He got home about one-thirty."

"Where the hell was he?"

"He didn't say. He looked as though he'd been on a bender." He started the coffee maker. "He accused Maureen and me of having an affair."

"Stupid bastard."

"We're not."

"Of course you're not. I meant him."

"I know you did."

He'd made enough coffee for both of them. He poured a cup and took a grateful slug, but it did little to revive him. His longing to go home to Vancouver and Muriel was an almost physical force. He wasn't scheduled to return until Friday, but a telephone call was all it would take to change that. The urge to make that call was almost overwhelming.

"You okay?" Rachel asked.

"Just tired," he replied. He drank more coffee. "What's on your agenda today?"

"There's a children's choir at ten and a kids' Irish dance group at eleven, then we start wrapping things up. Thank god. How 'bout you?"

"Not sure," he said. Involuntarily, he wondered if he should try to talk to Hal, beat some sense into his thick head. The desire to pack up and head for the airport became even stronger. "I'll lend a hand, if you like."

"Sure," she said.

"How are you holding up?" he asked.

"Okay, I guess." She paused, staring at nothing for a moment, then said, "It's weird. Yesterday, we were all but strangers. We'd seen nothing of each other in years and years, but all that changed the moment we started talking. I was looking forward to getting to know her again." Her voice thickened. "Now there's just this aching emptiness when I remember she's dead and that will never happen."

Shoe knew how she felt. He'd felt the same way too

many times in his life. He had no reason to believe he wouldn't again.

Down the hall, a door opened with a click and a soft creak of hinges, followed by shuffling footfalls. Shoe's father came into the kitchen. He looked at Shoe and Rachel, a slightly puzzled expression on his face.

"Mother said she thought she heard Hal's voice," he said. "Is he here?"

"No, Dad," Rachel said. "No one here but us chickens."

chapter forty-two

Hal woke up in increments, as if his brain were coming online bit by bit, neuron by neuron. At some point in the process, he looked at the digital readout of the clock radio on the bedside table. It read 11:22, but it took an inordinately long time for him to comprehend the meaning of the symbols. He also slowly became aware that he was ravenous; he'd eaten hardly anything at all the day before, just a couple of Big Macs after leaving Gord Peters's house with his overnight bag of money. Panic twisted in his guts when he couldn't immediately recall what he'd done with it. Then, with a rush of relief, he remembered that it was locked in his big tool chest in his basement workshop.

He heard voices from downstairs, muted and unintelligible. Who was Maureen talking to? he wondered with a flash of irritation. Had his brother stayed over? Had he and Maureen taken up where they'd left off when Hal had arrived home and interrupted them? He strained to make out the words, then realized it was just one of the inane talk radio shows to which Maureen was addicted.

His stomach rumbled and, with a grunt, he passed wind loudly into the bedcovers. So much for the myth that the noisy ones didn't stink, he thought, as he threw back the covers and got out of bed. Too tired to shower, he dressed in the clothes he'd purchased the day before and went downstairs. Maureen was in the all-white, blindingly bright kitchen, sitting at the table, doing some kind of paperwork. Her face tightened as he entered the room, but she otherwise ignored him.

He went to the refrigerator and yanked the door open. The jars and bottles rattled. He stared at the contents of the shelves, for the most part completely mysterious, no idea what to do next. With the exception of the barbecue, he didn't cook. He didn't have a clue how to turn on the oven, let alone operate the microwave. He could barely manage the toaster.

With a sigh, Maureen stood up. "I'll fix you something. What do you want?"

The martyred tone in her voice raised his hackles. "Forget it," he said. "I'll just have toast."

"Suit yourself," she said. She sat down again and resumed her paperwork.

He found the bread. It was that nasty, brown seedy stuff Maureen preferred, but he couldn't bring himself to ask her if there was any white bread. He put two slices in the toaster and depressed the lever. There were four margarine tubs in the fridge. The first one he opened contained something brown and lumpy. He wasn't sure what it was, but it definitely wasn't margarine. He put it back and opened another. Potato salad. He put that back.

"The butter is in the compartment on the door marked butter," Maureen said dryly, without looking up from her paperwork.

"I thought we used margarine."

"You haven't eaten margarine in years."

"Where'd all the margarine containers come from, then?" he asked, taking a stick of butter from the door compartment.

"Oh, for god's sake, Hal," she said, slapping the file folder closed. "Where do you think? You're not the only person who lives in this house."

Maureen stood, collected her paperwork, and started to leave the room, just as smoke began to rise from the toaster. Gripped by a sudden, uncontrollable rage, Hal grabbed the toaster. Yanking the cord from the wall outlet, he flung the appliance across the kitchen. It glanced off the edge of the doorway to the dining room and ricocheted onto the dining room table, tumbling and scattering crumbs and pieces of blackened toast across the polished surface. It fell onto the parquet floor and broke in half. Maureen stared at him in astonishment. Hal, his hands smarting, scorched by the hot metal of the toaster, turned on the cold water and thrust his hands into the soothing flow.

"That's just perfect, Hal," Maureen said.

"Why are you still here?" he growled, hunched over the sink. His hands were beginning to ache from the cold, but the sting had gone out of the burns.

"Pardon me?" Maureen said.

"Why are you still here? Why didn't you leave with my brother? It's obvious you'd rather be with him. Frankly, I'm in awe of your uncanny ability to land on your feet while spreading your legs." He knew he'd struck a nerve when the colour rose in her face.

"Give me a single good reason why I shouldn't rather be with someone else," she snapped.

He dried his hands with a dish towel. "Would it make any difference?"

"Probably not," she said. "Where did you go the other night? Where have you been?"

He looked at her and wondered what it was that made him want to hurt her, to punish her. "You don't really want to know," he said.

"I wouldn't have asked if I didn't want to know," she replied.

"All right," he said. "If you really must know, after I left my parents' house, I met Dougie Hallam at his bar, where we had a drink or two. Then we went to another bar, where we had more drinks. At some point during the course of the evening, Dougie rounded up a couple of women and we went to a motel somewhere out near the airport. I had sex with one of them, or perhaps both, I don't really remember."

Maureen's face was stony. Red and white blotches mottled her cheeks.

"I woke up yesterday morning," Hal went on, "alone in the motel room. I slept till about noon, bought some clean clothes at a Wal-Mart, dropped by a friend's place, then spent the rest of the day and evening just driving around. To be honest, I wasn't looking forward to coming home."

"No fucking shit," Maureen said, through clenched teeth.

"See, I told you, you didn't want to know."

"You're lying. You're saying those things just to hurt me, aren't you?"

"Maybe so," he agreed with a shrug. "But I'm not lying."

She looked at him as though he were something green and slimy she'd found in the back of the refrigerator. "Was Marty Elias one of the women you had sex with?" she asked, voice barely audible.

"What?" he said, not quite certain he'd heard her correctly.

"You heard me," she said. "Was she?"

He closed his eyes. He tried to visualize the faces of

the women with whom he and Hallam had partied, but they were a featureless blur. One had had dark hair, he remembered, and a tattoo at the base of her spine, but it hadn't been Marty Elias. Had it? No, he was sure of it.

"Well," Maureen said.

"No," he said. "Of course she wasn't. Why would you ask that?"

"She was murdered on Saturday night," Maureen said. "Shoe and Claudia Hahn found her body in the Dells yesterday morning."

Panic seized his heart and squeezed. He couldn't get his breath. He dropped onto a kitchen chair. "Jesus Christ, Maureen," he gasped. "You — you don't think I killed her, do you?"

"I don't know what to think anymore," she said. Tears streaked her cheeks. "*Goddamnit*, Hal."

She stalked from the kitchen, slamming open the sliding door to the back garden, slamming it shut again. Hal watched her depart with what he could only describe as a feeling of total indifference.

chapter forty-three

Shoe tossed the green trash bag into the cargo area of Patty Dutton's white Lincoln Navigator, on top of a stack of folding chairs.

"Thanks," Patty said, smiling at him as he closed the rear door of the Navigator. Her smile was a bit strained, he thought. She turned to Rachel. "Rae, next time I try to talk you into organizing something like this, just shoot me, okay?"

"You got it."

The small park was almost empty, almost back to normal. All that remained, besides a few overflowing trash barrels and recycling bins, was the big rented tent shelter. The rental company would be coming later to dismantle it and cart it away.

"You okay?" Rachel asked Patty.

"Yeah, I'm fine," Patty said, voice flat.

Earlier that morning, while Shoe had been helping Rachel and Patty strike the kitchen shelter, Tim Dutton had come by the park to pick up his solar power gear. The

tension between Dutton and his wife had been so intense
it all but hummed, like an electric motor on overload.

"Goddamned cops," Dutton had complained.
"You'd think they'd have better things to do than hassle
me about Marty. No wonder there are so many unsolved
murders in this city." He turned on Patty. "What the fuck
did you tell them, anyway?"

"Oh, for Christ's sake, Tim," Patty snapped, cheeks
flaming. "Your fucking *girlfriend* was murdered. You seriously think the police are going to accept what your
wife tells them without checking? And don't give me that
wide-eyed innocent look, you two-timing son of a bitch.
You've been screwing her practically since she started
working for you."

Muttering under his breath, Dutton had thrown
the solar gear in the trunk of his Audi and driven away.
Patty's relief had been almost orgasmic.

Patty climbed up into the driver's seat of the Navigator.
"See you later," she said, and drove off. Shoe picked up
the rolled-up kitchen tent and he and Rachel headed toward the park exit. Harvey Wiseman and Claudia Hahn,
walking side by side across the grass, a few feet apart,
each carrying a trash bag and wearing gardening gloves,
were making one last round of the park, collecting trash.
Rachel watched them, a wistful expression on her face.

"Something wrong?" Shoe asked.

She smiled. "No." She shrugged. "I dunno," she
amended. "I feel, well, I'm not quite sure what I feel. It's
not jealousy, precisely, although maybe there's a touch of
envy. Maybe it's regret, opportunities lost, chances not
taken. Not that I blame Doc. Claudia is very beautiful. I
wish them well."

"But … "

"Notwithstanding that both my marriages were
complete disasters, a state of affairs for which I'm not
entirely blameless — I can be a prickly bitch sometimes,

as you well know — I like waking up with a warm body beside me." She laughed. "Maybe I'll get a dog." She waved at Wiseman and Claudia, who both waved back. "Consider yourself lucky, Doc," she said, half to herself. "In more ways than one."

As Shoe was closing the garage door after returning the bulky roll of the kitchen tent to the rafters, Harvey Wiseman and Claudia Hahn walked up the driveway. They stood very close together, not quite holding hands.

"Shoe," Claudia said. "I spoke to Jake Gibson this morning. He'd said be happy to speak to you about Marvin, but it will have to be today. He's taking the train home to Winnipeg this evening. Shall I call him?"

"Yes, please."

Claudia took out her cellphone and made the call. After a brief exchange of pleasantries, she said, "Jake, I'm with Joseph Schumacher now. He'd still like to talk to you about Marvin Cartwright." She paused momentarily, then said, "Hold on." She lowered the phone and said to Shoe, "Would now be all right?"

"Yes, of course."

Claudia raised the phone. "Jake. We'll see you in about half an hour then." She closed her phone. "My car is on the other side of the park."

"We'll take my father's," Shoe said.

Rachel said, "Mind if I tag along?"

"Not at all," Claudia said.

Rachel turned to Doc. "I hope you don't mind if we borrow Claudia for a while."

"What?" Wiseman harrumphed self-consciously. "No, of course not."

Rachel popped onto her toes and kissed his bristly cheek.

Jake Gibson was staying with his daughter and son-in-law in a small, over-furnished townhouse in Etobicoke, just off Islington Avenue, within spitting distance of the ten-lane concrete slash of Highway 401. It had a narrow, walled patio with a retractable awning to provide some protection from the August sun. No breeze reached the patio, however, and in less than two minutes, Shoe's shirt was sticking to the plastic lawn chair.

Jake Gibson's daughter had made a big pitcher of iced tea for them. Emily St. Onge was a wiry, energetic woman in her early fifties, with bright blue eyes and a quick, infectious smile. Her husband, Len St. Onge, was a short, elfin-looking man of about sixty.

"You're Mr. Blizzard!" Rachel piped, when he smiled as he shook her hand.

"Ah, yes," he said, blushing slightly, smile widening. "How kind of you to remember."

"I loved your show," Rachel said. "I watched it every day after school till I was thirteen or fourteen." To a puzzled Claudia Hahn, she explained, "Mr. Blizzard was an old man who lived in a castle of ice at the North Pole with Wally the Walrus and Percy the Penguin, both hand puppets. Marvin Cartwright told us that Percy must have been lost, since penguins were indigenous to the Antarctic, not the Arctic." She turned back to Mr. St. Onge. "Pardon me, but you must be a hundred years old."

"Not quite," Len St. Onge said with a laugh. "They made me up to look older when I was doing the program. You're not the first one to notice that the makeup artist was amazingly prescient. It frightens me sometimes."

Emily and Len St. Onge excused themselves.

"They'll be happy to see the back of me," Jake Gibson said. He was burly and grey, with a ruddy complexion.

"I'm sure they won't," Claudia said with a warm smile. "What time is your train?"

"Six o'clock. Damned nuisance, not being able to drive, but I enjoy travelling by train, especially first class.

I can drink all the wine I want."

"Do you need a drive to Union Station?"

"Thank you, but Em and Len are taking me." He looked at Shoe. His eyes were a soft, mossy green. "So, how can I help you, Mr. Schumacher? It's been thirty-five years since I lost touch with Marvin and my memory isn't what it used to be."

"Anything you could tell us about him would be a help," Shoe said.

"That wouldn't be much, I'm afraid, even if my memories of him were clearer."

"Did he ever mention a woman named Ruth Braithwaite?" Shoe asked.

"Ruth Braithwaite," he said, as if trying the name on for size, seeing how it felt in his mouth. "Let me see. Hmm. No, not that I can recall. Which isn't to say, however, that he never did. Of course, he was an extremely private man. Not easy to get to know. Not easy at all. The only reason we were friends, and I use that term loosely, is that we shared an interest in birds. I was — still am, when I can get out — an enthusiastic birder and Marvin was an expert on the migratory, as well as non-migratory, birds of eastern Canada and the United States. He wrote a number of books on the subject that were required reading. He was less of a birder per se than a scientist, but still a good man to spend time with in the field. Unfortunately, he didn't get to spend as much time as he would have liked in the field, what with having to look after his mother."

"Did he have any other friends, birders or otherwise?"

"He must have had," Gibson said with a nod, "but I didn't know any of them. Except Claudia, of course. And the school librarian. What was her name? Gretchen? Gertrude?"

"Miss Scarlatti was librarian the year I was at the

school," Claudia Hahn said. "Her name was Carmen."

"Yes, of course. Odd woman. Always wore red. Something to do with her name, I suppose. Wrote satirical pornography in her spare time. Or was it pornographic satire? Ended up in Hollywood. Won an Oscar for Best Original Screenplay, I believe."

"Jake, stop it," Claudia admonished.

"It's true, I swear. Marvin may have helped her find a publisher. However, none of this helps Mr. Schumacher, does it? Outside of Miss Scarlatti, Claudia, and myself, I know of no one Marvin might have called friend. He was a very lonely man, I think. His mother, well, I suspect his relationship with her was not an altogether healthy one. He never said anything to me, of course, but I had the impression that she was a very demanding woman."

"Is there any other kind?" Rachel murmured to Claudia.

"There was one thing," Gibson added slowly, thoughtfully. "He showed me a sketch of a bird once. A common robin, I believe it was, but quite a good sketch, as I recall. When I asked him who'd drawn it, he told me it had been done by his fiancée."

"I didn't know he'd been engaged," Claudia said.

"He may have had second thoughts about telling me," Gibson said. "He asked me to keep mum about it. And it was around the time of your, uh ... " He coughed and cleared his throat, clearly embarrassed.

"I understand," Claudia said, placing her hand on his arm.

"Could his fiancée have been Ruth Braithwaite?" Shoe asked.

"He never told me her name," Gibson said. "Or, if he did, I've forgotten it."

"Did he tell you anything about her at all?"

"It was such a long time ago. Let me think." He fell silent, moss green eyes half closed, while Shoe, Rachel, and Claudia waited, sipping iced tea. After a moment, he cleared his throat, and said, "I recall asking him if they'd set the date. He said they had to wait until his mother passed away. She may not have approved. Marvin was close to forty and I think his fiancée was quite a bit younger." He hesitated, then added, "There may have been a child involved."

Claudia sat up straight.

"His fiancée was pregnant?" Rachel said.

"No, I don't believe so," Gibson said. He shook his head. "I'm sorry."

"There *was* a girl Marvin was concerned about," Claudia said suddenly. "I remember him talking to me about a girl he was certain was being abused. He wanted to help her, but he didn't know what to do about it without making matters worse."

"Could he have been talking about Marty Elias?" Shoe asked.

"No," Claudia said. "She was attacked after I was, and I didn't see Marvin again after my rape. The girl he spoke of was a student at the junior high school, I think. A year or two behind you. Her name was Janet or Jane."

"Could it have been Janey?" Shoe asked.

"Yes," Claudia exclaimed. "That was the name. Janey."

"Oh, shit," Rachel said. "Sorry," she added sheepishly.

"It's quite all right," Gibson chuckled. "I was a teacher and a school principal. I've heard it all and used most of it."

"Who was she?" Claudia asked.

Before Shoe could answer, Emily St. Onge came out of the house. "I'm sorry to interrupt," she said. "Dad, it's time we were going."

Shoe stood and shook hands with Mr. Gibson,

thanking him for his time, and his daughter for the iced tea. Claudia hugged Gibson's bulky form, kissed his grizzled cheek, and wished him a safe trip home.

The sun beat down as Shoe, Rachel, and Claudia walked to the car, and he could feel perspiration trickling down his sides. The interior of the car was like a sauna and they drove with all the windows open. After a few minutes of silence, Claudia turned to Shoe.

"So, who was Janey?"

chapter forty-four

Shoe dropped Rachel and Claudia off at his parents' house. His father was standing in the front yard, directing water from a garden hose onto the parched-looking flower gardens that ran along the front of the house on either side of the enclosed porch. The early evening sun cast golden highlights on his snow-white head.

"Taurus running okay?" his father asked.

"It is," Shoe said. "Thanks for letting me use it."

"No problem. It can use the exercise." He flipped the valve on the hose nozzle that shut off the water. "Help me put this away, will you?"

Shoe wound the hose onto the reel attached to the wall beside the outside hydrant, then walked his father to the backyard. Rachel and Claudia were standing by the fence, talking to Harvey Wiseman, who was watering a small stand of greyish, unhappy-looking tomato plants that bore only a few small, green fruit. When he saw Shoe, he shut off the water and lay down the garden hose.

"Do you have any plans for dinner?" he asked.

"No," Shoe said. He assumed he'd eat with his parents. However, it was already after six o'clock and he wanted to talk to Janey Hallam again first.

"Would you like to join Rachel, Claudia, and me? I have a friend who owns a restaurant in Bloor West Village. Best perogies in town. I have reservations for seven o'clock." He looked at his watch. "Which means we should get moving."

"Mum and Dad will be okay on their own," Rachel said.

"There's something I have to do," Shoe said. "Give me the address. I'll join you if I can."

"Are you going to talk to Janey?" Rachel asked, while Wiseman went into the house to get the restaurant address.

"Yes," Shoe said. "Then I want you to introduce me to Ruth Braithwaite."

Wiseman came out of the house and handed Shoe a business card. Shoe said he hoped to see them later.

Although the Hallam house was less than a kilometre away, easy walking distance, he drove, so he could go straight to the restaurant after speaking with Janey. There was a battered blue Pontiac Firebird in the driveway, but no sign of Dougie Hallam's Hummer. Parking on the street, Shoe went up the weed-choked flagstone walk, climbed the cracked concrete steps to the front door, and rang the doorbell. There was no answer. He went round to the side of the house. The property sloped steeply into the ravine, so that at the rear of the house, the basement was at ground level.

Shoe climbed a short flight of painted wood stairs to a side door. He pressed the bell button and waited. After what he thought was a reasonable time, he opened the aluminum screen door and knocked on the inner door. There was no window, just a peephole. And a sturdy lock. He knocked again.

"All right, all right," he heard Janey call. "Keep your shorts on." The lock rattled and the door opened a few inches, the chain lock still in place. Janey peered through the gap, her face in shadow. "Shoe," she said. "Um, look, maybe you could, um, come back later." Her breath was sharp and sweet with the tang of vodka and tonic. "I'm not really up to having company right now."

Her speech was distorted, as if her mouth were frozen after a visit to the dentist. He put his hand on the door, pushed it open as far as the chain lock would allow. She ducked back into the shadows, but not before he saw that her face was damaged.

"What happened?" he asked. "Are you all right?"

"I'm fine," she said. "I had an accident, that's all."

He didn't believe her. She looked as though she'd been beaten. "Janey, open the door."

"No. Shoe, go away. Please."

"Is there someone with you?" he asked, keeping his voice low.

She shook her head. "No."

"Then let me in, Janey. I'm not leaving until I know you're all right."

"I don't suppose you'd take my word for it."

When he didn't reply, she sighed, released the chain lock, and turned away. Shoe opened the door and stepped onto the landing midway between the half-flight of stairs down to the basement and the half-flight up to the main floor; the Hallam house was almost identical in layout to his parents' house. Janey descended. Shoe closed the door and followed her down into the kitchen of her apartment. She closed and locked the door at the bottom of the stairs, then went though the kitchen into the living room.

The living room was small and dark, the drapes drawn and the lights off. The air smelled fusty, as though something had died there a long time ago. "Do you mind if I open the drapes and a window?" Shoe asked. "Let in some light and air?"

"Sure, go ahead," she replied disinterestedly, still standing with her back to him.

He opened the drapes, flooding the room with northern light, tinged green from the thick woods behind the house. Unlatching a window, he cranked it open. The outside air was still hot, but fresher than that of the room, despite the pall of pollution trapped over the city.

He turned to Janey. Her back was to him, shoulders hunched, as if bracing herself for a blow from behind. He went to her, tread silent on the carpet. She flinched as he put his hands on her shoulders. Through the fabric of her T-shirt, the muscles of her shoulders were hard, more like stone than flesh. She didn't resist as he turned her to toward him.

A white-hot point of anger ignited within him. Her lower lip was split, her left eye was blackened and swollen almost shut, and her left cheekbone was red and raw. "Did Dougie do this to you?"

She tried to speak, but no words came. She gave up and nodded mutely, not looking at him. Tears spilled from her eyes, rolled down her bruised cheeks. Involuntarily, his hands tightened on her shoulders. She twisted away.

"Where is he?" Shoe asked roughly.

"I don't know." She moved away from him, as if seeking shadow, shelter from the light. "I don't care."

He unclenched his jaw. "Get your purse," he said.

"What?"

"I'm taking you to the hospital."

She shook her head. "I don't need to go to the hospital."

"You could have a cracked cheekbone," he said.

She looked at him, arms crossed below her breasts, hugging herself. Her cheeks were shiny with tears. "You don't understand," she said, turning away from him. "He didn't just beat me up. He — he raped me." The words ground from her, as if her throat were filled with broken glass.

The anger within him burned brighter and hotter. "Then it's more important than ever that you go to the hospital, so they can run a rape kit and document your injuries for the police. Then I'll take you to a hotel. Anywhere you want. I'll pay for it. You can't stay here. Go pack some things. I'll wait."

"I'm — I'm not worth all the trouble."

"Of course you are, Janey," he said. His anger seethed, threatening to consume him. He consciously relaxed, unclenched his fists, loosened his shoulders, slowed his breathing. "Don't ever let anyone tell you otherwise." His voice was strained, the tone harsher than he'd intended. "This isn't the first time he's raped you, is it?" he said.

She shook her head. "The first time was when I was ten," she said, so quietly he could barely hear her. "Freddy too."

The anger and the guilt were a physical pain in the centre of his chest. "How long?" he asked, voice tight and rasping.

"Freddy stopped when I was sixteen. Dougie didn't stop till — till Freddy and my mother were killed."

"Marvin Cartwright knew about it, didn't he?"

"Yes."

"Was he sexually abusing you?"

"No. No. He — he wasn't — he didn't." She raised her eyes and looked at him. "He tried to help me. He wanted to go to the police, but I begged him not to. I was too scared. And ashamed. I thought it was my fault. That's what my mother always told me, that it was my fault. She — she was having sex with Dougie." She turned away. "Marvin promised to take me with him when he left. He couldn't leave till his mother died, he said, but it wouldn't be long. She was very sick. But when she died, he left without me." She shuddered and a sob scraped from her throat like a rasp on steel. "It's my fault that he had to go away. Maybe if I'd told the truth about … "

Her voice trailed off. She would have fallen if Shoe hadn't caught her, held her, then lowered her onto the sofa. She clutched at his arm.

"How did he find out?" Shoe asked. "Did you tell him?" *Why didn't you tell me?* he wanted to ask.

"No, I didn't tell anyone. He caught me fixing up my little cave in the woods. You know, where we had sex the first time?"

Shoe nodded, not trusting his voice.

"I made him promise not to tell anyone. I told him if he kept it a secret, I'd let him have sex with me. He got angry — I didn't understand why at the time. I thought all men were like Freddy and Dougie. Until Marvin — and you." She looked up at him. "You liked me a little, didn't you? It wasn't just the sex, was it?"

"I liked you a lot," Shoe said. "And it wasn't just the sex." Had he loved her? He wasn't sure. Probably. It didn't matter. He'd cared for her. And did still. "Why didn't you run away?" he asked.

"I did," she said. "But Freddy always somehow found me and dragged me home again. He'd punish me, too. Eventually, I stopped trying."

"Besides Marvin Cartwright, did anyone else know?"

She looked at him for a long time, then averted her eyes before replying. "Freddy said if I ever told anyone, he'd kill them, then he'd kill me. That's why I never wanted anyone to know about you and me. I was afraid they'd think you knew."

"Joey knew, didn't he?" Shoe said. When she looked at him, he knew the answer. "When did you tell him?"

"You'd just started university," she said quietly. "He was visiting his parents and I ran into him somewhere. We got a little stoned one night and I told him. I'm not sure why. He wanted to take me away with him, but ... " She shrugged and picked up a glass from the coffee table. It was empty. She put it back down. "Except for Dougie and Freddy, you were the only one I'd ever done it with till — till later. Till Joey. All those other boys I went out with after we broke up, I never had sex with any of them."

Which explained why none of them lasted more than a week or two, Shoe thought. "You don't have to tell me any more," he said. "Let's get you out of here. You need to see a doctor."

"I don't need a doctor. It's not like I haven't been through this before." She kneaded her lacerated cheek with her fingertips. "Nothing's broken."

"It's the best way to document your injuries for the police."

"I'm not going to the police. What can they do?"

"They can arrest him," he said. "Put him in jail." He knew as he said it that he was being naive. Even if the police arrested Hallam and charged him with assault or rape, how long could they hold him? He'd be out on bail in a day or two, perhaps even on his own recognizance, upstanding member of the community that he was. Then what? Could the police protect her? Could he? He'd tried protecting Janey from her stepbrother once before, and it had only made it worse for her.

"I'll be all right," Janey said.

"I can't leave you here alone," he said.

"Don't worry about me. I let my guard down with him. It won't happen again. Believe me. You're a sweet guy, Shoe. Always were. Me? Well, you want to know what I did last night after you left the pub?"

"I don't care what you did. It doesn't matter."

"The kind of person I am, you don't want anything

to do with someone like me." She stood and went into the kitchen alcove. "Stop trying to be the hero," she said as she opened the freezer compartment of the refrigerator and took out a bottle of vodka.

"I stopped trying to be your hero a long time ago, Janey," he said.

Scooping ice from a bin into a glass, she added a generous splash of vodka, then put the bottle back in the freezer.

"I'm just trying to save your life," Shoe said. "The next time, he might kill you."

She walked to the sofa and sat down heavily. "There isn't going to be a next time," she said. "If he comes near me again, I'm going to kill him. Tell him that the next time you see him."

The next time he saw Dougie Hallam, Shoe thought coldly, he might kill him himself.

"Pack some clothes," he said. "And whatever else you'll need for the next few days. I can't stay with you and I'm not leaving you here alone. I'll check you into a hotel until we can make other arrangements. Don't bother arguing. You're coming with me if I have to drag you."

"You're bluffing," she said.

"Am I?" He pointed toward the door to another room. "Is that the bedroom?" Without waiting for an answer, he opened the door and went through into her bedroom.

"Hey," she protested, struggling to her feet and following him.

On a chest of drawers a small TV flickered silently. The queen-sized bed was unmade. Clothing was draped over the back of a chair. The louvred doors to the closet were open. There was a suitcase on the top shelf. He took it down and put it on the bed.

"Will you pack, or shall I do it for you?" he asked,

opening the suitcase. He went to the chest of drawers, opened the top drawer, and began to transfer handfuls of underwear and brassieres into the suitcase.

"All right, all right," she said, shouldering him aside. "Get out while I shower and change."

He went into the other room. He wasn't going to make it to dinner with Rachel, Claudia, and Wiseman after all. He took out the card Wiseman had given him and used Janey's phone to call the restaurant. The woman who answered had an eastern European accent. She said she'd relay his apologies to Mr. Wiseman and his guests.

Janey came out of the bedroom fifteen minutes later. She'd changed into a short T-shirt and snug-fitting jeans that rode low on her slim hips, revealing her flat, muscular belly. Shoe was struck by the apparent contradiction between her hard-bodied physique and hard-as-nails attitude and her almost childlike vulnerability. Her bleached white blonde hair was still wet from the shower, and she had applied makeup in an attempt to cover the bruises on her face. She had a small leather backpack slung over her shoulder. The suitcase was on the bed, closed.

"Okay, let's go." The drink she had fixed was on the coffee table. She picked it up. "For the road," she said, and downed it.

"Have you eaten today?" he asked.

"It hurts to eat," she said.

"You should eat," he said.

"Damnit, Shoe. I didn't agree to go with you just so you could mother me." He was somewhat surprised she had agreed to go with him at all. She put her hand on his arm. Her fingers were cool against his skin. "Sorry," she said.

He retrieved the suitcase from the bedroom and they went up the stairs into the bright slanting sunlight.

"What about my car?" she asked as he put her suit-

322   *Michael Blair*

case into the back seat of the Taurus.

"I don't think you're in any condition to drive. We can come back and pick it up later."

"Okay, fine," she said petulantly. She climbed into the Taurus.

chapter forty-five

It was almost eight o'clock by the time Shoe checked Janey into the Days Hotel on Wilson under his own name, booking the room for a week. He carried her suitcase up to the room. Inside, he said, "I wish you'd change your mind about the hospital and the police," even though he knew it was too late to run a rape kit. She'd taken at least one shower since her stepbrother had raped her, probably more, effectively washing away any DNA or trace evidence.

"Do me a favour," she said, surveying the room. "Forget it, all right? Please."

"It's not that easy," he said. He watched her open the mini-bar, examine the contents, close it, then sit on the edge of the single, king-sized bed and bounce gently, testing it. "You said Dougie hadn't touched you since Freddy and your mother died. What happened to set him off?"

"I dunno. Most of the time, he's predictable as gravity, but ... " She shrugged. "It was probably my own damned fault. I should never have moved into that house, except I couldn't afford to live anywhere else. Bankruptcy didn't erase all my debts and neither of my real jobs pays that well. The band management gig is actually costing me money."

"It wasn't your fault, Janey," Shoe said.

"But I should've known better than to stay there after the first time he came down to complain about my stereo being too loud. He never tried anything, but I could see what was on his mind."

"It wasn't your fault," Shoe said again. "Any more than it was when you were ten years old."

"Can we change the subject?"

"Let's get you something to eat," Shoe said.

She looked at herself in the mirror over the telephone desk, touching her bruised face. "I'm not going anywhere looking like this."

"We'll order," he said. "Or pick something up. We passed a noodle place on the way here. You should be able to eat noodles without too much trouble."

"I am kind of hungry," she admitted.

He left her in the room and drove to the noodle shop, where he bought an order of noodles in a half-litre plastic tub, plus two spring rolls and sauce. When he returned to the hotel, Janey was on the bed, fast asleep, wearing just her T-shirt and panties, revealing darkening, hand-shaped bruises on her upper thighs. There were two empty vodka miniatures and a can of tonic on the bedside table. Shoe put the noodles and spring rolls in the mini-bar refrigerator. He spread the extra blanket from the closet over her, then wrote her a note that included his parents' telephone number and left it on the desk with the key card. He made sure the door was locked behind him.

Shoe drove to Hallam's bar. Hallam's Hummer wasn't in either the front or rear parking area, but he went into the bar anyway. A different bartender was on duty, a doughy-faced man with an ill-fitting hairpiece and dentures that wobbled in his mouth when he spoke. He claimed he hadn't seen Hallam since shortly after opening up that morning, nor did he know where he was, or when he would return. He'd be happy to pass on a message, however.

"Tell him Joe Shoe is looking for him," Shoe said.

"Certainly, sir. That would be yourself then, would it, sir?"

"It would," Shoe replied.

On the chance that Hallam might take a woman to the Dells before dark, Shoe drove east on Sheppard Avenue. Just before Keele, Sheppard descended into Black Creek ravine, then climbed out again. The entrance to the Dells was at the bottom of the hollow, next to the short bridge under which Black Creek ran. He turned right onto the access road and drove through the open gate.

In the evening of the final day of the civic holiday weekend, there were still a lot of people in the park: picnic groups of every size and demographic makeup; dozens of cyclists and walkers, many with dogs; kids kicking soccer balls and flying kites; oil-basted sun worshippers who had evidently never heard of skin cancer taking in the last slanting rays of the setting sun; couples entwined on blankets, or under them. He did not find Hallam's Hummer.

A heavy-set black man in coveralls was removing trash bags from the roadside bins and throwing them into the back of a green John Deere utility vehicle. Shoe pulled off onto the shoulder of the access road, got out of the car, and walked back to him.

"You can't park there," the man said, as he put a fresh trash bag in the bin.

"I have a couple of questions for you," Shoe said.

"What now?"

If he believed Shoe was with the police, Shoe wasn't

going to correct his misapprehension. "Do you know a man named Douglas Hallam?" he asked.

"Yeah, I guess you could say I know him. Sort of. What about him?"

"Have you seen him?"

"Today, you mean? No."

"Are you aware that he has keys to the park gate and that he brings women to the park at night in his truck?"

"Yeah," the man replied warily. "I might be."

"Do you know he has keys to the gate or don't you?"

"Okay, so he's got keys. He didn't get them from me."

"When was the last time you saw him?"

"In the park, you mean? Not in a while."

"Did you see him Thursday night?"

"The night that guy was killed in the woods, you mean? No. Like I told the other detectives, when I locked up that night, the guy who died, his car was in the big lot, along with another car. The other car was gone in the morning. Someone must've let it out. It wasn't me. I guess it could've been Mr. Hallam, but I didn't see him that night."

"Could it have been Hallam driving the other car?"

"Could've been, sure, but it wasn't him I saw talking to the dead guy. Around nine. He was still alive then, o' course," he added with an impish smile. "It was another big guy. Maybe he was driving the other car."

"Can you describe him?"

"Six foot and a bit. Fat. Fifty, fifty-five. Dark grey hair. I think he was wearing glasses."

It was identical to the description Syd the bartender had given him of the man who'd left the bar with Dougie Hallam on Saturday night. While the description fit Hal, as in the bar, it fit a good many of the men in the park that evening as well.

"What kind of car was it?" Shoe asked.

"Toyota, maybe a Corolla or a Camry. Beige or grey."

"It wasn't a silver Lexus?"

"No, sir."

"Did you tell the police about the other car and the man you saw talking to Cartwright?" Shoe asked.

The man's eyes narrowed. "I thought you was the police."

"Whatever gave you that idea?"

"Gee, I dunno. I guess you did. Anyway, yeah, I told them about seeing the fat guy and the car. Gave them the first three numbers of the licence plate, too."

"Did you tell them that Hallam had keys to the gate?"

He shook his head. "I didn't remember about that till you mentioned it. I don't want trouble with that guy, though."

Shoe thanked him for his help, got into the Taurus, and drove back to his parents' house to grab something to eat before going back to the hotel to check on Janey.

chapter forty-six

On his way to his parents' house, Shoe drove past the Hallam house to see if Hallam had returned. Janey's blue Firebird sat alone in the fading light. When he got to his parent's house, Hal's silver Lexus was parked in the driveway, behind Rachel's yellow Beetle, leaving no room for the Taurus. Shoe was tempted to just keep driving, go somewhere, anywhere, anything to avoid facing his brother. He knew he'd have to face him sooner or later, so he parked on the street and went into the house. His parents were in the kitchen, his mother at the table, headphones on, listening to a CD. His father was perched on a tall stool at the sink, washing dishes.

"Hal's here?" Shoe asked.

"Downstairs," his father said, without looking up from the pot he was scrubbing.

Shoe went down to the basement. Hal was in the recreation room, slouched on his spine on the old sofa, head laid back, but eyes open, staring at the ceiling. At the sound of Shoe's tread on the stairs, he rolled his head to the side without raising it from the sofa.

"Where've you been?" he asked.

"Checking Janey Hallam into a hotel."

"Eh?" Hal grunted as he sat up.

"Dougie beat her up," Shoe said.

"Is that right? Well, wouldn't be the first time, would it? You were comforting her, were you? You're good at that, aren't you? Comforting women?"

"Is there something you want to see me about?" Shoe asked wearily.

Hal heaved himself to his feet with an effort that left him momentarily breathless. "I want to know what's going on between you and Maureen."

Shoe was not completely successful in suppressing a sigh of exasperation. "There's nothing going on between me and Maureen."

"I don't believe you."

"Nevertheless, it's true."

"She's left me, you son of a bitch," Hal shouted, as he swung at Shoe.

Shoe stepped out of the way. Hal staggered off balance and would have fallen if Shoe hadn't reached out and taken his arm. Hal wrenched himself free of Shoe's grasp, lost his balance, and fell heavily.

"Hal, I'm sorry," Shoe said, offering his brother his hand.

Hal ignored Shoe's hand, hauled himself to his feet, face red and breathing heavily. He wiped spittle from his lips. "You bastard," he said.

"Should I have let you hit me?" Shoe said. "All right. Go ahead, hit me, if it will make you feel better."

He didn't expect Hal to take him up on the offer, but Hal surprised him and hit him with a roundhouse right that caught him on cheek. Hal had never been quick, however, and Shoe had time to loosen up and let his neck and shoulders rotate with the blow. Nevertheless, it knocked him back a step.

"Feel better?" Shoe asked, touching his cheek. His fingers came away bloody; Hal's signet ring, worn on his right hand, had cut him.

"No," Hal said. "I guess not." He gestured to the cut on Shoe's cheek. "Sorry about that." He opened and closed his fist a couple of times. His knuckles were reddened and already beginning to swell.

"You should probably put some ice on that," Shoe said.

"Yeah," Hal agreed, flexing his fist.

Shoe regarded his brother for a moment.

"What?" Hal said.

"The police may have a witness that places someone answering your description in the Dells the night Marvin Cartwright was killed."

Hal did not look up from examining his swelling knuckles. "A witness? Who?"

"The park attendant."

"Well, he's either mistaken or lying. I was in my office till past midnight, then took the 12:43 train to Clarkson Station. It got in about 1:15 and I got home about 1:30." He took his wallet from his back pocket. "Would you like to see my cancelled multi-pass?" He removed a length of card stock about the size of two business cards end to end and held it out to Shoe. "Go ahead," Hal said, thrusting the ticket toward Shoe. "Check the cancellation if you don't believe me."

"That's not necessary, Hal," Shoe said. "I believe you."

"Right," Hal said skeptically.

Shoe regarded his brother for a moment, then turned and started toward the bedroom. He stopped.

"Now what?" Hal said.

"Did you know that Dougie and his father had been

sexually abusing Janey since she was ten?" Shoe said.

Hal was taken aback. "What? Did she tell you that I did?"

"No," Shoe said. "Did you?"

"Dougie used to brag about how he got her to show him her tits or jerk him off, but I figured it was bull, just Dougie being Dougie. Anyway, how do you know she wasn't a willing participant?"

"She was just a child," Shoe said, clamping down on his anger.

"You were having sex with her when she was thirteen," Hal said. "Correct me if I'm wrong, but doesn't that make you guilty of statutory rape?" Hal waved away Shoe's reply. "You know she came onto me once, eh? Let me cop a good feel, then kneed me in the nuts. She was a slut, just like her mother. Everyone knew it but you. Okay, now you want to hit me, don't you?"

"I don't want to hit you, Hal," Shoe said. He wasn't being entirely truthful.

"Well, if there's nothing else," Hal said. He started toward the stairs.

"Have you heard about Marty Elias?" Shoe said.

Hal stopped and turned. "Yeah," he said. "Maureen told me. The police have any idea who did it?"

"If they do, they haven't told me," Shoe said.

"She hung out with a pretty rough crowd when she was younger. Maybe she still did."

"Maybe," Shoe said.

"Anyway ... " Hal said. He did not finish the thought, shrugged, and started up the stairs.

"Hal?"

Hal stopped on the stairs, but he did not turn. "What?"

"I want you to know that my offer still stands," Shoe said.

"What offer is that?" Hal said, still looking straight

ahead.

"If there's anything I can do to help you out of whatever trouble you're in, you only have to ask."

"But that's the problem, isn't it?"

"What is?"

"Asking." He continued up the stairs, breathing hard and using the banister to pull himself up. Shoe hoped he wouldn't have a heart attack.

Shoe fixed himself a sandwich, washed up, then made his apologies to his parents and drove to the Days Hotel on Wilson.

chapter forty-seven

"Hello, Ruth," Rachel said, leaning close to the gap in the door. All she could see was a narrow slice of the woman's face, a single washed-out blue eye, curve of cheekbone, the merest fraction of her mouth. "Do you remember me? We spoke yesterday, about Marvin Cartwright." If Ruth remembered, she gave no sign. "This is my friend Claudia," she added, moving aside so Ruth could see Claudia.

"Hello, Ruth," Claudia said.

Although Joe had told Rachel he wanted to talk to Ruth, Rachel hadn't believed Ruth would answer the door if he were with her. Besides, she hadn't seen him since he'd gone to talk to Janey. She'd tried to talk Claudia out of coming, but as darkness gathered in the woods round the gloomy old house, she was grateful for the company. She'd make it up to Doc somehow.

"What do you want?" Ruth asked, voice thin and uncertain.

"We'd like to talk to you and your sisters," Rachel said.

"We're not allowed to have visitors," Ruth said.

"Yes, I know," Rachel said. "Your father will be angry. But do you always do what your father tells you? You don't, do you? You went into the woods, didn't you, even though your father told you not to?"

"I like to draw."

"And you met Marvin there too, didn't you?"

"Marvin."

"Did you meet him on Thursday night, Ruth?"

Ruth's expression grew troubled. "I stopped going into the woods after Father made Marvin go away."

"We don't want to get you into trouble," Rachel said. "But we'd like to talk to you and your sisters about Marvin."

"Marvin is my friend, not theirs."

"Okay," Rachel said. "But we'd like to talk to them too, if that's all right. I'm afraid we have some bad news." It was unlikely Ruth knew that Marvin was dead. Rachel wasn't sure if Ruth even knew that her parents were dead.

Ruth's face disappeared from the gap, but the door remained open. Rachel waited for Ruth to come back. After half a minute, when Ruth still hadn't returned, she looked at Claudia. The older woman shrugged. Cautiously, Rachel pushed the door open. There was no chain lock, and the door swung open with a creak of corroded hinges. Rachel leaned into the vestibule. It was about six feet square and unlighted. Three stairs led up to the main floor.

"Ruth?" Rachel called up the stairs. There was no answer. She looked at Claudia again.

"In for a penny … ?" Claudia said.

Rachel climbed the stairs from the vestibule into the front hall, Claudia behind her. She hesitated on the threshold of the living room, waiting for her eyes to adjust to the gloom. As they did, a figure materialized a few feet away, standing in the middle of the room, wrapped in shadow. Ruth's eyes were bright and wide with fear as she watched Rachel and Claudia enter the room.

"It's all right," Rachel said.

"He'll be angry," Ruth whispered.

"Who?" Rachel asked. "Who'll be angry?"

Ruth shook her head as her fingers clutched at the front of the thin, tattered housecoat that hung to her ankles and looked as though it hadn't been washed in a long time. She had shapeless cloth slippers on her feet, frayed and holed at the toes. Rachel was struck by the youthful smoothness of her complexion and the apparent robustness of her figure beneath the housecoat. She wasn't at all the frail elderly waif Rachel had imagined her to be. Still, it was hard to believe that she was a year or two younger than Claudia Hahn.

Rachel's nose itched. The house smelled of dust, mouldy wallpaper, mildewed carpets, unwashed clothing, and stale cooking oil. The only illumination in the living room was provided by the dying evening light that leaked through rents in the heavy brocaded drapes drawn tight across the front windows. It was like being in a cave, albeit one furnished from the Sears catalogue, circa 1945. None of the furnishings seemed more recent, and many were older. There was no television, but a big multi-band console radio dating from the thirties stood against the wall beside the entrance to the dark dining room. The living room set, a long sofa and two matching easy chairs, was Victorian drab, seat cushions stained and sagging. Next to the empty brick fireplace sat a big nineteenth-century oak rolltop desk that would fetch $2,000 or $3,000 in any antique store in the city. On the other side of the fireplace stood a tall, glass-fronted sectional bookcase, crowded with books, most of which appeared to be leather-bound, titled in ornate, gold-leaf lettering. Religious texts, Rachel supposed.

"Ruth, where are your sisters?" she asked.

"Gone," Ruth replied.

"Gone where?"

"With Mother and Father." Rachel wondered if that meant they too were dead. "To Africa," Ruth added, unhelpfully.

The gloom deepened. Ruth's slippers whispered as she crossed the carpet to the floor lamp by the end of the sofa. When she turned it on, the gloom was dispelled only somewhat by the low-wattage bulb.

"Rachel," Claudia Hahn said quietly. She gestured toward a table in the front hall, by the doorway to the kitchen. "Those seem a little out of place in this room, don't you think?"

Rachel looked closer. "They certainly do," she said. She picked up the stack of three unlabelled recordable DVDs in slim jewel cases.

With a suddenness that caught Rachel by surprise, Ruth leapt forward, snatched the discs from Rachel's hand, and fled down the dark hall toward the back of the house. Rachel hesitated, then followed, Claudia on her heels, past darkened bedrooms. Suddenly, dazzlingly bright light blazed from the room at the end of the hall. Rachel blinked, eyes watering. When she could see again, she and Claudia went into the room. They found Ruth standing by a king-sized bed surrounded by powerful lights and video cameras on heavy tripods. The bed was covered with a blue fitted sheet, stained and rumpled and strewn with sex toys of every size and description: vibrators and dildos and bizarre objects whose function Rachel did not want to guess at. There were three DVD recorders and small colour TV screens in a rack against the wall, next to a desk on which sat a black IBM computer with a flat LCD monitor, a round webcam clipped to the upper edge. On the front of the computer, a light glowed, indicating that it was running. LEDs glowed on the front of a high-speed cable modem and a wireless router.

"My god," Claudia Hahn said.

Rachel looked at Ruth. In the cruelly bright light, she could see bruises on her face and neck, and what appeared to be dried blood on her housecoat.

"You shouldn't be here," Ruth said. "He'll be very angry."

"Who, Ruth?" Claudia said. "Who will be angry?"

She didn't answer. Nor did she resist when Rachel reached out and took the discs from her hand.

"I don't think I want to see what's on that disc," Claudia said, as Rachel went to the rack of video machines and turned one of them on. One of the little TVs also came to life, showing a blank blue screen. "In fact, I'm bloody certain I don't want to see what's on that disc," Claudia added as Rachel pressed the button that opened the disc drawer of the machine.

chapter forty-eight

Janey opened the door in her underwear, pale and bleary-eyed.

"I was asleep," she said, as she climbed onto the bed and pulled the covers over her bare legs. The air conditioning was turned up high, and the room was chilly. "Where'd you go, anyway?" she asked. The empty plastic tub from the noodle place was on the bedside table, along with another empty miniature of vodka and can of tonic. The television flickered quietly on a music video channel.

Shoe told her, then said, "Earlier you said it was your fault Cartwright went away? What did you mean by 'If I'd told the truth'? Told the truth about what?" She didn't answer and she wouldn't look at him. "Janey?"

"I don't want to talk about it." She pointed the remote control at the television and raised the volume. A skinny white man in his twenties, wearing an oversized sports jersey and a baseball cap on sideways, intoned unintelligible lyrics while the music thudded and sweat-shiny, scantily-clad, and surgically-enhanced women writhed and gyrated against him.

"Did Freddy or Dougie know that Marvin knew they were sexually abusing you? Did they threaten to come after him if he took you with him? Is that why he left without you?"

She didn't answer. She just sat on the bed, head down, back bent. Shoe took the remote from her hand and turned off the television.

"Hey."

"Look at me, Janey."

She shook her head, refusing to look up. He sat down beside her on the bed. Perhaps a little shock therapy was in order, he thought.

"Did you kill Marvin Cartwright, Janey? Were you lying to me about being in Hamilton with your band? Did you meet him in the Dells last Thursday night and kill him because he didn't take you with him when he left?"

"No," she said, almost inaudibly, hugging herself. There were goosebumps on her arms.

"Tell me how it was your fault he left, then."

"Because I knew … " She paused. Shoe waited, afraid that if he spoke, she might not go on. After a moment, she said, "They told me they'd kill me if I ever told. And kill whoever I told. They would have, too, so I never said anything. To anyone. I just let everyone think it was Marvin who'd raped Daphne, your teacher, and killed that black girl." She looked at him. "Nice, eh?"

"You were just a kid," Shoe said.

"I stopped being a kid the first time I let Dougie fuck me," she said harshly.

"He raped you," Shoe said. Her breathing hitched. He gathered her into his arms. "It's not the same thing. It's not your fault."

He held her as she sobbed against his chest. It wasn't long, though, before she abruptly pushed him away and sat up. "Christ, I hate weepy women," she said, blotting her eyes with the corner of the bedsheet. Her makeup left dark smudges on the sheet.

"Was it Freddy or Dougie?" Shoe asked when she'd regained her composure.

"Dougie," she said.

"Did your mother or stepfather know?"

She took a deep, unsteady breath. "They both knew. They lied to the police, told them Dougie was away on business with Freddy when Daphne and the teacher were raped. Freddy was actually proud of him. Can you believe that? Then he killed the black girl. Freddy beat the crap out of him for being so stupid, then told him he'd kill him if he didn't stop. I guess he figured Dougie would eventually get caught and he didn't want the heat. He told him he'd just have to be satisfied with me and my mother. Dougie's lucky Freddy didn't just kill him and bury him in the Dells. I wish he had," she added.

Shoe had always considered himself to be fairly tough-minded, but felt sick with anger and self-recrimination. His voice was hoarse when he said, "I'm so sorry I was too stupid to figure out what was happening to you, Janey."

"You were just a kid too," Janey said. "In some ways more of a kid than me. Anyway, what could you have done?" She threw back the covers and swung her legs off the bed. Her colour wasn't good. "Excuse me a minute." She fled into the bathroom and closed the door.

He sat on the side of the bed, elbows on his knees, scrubbing his face with the palms of his hands. Through the bathroom door vents, he could hear Janey being sick. What could he have done? she'd asked. The answer was easy. More than likely he'd have tried his best to kill Dougie and his father, even if it meant going to prison. He'd have considered it a fair exchange.

Janey came out of the bathroom. Her colour had

improved, but she looked slack and de-energized. She slumped onto the bed beside him, pressing her shoulder against his, taking his left hand in both of hers, held it tight in her lap. The flesh of her thigh was cool against his wrist.

"Are you up to answering a couple more questions?" he asked.

"Sure. Why not? How much worse can it get?"

"Was it Dougie who molested Marty?"

Janey shook her head. "No. That time Dougie and Freddy really were away somewhere, fencing the stuff they stole, I suppose."

"Do you know who it was? Could it have been Joey?"

"Joey? Maybe. I don't know."

"After Freddy beat him up for killing Elizabeth Kinney," Shoe said, forcing the words out, "was he 'satisfied' with raping you and your mother?"

"For a while," Janey said. Her hands were cold.

"I don't remember any more rapes with his MO in the Dells after Elizabeth Kinney," Shoe said.

"My memories of that time are pretty mixed-up," she said. "Like when you wake up from a bad dream, you know, and it's hard to tell what's real and what was part of the dream. There was someone else, I think, before Daphne. Besides me and my mother, I mean. Whoever she was, she never reported it, but after Freddy and my mother were killed, I think Dougie raped her again. More than once."

"Do you know who she was?" Shoe asked, an icy coldness growing within him.

"No," Janey said. "For all I know, she doesn't exist, that they really are my own memories, projected onto an imaginary person because I just can't handle them. Or maybe it's what one of my shrinks called confabulation, when you make up false memories to fill in the blanks. A lot of my childhood is like that. Blank."

"I don't think she's imaginary at all," Shoe said. "I'm afraid she may be all too real."

"Then god help her," Janey whispered.

chapter forty-nine

After watching a few seconds of the video recording, Rachel turned off the DVD machine. Bile burned in the back of her throat. Although he had been wearing a ridiculous Lone Ranger mask, there was no doubt in her mind that the man in the video with Ruth was Dougie Hallam.

"We have to get her away from here," Claudia said.

"Ruth," Rachel said. Ruth seemed not to hear, stood staring mutely at the bed. "Ruth," Rachel said again. "Where are your sisters? Where are Naomi and Judith?"

"Gone," Ruth said. "To Africa. With Mother and Father."

"No, Ruth," Rachel said sternly. "Your sisters are not with your parents in Africa." She took a breath. "Your parents are dead, Ruth," she said gently.

"Mother and Father are dead."

"Yes, Ruth. That's right. Your mother and father

died in Africa a long time ago. You and your sisters have lived here alone for thirty years. Where are your sisters, Ruth? Are they here?"

"Naomi and Judith are with Jesus," Ruth said, with matter-of-fact calmness. "That's what he said. They are with Mother and Father and Jesus. In Africa."

"Bloody hell," Claudia whispered.

"Who?" Rachel asked. "Who told you Naomi and Judith were with Jesus, Ruth?"

"The man," Ruth said.

"What man? The man who hurts you? The man who makes you do things with him on that bed? Did he tell you your sisters were with Jesus and your parents?"

"He sent them to be with Jesus because they were bad and wouldn't do what they were told."

"Bloody hell," Claudia said again, louder.

Rachel shivered, but it wasn't from cold.

"Ruth," she said sternly. She gripped Ruth's arm. The woman looked at her, eyes wide. "Where are they, Ruth? Where did he put them?"

Ruth stared at Rachel, expression flat, devoid of any emotion, or even intelligence, it seemed. When Rachel released her arm, Ruth turned and left the bedroom, shuffling down the hall toward the dark living room. Rachel and Claudia exchanged looks, then followed. Ruth went into the kitchen, then proceeded down the back stairs to the basement. There was a door at the bottom of the basement stairs. Ruth opened it. Rachel blinked as bright light spilled into the stairwell. A heavy, damp aroma filled her nostrils. Rachel followed Ruth through the doorway, to find herself at the edge of a small forest of tall plants in big plastic pots. The plants gleamed a lustrous green under clusters of glaring 150-watt bulbs.

"Is this what I think it is?" Claudia said from behind her.

"If you think it's a marijuana grow-op," Rachel said,

perspiring in the stifling heat and humidity, "then, yes, it's exactly what you think it is."

Once the basement may have been finished like the basement in her parents' home, but now the floor was painted concrete, scabbed and wet, and the walls had been stripped to the studs and lined with heavy-duty polyethylene plastic. Similarly, the ceiling was lined with reflective Mylar plastic stapled to the joists. A sprinkler system constructed of black PVC tubing was suspended from the ceiling, sprinkler heads hanging below the lights. The PVC tubing was connected to a complex system of valves and what appeared to be a timing device installed over the deep concrete double sink against the wall. Bottles and bags of garden fertilizer were stacked on the floor by the sink. An old clothes washer stood next to the sink, enamel streaked with rust and ugly green stains.

"Ruth," Rachel said. "Why did you bring us here?"

Ruth didn't answer. She stared silently at nothing. No, not nothing, Rachel realized, following Ruth's gaze. She was looking at an irregular patch of the grey-painted concrete floor that was less uniformly smooth than the rest of the floor. The rougher area was about six feet long and three feet wide.

Despite the heat and humidity, Rachel's flesh puckered as a chill ran down her spine, and the fine hairs on her forearms actually stood on end. She looked around. Through the thick forest of marijuana plants she saw a rusting wheelbarrow leaning against a far wall. She made her way through the plants, which swayed and rustled as she pushed between them. Propped against the wall next to the wheelbarrow were a heavy pickaxe, a garden hoe, and a flat-bladed spade. The rusted blades of the hoe and spade were caked with a pebbly grey substance. Grasping the handles of the up-ended wheelbarrow, she lowered it. It was inordinately heavy. The barrow was thickly lined

with the same pebbly grey material that caked the blades
of the hoe and spade. She scraped at it with a fingernail.
It was hardened concrete.

"Oh, Christ."

"What is it?" Claudia asked, still standing by the
door with Ruth.

"They're here," Rachel said. "They're buried under
the floor."

"We need to get out of here," Claudia said.

"No shit," Rachel responded, beating her way through
the jungle of marijuana plants toward the door. Then she
saw something above the door that made her stomach
clench and her heart leap into her throat. Momentarily
paralyzed with fear, she thought, *How could I have been
so stupid?* Of course Hallam would have a security system to protect and monitor his investment.

"What?" Claudia asked, looking up. "What is it?"

"Move, move!" Rachel cried, pushing Ruth and
Claudia through the door toward the stairs. "That's a
wireless webcam, tied into the computer upstairs. There's
another webcam in the bedroom. *Go!* He's been watching us all along."

Ruth fell on the stairs. Rachel hauled her roughly
to her feet. She whimpered like a recalcitrant child as
Rachel pushed her up the stairs. She cried out as the back
door suddenly opened and Dougie Hallam stepped onto
the landing. He loomed above them. Rachel and Claudia
retreated to the bottom of the stairs.

"I tried to tell them," Ruth wailed, quailing before
him, clawing at his boots. "I tried to stop them. He'll be
angry, I said."

"Shut up," Hallam said, kicking out at her, sending her scuttling away. He slammed the back door shut,
twisted the inside deadbolt, and yanked out the key.
Grabbing Ruth and thrusting her into the kitchen, he
said, "You two might as well come up. There's no way

out down there. C'mon now. Don't make me come down
there and get you. You won't like it."

Cautiously, fearfully, Rachel and Claudia ascended
the stairs. Hallam stood aside, ever the gentleman, allow-
ing them to precede him into the kitchen. As if reading
each other's minds, Rachel and Claudia simultaneously
bolted toward the front door, but Hallam must have
read their minds too; he caught them before they'd gone
half a dozen steps. Holding each of them by the upper
arm, handling them as easily as if they were children,
he dragged them down the hall and threw them into a
bedroom across the hall from the makeshift studio. He
thrust Ruth in with them.

"Gimme that," he demanded, gesturing to Claudia's
bag, slung across her shoulders.

Claudia handed it to him. He pawed through it,
took out her cellphone and dropped it to the floor. He
stomped it to shards. Throwing the bag aside, he looked
at Rachel. She held out her arms. She wasn't carrying a
purse.

"Pockets," he said.

She turned out the front pockets of her jeans, turned
so he could see the back pockets.

Satisfied, he left the room, slamming the door shut
behind him. Rachel heard the snap of a lock, but tried
the door anyway. It was no use.

"What are we going to do?" Claudia asked, retriev-
ing her bag from the floor.

Rachel went to the window and parted the dusty
drapes. A piece of heavy construction plywood covered
the window, screwed to the frame every six to eight
inches. Even with the proper tools, it would take time
to remove it.

"You wouldn't happen to have a Leatherman multi-
tool in your bag, would you?" she said to Claudia as she
let the drapes fall closed.

"I don't know what that is," Claudia replied as she dug through her bag. Lowering her voice, she said, "I do have a Swiss Army knife." She handed Rachel a small red pocket knife. It had a single tiny knife blade, a nail file, and scissors, plus removable tweezers and a plastic toothpick.

"I was hoping for a .45 automatic."

"No gun," Claudia said with a brave smile. "Sorry."

"Father has a gun," Ruth said. "Mother doesn't like it, but Father says they need it for protection in Africa."

"Where is it now?" Rachel asked, thinking that Mr. Braithwaite must have been a very pragmatic man, for a missionary.

"With Father," Ruth said. "In Africa."

"Of course," Rachel said. Through the closed door she could hear Hallam's voice. She put her ear to the door.

"I don't give a fuck about that," she heard Hallam say. "We got bigger problems. Get your ass over here." A pause, then: "Where the hell do you think? Come through the woods to the side door. No one will see you." Another pause, followed by: "Tell them whatever you need to tell them, but get the fuck moving." There was a muted click, the sound of a cellphone being snapped shut.

Rachel straightened and looked around the bedroom. It was sparsely and simply furnished. A sagging single bed with a wood frame, a bedside table with lamp, a three-drawer dresser, and a straight chair. Rachel started going through the drawers of the dresser. They contained women's clothing — underwear, pullovers, nightwear — all neatly folded but dusty and musty smelling. The bedside table drawer contained a few personal items: old-fashioned eyeglasses, a hairbrush and comb, and a small plain wood box that held some hair pins and a religious medallion on a length of kitchen twine. The closet contained a few plain dresses, three blouses, three skirts, a cloth coat, and two pairs of cracked black leather shoes with laces. Other than the lamp and the chair, there was nothing in the room that could be used as a weapon or a tool.

"How you ladies doing?" Dougie Hallam called through the door.

Ruth whimpered, like a trapped animal.

"People know we're here," Rachel replied, leaning close to the door. "If we aren't back soon, this is the first place they'll come looking for us. You might as well let us go. Your little enterprise is going to get blown no matter what."

"We'll see about that," Hallam replied.

"Don't be any stupider than you have to be, Dougie," Rachel said. "Making and selling pornography isn't illegal and you'd probably get just a slap on the wrist for the pot farm, but assault and forcible confinement are more serious. You could do some hard time for that. Dougie? Are you there?" No answer. "Dougie?" Still no response. "Shit."

"How soon do you think it will be before Harvey starts to worry?" Claudia asked.

"We've been gone less an hour," Rachel said quietly. "He probably won't start to worry for another hour or so."

"We could be dead by then," Claudia said.

"Dougie isn't that stupid," Rachel said. "What would he gain by killing us? The police will come looking for us sooner or later and they'll find his little operation. He'll probably just keep us locked in here for a while to give himself time to get away."

"I hope you're right," Claudia said.

"Me too," Rachel replied.

chapter fifty

When Shoe and Janey pulled up in front of Shoe's parents' house in his father's Taurus, Hal and Harvey Wiseman were standing in the driveway by Hal's Lexus.

"What do you expect me to do about it?" Shoe heard his brother say as he got out of the car. "Kick the door down?"

"What's the problem?" Shoe asked.

"Doc thinks Rachel and Claudia Hahn have been poisoned by the crazy Braithwaite sisters and buried in the basement of their house," Hal said.

Harvey Wiseman scowled at Hal and said to Shoe, "Rachel and Claudia went to talk to Ruth Braithwaite over an hour and a half ago," he said. "Rachel said they wouldn't be more than half an hour — we were supposed to have dessert and drinks at my place. When they didn't come back after an hour, I got worried and knocked on the door of the house. No one answered."

"Have you tried Rachel's cellphone?" Shoe asked.

"Yes," Wiseman said, "but she left her phone in her purse, which is on my kitchen table."

"Claudia has a cellphone," Shoe said.

"I don't know the number," Wiseman said. "Do you?"

"No. What do you want to do, Harv? Do you want to call the police?"

"It might be, um, well, a bit premature for that," Wiseman said.

"You don't really want to kick the door down, do you?"

"No, of course not. But ... "

"All right," Shoe said. "Come with me. Janey, you stay here."

"I'm coming with you," she said.

Shoe knew there was no point arguing with her. "Hal, you stay with Mum and Dad."

"What? And miss all the fun? Not on your life. I want to see you in action."

chapter fifty-one

"It's about fucking time," Rachel heard Hallam say.

"Damnit, Dougie. We agreed I wouldn't ever have to come here. Jesus Christ, I don't believe this. What the hell were you thinking?"

"I'm getting really tired of your crap," Hallam replied. "You're so goddamned smart, you tell me what the fuck else I was supposed to do."

"Okay, okay. Shut up a minute and let me think, for Christ's sake."

"I know that voice," Claudia whispered in Rachel's ear as they hunched by the door.

"So do I," Rachel said, heart sinking.

"Who is it?"

"It's Tim Dutton."

"Think faster," she heard Hallam say. "We don't have all fucking night."

"We gotta get them out of here," Dutton said. "Before someone comes looking for them. I've got too much invested in these operations. I can't afford to have them busted."

"What do you suggest we do, let 'em go?"

"What? No. Christ, we can't do that. They'll go straight to the cops."

"So we kill 'em and dump their bodies in the Dells. That'll give us a little more time."

"Jesus," Dutton moaned. "We can't just kill them."

"Why not? You killed Marty because you were afraid she was going to blow the whistle on you. How's this different?"

"I didn't kill her." Dutton protested. "You did."

"I just gave her the 'coop de grass', like they say, because you were too fucking chickenshit to finish what you started. I don't give a shit what you decide. Kill 'em or let 'em go, it's the same to me. Either way, it's time for me to pull the plug. There's not much of Ruthie's trust fund left and sales of her videos haven't been so great lately. If I sell my house and the bar, I'll have more'n enough to keep me in booze and cooze in Mexico or some place for the rest of my life."

Hope bloomed in Rachel, only to be as quickly dashed.

"Well, I don't," Tim Dutton said. "I need the money from this and the other crops or I'll lose everything I've worked for. My business, my house, my standing in the community, everything."

You miserable little shit! Rachel wanted to scream. *Everything your old man handed you on a bloody silver platter, you mean.*

"I'll make it worth your while," Dutton added.

"Yeah? With what? I thought you were broke?"

"My wife's grandparents left her some money. I could get my hands on fifty grand, maybe a bit more."

"All right, fine," Hallam said. "Anything to stop your goddamned whining. Here, take these. Use 'em to tie 'em up. Just Rae and the teacher. I'll take care of Ruthie. You think you can handle that?"

"What about you? What are you going to do?"

"There's something I gotta check downstairs," Hallam replied. "Then I'll go bring my truck up to the garage. We can throw 'em in the back without anyone seeing."

Rachel heard footsteps approaching. Heart hammering in her chest, she backed away from the door, pulling Claudia with her. "Someone's coming." She opened Claudia's little Swiss Army knife. The tiny blade was razor sharp, but narrow and barely an inch and a half long. It was so ridiculously pathetic a weapon, she almost felt like laughing. Almost.

Tim Dutton did laugh when he opened the door and saw the little knife in Rachel's hand, but it was a hollow, nervous laugh. He was almost as frightened as she was, Rachel realized. He had a handful of narrow black plastic strips, about a foot long. Rachel recognized them. Cable ties. Not as sturdy as the disposable handcuffs she'd seen the police on television use, but just as effective. He tossed them onto the floor at her feet.

"Use these to tie her wrists behind her back," he said, gesturing toward Claudia.

"Go fuck yourself, Tim," Rachel said, holding the little knife out. She took a step toward him. He backed away a step.

"C'mon, Rae. I don't like this any more than you do. Don't make it any harder than it has to be."

"Jesus, you're an asshole, Tim," Rachel said. "I'll make it as hard as I fucking well can." She took step toward him, feinting with the tiny knife. He flinched, but stood his ground. She almost admired him for it. "Let us go, Tim. You don't want to do this."

"I can't let you go," Dutton said. "Don't you see? It's either this or lose everything I have. I'm sorry, Rae."

He kicked at the bundle of cable ties on the floor and to Claudia. "Tie her hands behind her, Rae. Then lie down on the floor so I can do you."

"Screw you, Tim. You're going to have to do it the hard way."

"What's taking so long?" Dougie Hallam said from the doorway behind Dutton.

"She has a knife," Dutton said.

Hallam snorted with disgust. "Christ, Dutton, you're such a fucking pussy."

He stepped past Dutton and, ignoring the knife, grabbed Rachel by the throat, choking off the air to her lungs, the blood to her brain. He wrapped his other hand around her wrist and squeezed. The knife dropped from her paralyzed fingers. He released her. She backed away from him, dizzy and gasping, wrist throbbing.

"I heard you talking," she wheezed. "You've got money, Dougie. Why don't you just take it and retire to someplace that doesn't have an extradition treaty with Canada. We'll even give you a couple of hours, more if you want, before we call the police."

"I'll write you a cheque for ten thousand dollars if you let us go," Claudia Hahn said as she opened her purse and took out a chequebook.

"I'll double that," Rachel said.

"Don't listen to them," Dutton said desperately. "They're lying. They'll go straight to the police."

"Do I look stupid to you?" Hallam said, but Rachel thought he looked as though he might be considering the offer.

A clock began to strike somewhere in the house. Rachel glanced at her wristwatch. It was almost nine-thirty. She prayed that Doc would begin worrying soon and come looking for them.

"Time to get this show on the road," Hallam said. He grabbed Rachel and thrust her into Dutton's arms.

"Hang on to her," he said, as he reached for Claudia. "You first. Turn around. Hands behind your back."

"No," Claudia said. She began to shout for help at the top of her lungs.

Hallam punched her in the face, chopping off the sound. He pushed her down onto her back on the bed. Claudia writhed and kicked and screamed. Rachel struggled in Dutton's grasp, but he held her fast.

"Hold still, goddamnit," Hallam growled, his words punctuated by the sound of his fist against flesh, and a grunt of pain from Claudia.

He flipped Claudia onto her face on the bed and twisted her arms behind her back. There was blood in her mouth and on her cheek. Suddenly, she was a wild-cat, thrashing, twisting free. Her teeth clamped on the fleshy edge of Hallam's hand. He clubbed her. She kicked and snapped and made sounds in her throat that didn't seem possible for a human to make. Then, as suddenly as her struggle had begun, it was over. Hallam picked her up by the throat and threw her across the bedroom as if she were a child's doll. She slammed against the wall, fell, and lay still. Dreadfully, bonelessly, breathlessly still.

Rachel began to scream. Hallam spun, his fist glancing off the side of her head. Stunned, she staggered as Dutton released her. She fell against the bed, and rolled face down onto the floor. A massive weight pressed against her spine. Hallam's knee. He grabbed her left wrist and twisted her arm behind her back. Through a haze of tears, Rachel saw the glint of metal on the floor by her face. The blade of Claudia's little Swiss Army knife.

She felt her left shoulder begin to dislocate as Hallam grasped her right wrist and twisted her arms together behind her back. Using every ounce of strength, she writhed beneath him, wrenching her right arm free. She grabbed the knife, rolled out from under Hallam's knee, and stabbed up toward his face. She felt the blade strike bone and break. Hallam howled and lurched to his feet, hand over his left eye, blood oozing between his fingers. Rachel scrabbled on all fours toward the door.

"Stop her!" Hallam shouted at Dutton. "Cunt almost put my eye out!"

Rachel made it to her feet and ran through the kitchen to the side door. Too late, she remembered that Hallam had removed the key from the deadlock. She twisted the handle. Miraculously, the door opened; Dutton had forgotten to lock it. She ran into the dark breezeway, but something snagged her legs and she fell, tangled in the rotting wicker lawn furniture by the door. One of her shoes came off. Desperately struggling to her feet, she kicked the other shoe off and ran down the rutted driveway toward the road, Tim Dutton close on her heels. If she made it to the road, she knew she could outrun Dutton without a problem.

Dougie Hallam burst from the front door and charged across the cluttered lawn, cutting her off from the road. She angled left and ran hard toward the entrance of the footpath to the woods. Hallam was twenty feet behind her. She was gaining ground, but slowly; Hallam was surprisingly fast for a man his size. She ran harder, ignoring the jabbing pain of pebbles and twigs on the soles of her feet, down the dark path next to Ruth's backyard, wondering where Dutton was.

She heard a sound to her left, from the direction of the path that led toward her parents' house. Dutton had flanked her by climbing the stone wall at the end of Ruth's yard. Turning, Rachel stayed on the main path and ran deeper into the dark woods.

chapter fifty-two

Although the Braithwaite house was less than two hundred metres away through the woods, it was almost a kilometre by road. For Hal's sake, Shoe opted to drive. The house did not show any lights, inside or out, and the small turnaround at the end of the cul-de-sac was dark. A vehicle was parked half in the trees on the edge of the woods. Hallam's black Hummer.

As Shoe swung the car through the turnaround, the headlights swept the front of the old house, illuminating the religious statuary on the overgrown lawn. A ghostly figure darted between the tilted figures, a woman with white hair and wearing what appeared to be a flowing nightgown. She ran into the house as Shoe turned the car into the rutted driveway. He turned off the engine and the headlights, plunging the yard into gloom, illuminated only by the distant street lights at the corner of Cabot Street. He got out of the car and picked his way across the shadowy, unkempt lawn, through the statuary, toward the front door. Janey, Hal, and Harvey Wiseman followed.

"I should've brought a flashlight," Wiseman said. Shoe remembered his father always kept a flashlight in the glove box.

"Jesus Christ," Hal swore, banging his shin on one of the cement figurines.

"I'm no expert," Wiseman said, "but that's the Madonna, I think."

"Ha ha," Hal said sourly.

There was no porch, just an apron of cracked and frost-heaved concrete in front of the door, the doorsill level with the ground. The door stood partly open.

"Looks like I won't get to see you in action after all," Hal said.

"Shut up, Hal," Janey said.

As Shoe's eyes adjusted to the dark, he could just make out a faint light from the interior of the house. He knocked on the half-open door and waited. After a moment, he knocked again, harder, leaned in and called out, "Hello. Miss Braithwaite. Rachel. Claudia."

"What was that?" Wiseman said.

"It sounded like a cat," Hal said.

"Be quiet," Shoe said. He listened. It came again. It did indeed sound like a cat.

"I told you," Hal said. "It's a cat."

Shoe leaned into the vestibule. He heard it again. It was not a cat. It was a faint cry for help. He pushed the door open and stepped into the musty, unlit vestibule. Straight ahead, steps led up to the dimly lit front hall.

"Help," a woman cried from somewhere upstairs.

"That sounds like Claudia," Wiseman said.

Shoe bounded up the stairs into front hall. The air was hazy with smoke. He smelled burning paper.

"Rachel," he called. "Claudia. Where are you?"

A reply came from down a dark hallway. Although

her voice was weak and rasping, Shoe recognized it as Claudia Hahn's.

The smoke was growing thicker.

"Hal," Shoe said. "See if you can find where the smoke's coming from."

With Wiseman and Janey on his heels, Shoe started down the hall. The smoke thinned somewhat. He ran his hand along the wall, finally locating a bank of light switches. He flipped one. The ceiling light in the vestibule went on. The second turned on a dim overhead light halfway down the hall. Nothing obvious happened when he flipped the third and fourth.

Shoe, Janey, and Wiseman moved down the hall, checking the bedrooms, turning on lights as they went. The first bedroom was simply furnished, clean and neatly kept, but unoccupied. The one across the hall was similarly furnished, but everything was covered in a thick patina of dust. When Shoe turned on the lights in the third room they were momentarily dazzled by the brightness. It appeared to be some kind of studio, with video cameras and powerful lights surrounding a big bed. The white-haired woman lay on the bed, curled into a tight fetal ball.

"From Rachel's description," Wiseman said, "that must be Ruth Braithwaite."

Shoe bent over the bed. "Ruth?" he said. She whimpered and curled into a tighter ball. "Ruth, where are the women who came to speak to you?"

"Hello," a muffled voice called through the door of the room across the hall. "Is someone there? Help."

Wiseman rushed across the hall and rattled the door before noticing that it was secured with a heavy sliding bolt. He slid the bolt and opened the door.

"Oh, Doc. Thank god," Claudia Hahn said, throwing her arms around his neck.

"You're hurt!" Wiseman said, alarmed.

Claudia stepped back. Her mouth was bloody, one eye was swollen shut, and her throat was beginning to bruise. She tried to smile, and winced. "I'm all right."

"Where's Rachel?" Shoe asked.

"I don't know. They took her."

"Who took her?"

"Dougie Hallam. And Tim Dutton." She became aware that her blouse was open, revealing a blood-stained camisole, and tried to refasten it, but most of the buttons were missing. "They've been making pornography with Ruth and growing marijuana in the cellar."

"Do you know where they took her?" Shoe asked.

"We overheard them talking about killing us," she said. "And disposing of our bodies in the Dells."

"How long ago did they leave?"

"I don't know. I was unconscious for a time, I think. It couldn't have been very long ago, though. Where's Ruth?"

"She's in the other room," Shoe said. "Where are her sisters?"

"Dead," Claudia said. "Interred in the cellar." She held her hand to her mouth; it obviously hurt her to talk.

"Let's get you out of here," Shoe said. "Go with Harv. I'll bring Ruth."

Shoe went into the makeshift studio. Ruth was still on the bed. She whimpered and fretted as he picked her up, but she put her arms around his neck. As he carried her down the hall to the living room, she whispered against his chest.

"She ran away."

"Who ran away, Ruth?"

"That girl. The boy's sister. Joe's sister. She ran way and he chased her. Him and the other one. Into the woods. He'll hurt her. He'll hurt her too."

He lowered Ruth onto the sofa. She clung to him. He

had to gently pry her arms from around his neck.

"We need to call the police," Wiseman said, casting about for a telephone.

Janey went into the kitchen. "There's a phone in here."

Shoe went into the kitchen as Hal puffed up the stairs from the basement, followed by the harsh stink of wet burnt paper.

"Someone's growing marijuana down there," he said, between ragged breaths. "They tried to start a fire with a space heater and some cardboard. I put it out." Through the doorway to the living room he saw Claudia Hahn and Ruth Braithwaite. "Jesus, what happened? Where's Rachel?"

"Harv will explain," Shoe said. He headed toward the front door, Janey going with him.

"Where are you going?" Hal asked, following Shoe and Janey out into the yard.

"I'm going after Rachel," Shoe said, as he opened the passenger door of the car. "Ruth said she ran into the woods, with Dougie Hallam and Tim Dutton after her." Sure enough, there was a flashlight in the glove box. More important, the batteries still held a charge.

"I'll come with you," Hal said.

"I need to move fast, Hal," Shoe said.

"She's my sister too," Hal said.

Shoe knew Hal would never be able to keep up. "All right, but when we find him, stay out of my way."

He ran down the footpath into the dark woods, Janey keeping up without any trouble.

chapter fifty-three

Rachel ran for her life, fear gibbering at the edge of her consciousness. She could easily succumb to panic, she knew, but she knew too that if she panicked, she would in all likelihood die. The fear gave her strength, however, as adrenaline raced through her. And so, ignoring the pain in her feet, she ran through the moonlit woods, undergrowth slashing at her upraised arms, whipping at her face, ripping at her clothing, snagging her ankles. Leaves and twigs and fallen branches crackled and snapped underfoot, sounding like gunshots in the stillness of the night. Suddenly, the ground dropped out from under her. She plunged down a hillside, fell, rolled, slammed against the trunk of a tree, and scrambled to her feet, still running. Through the trees she could see the lights of houses, but they seemed impossibly distant, and whenever she turned toward them, Hallam turned in the same direction, threatening to cut her off.

He was relentless. He bulled through the woods as though the undergrowth that slowed her was mere shadow to him. Despite her superior speed and agility, she could not shake him. What little distance she gained in the open, she lost when the tangled brush closed in again. He knew the woods better than she did, too, despite the dark, like a blind man in a familiar room. At least she could hear him, stamping and cursing behind her. At first, he had called to her, taunting her, telling her what he would do to her when he caught her, but he'd soon stopped, saving his breath for the chase.

She had to get out of the woods. If she could get to the street, any street, she could run full out, scream, call for help. He seemed to anticipate her every move, however, forcing her still deeper into the woods.

She scrambled up a steep hillside, feet slipping on old leaves and twigs, breaking nails as she clawed at the loose earth, rocks, and roots. The ground levelled and she found herself on a footpath atop a high ridge. She heard Hallam swear as he lost his footing and slid noisily a few yards down the hillside. She could see the lights from the backs of the houses along Cantor Street, less than two hundred metres away. She turned — and ran straight into Tim Dutton's arms.

"Gotcha," he said, gripping her upper arms. "I got her," he shouted.

Rachel struggled. She heard Hallam scrambling up the ridge. She clawed at Dutton's face and tried to knee him in the groin, but he turned her and held her in a tight embrace. She was caught. Hallam emerged from the trees. She drew a breath and opened her mouth to scream.

The darkness imploded.

chapter fifty-four

A few metres into the woods, Shoe stopped at the fork in the trail. To his left, skirting the broken-down wall at the bottom of the Braithwaite property, was the path to his parents' house. To the right, along the top of the rise, was the path leading deeper into the woods. He turned the flashlight off; it only impaired his night vision. The waning gibbous moon provided sufficient illumination.

"Which way did they go?" Janey asked.

Shoe gestured for her to be quiet, straining to hear. Rachel would have gone left, toward their parents' house, in which case she would likely be home free. If she'd been forced to go right ...

"What was that?" Janey said.

Shoe heard it too. Voices coming from deeper in the woods, and the sound of something large crashing through the underbrush.

"This way," Shoe said.

They took the right fork, running carefully along the

top of the rise, then descending into the shallow ravine. The path was indistinguishable in the moonlight, leaves rustling underfoot, twigs and dead branches snapping and cracking. Shoe stopped at the bottom of the ravine, at the base of the higher ridge. He stood still, listening intently. Had he heard a shout?

"What is it?" Janey whispered.

Suddenly, a shrill scream pierced the night, and was just as suddenly cut off. It had come from above and to his left. Shoving the flashlight into the back pocket of his jeans so he could use both hands, Shoe scrambled up the steep ridge. He was breathing hard when he reached the top, Janey right behind him. He turned left, and jogged along the trail, as quickly and as quietly as he could. Thirty metres away, a shadowy, many-limbed creature twisted and heaved grotesquely in the moonlight, changing shape as he ran toward it.

"Hallam?" Shoe shouted.

The shape momentarily froze, then a segment of it seemed to break off, separate itself from the main body. The new shape became a man, who ran away along the trail atop the ridge, until he disappeared into the darkness. The main shape stood its ground as Shoe closed.

"That's far enough." The shape resolved into Dougie Hallam, with Rachel on her knees before him. Her head was cocked at an odd angle, Hallam's left hand clamped on the back of her neck. Blood, black in the moonlight, covered the left side of his face, and his left eye appeared to be grotesquely swollen.

"Be careful," Janey whispered urgently, voice tight with fear. "He carries a butterfly knife … " She was standing close, but her voice seemed to come from a long way off.

"Let her go, Dougie," Shoe said.

"Sure," Hallam said agreeably. Shoe saw the gleam of metal in the moonlight as, with a flip of his right wrist,

Hallam deployed the blade of the butterfly knife. He held the blade against Rachel's throat. "Back off. Any closer and I'll slit her throat."

"Okay, Dougie," Shoe said, raising his hands. "Relax."

"He and Tim Dutton killed Marty," Rachel rasped. "And Claudia ... "

"Shut up," Hallam snarled, shaking her as though she were a rag doll. "Stupid cunt. When you gonna learn to keep your fucking mouth shut?"

"Take it easy, Dougie," Shoe said. "Don't hurt her. I don't care about Marty or Claudia. Just let Rachel go."

"Maybe I'll take her with me. To keep you honest. Least till I'm home free."

"No," Shoe said. "Let her go. That's your only option. You're free to leave. I won't try to stop you, but I can't let you take her with you."

"And what're you gonna do to stop me?"

"Whatever I have to."

"Let her go, Dougie," Janey said. "I — I'll go with you."

"Gimme a break," Hallam laughed. "Even if I believed you, what would I want with a worn-out skank like you? Nah, think I'll just hang on to little Rae, here. Her ass has a lot less mileage on it." He began to back away, dragging Rachel with him. "You two kids have fun now. Don't stay out too late."

"Dougie," Janey said.

Hallam stopped. "Now what?"

"Just this." Janey raised her right arm, fist clenched tight on a small, nickel-plated automatic pistol that gleamed in the moonlight. There was a flash and a sharp crack. Hallam ducked and swore, still holding onto Rachel, whose eyes were wide with terror as Janey took aim again, steadying the pistol in both hands.

Shoe reached for the gun, but Janey slipped aside,

stepping closer to her stepbrother. The pistol cracked. Hallam flinched, but Janey had missed again.

Hallam bellowed. He lifted Rachel, as if she weighed nothing at all, and threw her toward Janey. Janey stepped aside. Rachel fell hard on the ground. She raised herself onto all fours and scrabbled toward Shoe.

Janey aimed the pistol at Hallam's head. He cringed, raising his arms to protect himself. There was a dry snap as the pistol misfired.

Janey worked the slide, desperately trying to free the jam and recock the hammer. With a triumphant bellow, Hallam reached out, his left hand trapping Janey's gun hand. He closed his right fist around his knife handle and punched her in the face — once, twice. She tried to cover her face with her free arm, twist away from him, but he held her as he hit her again.

Shoe charged. Hallam wrenched the pistol from Janey's hand and stepped back. Janey collapsed to the ground. Hallam aimed the pistol at Shoe. The gun was ridiculously small in Hallam's hand. He pulled the trigger, but nothing happened. "Shit," he cursed and threw the pistol at Shoe. It bounced off his shoulder.

Shoe took at step forward. Hallam brandished the knife. Shoe took another step. Hallam lunged, driving the blade straight toward Shoe's chest. Shoe pivoted left, parrying the thrust with his right arm, lifting his left elbow as he continued to rotate. As he completed the rotation, he slammed his elbow into the back of Hallam's head. Hallam staggered, but did not fall. He turned to face Shoe in a crouch.

Shoe didn't wait for Hallam to recoup, but took the fight to him. Hallam backed away, holding the knife high, almost like a bullfighter holds his sword before the final thrust. He circled to his right, staying beyond Shoe's reach. In his peripheral vision, Shoe saw Janey crawl through the leaves toward Rachel. Shoe kept himself between them and Hallam, who continued to circle to his right.

Keeping an eye on Hallam, Shoe took a step back toward Rachel and Janey. As he retreated, Hallam advanced, bringing the knife down, holding it in front of him. The blade wove back and forth, glinting in the moonlight.

"Just go, Dougie," Shoe said. "While you've got the chance." He risked a quick look at Janey and Rachel, but he could not tell how badly either was hurt.

"It's time to finish it between you an' me," Hallam said.

"There's nothing to finish," Shoe said. He knelt beside Janey and Rachel. He felt the bulge of the flashlight in the back pocket of his jeans. He gently touched Janey's arm. "Are you all right?"

"Yes," Janey said. "But Rachel's hurt pretty bad, I think."

Rachel moaned and her eyes fluttered. "Joe?"

"She needs medical attention, Dougie," Shoe said. "I'm going to pick her up."

"I don't give a fuck what she needs," Hallam said, stepping closer, brandishing his knife.

"Joe," Rachel said again.

"Try and pick her up," Hallam said, "and I'll cut Janey. We're gonna finish this, whether you like it or not."

"All right," Shoe said. "Let's finish it."

As he stood, he pulled the flashlight from his back pocket. Flicking it on, he aimed the bright beam into Hallam's face. Hallam flinched, momentarily blinded. Shoe chopped the flashlight down onto Hallam's right wrist. He yowled and the knife fell from his hand. Shoe whipped the heavy steel cylinder across Hallam's face. The lens shattered and the light went out as Hallam sank to his knees. The backswing caught him a glancing blow on the left temple. He fell sideways, rolling away through the leaves and twigs. He lumbered to his feet with the help of a tree.

"Son of a bitch," he snarled, wiping the blood from his eyes. "You never could fight fair, could you?"

"And you've always had a unique interpretation of fair," Shoe said.

"Fuck you."

"It's over, Dougie. Finished."

"It ain't finished till I say it is." He took a step toward Shoe.

There was flash and a crack. A black spot appeared high on the right side of Hallam's chest. He staggered backwards as the spot began to spread. Another crack and a second spot appeared, a few inches to the left and slightly below the first. Hallam raised his hands to his chest as both spots continued to spread, a puzzled expression on his face, as if unsure what was happening to him. He took a step forward, then collapsed to his knees. Raising his head, he opened his mouth to speak as Janey stepped past Shoe and fired a final shot into her stepbrother's right eye. Hallam fell backwards, twitched once, twice, then lay still.

Shoe reached out and took the pistol from Janey's hand. The metal was warm to the touch and the smell of gunpowder was sharp in his nostrils. He squatted by the body and pressed his fingers against Hallam's throat.

"Is he dead?" Janey asked.

"Yes," Shoe said, standing.

"Good," Janey said. She slumped to her knees in the leaves. "Good."

Shoe looked at the pistol in his hand. Then he raised it, aimed it into the woods over the creek, and pulled the trigger. The pistol cracked and the slug rattled through the leafy undergrowth. He pulled the trigger again, but the hammer snapped down on the empty chamber. He slipped it into the back pocket of his jeans.

Shoe heard thrashing in the woods on the hillside below the ridge. He knelt beside Janey.

"Janey," he said quietly.

"Uh? What?" she replied, voice dulled.

"When the police ask you what happened, tell them it was your gun, and you tried to shoot Dougie to save Rachel, but that you missed. Tell it the way it happened, but that I killed him. I shot him twice in the chest, but when that didn't stop him, I had to kill him. Can you remember that?"

"You shot him twice in the chest, then killed him. Sure. Okay."

He looked at Rachel. Her feet were bloody. "Rachel?"

"Look, I — " She shook her head, as if to clear it. "All right. Sure. If that's what you want."

Shoe stood as Hal emerged from the woods. Huffing and grunting, he staggered a few feet then sat down in the leaves. "Did I — did I hear — gunshots?" he gasped. Then he saw Dougie Hallam's body. "Jesus," he said, scuttling away from the body like a massive crab. "Jesus. Who — ? Is he dead?"

"Yes," Shoe said.

"Jesus," Hal said again.

"Let's get out of here," Shoe said.

Hal struggled to his feet and stood looking down at Dougie's body. "You're just going to leave him here?"

"He's not going anywhere. Do you have a phone?" Hal shook his head. Neither did Janey or Rachel.

"Dougie has a phone," Rachel said.

Shoe looked at Dougie's body. He did not want to go through the dead man's pockets to look for his cell-phone, not because he was squeamish, but because he did not wish to disturb the crime scene.

"We'll call the police first chance we get." To Rachel,

he said, "Can you walk?"

"I think so." She struggled to her feet with Shoe and Janey's help, but was not able to stand without leaning heavily on Shoe's arm. Shoe gathered her up in his arms. It would be easier to carry her. They hadn't gone far when Hal stumbled and fell heavily.

"I have to rest," he gasped.

Shoe set Rachel down. He could see the lights of the houses through the trees. He could also see distant flashes of red and blue, the stroboscopic throbbing of the lights atop emergency vehicles at Ruth Braithwaite's house. "Janey, wait here with Hal," he said. "I'll send someone to help."

Janey slumped to the ground next to Hal. Shoe picked Rachel up and set off toward his parents' house.

chapter fifty-five

"Tell me again what happened," Hannah Lewis said.

It was early Tuesday morning. Shoe and Hannah Lewis were standing alone at the top of the yard, looking out over the wooded ravines. Shoe recounted once again how he'd shot Dougie Hallam. When he'd finished, Lewis looked at him for a long moment.

"You shot him twice in the chest with Janey Hallam's gun," she said.

"That's right."

"Then you killed him by shooting him through the right eye."

"Yes."

"Because two chest shots, one of which appears to have punctured his right lung, weren't enough to stop him from trying to kill her, your sister, and you."

"Yes," Shoe said. "Dougie Hallam was a remarkably tenacious man. Very strong and very determined."

She looked at him. It was a long and penetrating look that left Shoe feeling that she could see right through him. "I'm not sure I buy it," she said. "But I'm sure as hell not going to lose any sleep over it. Hallam got his just desserts, whoever served it."

When Shoe had told Lewis that Janey Hallam had been repeatedly raped by her stepfather and stepbrother from the time she was ten, Hannah Lewis's violet eyes had blazed.

"My brother will be happy to close the books on the Black Creek Rapist," she said. "Between Claudia Hahn's and Janey Hallam's testimonies, there shouldn't be a problem. What about Martine Elias's molestation? You said you were sure it was someone she knew. Could it have been Noseworthy?"

"I think it must have been," Shoe said. "Marty used to tease him a lot and he would get quite angry about it. Her teasing had a strong sexual component, too. Maybe things just got out of hand that day in the woods. And if it was Joey, she likely wouldn't have told the police, if only because he was my friend and she wanted me to like her. I think she liked him, too, in her way. She certainly came to like him."

"When we catch up to him," Lewis said, "we'll ask him."

"Any sign of him?"

"No. I'm guessing he just abandoned his bike and his gear and took off on Marty's bike."

"That's what he does," Shoe said.

"He'll show up sooner or later. At least he's off the hook for Marty's murder."

"What about Dutton?"

"Nothing so far." She shifted uncomfortably. "There's something else we need to talk about," she said.

Shoe waited. He had a feeling that he knew what it was she wanted to talk about.

"We have a witness who says he saw a man answering your brother's description talking to Marvin Cartwright in the parking lot of the Dells at about nine o'clock the evening Cartwright was killed."

"The park attendant?" Lewis nodded. "I spoke with him yesterday," Shoe said. "His description could fit any number of overweight, middle-aged men."

"Did he also tell you there were two cars still in the parking lot Thursday night when he locked the gate at ten, but that only Cartwright's Honda Accord was there in the morning?"

"Yes," Shoe said.

"He's supposed to record the license plate numbers of any cars left overnight, but he generally doesn't bother. It's not unusual, he says. Drunks sleeping it off. Local kids making out and losing track of time. Most people these days can't tell a Honda from a Hyundai, but he's pretty sure it was a light blue or grey Toyota Camry or Corolla. Common enough cars ... " She paused. "He did remember the first three digits, though."

Shoe waited.

"The partial he gave us matched the plate number of a car leased by your brother's employer. They have a fleet of half a dozen cars. All Toyota Corollas ... " She paused again. "I'm sorry to have to tell you this, but the parking garage security video shows him taking a car out at approximately 8:15 p.m. Thursday and returning at 12:05 a.m. Friday."

"Shit," Shoe said. Although he seldom resorted to profanity, under the circumstances, the sentiment the word expressed seemed appropriate.

"That doesn't prove he drove to the park and killed Cartwright," Lewis said, "but the park attendant picked him out of a photo array. It isn't dead bang, but enough to get a warrant for his clothes and DNA." She looked up at him. "Sorry."

"Not your fault," he said.

"No, but — well, look, maybe he used the car for business and whoever he went to see can provide him with an alibi."

"Perhaps," Shoe said. Except that when Shoe had told Hal that the park attendant may have seen him in the Dells on Thursday night, he'd insisted he'd been in his office all evening. It was possible that Hal had simply forgotten he'd taken out a company car. Shoe hoped that was the case. It was more likely, however, that Hal had been lying.

"When are you going to serve the warrant?" he asked.

Lewis looked at her mannish wristwatch. "We have to finish up here first. Probably around two this afternoon. Why? Look, you're not going to do anything, well, foolish, are you?"

"You've got him under surveillance, don't you?"

"Yes, of course."

"Then what could I do?"

Lewis left. Shoe went into the house. Rachel was in his father's recliner, feet up and swathed in bandages.

"How are you doing?"

"I may never play the violin again."

"Feel up to taking a ride?"

"Sure. Where to?"

"Oakville. I need to talk to Hal."

"What about? And why do you need me along? As referee?"

"You could say that. Can you walk?"

"I can manage." She slipped her bandaged feet into a pair of men's slippers and stood carefully. "Not bad. I could use an arm to lean on."

As Shoe helped her out to the Taurus, which he had retrieved first thing in the morning from the Braithwaite residence, a car pulled up in front of Harvey Wiseman's house. Wiseman got out and came over.

"How's Claudia?" Rachel asked from the passenger seat of the Taurus.

"Bruised. Shaken up," Wiseman said. "But she'll be fine. Are you all right?"

"Nothing a nice long vacation in the south of France won't cure."

"Mm," Wiseman said. He looked at Shoe. "How about you?"

"A vacation in the south of France sounds good to me too." Wiseman's expression darkened. "I'm fine," Shoe said.

Rachel smiled sympathetically at Wiseman as Shoe closed the passenger door and walked round the car to the driver's door. He got in and started the engine. He looked past Rachel. "We'll talk later, Harv," he said. He shifted into reverse and backed out of the driveway.

"You can trust him," Rachel said.

"I'm sure you're right," Shoe said. "But the fewer people who know what really happened, the better."

"I can't think of anyone who deserved to die more than Dougie Hallam," Rachel said. "And if anyone was justified in killing him, it was Janey. Why are you protecting her?"

"Because she needs it."

"You don't still care for her, do you?"

"Not in the way you're implying. But she's got problems enough without having her history dredged up for all the world to read about in the supermarket tabloids. Cut her some slack. She could use a friend or two about now."

"She doesn't make it easy to like her," Rachel said.

"Try harder."

chapter fifty-six

Hal got up that Tuesday morning feeling, if not great, then at least considerably better than he had the night before. More than once he'd been certain he was going to die in those damned woods, of a stroke or cardiac arrest. How bloody fitting, he thought, that Janey Hallam's voice would have been the last thing he heard. "Come on, Harold. Move your fat ass. Don't you pass out on me, you bastard, or I'll leave you here to fucking die. Come on! Just a little farther, goddamnit." Christ, she was worse than Maureen, and Maureen was in a class by herself when it came to badgering. At least she never called him Harold ...

Thoughts of Maureen turned his feeling of well-being, such as it was, to crap. He'd really done it this time, hadn't he? Bad enough that he'd had sex with that woman, whoever the hell she was, in that motel, but what on Earth had possessed him to tell Maureen about it? Was she right? Had he done it just to hurt her? He couldn't even remember if he'd had a good time. *If you're going to throw away twenty-five years of marriage on a one-night stand,* he berated himself bitterly, *you could at least remember if it had been worth it.* As it was, all he could recall of the woman were her massive, flexing thighs and her pale, flaccid breasts. He shuddered at the memory.

He and Maureen had been through some rough patches over the years, each slightly worse than the one before, but they had always managed to work things out, reach a state of marital equilibrium. Each had been slightly less stable than the one before, but they'd soldiered on, as they say. Not this time, he thought. This time, he knew, it was over for good. All things considered, perhaps it was for the best, he thought dolefully.

He was in the kitchen when heard the front door open and Maureen call out, "Hal, are you here?" He went into the hall.

"Where the hell else would I be?" She flinched at the anger in his voice. He savagely suppressed any feeling of remorse or guilt. "What do you want?"

"I've come for some of my things," she said, eyes glistening.

"Fine. Take whatever you want. I won't get in your way."

"I won't be long." Her voice was a strained whisper.

"Whatever," Hal said, and retreated downstairs, to the sanctuary of his basement workshop.

He heaved his bulk onto the high stool at his workbench. The Formica surface of the bench was smooth and cool beneath his hands. Dozens of hand tools and small power tools hung from the pegboard panel above the bench. A red LED on a battery charger winked out as he watched, indicating that the spare battery for his set of cordless power tools was fully charged. An elaborate mitre saw was mounted at one end of the bench, a wood vice at the other. A band saw, table saw, drill press, and a planer stood in a row against the wall, next to the big red rolling toolbox that held even more hand and power tools. Wood for his next project — a wardrobe for the guest room — was stacked in the corner, the scents of knotty pine and B.C. cedar mingling pleasantly. Although it had been weeks since he'd done any work, Hal was stung by the realization that he was going to miss his workshop, perhaps even more than he was going to miss Maureen.

The "down payment" he'd got from Gord Peters — extorted, really; there was no other word for it — was again safely stashed in the bottom of the big toolbox. Dougie Hallam wouldn't be needing it now, thanks to Joe. Hal looked at his watch. It was almost time to leave to meet Peters at the bank. Half a million dollars wasn't quite enough to entirely solve his financial woes, but added to his bonus — the "Oscar" — it would go a long way toward alleviating them. A sick feeling twisted in his guts as he realized he might never get the chance to collect his bonus, if what Joe had said about the park attendant was true.

He gripped the edge of the workbench as the wave of dizziness washed over him. His chest heaved, as if all the oxygen had been suddenly sucked out of the room.

Marvin Cartwright had called Hal's office the previous Thursday, asking Hal to meet him that evening in the parking lot of the Dells, that they needed to talk.

"What do we have to talk about?" Hal had asked.

"Atonement," Cartwright said.

"Atonement for what?"

"For our sins," Cartwright replied. "Mine. And yours."

"What are you talking about?" Hal asked.

"I'm talking about that day in the woods," Cartwright said.

Hal's heart stuttered. "For god's sake," he said.

"That was thirty-five years ago. Who cares anymore? Who even remembers?"

"I remember," Cartwright said. "So does Marty. And so do you, Hal. You must atone. You must go to the authorities and tell the truth about what happened."

"Why? What difference will it make now?"

"Redemption, Hal. It's the only way."

"And if I refuse?"

"If you won't save yourself," Cartwright had said, "I will have to do it for you."

He could have hung up, of course, and taken his chances. After all, the old man hadn't exactly had all his oars in the water, had he? But even if the police hadn't taken him seriously, they would have been obliged to re-open the old Black Creek rape/homicide case. And while Hal hadn't raped or murdered anyone, that wouldn't have mattered a jot to Jerry Renfrew, to whom appearances were paramount. At the merest whiff of scandal, Jerry would have cut Hal loose "faster than you could say 'family values,'" as Gord Peters had put it. Hal would have kissed his job, his promotion, and the "Oscar" goodbye.

So, instead of hanging up, Hal had agreed to meet him ...

Hal raised his head at the sound of a car pulling into the drive. Peering through the high window over the workbench, he saw his brother help his sister out of his father's car. Oh, shit, he groaned. What do they want? He heard the doorbell ring and Maureen's tread on the carpet as she went to answer the door.

chapter fifty-seven

Maureen's car was parked in the driveway. Shoe parked beside it, then went round to the passenger side and opened the door for Rachel.

"Do you think she's changed her mind about leaving?" Rachel asked as Shoe helped her out of the car.

"I don't know," Shoe replied. For Hal's sake, he hoped so.

Shoe helped Rachel up the walk to the front door and pressed the bell. A moment later, Maureen opened the door. There were three sealed cardboard cartons and two green plastic garbage bags stacked in the front hall. Rachel and Maureen exchanged hugs and sisterly kisses.

"You're serious about moving out then?" Rachel said.

"Yes," Maureen replied. Looking down, she said, "What happened to your feet?"

"Didn't Hal tell you about last night?"

"No. What about last night? What happened?"

"Is Hal here?" Shoe asked.

"He's downstairs, in his workshop. What happened last night?" Maureen asked insistently.

Shoe left Rachel to explain and went downstairs. Hal's basement workshop was behind the family room Hal had built for the family he and Maureen had never had, and likely never would. It appeared to be equipped with every hand and power tool known to man. "If Stanley or Black & Decker makes it," Maureen had once said to him, "Hal owns it, sometimes two or three." Shoe could believe it.

Hal sat on a stool before a long Formica-topped workbench, spine bent, great stomach sagging, a compartmentalized plastic container the size of a large pizza box in front of him. He was lackadaisically sorting assorted screws and plastic anchors into the compartments of the container.

"You don't look any worse for your ordeal," Shoe said to him.

Hal looked up from his sorting. "Do you want something? Or did you just come here to remind me what a big hero you are?"

Shoe tried to ignore the bitterness in his brother's voice, but was stung by it nonetheless. "What happened between us, Hal?" he asked. "When did we stop being friends?"

"We were never friends," Hal said. "Just brothers." He went on with his sorting, yellow plastic anchors in one compartment, red in another, white in another.

"That's not true," Shoe said. "Once upon a time we were much more than 'just brothers.' I'm no hero, Hal, but I used to think you were one. Rachel thought so, too."

Hal snorted.

"You used to stand up for us, Hal. Both of us. Do you remember when I was ten and accidentally released the handbrake while playing in Dad's car and smashed in the garage door? You took the blame for me."

"I don't remember that," Hal said, but Shoe could tell from the look in his eyes that he did.

"I've never forgotten it. And when Rae was seven you walked her to school for a month because some kids were teasing her about having her head shaved."

"That I remember," Hal said. Shoe's father had been painting the kitchen cupboards when Rachel had run into the room and bumped the ladder, upsetting a gallon of white oil-based paint over her head.

"So what happened?" Shoe said.

"You grew up," he said with a shrug. "What's that old saying about gods with feet of clay? You realized I wasn't perfect."

"I hate to break this to you, Hal," Shoe said, "but I don't think either of us ever thought of you as perfect. We admired you, looked up to you, but we knew you weren't perfect. No one is."

"Everyone seems to think you are," Hal said.

"Well, everyone is wrong, believe me."

"Oh, I believe you." Hal said. "Is that what you came here for, to remind me that I'm a loser? I don't need you to tell me that."

"You're hardly a loser, Hal," Shoe said. "You have a successful career, a nice house in a good neighbourhood, and a wife who, if you'll let her, loves you." All of which, Shoe reminded himself, Hal seemed determined to throw away.

"You've got Maureen now, don't you?" Hal said bitterly. "You can have the house and the job, too."

Maybe he should just let him stew in his own juices, Shoe thought. He knew he couldn't do that, though. It wasn't an option. His brother was in trouble and Shoe would do whatever he could to help him find his way out of it, whether Hal liked it or not. But Hal wasn't making it any easier.

"You lied about not leaving your office till midnight on Thursday," Shoe said. "You were caught on video taking a company car out of the garage a little before 8:00 p.m. and returning a few minutes after midnight."

"So I went for a drive."

"The park attendant at the Dells picked you out of a photo array."

"Like I told you yesterday," Hal said. "He's either mistaken or lying."

"Why would he lie?"

"Okay, so he's mistaken. I wasn't there."

"I want to believe you, Hal, but the police have enough circumstantial evidence to get a warrant to seize your clothes and shoes, fingerprint you, and compel a DNA sample from you."

Hal shrugged. "If you say so."

Shoe struggled to keep his anger under control. He wanted to take his brother by the shoulders, shake some sense into that thick head of his. He came very close. He came even closer to simply turning and walking away.

"Look at me, Hal," Shoe said. Hal turned his head, but his eyes were deeply hooded, almost unreadable. Shoe asked the question anyway. "Did you kill Marvin Cartwright?"

"What's the point in denying it," Hal said, looking away as he said it. "You wouldn't believe me anyway."

"Hal, if you tell me you didn't do it, I'll believe you." Would he? Could he? The evidence against his brother, circumstantial as it was, seemed almost overwhelming, but if Hal swore to him that he hadn't killed Cartwright in those woods, Shoe would do his best to take him at his word, to ignore the nagging doubt in the back of his mind. After all, when all was said and done, Hal was his brother. But what if his best wasn't good enough?

Hal finally looked at him, and what Shoe saw in his

brother's eyes was like a knife in his soul. Hal must have also seen something in Shoe's eyes.

"You think I killed him, don't you?" he said.

"Tell me I'm wrong," Shoe said.

"The great and powerful Shoe," Hal said with mock astonishment. "Wrong? Can it be?" He waved his hands in the air above his head. "Repent all ye sinners, the end of the world is nigh." He dropped his hands and returned to sorting screws and anchors.

There were footsteps on the stairs. A moment later, Rachel and Maureen came into the workshop. With bitter, mocking heartiness, Hal said, "Ladies. Join the party. My brother has just accused me of murdering Marvin the Martian. How 'bout that, eh?"

"Joe!" Maureen gasped, face registering shock.

"Oh, don't look so surprised," Hal said. "I'm not buying your act for a minute. What about you, Rae? I can't remember the last time you were at a loss for words. Surely you must have something to say? Cat got your tongue?"

Shoe said, "This isn't helping, Hal. Tell me you didn't kill him and I'll accept it."

"But will you believe me?"

"Don't be an idiot," Rachel snapped. "Of course we'll believe you."

Maureen turned to Shoe. "Why would Hal kill Mr. Cartwright?" she asked.

"This ought to be good," Hal said.

"I don't know that you did kill him, Hal," Shoe said. "Look at it from the point of view of the police. They have a witness that places you with Cartwright a few hours before his death. They have proof you lied about not leaving your office."

Hal threw up his hands. "Well, there you go, then. Open and shut. I did it."

"Oh, for god's sake, Hal," Maureen said. "What's

wrong with you? Just tell him you didn't do it. He'll believe you."

Hal hunched in silence over the box of screws and anchors.

"You did it, didn't you?" Rachel said. "You stupid, stupid bastard."

Maureen sobbed, "No. Please, Hal. Tell her you didn't do it. Tell *me* you didn't. Please."

Hal's face crumpled and a sob broke in his chest.

"Oh, god," Maureen moaned, hunching and clamping her arms across her middle as though she had been punched in the stomach. She slumped to the hard concrete floor. Rachel knelt by her, wrapped her arms around her shoulders. "Why? Oh, god, why?" Maureen sobbed.

Hal put his face in his hands, breathing heavily and noisily through his nose. Then he raised his head from his hands. He looked from Maureen to Rachel to Shoe. His eyes were tormented, like those of a coyote caught in the steel jaws of a leghold trap, too weak and close to death to chew a leg off to escape. He looked down at Maureen.

"I'm sorry," he said. Maureen moaned. Hal lifted his gaze to Shoe. *Don't make me do this*, his eyes pleaded. *Please*.

Shoe's throat was tight, as if he were being strangled by an invisible hand. He desperately wanted be somewhere else, anywhere but in that cramped, musty space, surrounded by the useless devices of his brother's life. Black & Decker wasn't going to be able to fix this mess, he thought, as tears rolled down his brother's pale, sagging cheeks.

"I didn't go there with the intention of killing him," Hal said, forcing the words out, voice strained almost to breaking. "God, if only ... " He shook his head. "He was obsessed with the idea of atonement. Of making things right with everyone he'd failed. His mother. Ruth

Braithwaite. Joey Noseworthy. Janey Hallam. Me. And … " He hesitated, took a deep, unsteady breath, then let it out. "And Marty," he said.

"Marty?" Rachel said. "What does she … ?" She paled. "Oh, shit."

"He told me I had to go to the police and tell them about — about what happened, that it was the only way I could atone for — for what I'd done. And that if I didn't, he would. I … " He looked at Maureen. "We'd have been ruined, Moe. We'd have lost everything." He fell silent for a moment, eyes half closed. "I tried to talk him out of it," he said. "Make him see reason. But I couldn't get through to him."

"So you beat him to death with a goddamned tree branch," Rachel said, with savage intensity.

"I didn't mean to. I'd picked up a branch to use as a walking stick. It was in my hands. I hit him with it. And just kept on hitting him until — until I thought he was dead. I couldn't let him destroy our lives because of a silly mistake I'd made thirty-five years ago."

"A silly mistake," Rachel repeated bitterly. "Is that what you call it. Goddamnit, Hal. She was just a little kid."

"It wasn't like that," Hal said. "I — "

"I don't want to hear it," Rachel snapped, cutting him off. "You can't rationalize pedophilia."

"I'm not a pedophile," Hal cried. "Jesus, Rae."

"What do you call it, then?"

"I didn't molest her. Not — not like you're thinking. I was sneaking a smoke in the woods when I saw her collecting bugs in a peanut butter jar. 'It's not safe to be in the woods alone,' I told her. When she asked me why not, I said, 'That teacher from the junior high school was raped near here.'

"'Mr. Cartwright said a friend of his was hurt by some man,' she said. 'Was that her?' I said I supposed it was. She just shrugged and continued down the path toward the old tree across the bend in the creek. I followed her. Just to keep an eye on her. When she got to the tree, she turned to me and said, 'Do you want to play a game?'

"'What kind of game?' I asked.

"'Give me some money and I'll show you my wee-wee,' she said.

"I was totally dumbfounded. Dougie Hallam had told me he'd given her money to masturbate him, but I hadn't believed him, any more than I'd believed him about Janey. But then she giggled and I realized she was just teasing me again."

"What do you mean, again?" Rachel said.

Hal shook his head. "It doesn't matter. Anyway, I thought I'd teach her a lesson. I asked her, 'How much?' She said, 'Five dollars.' I said, 'For five dollars you've got to do more than show me your wee-wee. How about you pretend my thing is a lollipop?'"

Rachel made a sound of disgust deep in her throat. Maureen looked as though she were going to throw up. Shoe just wanted his brother to stop talking, but he seemed compelled to continue.

"She didn't want to do it, of course," Hal said. "She offered to let me touch her, but I said for five dollars, I expected more than that. She finally agreed to masturbate me and let me touch her vagina. 'Gimme the money,' she said."

"'Uh-uh,' I said. 'You first.' I showed her the money, but I wouldn't give it to her. She looked scared."

"No shit," Rachel said.

"I *wanted* her to be scared," Hal said. "I was trying to teach her a lesson."

"Keep telling yourself that," Rachel said disgustedly. "I'm sure you'll start to believe it."

"It's true," Hal said.

"So what happened?" Rachel said. "When she refused to comply, you molested her — to teach her a lesson. You sick son of a bitch ... "

"That's enough," Shoe said. He did not want to hear
the answer, even though the truth was clear enough from
the expression of shame and misery on his brother's face.
"Cartwright caught you," he said.

"Yes," Hal said. "He came howling out of the woods
like a wild man and grabbed me. He wasn't big, but he
was quite strong. He threw me down and accused me
of statutory rape. I told him it wasn't what he thought.
I tried to get Marty to tell him we were just fooling
around, but she took off. He pulled me to my feet asked
me if I could think of any reason he shouldn't report me
to the police. I said I hadn't really done anything. That
only made him more angry. I begged him not to tell the
police, that they'd think I was the Black Creek Rapist. I
was terrified he did too, but he said he knew I wasn't. He
wouldn't go to the police, he said, on the condition that
I promised never do anything like that again. I swore to
him I never would. And I never did."

Rachel helped Maureen up. She stumbled toward
the stairs, leaning on Rachel. Hal struggled to his feet,
wobbling unsteadily, supporting himself with a hand on
the workbench.

"Moe, I'm sorry."

Maureen stopped, stood with her back to him shoulders hunched. "It's too late for apologies," she said. She
turned. Her face was pale and loose, eyes red-rimmed
and bloodshot.

"Maybe you're right, but I'm going to try anyway.
I — I'm sorry, Moe. For everything."

Her mouth twitched and her eyes shone, but otherwise she did not speak or move or show any sign of
having heard him.

"Moe, I — "

"No," she said. "I don't want to hear it. It's not enough, Hal. It's too little, too late. You can apologize all you want to, but it's not going to fix things. It's not going to change anything."

He tried to go to her, but he staggered back against the workbench. "God, Moe, you've got no idea what I've been going through lately."

"No, of course not. For god's sake, Hal. You killed a man just to save your reputation and your fucking job."

Maureen turned and went up the stairs, Rachel helping her, despite her injured feet. Hal slumped onto the stool, looked at Shoe. Tears welled in his eyes and Shoe felt something he hadn't felt for his brother in a long, long time.

"I can't bear the thought of losing her," Hal said. "I don't think I can live without her."

"You're going to have to learn how, I think," Shoe said. He went to his brother, took his arm. "Let's go upstairs."

Hal nodded meekly and let Shoe lead him up the stairs and into the living room, where he slumped onto the sofa.

"Do you think I could have a glass of water?" Hal said.

Shoe went into the kitchen, filled a glass at the sink, and took it to Hal. Hal gulped greedily, spilling water on his shirt. He finished the water and put the glass on the coffee table, carefully placing it on a coaster. He sat back, squirmed, and passed wind softly into the sofa cushions. He smiled crookedly at Shoe.

"What should I do, Joe?"

"I don't know, Hal," Shoe said. "I wish I did."

"I don't want to go to jail. I have some money. I can go away. Is that what I should do?"

Shoe shook his head. "Even if you could get away," he said, "how long do you think you'd survive as a fugitive? I don't want you to go to prison, but running isn't the answer. You may have to reconcile yourself to spending a few years in prison."

"Fuck," Hal said dully.

"Yeah," Shoe said. "That sums it up pretty well."

Hal smiled weakly. "You didn't kill Dougie Hallam, did you? Did Janey kill him?"

"I killed him," Shoe said.

"I don't believe you, but if that's the way you want to play it ... " He shrugged. "God knows why, though. I never did understand you, this compulsion you have to protect people from themselves. Did you expect gratitude from the likes of Joey Noseworthy, Janey Hallam — or me? I don't think so. All it's ever brought you is grief, hasn't it?"

"Not always," Shoe said.

chapter fifty-eight

Rachel and Maureen came into the living room, but Hal didn't look up as he spoke.

"After he caught Marty and me, I did everything I could to convince him that he hadn't made a mistake by not going to the police. I ran errands for him and did his yardwork. I got to quite like him, actually. He was a nice, kind man, despite how his mother treated him. Marty didn't report the incident either, but her parents must have sensed something was wrong and called the police, figuring she'd been another victim of the Black Creek Rapist, which was just what she let her parents, the police, and everyone else in the neighbourhood believe." He looked at Rachel. "I'm sorry she's dead."

"Did it occur to you that the police might not have believed him?" Shoe asked.

"Yes, of course," Hal replied. "Even so, if allegations of child molestation had been made public, it wouldn't have mattered if I was innocent or not. It would have cost me my job and hung over my head for the rest of my life. It would have killed Mum and Dad."

"They're made of sterner stuff than that," Rachel said.

"How did you get your car out of the Dells?" Shoe asked.

"I knew Dougie Hallam had keys to the gate," Hal said. "So I called him on my cell. He came and let me out, but of course he wanted to know what I was doing in the park after closing. I told him some lame story about parking there to watch the sunset and falling asleep. He realized the truth as soon as he heard about Cartwright's murder, of course. Naturally, he saw it as an opportunity to blackmail me." He looked at Shoe. "You did me a favour by killing him." He looked at his watch, then stood up from the sofa. The effort left him momentarily breathless. "I'm late for an appointment," he said.

"If you're still thinking of running," Shoe said, "you should know that the police are watching the house."

Hal went to the living room window and peered out.

"You probably won't see them," Shoe said.

"What should I do?" Hal said. "Maybe if I went out through the backyard."

"They'll be watching that route, too," Shoe said.

"I know a little about the law," Rachel said. Her second husband had been a lawyer, Shoe recalled. "If you save them the cost of a trial and cop a plea, a good lawyer could probably get you off with manslaughter, diminished capacity, or something. You'd get ten, twelve years, most likely less. You'd be out in four or five."

"Five years," Hal moaned. "I'd rather take my chances and run for it."

"Don't be stupid," Rachel said. "How much money do you have? A couple of hundred thousand? How long do you think it would last? You'd be destitute in four or five years. Living on the goddamned street. Hell, maybe even dead. A few years in prison and you'd be free to resume your life. Besides, if you run, you'll never see Mum or Dad again."

"Better that than what it would do to them seeing their eldest son going to prison for murder."

"It's always about you, isn't it, Hal?" Maureen said. Without waiting for a reply, she left the room and went up the stairs.

"Rae's right," Shoe said. "I know five years seems like a long time, but if you try to run, you'll only make matters worse. Even if you did manage to get away, you'd be sentencing yourself to life in a different kind of prison."

"I don't want to go to jail."

"No, of course you don't. Who would? But it's time you grew up, Hal, and started taking responsibility for yourself. There's a saying some criminals have: do the crime, do the time. My advice to you is to do the time, Hal. Then you can put it behind you and get on with your life."

"Easy for you to say," Hal said.

"No," Shoe said. "It's not."

chapter fifty-nine

Maureen came out of the house as Shoe was getting into the Taurus. He wanted to check on his parents. Rachel was in the house with Hal, who was trying to make up his mind what to do. A few metres up the street from the house sat an old station wagon with fake wood side-panels, a man and a woman in the front seat, trying to look as if they belonged there.

"You were going to leave without saying goodbye," Maureen said.

"I'm not going to abandon my brother," Shoe said. "I'll have to go home to Vancouver for a few days, but I'll be back."

"You'll stand by him," Maureen said. "You'll do everything you can to help him get through this."

"Of course," Shoe said.

Maureen looked at the ground between them. "I don't think I can do that," she said. "Not now, not after what he's put me though. Maybe if I still loved him ... "

She looked up at him. "Do you think I'm being horribly selfish?"

"You'll do what you have to do," Shoe said.

"You're disappointed in me, though, aren't you?"

"It has nothing to do with me. Hal needs you, Maureen. More than he needs me or Rachel or our parents. If you abandon him, he'll probably die in prison. But if you tell him you'll stand by him, he'll see it through, especially if he knows you'll be waiting for him when he gets out. Can you do that for him, Maureen?"

"If that's what you want me to do."

"It has nothing to do with me," Shoe said again, an edge on his voice that brought her close to tears.

A plain grey Sebring pulled up in front of the house, followed by two Halton County patrol cars. Hanna Lewis got out of the passenger side of the Sebring and her partner got out of the other. Four Halton County constables got out of the two patrol cars.

"Mrs. Schumacher," Hannah Lewis said. "Is your husband here?"

Maureen looked at Shoe. "I can't do this," she said.

Shoe watched Maureen walk stiffly to her car, open the door, and get in. She started the engine. The brake lights flared and the backup lights lit as she put the transmission into reverse, but the car did not move. She sat with her hands on the steering wheel, looking straight ahead.

Lewis looked at Shoe. "We found Timothy Dutton," she said quietly. "He was in the trunk of his Audi, wrists wired together and a .22 bullet hole in the back of his head. A witness saw a man with long grey or dirty blond hair set fire to the car then drive away on a motorcycle that burned oil. We have a bulletin out on Joey Noseworthy."

"You'll understand if I don't wish you good luck finding him," Shoe said.

"We also got the final autopsy report on Marvin Cartwright. He was a dead man walking, according to the pathologist. He had an advanced inoperable brain tumour. He probably didn't have more than a few weeks left. The pathologist reckons he must've been one tough son of a bitch to even be walking around, but likely a lot of what he said wouldn't have made a lot of sense."

Shoe and Lewis both turned as Maureen shut off the engine and got out of her car. She looked at Shoe, then went into the house.

"My brother's inside," Shoe said to Lewis. "He's waiting for you."

Acknowledgements

Thank you to the following people for helping make this a better story: Alan Annand, Marc Cassini, David Hanley, and Mark Mendelson. Thanks also to Barry Jowett, Alison Carr, Marja Appleford, and the rest of the staff at Dundurn Press. I take full responsibility for all literary thuds, grammatical clangs, and factual and procedural errors. A heartfelt thank you, too, to Pam Hilliard, for her love, support, and endless patience. Lastly, I dedicate this book to my father, Hugh Fairlie Blair, who shared with me his lifelong love of the printed word. If there's a heaven, it's a library filled with books he's never read.